Fever season /

F H174f   3420110089392%

Fever
Season

Also by Barbara Hambly

A Free Man of Color

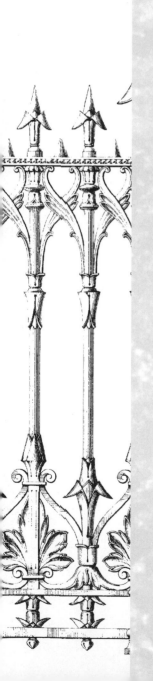
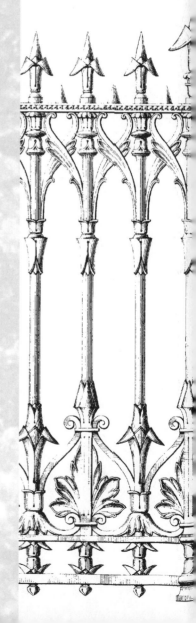

BANTAM BOOKS

New York
Toronto
London
Sydney
Auckland

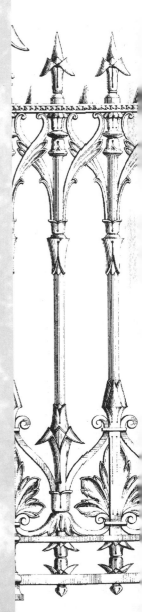

Fever
Season

———〰———

Barbara
Hambly

Fever Season
A Bantam Book / July 1998

**Library of Congress Cataloging-in-Publication
Data**
Hambly, Barbara.
   Fever season / Barbara Hambly.
      p.   cm.
   I. Title.
   PS3558.A4215F4   1998
   813'.54—dc21   97-49319
                                                        CIP

      ISBN 0-553-10254-0

*Published simultaneously in the United States
and Canada*

Bantam Books are published by Bantam Books, a
division of Bantam Doubleday Dell Publishing Group,
Inc. Its trademark, consisting of the words "Bantam
Books" and the portrayal of a rooster, is Registered in
U.S. Patent and Trademark Office and in other
countries. Marca Registrada. Bantam Books, 1540
Broadway, New York, New York 10036.

PRINTED IN THE UNITED STATES OF AMERICA

BVG   10 9 8 7 6 5 4 3 2 1

For Laurie

Special thanks to the staff of
the Historic New Orleans Collection
for all their help; to Kate Miciak for her
assistance and advice in redirecting
the story; to O'Neil deNoux;
and, of course, to George.

NOTE ON TERMINOLOGY

As in my previous book of this series, *A Free Man of Color,* I have employed, as far as possible, the terminology of the 1830s, which differs considerably from that in use today. In the 1830s, as far as I can tell, *creole* was generally taken to mean a native-born white descendant of French or Spanish colonists. If a person of African parentage was being referred to, he or she was specified as a *creole Negro,* that is, born in the Americas and therefore less susceptible to local diseases than *Congos*—African-born blacks.

There was a vast distinction between *black* and *colored.* The latter term had a specific meaning as the descendant of African and European ancestors. *Sang mêlé* was one of the French terms: "mixed blood." Any colored person would have been deeply offended to be referred to as "black," since *black* meant "slave"; and the free colored had worked long and hard to establish themselves as a third order, a caste that was neither black nor white. Likewise, they were careful to distinguish between themselves and slaves of mixed race and between themselves and freedmen, whatever the percentage of African genetics in their makeup. Given the economics of the time and the society, this was a logical mechanism of survival. That they did survive and thrive, and establish a culture of amazing richness that was neither African nor European, is a tribute to the stubborn and wonderful life force of the human spirit.

Fever
Season

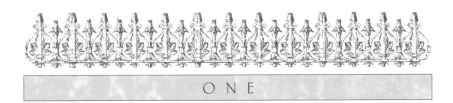

O N E

In fever season, traffic in the streets was thin. Those who could afford to do so had left New Orleans with the ending of Lent; those who could not had all through the long summer hurried about their business as if Bronze John, as they called the sickness, were a creditor one could avoid if one kept off the streets.

Midday, the molten September heat raised steam from the water in the French town's cypress-lined gutters and the rain puddles in the soupy streets. Mephitic light filtered through clouds of steamboat soot from the levees and gave the town the look of a grimy but inexplicably pastel-walled hell. Only those whose errands were pressing walked the streets then.

So it took no great cleverness on Benjamin January's part to realize that he was being followed.

Charity Hospital, where he'd spent the night and all the morning among the dying, lay on the uptown side of Canal Street, the American side. It was against January's nature to spend more time on that side of town than was absolutely necessary, to say nothing of the fact that Americans seemed to regard all free persons of color as potential slaves, money on the hoof going to waste that could be going into their pockets in the big markets along Baronne and Levee Streets. Americans made no distinction, as the French were careful to do, between African blacks—be they slaves or freedmen—and the free persons of color whose parents had been both colored and white. Not, January reflected wryly, that it made a great deal of difference in his case.

But even in fever season, when men and women, black and white and colored, were only hands to hold off Bronze John from one another—to carry water and vinegar and saline draughts, to fan away the humming swarms of mosquitoes and flies—he felt uneasy up-town.

Maybe that was why he realized so quickly that someone was dogging his steps.

His head ached from twenty-four hours without sleep. His senses felt dulled, as if someone had carefully stuffed his skull with dirty lint soaked in the stinking fluids of the dying; his very bones weighed him down. His last patient that day had been a nine-year-old girl who'd walked the twelve streets to the hospital from the levee where she'd been selling oranges. Her mama, she said in English, before delirium claimed her, would whale her for not staying on to finish the day. The child had died before she could tell anyone who her mama was or where that lady could be found.

As of that morning, no newspaper in the town had yet admitted that there was an epidemic at all.

The fever had first come to New Orleans in January's sixteenth year. In those days you never heard English spoken at all, though the city already belonged to the United States. He'd been studying medicine then with Dr. Gomez and had followed his teacher on his rounds of the hospitals; it seemed to him now, twenty-four years later, that the ache of grief and pity never grew less. Nor did his fear of the fever itself.

He wasn't sure exactly what it was that made him realize he was being stalked.

A glimpse from the corner of his eye as he dodged across Jackson Street among the ambulance wagons, the produce carts, the drays of sugar and indigo on their way to the levee from the inland plantations along the lake. A horse lurched to a stop, tossed its head with an angry snort. A driver cursed in Spanish. Steps away, Freret Street lay deserted under the hot weight of brazen sky, but January knew he wasn't alone. He quickened his stride.

If he walked down Canal Street, among the hip-high weeds, strewn garbage, and dead dogs of what French and Americans alike called the "neutral ground," he would be spared at least some of the stenches of the cemeteries. There seething corpses lined the walls three-deep, like bales on the levee, waiting for tomb space and the men to bear them in. But though he was an accredited member of the Paris College of Surgeons who had practiced at the Hôtel Dieu in that city for six years, January was perfectly well aware that he looked like a field hand: six feet, three inches tall, powerfully built despite the dust of gray that now powdered his short-cropped hair, his skin as glossy black as his African father's had been. That was one reason why it was only in the fever season that he practiced medicine. The rest of the year he played piano to earn his bread. It was an injustice he'd accepted, upon his return to New Orleans from Paris, nearly a year ago.

And things had changed in the city since his departure in 1817.

So he followed Rue Villere downstream, past shabby cottages and grubby shacks in rank jungles of weed, the stench of untended privies, of gutters uncleaned for weeks, and of sties and coops, neglected by their owners, thick as fog around him. An unpaved path, mucky from the morning's rainstorm, led him toward the river.

He was definitely being followed. He didn't want to look back; he couldn't tell by whom.

Rue Douane, the first street of the French town itself, was usually alive with cart and foot traffic. Today, there were only two women in the faded calico of poverty, hurrying with bowed heads. Those, and the dead-carts that lurched toward the cemeteries with their stiffened cargoes wrapped in cheap Osnaburg sheets and their throbbing armies of attendant flies. Like the Americans uptown, the householders here burned piles of hair and hooves from the slaughteryards or smudges made up with gunpowder, to clear the disease-ridden miasma from the air. The smell was foul—charnel house and battlefield rolled into one. The Four Horsemen, January thought, coughing, would bear that smell on their wake when they reaped the plain of Armageddon with their swords.

He cut across Rue Douane midway between two streets, mud sucking his boots. Just before he sprang across the gutter he glanced back. He saw no one.

What do I do? he wondered. *What do I do?*

The houses on the other side of Basin Street were mostly small, but built better than those that bordered the swampy town pastures. Neat cottages of plaster and brick lined Rue des Ramparts and Rue Burgundy, pale yellows and celery greens, pinks and sky blues under the savage light. For years, wealthy bankers and planters and brokers had been buying their quadroon and mulatto mistresses dwellings like these, along the back edge of the old town. These days just as many belonged to respectable craftsmen and artisans, clerks and tailors, whose wives and families turned their eyes from their sisters and cousins and neighbors of the demimonde.

His mother's protector had bought her such a house, when January was eight and his full-sister, six. The daughter his mother had subsequently borne to St. Denis Janvier had recently been given the deed to such a house herself, by a fat, indolent Creole named Viellard.

Most stood empty now, shuttered tight in the hot glare of morning. When Bronze John came calling, a lot of people, no matter how strait their circumstances, came up with the money to remove for the summer to one of the hotels or cottages on the shores of the lake, where the air was cleaner, in Milneburgh or Mandeville or Spanish Fort. Those who hadn't done so from fear of the fever, which came nearly every year—or from the horrible combination of summer decay and summer insects—reconsidered the matter when the first cases of the cholera were diagnosed.

As he walked along Rue Burgundy, January counted off houses. After sixteen years' absence he was just coming to know these people again. The yellow cottage belonged to his mother's dressmaker; the two-and-a-half-story town house occupied by Dr. LaPlante and his family (currently residing at his cottage in Milneburgh); the pink cottage owned by the perfumer Crowdie Passebon. The planks that ordinarily bridged the deep gutter from the unpaved street to the brick banquette were one and all propped beside the high brick steps. If anyone was home, no one was receiving visitors. Narrow spaces gapped between house and house, pass-throughs, leading back to the yards behind where slant-roofed outbuildings, of a sort January had never seen in any other city, housed kitchens, laundries, storerooms at ground level and slave quarters above. Each house, even the cottages, was an enclave; each a little fortress walled into itself. In New Orleans there was no such tangle of alleys as had cut and twisted through the inner arrondissements of Paris, enabling a man to duck inconspicuously from one street to the next.

But January had been brought up on this street and knew the quirks and features of any number of those hidden courts. As he approached the pale green cottage belonging to his mother's bosom-bow Agnes Pellicot, he found his muscles growing tense.

Agnes and her daughters had departed, like January's mother, when the first cases of cholera were rumored in June. But the cottage, given to Agnes by her protector—with a sizable annuity—when they had terminated their relationship upon the occasion of his second marriage, had undergone a number of remodelings in the years before Agnes owned it. One of these had included the erection of an outside stairway up the rear wall of the building and the enlargement of one of the attic gable windows to form a door.

That door was kept firmly locked, but the window of the gable beside it had only a catch. He might be perilously close to his forty-first birthday, but January was fairly sure he could make the short scramble across the roof to effect an entrance.

Whether he could do so with sufficient speed to trap his pursuer was, of course, another question.

He counted steps in his mind, tallied details. The possibility that whoever dogged him might be armed tugged uncomfortably; so did the thought that there might be more than one of them.

He carried his medical bag, part of his persona as surgeon, like the tall-crowned beaver hat or the threadbare black wool coat that became a portable bake oven in heat like this. Casually he brought the bag up under his arm and fumbled at the catch like an absentminded man trying to open it while pondering something else, just as he turned into the pass-through that led to the Pellicot yard.

The moment he was out of sight of the street he bolted down the narrow space like a spurred horse, tearing off his hat as he ran, clutching the black leather satchel tight. He whipped through the wooden gate and shucked his coat as he darted across the dusty yard, flung himself up the outside stairs as though the Platt-Eye Devil of childhood legends ran behind. At the top he paused only long enough to find his longest-bladed scalpel, then tossed bag and hat and coat on the topmost step to make the quick, careful scramble across twenty feet of roof to the other gable.

With the back edge of the scalpel it was ridiculously easy to flip the window catch. All these cottages were built the same, and he knew the layout of the Pellicot attic was identical to that of his mother's home. Two chambers and a perilously steep wooden stair-way that led down through the *cabinet* tacked onto the back of the house, a little pantry-cum-warming room opening in its turn into the rear parlor, which served as a dining room. Within moments January crossed through the dining room, through the archway to the front parlor, and flipped the catch on the shutters of the tall French doors that looked onto the street. Stepping out, he closed the shutters silently behind him and rounded the corner of the house into the pass-through again.

"You wanted to have a word with me?"

The woman—girl—who stood peeking cautiously through the gate into the yard spun, her hand flying to her mouth. She blundered back against the fence, catching the gate for support. January said, "There's no way out, that way."

He walked down the passage, more wary that she'd try to bolt past him or that someone else might come in behind, than from any fear that she might be armed. As he got close he saw that her clothing was plain but very well cut. The dark red cotton gown, high waisted and with narrow sleeves made down to the wrists, was the kind a young girl of good family might wear. By the fit of the bust, it hadn't been made for her. The headcloth mandated by law for all black or colored women was dark red too, but tied as a servant, or a country-bred slave, would tie it. His younger sister Dominique had tried to initiate him into the intricacies of the proper tying of tignons into fanciful, seductive, or outrageous styles in defiance of the law, but without much success. January knew a confection when he saw one, though, and this wasn't a confection. It was a headcloth, the mark of a slave's humility.

"Why did you follow me?"

"Are you M'sieu Benjamin Janvier?" The girl spoke the sloppy Creole French of the plantations, more than half African. Any town mother would have whaled the life out of a girl who used *vo* for *vous,* at least any mother who'd have been able to afford that dress.

"That's me." He kept his voice as unalarming as possible. At his size, he was aware that he was alarming enough. "And I have the honor of addressing . . . ?"

She straightened her shoulders in her red dress, a little slip of a thing, with a round defiant chin and a trace of hardness in her eyes that may have been fear. *Pretty,* January thought. He could have picked her up in one hand.

"I'm Cora . . ." She hesitated, fishing, then went on with just a touch of defiance, ". . . LaFayette. Cora LaFayette. I needed to speak with you, Michie Janvier. Are you a music teacher?"

"I am that," he sighed.

After ten years he still didn't know whether to feel amused or angry about having to work as a musician. There were free men of color who made a living—and a good living—as physicians and surgeons in New Orleans, but they were without exception light of skin. Quadroon or octoroon, they were for the most part offspring of white men and the women for whom they bought these pastel houses along this street.

In his way, St. Denis Janvier had been as much an optimist as his mulatto plaçée's son had been, concerning the chances a man with three African grandparents would have of earning his living in medicine in New Orleans or elsewhere, Paris training or no Paris training.

Cora LaFayette looked down, small face a careful blank, rallying her words, desperate to get them right. January relaxed a little and smiled, folding his big arms in their sweat-damp muslin sleeves. "You followed me all the way from Charity Hospital to ask what I charge for lessons?"

Her head came up, like a deer startled in the woods, and she saw the gentle teasing in his eyes. Something eased, very slightly, in the corners of that expressionless little mouth.

But she did not smile. She dwelled in a country where smiles had been forgotten years ago. "Do you teach the daughters of a lady name Lalaurie? Great big green house on Rue Royale?"

January nodded again. He glanced around him at the narrow tunnel they stood in, between Agnes Pellicot's house and that of Guillaume Morisset the tailor, also out of town. The slot of shadow stank of mud and sewage where mosquito-wrigglers flickered among the scum. "You want to go somewhere a little more comfortable, Mademoiselle LaFayette? The town's half closed up, but at Breyard's Grocery over on Rue Toulouse I can get you a lemonade."

Eyes that seemed too big for that pointed, delicate face raised quickly and as quickly darted away. She shook her head, a tiny gesture, and January stepped past her, still cautiously, to push open the gate that led into the Pellicot yard. The French doors into the house were shuttered, as were the doors of the service building at the back of the yard. The brick-flagged porch below the slave quarters' gallery was a slab of blue-black velvet. January led the girl to the plank bench outside the kitchen where Agnes's cook Elvire would sit to shell peas or pluck fowl, and said, "Wait here a minute for me, if you would, Mamzelle."

She stiffened, panic in her eyes.

"I'm just going around to latch the door. I'll be back."

He was conscious of her, bolt upright and motionless as a scared cat, on the bench as he crossed through the yard again, down the blue tunnel of passway, and out to Rue Burgundy. He stepped back through the French doors into Agnes Pellicot's parlor and latched them; and on the way through the *cabinet* pantry to the stairs, he found a cheap horn cup on a shelf beside the French china dinner service. This he carried in his waistcoat pocket up the stairs, through the attic, out the window, across the roof, and down the outside stairs, marveling that he'd made that circuit earlier at a dead run. It was a wonder what you could do with a good scare in you.

When he returned to the yard Cora LaFayette was gone. He saw her a moment later just within the gate to the pass-through out to the street, poised to run.

He waited in the middle of the yard, as he'd have waited not to startle a deer in the cypress swamps behind the plantation where he'd been born. In time she came away from the gate and hurried to the bench again, keeping close to the wall.

Runaway, he thought. And making more of it than she needed to. Did she really think that with the fever and the cholera stalking the streets, with the town half-empty and fear like the stench of the smoke in the air, that anybody would be chasing a runaway slave?

He filled the horn cup from the coopered cistern in the corner of the yard and held it out to her. Cora drank thirstily, and he sat on the other end of the bench, laying coat, hat, and satchel down beside him. Aside from her dress, which was not a countrywoman's dress, her hands and face were clean. She'd been in town a little time.

"Do you know Madame Lalaurie?" he asked her, when she set the cup aside. "Or know of her?"

The girl shook her head. "That is, I know she's a rich lady, if she's got a big house like that, and bought slaves." She looked down at the toes of her shoes, black and red, to match the dress, with frivolous white lacings. "She bought a houseman, only a week or so ago, name of Gervase, from my master—that used to be my master, before he freed me," she added hastily. "Michie . . ." She hesitated, fishing around for corroborative detail again. If her name were LaFayette her master's would probably be, too, so she said, "Michie Napoleon LaFayette. But Michie LaFayette, he set me free, and I come to town looking for Gervase. We were married, me and Gervase. Really married, Michie Janvier, by a priest and everything."

Her dark eyes were childishly earnest, looking into his, but he saw in the flinch of her mouth, heard in the inflection of her voice, that she lied. Not that it was his business. There were a lot of men who didn't want their people to marry, or even to become Christians. But it wasn't any of his affair, though as a Christian he hoped this girl had at least been baptized. He asked, "So why didn't you try to see Gervase yourself?"

"I did!" She spread out her child-small hands, with the roughened skin of washing-up on the fingers and backs. "I tried. I went to the house on Rue Royale, and they always keep the big gate there shut. That coachman of Madame's there, he wouldn't let me in. I asked him." There was anger in the set of the little mouth. "He just smiled at me nasty and said Gervase was busy and Madame wouldn't have her people taking time off from their work to chat with girls in the street. I told him I was his sister," she added naively, and sighed.

January forebore to mention how many "sisters" and "cousins" and "brothers" came loitering around to speak to servants in the twilight. Only the slackest of mistresses would permit such dalliance, and Madame Delphine Lalaurie was known for the silent efficiency of her servants.

"So you want me to talk to Gervase?"

Cora nodded. "If you would, M'sieu. After the second time that coachman—that Bastien—turn me away, I watched the house, and I saw you go in. The cripple-man selling water across the street, he say you was the music teacher for Madame Lalaurie's two girls. He say you also work at the Charity Hospital during the fever season, so when I . . . I couldn't wait for you to come out of the house, I look for you at the Hospital."

Where there was too much of a crowd for you to want to come up to me, thought January, studying that wary, triangular face. It didn't surprise him that the water seller would know everything about him. In New Orleans, the vendors who sold everything from strawberries to fire irons through the narrow streets knew everything about everyone.

But that, too, was none of his business. This girl's lover had been sold, and she had run away to see him again. For all his mother's talk about the unruliness of blacks (not that his mother was so much as a half-shade paler than Cora LaFayette) he could not blame her for it.

"What would you like me to tell Gervase?"

Her smile transformed her like spring dawn, not just her face but her tense little body as well. Joy became her. Then she swallowed, again, thinking hard and contemplating once more the toes of her red-and-black shoes. "Could you ask him if there's a way we can see each other? If there's a way he can get out? Just for an evening, I mean, M'sieu. They keep that gate closed tight all the time. I'll meet you here," she went on quickly. "If that's all right with you, Michie Janvier. Tomorrow night?"

"Wednesday," said January. "Wednesday afternoon. I teach the Lalaurie girls Tuesdays and Fridays, and I'm working at the Hospital Tuesday night."

"Wednesday afternoon." She got to her feet, her smile coming and going, like a child fearing to hex a wish. "I'll be here, Michie Janvier. Thank you."

She looked so fragile, standing poised in the brazen sunlight, that it was on January's tongue to ask her if she had a place to stay. But if she were a runaway, he thought, she wouldn't tell him. And if she were a runaway it was better that he didn't know. Still he felt a pang of worry for her, as she darted away like a small rusty damselfly into the dark beyond the gate.

He shrugged his coat back on, shifting his wide shoulders beneath it, shirt gummy with sweat. As he donned his hat again, tucked his bag under his arm and crossed Agnes Pellicot's yard, he thought of his own room behind his mother's house, his own bed, and a few hours' sleep without the stink of death in his nostrils, without the whimpers of the dying in his ears.

Mostly the runaways went back home. They had nowhere else to go. Their families and their friends were all on the home place, wherever the home place was, like the villages in Africa from which their parents and grandparents had come. He remembered some-one—his father?—telling him about how in old times there'd been whole villages of escaped Africans in the *cipriere,* the cypress swamps that lay behind the line of river plantations. They'd raised their own food, hunted, and set scouts, hidden from the eyes of the whites. But that was long gone even in his childhood.

Still, at Bellefleur where he'd been born, there were a couple of the hands who ran off two or three times a year, to live in the woods for a few days or a week. They never went far.

Maybe that was because they knew they wouldn't get more than a beating. A beating was worth it, as far as they were concerned. It was the price they were willing to pay for earth and peace and silence of heart. Try as he would, January could not recall whether his father had been one of them.

He let himself out the gate. Cora LaFayette—or whatever her name actually was—had vanished from the empty street. January strode quickly toward his mother's house, sweating in the penitential coat. Twice he looked around, as if he half expected to see the black, tall, smoky form of Bronze John himself stepping through the thin scrim of gutter steam. But he saw only Hèlier the water seller, with his buckets and his yoke on his twisted back, calling out hopefully, "Water! Water! Clean cold water!" to the shut and bolted houses.

Benjamin January prayed that when he slept, he would not dream.

January drew the ragged sheet up over the face of the man on the floor before him and sat back on his heels. Toward the end the man had begged for something, January didn't know what, in a language he could not understand. Dr. Ker, the head of Charity Hospital, guessed he was a Russian, a sailor who'd jumped ship hoping for a chance of making a better life for himself ashore.

Poor fool.

"You stupid dago, I'm doing this for your own good!"

January turned his head at the sound. Emil Barnard, a gangly young man who had styled himself "a practitioner of the healing arts" when he'd volunteered his services to Dr. Ker, backed nervously from the cot of a man who'd been brought in that afternoon. The patient's face was flushed the horrible orange of the fever, and black vomit puddled the floor beside the rude wooden bed. The sick man was cursing weakly in Italian, swearing that no priest should come near him, no murdering government spy.

"Own good, you understand?" yelled Barnard, more loudly. "You understand?"

It was quite clear, of course, that the Italian didn't understand.

Probably even if he knew French when he was in his right mind, the fever's delirium had sponged such knowledge from his screaming brain. All he knew—he was shouting this over and over again now—was that he was in hell. In hell with all the murdering priests.

January closed his eyes. He knew he should get up and go over to them—his Italian was good enough to make himself understood—but exhaustion held him like a chain. Maybe they *were* in hell.

It was hot enough, God knew. In the long upstairs ward, the clotted black heat was imbued with the stenches of human waste and fever-vomit and the peculiar, horrible stink that reeks from the sweat of those in mortal fear. The long windows that gave onto the gallery were shut tight and heavily curtained in the hopes of excluding the pestilence that rode the air of night, and January's face ran with sweat as if he'd put his head in a rain barrel. Like hell's, the dark was smudged with fire. The lamps were too few and burned the cheapest oil obtainable; smoke hung beneath the high ceiling and the smell of it permeated clothing, hair, flesh. Like hell, even in this dead hour of the night, the room murmured with a Babel of voices: German, Swedish, English . . .

Like hell, it was a place without hope.

"He thinks you're a priest." January got to his feet, slowly, like an old man. "He has no use for priests."

"An Italian?" Emil Barnard straightened indignantly. He spoke the singsong French of the Midi, with its trilled vowels and rolled *r*'s. "Absurd. They're all priest ridden, Romish heathens. You are mistaken." Yet Barnard did look a little like a priest, in his long, old-fashioned black tailed coat and his shirt of biscuit-colored calico that looked white in the lamp glare and smoke.

"He thinks that's the viaticum—the Host—you have . . . sir." In his days in Paris, January had called no man "sir" unless he thought they deserved it: the physicians at the Hôtel Dieu, the wealthy men who had hired him to play, the Director of the Opera. It was hard to return to his childhood, to call even a street-sweeper "sir" if that street-sweeper happened to have been born white, to look down or aside so as not to meet their eyes. "What *is* it?"

"Onion." Barnard had a very long narrow face that was carefully shaved, light brown hair a trifle too curly for Nature's unaided hand. "Placed near or under the bed of a sufferer from the yellow fever, it is a sovereign remedy against the miasmatic influence of fever-air." He stepped aside a pace as a woman came to mop up the Italian's vomit from the floor by the cot; he didn't even look down at her as he continued his lecture. "The onion is a near-perfect remedy for all imbalances of the bodily humors. Its wonderful absorptive powers will draw forth the febrile vapors from the lungs and gradually purify the lymphatic and bilious systems. It was a common remedy among the great Indian nations that anciently inhabited these countries, and was written of in papyri of Egypt in the reigns of the Pharaohs, long before the birth of Christ."

"Get him away from me!" screamed the Italian. "Clerical scoundrel! Starver of babies! Thief of a poor man's belongings! You stole the bread out of the mouths of my children and left them to die!"

"Here, now, what have we here?"

Dr. Jules Soublet, in charge of the ward by night by virtue of having one of the oldest practices in the French town, approached them, a tall, brisk, bustling man only a few years January's senior. His coat of black superfine wool was expensively tailored over heavy shoulders, his linen immaculate—Soublet changed it every few hours. His servant followed him, bearing on a japanned tray a jar of slow-squirming brown leeches, six knives of German steel, an array of cupping-glasses and a bleeding-bowl whose white porcelain was daubed and splashed with red.

"Mary, Mother of God, save me!" shrieked the Italian. "I have not loved those fat capons of Satan but I always loved Thee! Do not leave me in Satan's hand!" He began to vomit again, clotted black rivers of spew. Barnard and Dr. Soublet both stepped back in alarm; January caught the man's shoulders to steady him, helped by the tall woman who'd been mopping up. The vomit spattered her calico skirt. Her face, beautiful and impassive under an elaborately folded tignon, did not change, dark eyes like a serpent's, registering neither disgust nor pity.

"This man doesn't need your silly Thompsonian trash," Soublet said to Barnard, not sparing a glance for the sick man. "Weeds and vinegar and cinchona bark—fie! It's clear that his constitution needs to be lowered. Boy . . ." The doctor addressed January. "Hold him down."

Barnard backed away, clutching his slice of onion, which in the dim light did indeed resemble the Eucharist. The Italian, too spent to struggle, only wept a little as January gripped his right arm and shoulder, Soublet's servant his left. Soublet opened the patient's vein at the elbow. The blood was inky in the semidark.

"There. He should do now. Bind that up." Soublet turned away. "I'll leave instructions to Ker to take another pint at noon."

The servant gathered up the reeking bowl and moved off in his master's wake.

January muttered, "I saw less blood when Jackson beat the British than I do on any night he's in charge." The tall woman, turning away, paused, a flick of a smile in the ophidian eyes.

There was no one else to work the ward that night. January and Barnard moved the dead Russian—or whoever he had been—out onto the gallery and, later, when they had time, down the stairs to the yard. Three women and four men were already there, rough sheets drawn up over them, waiting for the dead-cart man. The night was as hot outdoors as in, the roar of cicadas rising and falling like demon machinery in the dark beyond the wall. Smudges in the yard—and the fact that the municipal contractors in charge of cleaning the gutters of Common Street hadn't done their job in weeks—rendered the air nearly unbreathable. A woman moved about the courtyard, lifting the corners of sheets to see the dead faces underneath.

"Can I come upstairs and look?" she asked January when he went to her. "I'm lookin' for a man name of Virgil, big man, but not so big as you?" She put an inflection of query in her voice. By her clothing she was either a slave or one of the dirt-poor freedwomen trying to make a living in the shanties at the ends of Girod or Perdido Streets, maybe a prostitute or maybe just a laundress. "Virgil, he slave to Michie Bringier over by Rue Bourbon, but he sleep out and work the levee. He pay Michie Bringier his cost, pay him good. He didn't come to the shed he rent behind Puy's Grocery, not night before last, not last night . . ."

She nodded down at the dead around her feet. "These folks all white."

Though Bronze John's hand touched everyone, white, black, and colored, it was mostly the whites who died of it and, of them, more often the whites who'd flocked into New Orleans from the United States—the *rest* of the United States, January corrected himself—or from Europe.

In Europe, January had known dozens of men whose aim was to come here and make fortunes impossible to find in the overtaxed, overcrowded, politically watchful lands of Germany, Italy, and France. They'd meet and read *The Last of the Mohicans* together or New York newspapers a year old. And there were fortunes to be made, in sugar, in trade, in the new, phenomenally profitable cotton.

But there was a price.

And with the coming of the cholera, even the blacks and the colored found no immunity, no recovery, no hope.

January led the woman up to the ward, as he had led so many since June. The arrival of the ambulances called him away: those who had been found, as this woman feared her friend had been found, in the shacks or attics or on street corners where they had fallen. One of those carried in was Hèlier the water seller, who raised a shaky hand and whispered, "Hey, piano teacher," as he was borne past. In a different voice he murmured, "Mamzelle Marie," to the woman who had cleaned the floor. And, "Hey, Nanié," to the ragged woman . . . Even *in extremis*, the man knew everyone in town.

"You seen Virgil?" she said. "He sleep out, you know, alone in that shack . . ."

The water seller shook his head. He was fine boned and older than he looked, the creamy lightness of his skin marred by a clotted blurring of freckles. His shoulders, though broad and strong, were uneven with the S-shaped curvature of his spine. Now his face was engorged with the fever jaundice. Dark in the glower of the oil lamps, he trembled, and there was black vomit down the front of his shirt.

"I ask around," the water seller whispered, as they bore him away.

When January went down to the court again he saw Emil Barnard crouched over the bodies of the dead. Barnard heard the creak of his weight on the steps and straightened quickly, jerked the sheet back into place, and shoved something up under his coat. "I saw a . . . a black man come in just now." Barnard pointed accusingly out the courtyard gate. "He was doing something with the bodies, but I didn't see what. I must go and report it at once." He almost ran, not up the steps to where Soublet would be, but through a door into the lower floor of the Hospital, where those unafflicted with the fever were cramped together in emergency quarters.

January pulled back the sheet. The Russian's boots were gone. So were his teeth. His jaw gaped, sticky with gummed blood; little clots of it daubed his pale beard stubble, the front of his shirt. January whipped aside the other sheets and saw that all the corpses had been so treated. One woman's lips were all but severed, bloodless flaps of flesh. Ants crept across her face. Both women had been clipped nearly bald.

January stood up as if he'd been jabbed with a goad, so angry he trembled.

A hand touched his arm. He whirled and found himself looking into Mamzelle Marie's dark eyes.

"Don't matter no more to them, Michie Janvier."

Wheels creaked in the ooze of Common Street outside, harness jangling as the horses strained against the muck. The dead-cart.

"It matters to me."

Mamzelle Marie said nothing. Where the orange light brushed a greasy finger her earrings had the gleam of real gold, the dark gems on the crucifix suspended from her neck a true sapphire glint. "It's nowhere near so bad as it was last year."

And that's supposed to comfort me? "No."

Last year.

It had been almost exactly a year.

Paris in the cholera. January felt again the dreadful stillness of those suffocating August days, the empty streets and shuttered windows. Though he'd been working then for ten years as a musician, he'd gone back to the Hôtel Dieu to nurse, to do what he could, knowing full well he could do nothing. That epidemic had recalled to him all the memories of fever seasons past: the families of the poor brought in from the attics where two or three or seven had died already, the stench and the sense of helpless dread. Whenever he'd stepped outside he had been astonished to see the jostling mansard roofs, the chestnut trees, and gray stone walls of Paris, instead of the low, pastel houses of the town where he had been raised.

One day he'd walked back to the two rooms he and his wife shared in the tangle of streets between the old Cluny convent and the river, to find them stinking like a plague ward of the wastes Ayasha had been unable to contain when the weakness, the shivering, the fever had struck her. To find Ayasha herself on the bed in the midst of that humiliating horror, a rag doll wrung and twisted and left to dry, the black ocean of her hair trailing down over the edge of the bed to brush the floor.

Death had spared her nothing. She had died alone.

"No." Though January had never spoken of this memory to his sister—who he knew was a disciple of Mamzelle Marie—or to anyone else, he thought he saw her knowledge of the scene in this woman's serpent eyes. Maybe she really did read people's dreams. "No, it's not so bad as last year," agreed January again, softly.

January didn't really expect to be allowed to speak to the houseman Gervase. His query met a bland, sleek smile and a murmured "Oh, Gervase is at his work right now. Madame doesn't hold with servants leaving their work."

He'd never liked the Lalaurie coachman, Bastien. The round-faced, smooth-haired quadroon had a smug insolence to him, a self-satisfaction that boded ill for the other servants of the Lalaurie household, despite all that Madame herself might try to do.

Born a slave and raised in slavery until the age of eight, January had always found it curious that colored masters so frequently worked their slaves hard and treated them cruelly, even if they had once been slaves themselves. Given a chance, he suspected that Bastien would have been such a master, exercising petty power where he could. He knew the coachman had been with Madame Lalaurie a long time, perhaps longer than Dr. Nicolas Lalaurie himself. Upon those occasions when he'd seen them together, it was clear to January that the face Bastien showed his mistress was not the face his fellow slaves saw.

The two Blanque girls—daughters of Delphine Lalaurie by her second husband, the late banker Jean Blanque—were older than one usually found still unmarried Creole belles of good family. Though they were soft-spoken and polite, as Creole girls must be, January liked neither of them. Even Louise Marie, the cripple, for whom he had expected to develop sympathy when first he had been introduced to the household last spring, made him uneasy. She was clinging and self-pitying, constantly referring to her twisted back and misaligned pelvis.

"I do my best," she said with a sigh, blinking her large hazel eyes up at him from the piano stool. "But as you see, I'm no more a musician than I am a matrimonial catch." Her lace-mitted hand, thin to the point of boniness, strayed for the thousandth time to the bunches of fashionable curls that hung over her ears, readjusting the ribbons and the multifarious lappets of point d'esprit. Louise Marie was dressed as always in the height of Paris fashion, the bell-shaped skirt of girlish yellow jaconet trimmed with blond lace, flounces, and far too many silk roses. The bodice was specially cut, and the skirt specially hemmed, to accommodate the twist of her spine and the uneven length of her legs.

"As long as you do your best, Mademoiselle Blanque," replied January, with the patient friendliness he had long cultivated to deal with pupils he didn't much care for personally, "you'll make progress. This isn't a race," he added, with a smile. "It's not like you have to be ready to open in *Le Mariage de Figaro* at Christmas."

"Well, that's a blessing," muttered Pauline, prowling from the shuttered windows of the second-floor front parlor where the piano stood. The younger sister slapped her fan on the piano's shining rosewood top, then a moment later caught it up and beat the air with it again, as if the necessity to do so were unjust penance imposed upon her alone. Though he had bathed before coming here, January felt the stickiness of sweat on his face and under his shirt and coat.

In April or October, all the long windows onto the gallery would have been thrown wide at this time of day to catch the breezes of coming evening. But now that was a luxury that could not be risked. Fever rode the night air, invisible and deadly—that was all that anybody knew of it.

The winter curtains of velvet and tapestry had been exchanged for light chintz and gauze, but those were drawn closely over the tall French doors; and the light they admitted was wan and sickly gray. The woven straw mats underfoot, and the muslin covers masking the opulent furniture, did little to lighten or cool the room. With its mirrors swathed in gauze, its ornaments veiled against flyspecks, the place had a shrouded atmosphere, tomblike and drained of color.

"Oh, darling, please . . ." Louise Marie made a feeble gesture toward her sister's fan and produced another cataclysmic sigh. "If you would . . . The heat affects me so!"

Any other family would have been in Mandeville, where January knew Madame Lalaurie owned a summer cottage and a good deal of property. Nicolas Lalaurie was a doctor—a partner at Jules Soublet's clinic on Rue Bourbon—but somehow January suspected the small, pale, silent Frenchman would have had no objection to leaving a town where only the poor remained to fall ill. But Madame Lalaurie, almost alone among the high Creole society, had chosen to remain in town and nurse the sick. January guessed that Dr. Lalaurie—not a native Creole himself—knew his reputation would never survive flight from a danger that his wife faced with such matter-of-fact calm.

He guessed, too, that one or the other of the Lalauries had decreed that the two girls should remain as well: the doctor out of wariness about how things looked, or Madame simply because the possibility of falling ill had never entered her mind.

Her face like bitter stone, Pauline slapped open the sandalwood sticks and began to fan her sister, while Louise Marie, a long-suffering smile of martyred gratitude and a gleam of satisfaction in her eye, jerked and hobbled through a Mozart contredanse in a fashion that amply demonstrated that she had done none of her appointed practice during the previous four days.

But January was used to pupils not practicing, and there were things he could say to praise without condemnation, which he knew would do him no good. All girls of good family studied the piano from childhood, though few kept up lessons into their twenties. Madame Delphine Lalaurie, however, was as renowned for her piano playing as she was for her hospitality, for her business acumen, for her beauty and social connections, and it was unthinkable that her daughters should fall below the standard she set. Watching Louise Marie's exaggerated winces at her mistakes—as if they were catastrophes imposed upon her by a spiteful Muse instead of the result of her own negligence about practice—January felt a pang of pity for them.

Madame's very perfection was probably not easy to live up to.

"That was good, Mademoiselle Blanque. May I hear Mademoiselle Pauline on the Haydn now?" Their mother had been the daughter of one of the wealthiest men in New Orleans; Marie Delphine de McCarty's first husband a city intendant, a Spanish hidalgo of great wealth, and her second, Jean Blanque, a banker whose signature underwrote nearly every property deed in the city. Their two older sisters were the wives of two of the most influential men in the parish. With the early death of their little brother these girls became heiresses to a sizable fortune in city rents and land; to an unshakable position in Creole society; and to this huge and almost oppressively opulent house, with its gilded ceilings and French furniture, its marble stairs and crystal lighting fixtures.

But as he watched the older girl—a young woman, in truth, in her early twenties—make an elaborate business of limping across the parlor to the most comfortable chair; clutching heavily on her sister's arm; sending Pauline to fetch a fan, a cushion, a kerchief, to call for Babette to fetch some lemonade from the kitchen—summoning Pauline back when she had gotten started on the Haydn march, because she suddenly felt faint and needed her vinaigrette—he knew Louise Marie would never marry.

And Pauline?

She was still what they would consider marriageable in any society, eighteen or nineteen, and would have been pretty had she not been so thin. Some wasting sickness there, thought January, studying her rigid profile with a physician's eye. Not consumption. Her color looked good, and she seemed to have no trouble drawing breath. An inability to digest certain foods, perhaps? Her hands were stick thin, wrist bones like hazelnuts standing out under the gold of her bracelets; her whole body seemed brittle, stiff as wood as she played, mechanically and badly. Resentment rose off Pauline like steam from the mosquito-wriggling gutters.

At her sister? January had seen other households rendered twisted and tense by the manipulation of a chronic invalid, and Louise Marie certainly seemed to take delight in interrupting her sister's practice. "Oh, here's Babette; darling, will you bring the lemonade here?" Pauline must have had a lifetime of being admonished to obey her sister: she stopped playing immediately, stalked to the parlor door where an emaciated servant woman stood with a single German crystal goblet of lemonade on a tray. This Pauline snatched without so much as a word of thanks and brought it across to the invalid.

January, who had hoped to have a quick word with the servant, watched the woman depart, a dark-clothed ghost whose plain white muslin tignon brought back a memory of petite Cora, who dressed like a freedwoman's daughter but arranged her headscarf like a slave.

For the remainder of the lesson January watched for his chance to have a moment alone, to slip away and find another servant, to ask discreetly that word be got to the houseman Gervase to meet him. But only in so watching did he become aware of how bounded he was by the regulations of society. A guest in the house never spoke to the servants, be that guest white or free colored. Neither was expected to have the smallest inclination to speak to a black, a slave. And well-trained servants, for their part, never came into the presence of guests unless specifically sent for. Listening, he was aware of how quiet the entire floor was. Now and then he heard a soft tread in one of the rooms above, but no one entered the big front parlor in which the piano stood or the smaller sewing parlor, which opened from it through an arch of cypress wood painted to resemble marble. The shadowy hall that divided the house, American fashion, from front to back, was still. If any servants moved about, laying the table in the long dining room or cleaning the lamps in Dr. Lalaurie's library behind it, they did so without sound.

And January was very conscious that he was being paid to teach Mademoiselle Blanque and Mademoiselle Pauline to play the piano, however little they might wish to learn. They were his priority, taking precedence over a favor promised to an untruthful young woman he barely knew. So, though he watched for his chance, he kept the greater part of his concentration on them.

Were they obliged to play, he wondered, at the dinners and danceables that made their mother so famous in the upper levels of Creole society?

At the end of the allotted hour, Bastien materialized like a round-faced smiling genie in the parlor door, holding the carved cypress panels open for Louise Marie and Pauline to exit. Louise Marie gasped with restrained agony as she rose from her chair, her hand going now to her twisted back, now to her narrow chest. Once the demoiselles had gone, the coachman handed January his Mexican silver dollar.

"This way, M'sieu Janvier."

The servant woman Babette slipped across the hall and through the door of the rear parlor as January and Bastien passed through that of the front; from the corner of his eye January saw her nip up the lemonade goblet from the marble-topped occasional table beside Louise Marie's daybed as if she feared to let it remain out of her custody one moment longer than necessary. He tried to formulate an excuse to turn back, but was very conscious of the watchfulness in the coachman's eye, and in the end did not.

The brick-paved courtyard's size was itself an ostentation in the crowded French town, and though the house was less than three years old, it was already lush with foliage, paint-bright bougainvillea and the banana plants with their pendulous fleshy blooms that seemed to spring up overnight. Piles of hooves, horn, and hair from the slaughterhouses smoldered fitfully in terra-cotta tubs, and the doors of the kitchen, the laundry, and the slave quarters above were shut against the smoke. *That kitchen must be an inferno!* thought January, looking back at its closed doors with a shudder of pity for any cook condemned to work there. The rooms above it would be worse: three servants' rooms looking onto a narrow gallery and three more garrets and another gallery on top of those. Below the slates of the roof, the heat would collect like a bake oven. Even the stables, where Madame's famous team of matched coal black English carriage-horses was housed, seemed almost hermetically fast.

From a little ways up Rue de l'Hôpital, it seemed to him that the tall house, with its tiers of galleries and watchful doors, had the look of a fortress, wreathed in smoke and towering above all buildings around it.

A fortress against Bronze John, he thought. Against the cholera. Locked and shuttered, like every other house on the street, in the hopes of thwarting nightborne, drifting enemies no one could see.

January shook his head, and proceeded up Rue de l'Hôpital through gathering dusk.

When Benjamin January left New Orleans in the spring of 1817, twenty-four years old, to study medicine in Paris, he had vowed in his heart as Louisiana's long flat malarial coastline settled into sullen mist behind the boat's wake that he would never return. Even in those easygoing days the dense African darkness of his skin guaranteed that he would be regarded as little better than a savage by white and colored alike, no matter how skilled he became. Not for him, he had always known, the affluent practices of the free colored physicians and surgeons in the town.

He had made Paris his home. Even when he became a musician, trading on the other great love of his life to earn sufficient money to marry the woman he found there, the woman he loved, he had regarded Louisiana as a country of the past. Its memories of smothering heat, of going to bed too exhausted to eat were things he wished to put aside forever: of taking care never to meet a white man's eyes and always to appear slightly stupid, slightly lazy. Of avoiding anything that might possibly be construed as a threat. And hand in hand with all that had gone the knowledge that anything in his life could be taken away from him without warning, explanation, or recompense.

In France it would not be so, he had told himself. In France he would be truly free.

Then Ayasha had died. As if the wall between past and present had shattered like a pane of glass, pestilence flowed through the streets of Paris. The city took on for him the aspect of nightmare, a nightmare in which she was always about to come around the corner, she was always just a stall ahead of him in the market buying apples . . .

she was always lying on the reeking bed amid the filth in which she had died, reaching for the empty water pitcher, praying for the strength to hang on until he returned home.

Like a termite-riddled post under a hammer blow, his life had crumbled with her death. He had returned to New Orleans, to the world that, if it had not cherished him, at least was one he knew. He was forty. Some day, he thought, springing over the offal of the gutter and seeing ahead of him the pink stucco walls of his mother's house, some day he might collect the strength to leave Louisiana again. To return to France—though probably never Paris—or Vienna, or London, or Rome.

But right now he was like a man with fever who can crawl no farther than his bed, where he lies waiting to heal.

Someday, maybe, he would heal.

He didn't know.

His mother still owned the house on the Rue Burgundy given her by St. Denis Janvier, when that gentleman had died in 1822. Livia January had married a respectable upholsterer named Levesque, and a few years ago he had died, too. Though January had the impression she was less than pleased about admitting she'd ever borne a son in slavery—to hear his mother talk she had never cut cane in her life—she had extended a temperate welcome and agreed that he could reoccupy his old room above the kitchen, the room next to the cook's quarters. These rooms—garçonnières—were the custom in a country where the presence of growing sons under the same roof was regarded with less than enthusiasm by their mothers' protectors. Being his mother, she charged him three Spanish dollars a week.

Livia Levesque was currently renting chambers in a comfortable boardinghouse in Milneburgh with a number of her better-off cronies, having let the cottage she owned there to a wealthy, white sugar broker. She had taken Bella, her cook, with her. January's shift at the Charity Hospital officially ended at eight in the morning, though it was frequently noon before he left. He was usually too exhausted, and the day too sweltering, to even attempt to start up the open brick stove in the kitchen: he either had beans and rice bought out the back door of one of the local groceries or went without.

Today he had gone without and was wondering if he should seek out a meal at Gillette's Tavern, or bribe the cook at Breyard's for a dish of something, before returning to the Hospital in a few hours. First, he thought, pushing open the gate into his mother's yard, he wanted to get rid of this hell-begotten wool coat and waistcoat and cravat. What lunatic Frenchman had dictated that the formal dress that marked him as a professional had to be the same in a tropical city like New Orleans as it was in London or Paris? He couldn't dispense with it, of course. Leaving out the fact that his mother would kill him if she heard he'd been abroad in his official capacity less than fully and formally attired, he could say good-bye to any chance of professional employment as a musician if those who hired him saw that he dressed like a day laborer.

But at least he could sponge off again and put on a clean shirt and a slightly less excruciating garment.

It wouldn't do to be seen dressed like (for example) the verminous, long-haired scarecrow currently lounging on the steps of the garçonnière, spitting tobacco and reading the *New Orleans Courier* while he waited, quite clearly, for January to come home.

"You're lucky my mother's away," January remarked, closing the gate behind him. "She'd order Bella to chase you off with a broom. Sir," he added.

The scarecrow spat a dark stream of expectorant onto the bricks. "I been chased off better." He spoke in a mild, rather scratchy tenor and blinked up at January from under the wide brim of a countryman's rough hat and a greasy curtain of hair the color of dried onion tops. "And worse," he added, carefully folding up his newspaper and rising to a height barely half an inch less than January's own. There was a hole in the skirts of his old-fashioned coat. "Sorta comes with workin' for the law. Now what's all this truck"—he gestured with the paper—"about there bein' 'no sign yet of any epidemic fever in the city'? These newspaper fellers live in the same town as the rest of us, or what? 'Some few of the weak-kneed have ignominiously fled at the sound of a rumor. . . .' "

"The newspapers always say that," said January. "The businesses in town won't have it any other way."

Lieutenant Abishag Shaw of the New Orleans City Guard widened his eyes in momentary startlement at this piece of journalistic cooperativeness, then shrugged. "Well, I don't suppose it's any news to anybody in town." He tucked the paper away. "I understand yore laid out, Maestro, and gotta be back at the Hospital tonight, but there's sort of a matter I gotta take up with you." He spat again and wiped his bristly chin. "You acquainted with a gal by name of Cora Chouteau?"

He pronounced the French name correctly, something one wouldn't have expected from the raspy, American flatboat-English he spoke, and January tried not to react. By the sharpening of those rain-pale eyes, he didn't think he succeeded.

"Chouteau?" He shook his head. "The name isn't familiar."

"Little gal so high, 'bout as dark as yore ma." Shaw had made the acquaintance of the redoubtable Widow Levesque last Mardi Gras. "Skinny. Sort of pointy chin they say. Twenty-two, twenty-three year old."

January manufactured furrows of thought in his brow, then shook his head again. "Why are you looking for her? A runaway?"

"In a manner of speakin'." Shaw gently scratched under the breast of his coat. "She did run away, yeah. But when she left she helped herself to five thousand dollars from the plantation accounts and the mistress's pearl necklace and poisoned the master an' the mistress both for good measure. The mistress'll live, they say. They buried the master Friday."

THREE

"It isn't true!" January thought that Cora would flee from him entirely, but in fact she only turned her back on him sharply and went a few steps, her arms folded over her breast, hands clasping her skinny shoulders. In the dense noon shadows under the Pellicot kitchen gallery her face was unreadable, like a statue, always supposing some Greek sculptor would have expended bronze on the pointed, wary features of an urchin and a slave. A wave of trembling passed over her, an ague of dread.

January leaned against the rail of the gallery stairs. What was it, he wondered, that she feared he would read in her face?

"What this policeman tell you?" She flung the words back at him over her shoulder.

"Why don't you tell me?"

Her breath sipped in to spit some counteraccusation, but she let it go. She rubbed one hand along her arm, as if trying to get warm.

"Did this Otis Redfern rape you?" January asked.

Cora sniffed. "What's rape?" she demanded. "My . . . a girl I knew, a friend of mine, she was raped. She was sick after for a long time. I took care of her. . . ." She shook her head. "She fought him, and he hurt her." The softness of her mouth hardened again. "So you don't fight, and it's not so bad. But if you don't fight, it's not really rape, is it? And what's the sense of fighting anyway? He'd just have one of the men come in and hold me down. That's what he said. He said he'd have Gervase do it. You think I'd kill him over that?"

"There's women who would."

"If every woman killed every master who had her against her will, there'd be dead men lying like a carpet from here to the Moon. And that M'am Redfern, she wouldn't get after him about it. Just made my work harder for me, like I liked being fingered and poked and pestered by that smelly old man. If it wasn't for Gervase I think I'd have gone crazy."

She made a quick gesture with her small hands and faced back around. Beyond the shade of the gallery the sun smote the yard like a brass hammer. The dead-carts had finished their morning rounds, and the voice of a man or a woman in the street, or the creak of a wagon, fell singly into the hush.

"You know how they do," Cora said. "She tried to get me sent out to the fields, he said I was to work in the house. She said if I worked the house I'd do the chambers and the lamps. He said no, I had to do something genteel, like sewing. Me, I'd rather have cut cane than be under the same roof with her all day. She puts me hemming sheets and then makes me pick out every stitch 'cos the hem's too wide, she says. And then he says, to *me* he says, 'Don't rub up against her, don't be always givin' her trouble, can't you see what you do'll come back on me?' What *I* do comes back on *him*?"

She drew another breath, anger narrowing her dark eyes. "I never killed him. I ran away. I had to run away. It's her that was out to kill *me*."

January raised his eyebrows. "If every woman killed every wench her husband had, there'd be dead women lying like a carpet from here to the Moon."

"Yeah." Cora's mouth quirked with a kind of grim humor. "But I heard them fighting. I heard her say, 'You sell that slut of yours if we're so hard up for money from your gambling'—and he was a terrible gambler, Michie Redfern was. And Michie Redfern says, 'You're not telling me what to do, woman, and if you take and sell her

I swear to you I'll find her again and it'll be the worse for you.' Not that he cared about *me*, Michie Janvier. But M'am Redfern is an overbearing woman, a Boston Yankee woman, always on about how much money her daddy had had, and Michie Redfern wasn't going to take anything off her. You known men like that."

January had known men like that.

"That's still a long way from her killing you."

"Michie Janvier, I swear what I'm telling you is true." She came back and sat on the end of the bench that was drawn up near the stairs where he stood. She wore a green dress today, though she still had on the red-and-black shoes. The skirt's folds hung limp, for it had been cut to accommodate several more petticoats than she was wearing; cut to accommodate a corset, too, as the red dress had been. No servant wore corsets, and Cora was not wearing one now.

Where had she gotten those? he wondered. And the soap and water to wash her face this morning. Not in the Swamp, the squalid ag-glomeration of grogshops and brothels that festered a few unpaved streets behind the Charity Hospital: that was the place most runaways went. But hers weren't dresses that could be acquired, or kept in good condition, in that maze of mud-sinks and cribs. He remembered the woman Nanié two nights ago, looking for her Virgil among the sick. Her stained dirty clothes had the stink of sweat ground into them, not because she was a particularly unclean woman but because spare labor and time and the fuel to heat water were luxuries among the poor, and their clothes went a long time between washings. Neatness of appearance was something that could be maintained only with great care and with a certain minimum of money.

His own coat and waistcoat, folded tidily over the rail of the stairs behind him with the cravat tucked into a pocket, were one badge of his freedom. Even more than the papers the law demanded he carry— and as much as the well-bred French his tutors and his mother had hammered into him as a child—they said, This is a free man of color, not somebody's property to be bought and sold.

A woman dressed like a slave on the streets would be noticed, especially by someone looking for a runaway.

The dress was a disguise.

The cleanliness was a disguise.

Both depended on money and a place to stay.

After a long time of silence, Cora said, "Me and Gervase, we used to meet over by Black Oak. That's the place next up the river from Spanish Bayou—Michie Redfern's plantation just south of Twelve-Mile Point. Black Oak isn't hardly a plantation, just a little bit of land, but M'am Redfern's pa bought it for her when she came down from Boston to marry Michie Redfern. At least that's what Leonide told me, Michie Redfern's cook. They was gonna go to business together, M'am Redfern's pa and Michie Redfern, only he died. Michie Kendal, I mean."

She took a deep breath, not meeting his eyes, folding carefully the pleats of her green cotton sleeve where they ran into the wristband. There was a thin line of tatted cotton lace there, pale ecru, the kind schoolgirls produced by the yard while their governesses read to them from edifying books.

"That's where Gervase and I went, after Michie Redfern told him and the others—Laurent, and Randall, and Marcel, and Hermes, and Sally—that he was selling them on account of what he owed Michie Calder and Michie Fazende. Michie Redfern, he found us there. He sent Gervase back to the house and he hit me a couple times, then he had me, like your policeman said; though what that was supposed to prove I don't know. That a big man can stick it into a little girl my size when he can have her whipped if she don't let him? We both of us knew *that*."

Contempt blazed in her eyes.

"A couple days later he takes Gervase and the others on into town. Gervase told me he'd been sold to M'am Lalaurie, on Rue Royale—the others was gonna go to the Bank of Louisiana, and be sold up north in Missouri and Arkansas Territories, where they need cotton hands something bad. M'am Redfern, she doesn't say much to me, but she looks at me like the Devil looks at a little child out lost in the swamp. I slip out of the house and walk over by Black Oak again in the afternoon. I'm feeling bad, missing Gervase and wondering if I can get away long enough to come down to New Orleans and see him now and then, or he can come back maybe and see me.

"It's hot, and I start lookin' around the house for a cup or something to get me some water."

The look of calculation had disappeared from her face, replaced by a pucker in her brow as she called back the events to her mind. She was no longer thinking, January thought, about her story, no longer tailoring it for what she thought he wanted to hear.

"Black Oak's a little house," she went on after a time. "All the furniture and dishes and that been cleaned out a long time ago, but I thought there might be something. Mostly Gervase and I just layed in the bedroom, where it's cool, and didn't go in the other two rooms. But there's this cupboard in the parlor by the fireplace, that's always locked with a key. Only this time when I went in it wasn't locked, and inside I found this tin jar, like they sell candy in. It was new—it wasn't rusty nor chipped nor nothing—but when I opened it, there was a little sort of bag inside, made out of black flannel, full of crushed-up dry leaves and some seeds. I knowed the smell of it, 'cos one of the women on Grand Isle where I grew up was a conjure, and she told all us children what to stay away from in the woods. It was monkshood, and poison, and I knew then it had to be M'am Redfern that hid it there, in the little house where she had the key to, to keep it away from her husband finding it. I remembered how M'am Redfern had looked at me, all day, when her husband was gone."

She looked down again, tugging the ruffle of her sleeve.

"And what did you do?"

"I was scared." Cora raised those great dark eyes, under a fringe of thick-curled lashes. "I slept out in the swamp that night, and in the morning I hid in the trees near the steamboat landing by Spanish Bayou. They'd said there was a boat coming in that day—Michie Bailey had said, that rode over the day before because he was bringin' down these horses of his to sell in town. When the boat came in, I slipped in the water and swam around the far side of it. The men down on the engine deck pulled me up and hid me in the hay bales, for Michie Bailey's white horses. And, Lordy, you'd have thought they'd give those horses feather beds, the fuss they made over 'em."

January studied that guarded face. Wondering how much of what she told him was truth.

"And you didn't go back to the house for anything before you went down to the boat?"

She shook her head vehemently. "I didn't steal no money. Nor no pearls. Michie Redfern, he probably took them pearls himself and sold them for gambling money or to pay off some more money he owed. He owed everybody in the Parish. That's what probably happened. And I sure didn't kill anybody. But I had to run away, Michie Janvier. She'd have killed me. I know she would have. I had to find Gervase . . ."

"And what?" asked January softly. "Get him to run away, too?"

Her eyes remained on her sleeve ruffle, which she stroked and smoothed, stroked and smoothed with her tiny, work-roughened fingers. "I don't know. Maybe we can—can find some way to make us some money. To buy him free. Sometimes white folks lets their servants work out—sleep out, too, long as they come back and pays 'em. But I just want to see him. To talk to him."

For a time January said nothing. Madame Lalaurie was an astute businesswoman, and it wasn't outside the realm of possibility that she'd let a slave operate independently, though not, probably, a trained houseman. But looking at that down-turned little face, the careful deliberation of those little fingers tracing the folds of the cloth, he knew those were not Cora's thoughts.

He'd seen monkshood poisoning, in Paris, at the Hôtel Dieu; a woman named Montalban had poisoned the brother with whom she lived. He thought about the agonies of vomiting and blindness, the sweating, convulsions, pain. Thought about Shaw sitting on the steps of his mother's gallery, spitting tobacco and recounting the facts of the case without ever asking why or if January had made inquiries about the purported murderess's lover scant days after the woman herself had been seen at the Lalaurie house. Bastien the coachman would have reported her to Shaw, he thought. Would have reported, too, January's request to speak to the young man.

It didn't mean Shaw didn't have other information, held back as a speculator holds sugar or cotton, against a rise in prices.

"Cora," said January slowly, "whether or not you put poison into Otis Redfern's supper, Madame Redfern thinks you did. The police think so, too. Now, I told them I hadn't met you, hadn't ever heard of you, and I implied I hadn't ever been asked to take any kind of message from you to Gervase. At least when Lieutenant Shaw asked me to notify him if you did ask me, I said I would. All this is illegal. I could get into serious trouble for it."

Cora licked her lips and folded her arms again, as if chilled despite the day's burning heat. "You mean you can't help me anymore." It was not phrased as a question.

That's what he meant.

And that, he thought later, should have been the end of it. For everyone's good.

That's when he should have walked away.

Last night he had dreamed about his father.

He didn't often. His memories of his father—or the man he believed to have been his father—existed only in flashes, isolated incidents of time: being picked up, up and up and up at the end of those powerful arms, and the coal black face with the gray shellwork of tribal scars grinning joyfully below him, or walking along the edge of the bayou, listening to the deep bass voice hum-sing songs he barely recalled. He didn't even know where his father had been when he was told that his mother was being sold to St. Denis Janvier, whether his father had still been on Bellefleur Plantation then or not.

But he did remember, hot summer nights, creeping out of his room to sit on the gallery of the garçonnière, waiting for his father to come for him.

That had to have been shortly after they'd moved into the pink cottage on Rue Burgundy. January was eight. His father wouldn't let them leave him, he had told himself. He'd come slipping through the passway into the yard, to tap on his wife's shutters, to stand below the gallery of the garçonnière, white teeth gleaming in the moonlight, waiting for his son to come running down to him and be lifted up in those powerful arms.

January had crept out of his room most nights for a year, he remembered—except those nights when St. Denis Janvier would come to visit his mother—to sit on the gallery in the darkness and wait. The town had been smaller then, with vacant land between the cottages on Rue Dauphine and Rue Burgundy, and between Rue Burgundy and the old town wall, rank marsh where moon-silvered water gleamed between forests of weeds. January had given names to the voices of the frogs crying in the darkness and made up words to the heavy, harsh drumming of the cicadas and the skreek of crickets; the drone of mosquitoes in the blackness. His sister Olympe jeered at him, but he'd waited nonetheless.

His father had never come.

"You have to lie low," he said slowly. Cora looked up, startled, at the sound of his voice. "You have to stay quiet. You can't even think about 'making money somehow' to help Gervase." Even as the words came out of his mouth he couldn't believe he was saying them.

"Slaves are just too expensive these days for them to let him go— or you either. They're watching for you, Cora. You have to get out of New Orleans if you possibly can, and remember that even with the fever on they'll be watching the steamboats on the river and on the lake. You think you can do that?"

She made no reply, neither nodded nor shook her head. But trembling passed over her again, a long silvery shiver, like a horse at the starting line of a race, before they whip the flags down to let them run.

"You send me a note under another name," said January. "Post it after you get to some other city. Set up some way for me to send a letter to you. Can you write?"

"A little," Cora whispered. "My friend taught me."

The girl who'd been raped?

"My next lesson with the Lalaurie girls is Friday. Can you be here Friday evening about sunset?" It meant going to the Hospital again without sleep, but these days that was common enough.

She nodded. Her lips formed the words *thank you,* without sound. She waited in the dark of the gallery while he slipped away up the pass-through between houses, still as a mouse waiting for the cat to go by.

Idle to suppose that a slave girl accused of murdering her master could turn the accusation on her master's wife.

He thought again about poor Anne Montalban, trying to convince her neighbors, and later the police and the press, that Brother Jean, professor of law and pillar of the community, had raped both her and her daughter (and possibly three other local girls who could not be brought to testify) and was in the habit of keeping his niece locked in her room for weeks on end "for the good of her soul."

Lying naked on his bed in the heat, hearing the roaring of afternoon rain on the slates, he tried to sleep, and his mind returned to the small, taut face, the wary eyes, of Cora Chouteau.

If you don't fight it's not really rape.

According to Shaw, the Redfern cook had seen Cora slip back into the house, some time after she was supposed to have run away. How long after? In the twilight, Shaw had said. *I slept out in the swamp.*

Then after supper Wednesday night Otis Redfern had stumbled against the wall, trying to get outside to the outhouse, gasping and crying with a mouth half-paralyzed, pleading in the heat that there was ice water in his veins. Madame Redfern was found sick in her room only half an hour later, having collapsed from dizziness, too weak to call for help.

Had Cora returned only to steal five thousand dollars and her mistress's pearls? What the hell was five thousand dollars doing lying around the house? Money and credit were impossibly tight this year (his mother had investments, and he'd been hearing about the tightness of money at great length for months). Most plantations dealt in letters of credit. In the best of times it was rare that even the richest of the planters, the Destrehans or the McCartys, had a thousand dollars cash money readily available.

Or had she gone back to slip powdered monkshood into whatever was being prepared for that evening's meal?

Shaw had made no mention of the candy tin. January wondered if he knew about it. He could not imagine a Boston-raised merchant's daughter knowing how to identify monkshood in the woods, much less how to cull and dry it. If Cora didn't prepare the stuff herself, Emily Redfern would have to have acquired it somewhere.

And after all that, were Cora to testify that Emily Redfern kept powdered monkshood in the locked cupboard on her own property, and her case failed, she would be in serious trouble indeed.

He closed his eyes. The rain eased off, and a breeze walked across his bare belly and thighs. Why Cora Chouteau concerned him he didn't know. It was madness, insanely risky. He'd learn what he could, but there were things he simply could not do.

At least it was better than lying here obsessively inventorying his own body: did his head ache? *(That's just lack of sleep.)* Was he thirsty? *(That's nothing. It's hot. No worse than yesterday.)* Were his joints sore? Nausea? Belly cramps?

Was he hot with fever or was it just hotter today?

There had been a time when he'd wanted to die, wanted some shining angel from his childhood catechism to appear and tell him he didn't have to be in pain anymore, didn't have to deal with loss and grief and wondering why. But the only psychopomp in town these days was old Bronze John. At the memory of those bloated orange faces, the protruding tongues, the horrible feeble picking of the hands on the coverlets, he'd grope his cheap blue glass rosary from beneath the pillow and whisper, "Be mindful, Oh Lord, of Thy covenant, and say to the destroying Angel, Now hold thy hand . . ."

Like the choir at Mass the dreary voice of the dead-cart man replied from the street, "Bring out yo' dead!"

January rose, and washed, and made his way through streets stinking of summer heat to the Charity Hospital as it was growing dark. The ward was like the waiting room in hell. By lamp glare the color of the fever itself, Dr. Sanchez, another of the physicians volunteering his services, mopped down a withered shop-woman with cold vinegar and niter, the smell of it acrid in the murky dark. There were slices of onion placed under every bed.

Dark forms fidgeted like ghosts, conferring in a corner; and coming close January saw it was Dr. Soublet and Dr. Ker, the former British Army surgeon who over the protests of the Creole community had been given the post of Director of the Hospital. "I don't see that," Soublet was saying, voice rising with anger. "I don't see that at all." He spoke French, being one of those Creoles who not only had refused to learn English with the advent of the Americans but had deliberately expunged from his memory any English he had ever known.

His servant stood beside him, holding open a box the size of a child's coffin. In it January could see an apparatus of braces and straps, ratcheted wheels and metal splints. Equipment from Soublet's clinic. He'd seen the like in every medical journal for the past dozen years, accompanied by long articles about scientific advances in re-aligning the bones.

"This man came to this Hospital because he wished to be treated *gratis,* with the skills we have worked to acquire and the medicaments purchased by the city. He owes us something." On the bed between them, Hèlier the water seller moved his head vaguely. His eyes glimmered horribly bright between bloated lids. January guessed that the sick man had only the dimmest notion of what was going on. "Moreover, such an experiment can only be beneficial to him! I have had nearly miraculous results from the use of scientifically applied force in the realignment of the skeleton and limbs."

"This is a hospital, man," retorted Ker, in excellent French, "not the headquarters of the Spanish Inquisition! Take that thing away! *Charity* means 'out of love,' not 'for the sake of finding some poor soul to test your theories on.' "

"Theories, sir!" Soublet drew himself up, a tall man with a sort of coarse sturdiness to him and skin like a very bad road surface in the jumpy light. "I do not deal in theories! My work is soundly based on observation, facts, and the latest findings of the medical fraternity—"

He stopped, his attention arrested by someone at the door of the ward. Turning, January saw Madame Delphine Lalaurie.

The first thing that anyone ever said of her—the thing that most of Marie Delphine de McCarty Blanque Lalaurie's admirers always mentioned—was that she glowed. With energy, with intelligence, with strength. There were other beautiful women in the city, possibly others more beautiful by conventional standards, but had she been plain, Delphine Lalaurie would still have drawn all eyes. January had never figured out how some people could do that.

She was a tall woman, imperially straight; and though nearly every Creole woman of her age had surrendered to rich food and *embonpoint,* she retained the slim figure of a girl. She was clothed in a plain gown of black merino, such as wealthy women wore to nurse in, spotlessly clean even to its hem, as far as he could tell in this light, and unobtrusively on the leading edge of Paris fashion. The linen apron pinned over it, and the linen veil that covered her lustrous dark hair, gave her a nunlike air, as if a queen had taken vows.

Soublet and Ker immediately went to greet her, but before they could reach her she turned, hastening to the bedside of a delirious, bewhiskered young sailor who had begun to struggle and shout. A harassed nurse was trying to calm him, but he flung her back, eyes staring in horror and agony. Madame Lalaurie caught his shoulders, pressed him back to the bed with surprising strength, whispering to him, gentle words, soothing words. After a moment's desperate thrashing the man settled back, gasping, then turned and began to vomit. Madame Lalaurie and the nurse held him, and in the livid lamp glare January saw the expression of Madame's face: a deep intense pity, mingled with something else. An inward look, yearning, longing, ecstacy, as if she knelt in meditation at the Stations of the Cross.

The man collapsed, sobbing, exhausted. Madame and the nurse wrung rags in a basin of grimy water, sponged his fouled and tear-streaked face. *"Kösönöm,"* the man whispered, or something like it, a language January did not know. *"Kösönöm."*

"It's all right," she breathed, and stroked the crawling hair, "you'll be all right."

Then in a whisper of petticoats she rose, greeted Soublet with a warm smile and turned her back on Ker without a word. But she did not stop to speak with her husband's partner, crossing instead to where January stood.

"M'sieu Janvier?" Her voice was a lovely mezzo-soprano. He had heard that she sang like an angel. Like her daughter Pauline, her eyes were large, coffee dark, and brilliant. Like Pauline she seemed to burn with energy; but instead of the girl's restless, dissipated resentment, hers was a focused vigor that seemed to fill the room. "I realize it's an imposition, with as much as you have to do here," she said, "but might we speak?" Without seeming to, she glanced back at Dr. Soublet and Emil Barnard, hovering just out of earshot, and lowered her voice. "It concerns my houseman, Gervase."

There was little space in the Hospital that wasn't chockablock with the dying. January unlatched the long windows that led to the gallery. "Shut those!" roared Soublet. "Do you wish to kill all these people?"

You should talk of killing all those people, thought January dourly.

Nevertheless, he closed the shutters behind them quickly as he and Madame stepped into the steamy rankness of the night.

"I'm sorry to have to bring you out here, Madame."

She chuckled softly. "We walk back and forth through the night miasma coming here, M'sieu. If it's the night air that causes the fever at all, a little more can scarcely harm us." She coughed with the smoke of the smudges burning in the courtyard below them and waved her hand. Her gloves were French kid at fifty cents the pair, as immaculate as her apron when she had come in. Having seen the promptness with which she attended the delirious sailor, January couldn't imagine this woman going through a shift at wherever she nursed without getting as fouled as he was—apron, dress, and gloves were now spotted with water and filth. She must have changed the entire outfit before coming here.

"Sometimes I don't think doctors know anything. One can only care for the sick, and pray for their poor disobedient souls." She crossed herself; January did, too. Her one ornament was a gold crucifix on a slender chain around her neck. "I take it the girl Cora came to ask your help?"

"I know no one by that name, Madame." So that sleek bastard Bastien had told her. "It was on another matter that I wished to speak with Gervase. He's a friend of my sister Olympe. And it wasn't important. I'm sorry that you were troubled."

"M'sieu . . ." The twinkle in her dark eyes mocked him gently. "The boy's never been in this city in his life before I purchased him. And I happen to know that spiteful harpy Emily Redfern is looking all over the Parish for someone to blame for her husband's death besides her own parsimony in keeping her meat hanging too long in the summer. I gather she's talked her Yankee compatriots in the City Guard into wasting their time and citizens' money in pursuit of some poor child who had no more to do with Otis Redfern's death than you did—and paying off old scores onto her."

Regarding her, January guessed there wasn't a great deal about the personal lives of anyone in New Orleans society that Delphine Lalaurie didn't know. Related to everyone of wealth and breeding, she was in a position to hear everything. Still he said nothing. In the courtyard below them, Emil Barnard emerged from the Hospital, made his way toward the piled bodies near the gate, then stopped and glanced up to see January standing on the gallery. Barnard coughed self-consciously, shoved the empty flour sack he carried into his pocket, and strolled casually away.

January was aware of the woman's eyes on his face. Under the rouge and powder that all Creole women wore, the torchlight showed up lines at the corners of her mouth and eyes, fine lines gouged deep, more than simple weariness could account for. Juxtaposed with that slender figure, those brilliant eyes, they were almost shocking. Was it so hard, then, to carry the burden of a crippled daughter, to deal with whatever illness made Pauline so wasted and thin? Did it tell on one so terribly, to rule the household with such exactness and splendor? To be so perfect oneself, beyond weeping or fear or regret?

"I know that you can't admit to having spoken to the girl." Her voice was soft but brisk, matter-of-fact, and the lines in her face were suddenly only the marks of fatigue again. "Bastien tells me he turned you away. Very properly, of course. One can't have one's people interrupted in their work. That kind of thing upsets the other servants, as I'm sure you know; and any little disruption in the routine spreads like a mildew, until it's nearly impossible to bring everyone back up to their best. But as I'm sure you've also guessed, my Bastien is officious. He wants only the good of the household, but there! What can one do? I've spoken to him about telling that lout of a Guard that Cora came asking after poor Gervase. He will mind his tongue hereafter."

Still January made no reply.

"One cannot approve, of course, under most circumstances, of runaways," Madame Lalaurie went on. A mosquito hummed in the torchlight, close to her face, but such was her breeding that she didn't flinch, let alone swipe at it with her gloved hand. "But sheerly as a human being one cannot but feel for anyone who lives under the heel of a woman like Emily Redfern."

"I know nothing of her, Madame."

"Pray God you never have the occasion to learn, M'sieu." She sighed, as if about to add something else, then changed her mind and put the remark aside. "Be that as it may, M'sieu, Friday night I will order Bastien to leave the carriage gate open—though he will naturally be watching for thieves—from eleven o'clock until midnight. Gervase will be in the yard. I don't wish to know anything further."

January inclined his head. "Of course, it's your own business whether the gate is open or closed, Madame."

Wry amusement pulled at the corner of her lips. "I like a man who's discreet. Monsieur Blanque was like that. I don't believe, in all the years we were married, that he ever said, 'I am going to play cards with so-and-so.' Only, 'I am going out.'"

Jean Blanque, January recalled, in addition to running one of the largest banks in the city, had had connections with half the smugglers who brought illegal slaves and other goods into the city. It was to Blanque that Jean Laffite had come to begin negotiations with the Americans in the face of the British invasion. Discreet indeed!

"I trust I shall be able to rely upon your discretion in the future?" She made as if to go, then hesitated, her hand going to the reticule on her belt. After a pause she opened it and withdrew a smaller purse that clinked heavily in her hand. "Please give her this."

"I don't know who you mean, Madame."

Her smile widened, the twinkle brightening in her dark eyes. "Ah. Very well, then." She opened her hand and let the purse fall to the planks of the gallery and, with the toe of her slipper, nudged it into the shadows next to the door.

January saw her to the street. Bastien waited with the black-lacquered carriage and the four-in-hand of black English geldings that were the admiration and envy of Creole and American society alike. A long cardboard dress box lay on the driver's seat—Madame had changed her clothes before coming, then. The coachman sprang from the box to help her inside, with a combination of obsequiousness and tenderness; and as he shut the door, Madame Lalaurie smiled her thanks.

The grimy lantern light of the Hospital's porch glinted on harness brasses, polished like gold, and they were gone.

Emil Barnard straightened up quickly from the corpses by the gate as January came back through and yanked the sheets into place before hurrying away. Flies roared up in a cloud. Sickened, January didn't even look this time. When he climbed the stairs and passed through the ward he saw that Soublet, his servant, and their apparatus for the straightening of the skeleton and the limbs were all gone: Hèlier the water seller, with his crooked spine and uneven shoulders, was gone, too.

He stepped out onto the gallery again and retrieved the purse from the shadows. It contained ten Mexican silver dollars and assorted cut bits.

FOUR

For the next thirty hours January felt like a fugitive, as if Madame Lalaurie's money glowed in the dark and could be seen by all through his pocket.

Slave stealing was what white law called assisting blacks to steal themselves from those who'd paid hard money for their bodies.

And to that was added *Accessory After the Fact.*

Through the remainder of the long night in the Hospital, and walking home between houses shuttered and mostly empty in the blinding light of morning—climbing the garçonnière stairs to his bed and later waking and walking over to his sister Olympe's house on Rue Douane for dinner—he felt as if at any moment Lieutenant Shaw would step out from between the houses and say in that mild, scratchy voice, "I'd like a word with you, Maestro."

"Why would she do a thing like that?" Olympe Corbier took a pan of bread pudding from the brick-and-clay oven and set it under a little tent of newspaper to keep the flies off.

"Do what?" Straddling the kitchen's single wooden chair, January sat up a little straighter. "Give her money?"

"Help her at all." His middle sister turned from the hearth, tall for a woman and thin, her face like a coal black marsh spirit's in the furled fantasia of a blue-and-pink tignon. Olympia Snakebones, she was called among the voodoos: his true sister, his mother's child by that father who had never emerged from the darkness of St. Denis Janvier's yard. "Bernard de McCarty's daughter? Mama-in-law to one of the descended-from-God Forstalls? Jean Blanque smuggled in slaves by the boatload from Cuba."

"Why would she risk her life to mop some sailor's vomit off a hospital floor?" countered January. "You work in the clinics—if helping out other folks isn't enough for you—in order to give your work up to God, to school your pride. Who knows what she thought about what Jean Blanque did? The money may have been part of that." He shrugged, seeing the disdain in his sister's eyes, as it had been from childhood every time St. Denis Janvier's name was mentioned. "She may just have wanted to score points off Emily Redfern."

It surprised Olympe into grinning, something she'd never have let herself do as a girl, and she dropped him a curtsy. "I concede you a point, Brother. You ever met Emily Redfern?"

He shook his head.

"There's a woman," his sister said, "wants to be Delphine Lalaurie when she grows up. Fetch me the blue bowl there behind you, would you, Brother?"

She ladled jambalaya from the iron pot that hung above the coals. Even with all its shutters thrown wide—opening the whole side of the little room to the yard—the kitchen was baking hot, though with the sinking of the sun below the roofs of the American faubourg a little breeze flowed up Rue Douane. The houses on either side of Olympe's were empty, shuttered fast; traffic in the street had ended with the coming of evening; and the oppressive silence, broken only by the far-off whistle of a steamboat, breathed with the presence of Bronze John. He waited out there in the darkness. When Gabriel, Olympe's eleven-year-old son, came darting across the yard to the kitchen from the lighted house, January had to suppress the urge to tell the boy to stay indoors where it was safe.

Nowhere was safe.

"Delphine Lalaurie, she has the best of everything." Olympe muffled her hand in her bright-colored skirts, to keep from her skin the heat of the iron hook with which she rearranged tripods and pots above the fire. Her sloppy, *mo kiri mo vini* French reminded January of Cora's. It was the French of Africans who'd made the language their own as they'd made what they could of the land. Their mother would faint to hear her—but then, Livia Levesque had not heard her daughter's voice for nearly twenty years.

"When a boat comes in from France with the latest shade of silk, or some kind of bonnet they're all wearing in Paris, Delphine Lalaurie's got it. Either for her or for her daughters, for all it's said she don't let those poor girls eat enough to keep a cat alive. When Michie Davis brought in those French singers for his Opera, Delphine Lalaurie had them to her parties, to sing for her guests, before anyone else in town; and when she gives a ball, no other lady in town dare hold any kind of party that night, knowing it won't be no use."

She wiped her face with one of the threadbare linen towels. "Hell." She chuckled. "I bet if Delphine Lalaurie were caught red-handed taking runaways out of town by the coffle there'd be folks falling over themselves to say it wasn't so. She does what she pleases. And that's what just about rots Emily Redfern's heart."

She scooped greens from a cauldron at the back of the hearth, handed the white porcelain bowl of them to her son to carry back to the house, and shifted the coffeepot a little farther to one side, where it would warm without boiling. "The voodoos know everything that goes on in this town, Brother," Olympe said. "Emily Redfern wants to have that same power Delphine Lalaurie has. Wants to have it with everyone, not just with the Americans. That's what ate her about her husband's gambling. Not that it might lose them their home—that little place at Black Oak was *hers,* not his, and couldn't be took for his debts. But his gambling took away from what she could spend on having the best in town, on being the best."

"Ate her enough to poison him?"

Olympia Snakebones's dark eyes slid toward her young son, but the boy was already out of the kitchen, skipping across the dark yard to the house with his bowl of greens. "The voodoos know everything in this town," she said again, her face enigmatic. "But sometimes we don't tell even each other what we know. Tell your little Cora to be careful, dealing with that white woman, with any white woman. And you, Brother—you watch yourself too. You get yourself mixed up with the whites, French or American, and you'll be hurtin', too."

They crossed the yard together, Olympe taking off her apron, leaving it on the kitchen table. The smell of burning was thick in their nostrils.

"Tell her there's a man name of Natchez Jim down by Rue du Levee." They paused in the molten light from the dining-room door. "She'll find him near the coffee stand under the arcade of the vegetable market, when he's not out freighting firewood in his boat. He'll get her up the river safe. Tell him I said it's a favor to me."

Dinner was a lively meal, with Gabriel and thirteen-year-old Zizi-Marie up and down, back and forth to the front bedroom where their father, Paul Corbier, was slowly convalescing from a brush with the fever. While listening to Zizi-Marie's account of how she'd done the finishwork on Monsieur Marigny's yellow silk chairs while her father was ill and thus helped rescue the family finances—which turned out to be quite true, for she was a good upholsterer already—and explaining correlations to Gabriel between Olympe's herbal remedies and his own medical training, it was difficult for January to remember his own worries or to feel anything but joy in the warm haven of that little house. Halfway through the meal there was a knock at the door, a woman from the shacks out toward the swamps, asking Olympe's help with her children taking sick; Olympe said, "I'll have to go."

January nodded. He was on his way to the Hospital himself. Even this haven, he thought, looking around the candlelit parlor, was not safe. It could be taken away at any time, as Ayasha had been taken.

"I'll put up extra for you, borage and willow bark," Olympe said, going into the parlor where the shelves were that contained the potions of the voodoo: brick dust and graveyard dust, the dried bones of chickens and the heads of mice, little squares of red flannel and black flannel, colored candles and dishes of blue glass beads.

"We can't stay, either," Gabriel announced, as Chouchou gathered the dishes to carry back to the kitchen with the solemn care of an eight-year-old, and Olympe lifted Ti-Paul down from the box on the chair seat that raised him up to the level of the table. "Zizi and I, we got to help Nicole Perret and her husband pack up. Would you know it, Uncle Ben? Uncle Louis says now his cook and yard man gone over to Mobile, Nicole and Jacques can stay on the porch of his house out by Milneburgh, that he rent for the summer, and work for him. Now the fever here's so bad, Nicole and Jacques will do that just to be away from town."

He pulled on his jacket, ran quick fingers over his close-cropped hair, a tall, gangly boy, like January had been, but with the promise of the gentle handsomeness still visible in Paul Corbier's face. "I ain't scared of no fever, me. Just it's so hot here I wish we could go, too. You think Grand-mère might let us, just for a while?"

January couldn't imagine his mother inconveniencing herself to the extent of giving her elder daughter floor space in her lovely rented room at the Milneburgh Hotel—let alone her elder daughter's decidedly working-class husband and four children—to save her had Attila the Hun been on the point of sacking the town. "Stranger things have happened," he told his nephew.

But probably not since the Resurrection of Christ.

"Take a smudge with you," he cautioned, as Zizi-Marie came out of the bedroom with her jacket, her father leaning on her shoulder. "And a cloth soaked in vinegar." He tried to think of anything that actually seemed to have some effect in deflecting the fever, the poisons that seemed to ride the stinking, mosquito-humming darkness.

Slices of onion?

Get out of this town, he thought despairingly. *Get out of this town.*

"You could do us a favor, if you would, Ben." Paul Corbier sat carefully on the parlor divan. He was breathing hard just from the effort of coming out to bid his brother-in-law good night. "Alys Roque was here this afternoon, Olympe's friend. She says her husband, Robois, didn't come in last night from working the levee. She's already been to Charity, and the Orleans Infirmary, and Dr. Campbell's, and that clinic the Ursulines have set up where the convent used to be, but . . . it strikes so fast, sometimes. And if it's the cholera, it's all the worse. Me, I was shaping an arm cushion one minute and the next thing I knew I was lying on the floor, without the strength to so much as call out."

He shook his head. His face, round when January had first met him in the spring, had thinned with the effects of the disease; and it would be some time before he'd recover the lost flesh. By the look of him he had a good deal of African blood, which had probably been the saving of him. The lighter-skinned colored, quadroons and octoroons, suffered more with the fever. The exquisitely pale musterfinos and mamaloques were as susceptible to its effects as the whites.

"You were lucky," said January softly. *Not least,* he added to himself, *in having a wife who knew about herbs and healing and wouldn't call in some sanguinary lunatic like Soublet to bleed you to death.*

Soublet was at the top of his form that night when January returned to the hospital, opening veins and applying leeches with the pious confidence of a vampire. "Balderdash, sir," January overheard him saying to Dr. Sanchez. "Salts of mercury are all very well in their place, but fever resides in the blood, not in the nervous system."

"Salts of mercury mixed with turpentine have been shown to be of sovereign benefit—sovereign, sir!—in cases of fever!" Sanchez retorted. "But the dosage must be heroic! Nothing is of any benefit unless the patient's gums bleed. . . ."

Balderdash? wondered January, as he lifted the half-dead Italian, waxen with phlebotomy, to sponge him clean. The heartbreaking, terrifying thing about the fever was that he didn't know. Nobody knew. Maybe Soublet and Sanchez were right.

On the bed next to the Italian's a dead woman lay. Her face was covered with a sheet, but her hair, long and black, hung to brush the reeking floor, and the sight of it cut his heart. Had he returned soon enough to find Ayasha still alive, could he have saved her by bleeding? By forcing calomel and turpentine down her throat until her gums bled?

Why did one person recover, and another succumb? Might Monsieur A have recovered without the remedy, and did Madame B perish in its despite?

"Stick to surgery, my son," Dr. Gomez had said to him, all those years ago. "These physicians, they know nothing but calomel and opium, the clyster and the knife. When a man breaks a bone, by God, you know what you've got."

What you had, of course, thought January, as he was summoned to hold down a laborer who wept and fought and cursed at them in Gaelic, was a mechanic of the body's armature who had to sit by while a man he was certain was an imbecile opened the patient's veins for the fifth time in as many days.

Rain began to fall: hard, steady, drenching rain that abated not an atom of the suffocating heat. Ants crawled steadily up the walls and over the floor, in spite of the red pepper sprinkled along every baseboard. A man came in, his coat of fine tobacco-colored wool sticking to his broad shoulders with wet and his fair hair and extravagant sidewhiskers dripping on his shoulders, and searched among the sick, as the woman Nanié had searched a few nights ago. Handsome face impassive, he passed once through the ward and then made a second circuit, as if not believing the one he sought was not there. January saw that it was the men of color he went to, lifting the sheets over the faces of the dead, looking down at them for a few minutes before moving on.

"Can I help you, sir?"

The man turned, and met his eyes with eyes of bright Irish blue. "Thank you kindly, no." His voice had the soft lilt of the well-bred Irish gentry, like that of January's friend Hannibal the fiddler when Hannibal was more than usually drunk. "Just seekin' after a friend."

There was a jewel in his stickpin the size of little Ti-Paul's fingernail—what kind, it was too dark to tell—and except for the soak of the rain his linen was clean and very fine. His coat, with its wasp waist and lavishly wadded shoulders, was too flashy for a broker's or a planter's. A gambler, January guessed, or someone in the theater.

"Does he have a name, if they bring him in after you've gone?"

The man hesitated, then shook his head. "I'll be back," he said.

There were many people who came in, seeking those they knew among the dying or the dead. Later in the night January thought he saw the woman Nanié return, but through the grind of exhaustion and the haze of smoke could not be sure. He himself studied the faces of the patients, asked the names of those still conscious enough to reply, searching for Robois Roque, as his brother-in-law had requested. When the ambulance came in, toward midnight, he looked again. There was no one he sought, but there was an elderly German woman with a withered and shortened leg, and Soublet descended upon her at once, rubbing his thick-muscled hands.

"Would you like to have the affliction of your limb cured?" the doctor murmured—he had a beautiful voice when he chose to soften it—and the woman thrashed her head giddily and muttered something in her own tongue. January saw Soublet look around quickly for Ker, and then wave his servant over. "If you consent to come to my clinic, you can be better cared for there, and not only will you be cured of the fever but full use of the limb will be restored to you within a matter of weeks."

January shuddered, but knew if he interfered he might be put out of the Hospital altogether. It was not for surgeons to question the work of actual doctors, and certainly not for a black man to question the opinion of a white. He looked around for Ker, as Soublet had done, but the Englishman was not to be seen.

"M'sieur?"

A woman had been standing beside him for some time, a wet cloak hanging from her square, slender shoulders and a look of sickened horror on her face. And well she might look so, thought January, seeing anew the smoky hell of the long room, roaches rattling ferociously around the lamps, the dying laid on pallets along the wall for lack of beds. Barnard crouched beside one old man and shoved what looked like garlic tops into his ears while Soublet and his servant hovered like a pair of sable-cloaked vultures above the delirious German woman. "Do you need help, Madame?"

She raised her eyes to his. Not far—she was a tall woman. Her eyes seemed dark in the shadows, behind thick slabs of gold-rimmed spectacle lenses, but when she turned toward the lamps, they showed their true color, cindery gray flecked with green.

"I need a doctor," she said. She wore a free woman's tignon, and in the dusky half-light she had a free woman's complexion. Her face was a long oval with a mouth too prim and a chin too pronounced for real beauty. All arms and legs, she moved as if she were always going to trip, but never did.

January glanced back at Soublet and the beggar woman. "I'm a doctor." He went to fetch his satchel from behind the door.

The rain had eased to a patter, but the air outside smelled thick of it. It was only a break in the storm. An electric wild warmth charged the night, monstrous clouds advancing over the lake like the siege

engines of some unimaginable army. He wondered where the girl
Cora Chouteau was tonight, and if she was sleeping dry.

"Three of my girls are down sick." The wind caught the woman's
cloak, whirled it like a great cracking wing. "I'm sorry," she added, as
they passed through the gate of the Hospital courtyard, and he
handed her across the gutter and into the morass of Common Street.
"You've got as much as you can do here, I know. But I've done
everything I can, everything I know how to do. I'm not . . . I'm not
very good with the sick."

She had a small school on Rue St. Claude, not far from the Bayou
Road. Her name, she said, was Rose Vitrac.

"Sometimes this past year I've felt like a peddler trying to sell
Sèvres teacups to the Comanche," she remarked ruefully, taking off
her spectacles to wipe rain from the lenses. Away from the Hospital
she seemed to gain back some of her poise, to be less like a very young
egret trying to balance on its long legs. There was a wry little fold in
the corner of her mouth and, even in this time, a dry capacity for
amusement. "It's difficult enough to find Creole girls, let alone girls
of color, whose parents are willing to pay for them to learn Latin—or
proper French, for that matter, much less, God help us, natural
philosophy. But there have to be a few Comanche warriors out there
who like . . ." She hesitated, fishing for exactly the proper word,
and January smiled and suggested,

"Tea?"

Rose Vitrac chuckled. "Beautiful things, I was going to say." She
put the spectacles back on. "Learning for its own sake, for the joy of
knowing how the universe is put together. Things that have nothing
to do with hunting buffalo or scalping people."

"You're probably in the wrong town for that," he said, still smiling.

The face she turned to him, as they stopped before a crumbling,
galleried Spanish house, post-and-brick raised high off the ground,
was suddenly serious again. Quiet intensity illuminated her eyes.
"No," she said. "I'm in the right town for that. If you're a colored
boy—if your father is a rich white man—he'll see to your education if
you say you want to study Hebrew, or optics, or how logarithms

unfold invisible universes that you never even suspected. But if you're
a girl? If you're hungry to know, to learn? To see the magic in cosines
and radii, to learn how to call lightning out of water and steel and
copper wire? This is the only town where that fulfillment is even
possible."

"You teach all that?"

"If they want to learn, I find a way to teach it." She looked away
from him, suddenly embarrassed, and drew a key from the reticule at
her belt. Dawn was just coming, down the river and above the clouds,
enough light to show him the freckles that dusted her nose and
cheekbones, and to turn the oil lamps in their iron brackets along the
wall to fey shreds of torn silk. "I'm sorry," she said. "I'm lecturing
again. It's a noxious habit."

January shook his head, recalling Dr. Gomez's quiet study, with
its glistening jars of specimens preserved in brandy or honey, its worn
medical books and ferocious-looking galvanic battery. He climbed the
tall steps beside her to the gallery, the warm damp wind smiting them
again as he scraped the mud from his boots, and she unlocked the
door. "And did you find buyers for your philosophic tea sets?"

She glanced up at him, the fear that had come into her eyes with
the touch of the door handle leaving them for a moment. She smiled.
"A few."

The smell of fever and sickness flowed from the black dark of the
house, vile and frightening. Just enough light trickled in from outside
to show up a branch of candles on a table just beside the door.
Mademoiselle Vitrac kicked her feet out of the wooden patterns that
guarded her shoes, took a match from her reticule, scratched it on the
match-paper. By the growing light January was just able to discern
looming bookcases, a blackboard, a globe, and a couple of straight-
backed chairs. Saw, too, the knot of fear bunch at the corner of the
schoolmistress's jaw. He remembered coming into a house in Paris,
smelling that smell as he ascended the stairs.

"It will be all right." He took the candelabra from her unsteady
hand.

There were eight beds in the long, low attic above the school's
three rooms. Three were occupied. A girl of thirteen—Zizi-Marie's
age—sat beside one of the beds, a china basin of water and a candle

on the floor beside her. She turned, gratitude flooding her round, pug-nosed face as she heard the steps on the stairs, saw the light of the candles imperceptibly brighten the terrible blackness of the room.

"Mamzelle Vitrac, I think she's worse."

Mademoiselle Vitrac bent to hug her reassuringly before going to look at the girl on the bed.

"She's thrown up twice," the girl went on, fighting tears. "The second time I didn't think she was ever going to stop. She's so hot. Geneviève keeps thinking I'm her sister, and Victorine—I've checked a couple times to see if she's still breathing, with a feather like you showed me, but she hasn't moved or made any sound or anything. And Isabel left and I don't know where she went, but she said she wasn't going to stay and catch the fever from the others."

Her dark eyes begged for reassurance. "It isn't catching, is it? Will I catch it from—from Geneviève and Victorine and Antoinette here, from staying and taking care of them?"

"No, you won't, Mamzelle," said January firmly. He set down his satchel beside the girl Antoinette's bed. "I take care of people every day at the Hospital, and I haven't got the fever yet."

"And anyway, you don't get fever from people who have fever, Marie-Neige." Mademoiselle Vitrac gently took the sponge from the girl's hand. "You get fever from swamp mist and night air, and you see we've got all the windows closed up tight. The fever can't get in and get you. Marie-Neige, this is Dr. Janvier. He's here to help us take care of the girls this morning."

"M'sieu Janvier," corrected January. "I'm just a surgeon, not a doctor . . . and I think Marie-Neige and I have met already, at her mother's house. It is Marie-Neige Pellicot, isn't it, Mamzelle?"

The youngest Pellicot daughter nodded. January calculated he'd probably climbed through the window of her attic bedroom last Saturday. He remembered Agnes Pellicot complaining to his mother, "What earthly use is it to educate a girl? It costs a fortune and in the end to whom is she going to speak in Greek or Italian or whatever it is?"

"Well, you can go find Isabel now," said Mademoiselle Vitrac gently. "Tell her I'm not angry at her for leaving. And don't you rip up at her for it, either, Marie-Neige, please. Everything turned out all right in the end. Is there anything you can do for them, M'sieu Janvier?" She asked this as Marie-Neige took up her candle in one hand, gathered her voluminous petticoats in the other, and made her careful way down the ladderlike stairs.

"Only what you've been doing." January walked to the pink-and-green china veilleuse that stood on one of the room's plain cypresswood dressers, its candle providing the sole illumination in that corner of the long attic. He touched the backs of his fingers to the vessel's smooth side, and found it warm. From his satchel he took the powdered willow bark and herbs Olympe had recommended, and poured the heated water over them in one of the bedroom pitchers.

"It's all anyone can do," he went on. "The fever is like a hurricane. It passes through the body, tearing up everything in its path, and it's going to take as long as it takes to pass. All we can do is keep the girls alive, keep the fever down by whatever means we can: cool water on the skin, vinegar, herb draughts like this one, saline draughts. Nothing is going to rebalance the body's humors or drive the fever out."

He saw her relax, and nod. "Can I get you water?" she asked. Later, when she brought it, she said, "My mother died of fever, but she suffered cruelly at the hands of the doctors before she died. They bled her; and after they'd gone, my grandmother thought it would be a good idea to blister her, to 'revive her,' as she said. I was afraid . . ." She hesitated. "I was afraid that in not seeking a doctor yesterday, or the day before, I might have . . . have done them harm. As I said, I'm not very good with the sick. They seemed to be getting better yesterday."

"That happens," said January. Wind scratched at the dormer shutters, and the thunder of rain sounded very loud on the Spanish-tiled roof.

"I thought—I hoped—we actually could get through the summer here without anyone falling sick." She propped her spectacles more firmly on her nose with her forefinger, then stripped back the sheets, and wrung a sponge in the vinegar-water she had brought. "We did last summer, four girls and I. Geneviève over there . . ." And there was in her eyes the special smile teachers have when they speak of pupils who have become their friends, ". . . and Victorine were two of them. Looking back, I can't imagine how we did it. But entire families survived, you know. And quite frankly," she added, "I had nowhere else to go. Neither did most of the girls."

She bent to her task, mopping down the girl Antoinette's thin body, gently, slopped water dripping onto the sheets. "Every penny I own is tied up in this building, and these girls. . . . Their parents mostly wanted to know they're 'in good hands.' Being educated, and out of their way. You know what it costs to leave the city in the summer, to take a room in anything like a decent hotel or boarding-house in Milneburgh or Mandeville."

A trace of bitterness crept into her voice. "Antoinette is a day student. Her mother asked me to board her here while *she* left the city, when she heard I was going to stay."

January thought about his mother. When Olympe was sixteen years old she had run away from home. His mother had made no effort to learn where she had gone.

Rather wistfully, Mademoiselle Vitrac added, "These are mostly not girls whose parents understand them or know what it is they want out of life."

"Did yours?"

She hesitated, looking across at him as he tipped the herb tea into a spouted invalid's cup. Then she shook her head, briefly, and re-arranged Antoinette's nightdress so that he could half-lift her and force her to drink. "What is it?" she asked.

"Borage and willow bark. My sister's remedy for fevers. It works, too."

"She's a follower of Dr. Thompson's theories?"

"She's a voodooienne."

"Ah." Mademoiselle Vitrac didn't appear shocked, a little surpris-ing considering her prim appearance. "Myself, I'd trust a voodoo as much as I'd trust some of the doctors I've met. One of them's one of my financial backers—a doctor, I mean. He insisted I accept a 'Pos-tural Remediant' that reminds me of nothing so much as woodcuts I've seen of the Iron Maiden. It's downstairs. I'll show it to you—I have to keep it out because he sometimes comes by."

She smiled faintly, looking down into Antoinette's flushed,

wasted face. "I'm always threatening to lock the girls into it for punishment—as a joke, you understand. We made games of what kinds of crimes merit imprisonment. I think the longest was five years for poisoning Monsieur Heymann, that tenor at the Opera the girls are all in love with. Poisoning the Pope was good for three years, as I recall."

The muscle of her jaw stood out again, fighting the knowledge of how close death stood to those giggling schoolgirl games. She propped her spectacles again and went on calmly, "It's supposed to force one into a correct posture while writing, but I can't imagine it doing anything except making one never wish to touch a pen again."

She followed him to Geneviève's bed, holding the girl, who was very restless, while he dosed her with the herbal tea, then sponging her down with vinegar-water while January went on to dose Victorine, who looked, he thought, far too young to be sent away to school.

"Give them this three or four times a day," he told Madamoiselle Vitrac, digging in the half-darkness of his medical bag for the linen packet of herbs, which he set on the dresser top next to the veilleuse. "Made up in tea, as I've done, medium-dark. The disease is going to take as long as it takes, to pass through them. All we can do is keep it from killing them on the way."

She drew up the sheets over the girls' bodies, and rearranged the mosquito-bars, then followed him down the black ladder of the stairs.

Full daylight leaked through cracks in the shutters and partings in the curtains that covered the tall French doors onto the gallery. It showed January again the books shelved floor to ceiling in the school-room and in a corner, as promised, the Postural Remediant, an elaborate cage of metal, straps, and delicate boxwood rollers designed to force a girl to sit upright with her wrist properly raised to the task of writing.

"Five years for poisoning Heymann, at the very least," he agreed judiciously, pausing to study the thing. "Odd," he added, "one never sees boys forced to sit and write a certain way. Only girls."

"You notice," replied Mademoiselle Vitrac, with a touch of astringency in her voice, "which sex wears the corsets." She crossed to the divan set at right angles to the desk, where two girls slept in a mussy, crook-necked heap: Marie-Neige and a delicately pretty adolescent who was presumably the truant Isabel. The schoolmistress bent and brushed aside a strand of Isabel's coarse black hair, which, unbound and uncovered, had caught in the corner of her rosebud mouth. Both children looked desperately young.

"It must be very difficult for them," January said softly. "Coming here. Choosing this road."

"It is," she replied. "I hope at least that I've given them somewhere to come. Let them know that there *is* a different road to choose. It isn't an easy road. No one I've ever met seems to believe that a woman can want anything more than some man and children of her own to make her blissfully happy." There was bitterness in her voice again, the utter weariness of a warrior who has gone into battle every day of her life, in the knowledge that she will have to fight and refight for the same few feet of ground each day until she dies.

He wanted to ask her how she had come to it, how she had won the right to pursue her own strange dream of knowledge for its own sake. He had met women intellectuals in Paris and knew their path was difficult enough. What it must be for a woman here, and a woman of color at that, was almost beyond imagining.

But weariness overwhelmed him, and he guessed that she, too, was close to the edge of collapse. So he only asked, "Will you be all right?"

"Oh, yes. Marie-Neige and Isabel help me—I have other friends, too, who come in to nurse. But nursing isn't the same as having someone who knows what he's doing look at them." She held out her hand, long-fingered and slim, but large of bone, strong to grip. "Thank you," Rose Vitrac said. "Beyond words, thank you. The medicine you gave me—will that be enough?"

"I think so." January set his satchel on the gallery rail again, tilted it to the daylight. "My sister said she'd give me more of them . . ."

He paused, bringing out the tin of herbs in his hand. It was easy to recognize, for it was the one thing he hadn't put into the bag himself: it had to have been placed there by Olympe. And opening it, he smelled the comforting familiarity of the fever remedy.

It was the tin itself that caught his eye: bright red and gold, new and shiny, with WILLET'S BOILED SWEETS inscribed on its lid.

And remarkably similar to the tin Cora Chouteau had described as containing Emily Redfern's stock of poison.

It didn't mean anything of itself, of course.

The Willet's Company of England must export thousands of those little red-and-gold tins every year, and they were precisely the right size to put things in. Everyone in New Orleans from the Ursuline Sisters to the gamblers in the Swamp must have little red-and-gold candy tins in their houses, full of coffee beans, sugar, pins, and blotting sand. It didn't mean Olympe was a poisoner. It just meant that Olympe had four children.

He intended to go to her house immediately, to ask her whether her practice of voodoo included selling powdered monkshood, but exhaustion draped him in chains as he traversed the rough planks that served as a banquette along the Rue des Ramparts; and in the end he turned left, toward home. In his dream he found himself again on the gallery outside the garçonnière, staring out into the pitchy darkness of those hot, silent, heavy summer nights, listening to the baying of dogs in the swamp.

In his dream he ran down the steps, bare boards splintery as they always had been beneath his bare feet. Ran into the house, where his mother sat at the open front window, sewing on a man's white shirt.

She had work candles behind her, the smell of burning tallow strong. She didn't look up from her work. In here the baying sounded louder, and January saw that outside the windows lay, not Rue Burgundy, but the crisscross maze of swamp and bayou, trailing moss and cypress knees, and he knew his father was out there, running toward the light of the house, running with dogs on his track.

> *They chased, they hunted him with dogs,*
> *They fired a rifle at him . . .*

In his mind he heard the words of the old song about St. Mâlo, the rebel slave.

> *They dragged him from the cypress swamp,*
> *His arms they tied behind his back.*
> *His hands they tied in front of him.*
> *They tied him to a horse's tail . . .*

He saw him in the darkness. Saw the tribal scars on his face, the whip marks on his sides and back. Saw also the face of the man who ran behind the dogs, and recognized the long jaw and pale glitter of beard stubble as Lieutenant Shaw's.

He ran to the window, called out, "Father! Here!"

But his mother—and she was as he first remembered her, as he always saw her in his dreams, slim and fragile, young and breathtakingly beautiful—rose from her chair with the slow languor she had affected then, laid aside her sewing, and closed the shutters fast. "It's time to come to bed, Ben," she said, and took his hand. "It's time to come to bed."

He wrenched his hand from her—he was only eight—and flung himself against the shutter, trying to wrestle loose the heavy latch. "Father!" he shouted again. "Father, here! I'm here! Come and get me!"

His muffled cry woke him. He lay in the garçonnière where he had lain as a child and heard the voice of the dead-cart man: "Bring out yo' dead!"

Afternoon sun glared through the jalousies. It must be close to three.

It was smotheringly hot outside, the air unstirring. He ran water from the cistern in the yard and sponged off in the kitchen, the silence of the town sawing at his nerves. When he'd returned from Rose Vitrac's school that morning he had checked beneath the floorboard in his room for Madame Lalaurie's purse of money, and he checked it again now; checked also the little chips of wood he'd placed just so on the edge of the loose floorboard, as if accidentally. They were in the same place. That didn't mean Shaw hadn't been in and seen them.

Slave stealing.

Accessory After the Fact.

Olympe putting a red-and-gold candy tin in his satchel.

His father running exhausted through the darkness to see his son.

Somehow he got through his lesson with the Lalaurie girls, who as usual hadn't practiced and who as usual looked brittle and waifish as children off the wharves. Only Olympe, with her bone-deep mistrust of any white, let alone Jean Blanque's widow, would have accused Madame Lalaurie of starving her own daughters. *Their mother doesn't let them eat enough to keep a cat alive.*

Madame Lalaurie was renowned for setting the best and most lavish table in town.

But for all Delphine Lalaurie's goodwill, January was under no illusion that she would take his part were he caught helping an accused murderess and runaway slave. Nor would Madame have to do more than deny indignantly that she had anything to do with the matter, should he be so foolish as to accuse her of giving him the purse that seemed to be burning a hole in his clothing. Police Chief Tremouille was related to the Joncheres, who were related to the d'Aunoys, who were related to the McCartys—not to speak of having a daughter to marry off.

All the way up the Rue de l'Hôpital and along the Rue Burgundy, he kept glancing over his shoulder, expecting to see Lieutenant Shaw ambling with his loose-jointed walk, as if he simply chanced to be there, watching, waiting. But in fact the only person he saw was

Mamzelle Marie, strolling along the banquette, remote and beautiful, her yellow seven-pointed tignon like a halo of flame.

"M'sieu Janvier."

He tipped the beaver hat he wore. "Madame Pâris."

She paused, and inclined her head. A smile touched the serpent eyes, that in the muck and stink of the charity wards were so calm and unpitying. "I haven't gone by poor Pâris's name for some years now," she said. Her French was good, though her deep voice had a soft Creole burr to it. "You may make that Laveau, if you wish, or call me Mamzelle Marie, as your sister does. I take it your sister's well?"

"As of last night." It seemed a hundred years ago. *The voodoos know everything in this town. . . .* "Have you heard word about this Robois Roque, who vanished off the banquette? My sister asked me to watch for him."

"And me." For a moment he thought she'd been about to say something else, for she turned her head to sweep the street with those dark eyes. But whatever it was she put it aside, and looked back at him. Her strongly drawn brows pinched in a frown. "Now they're— What? The third or fourth people—who've asked me about someone who disappeared. Taken sick, they said, or thought. . . . Nobody knows for sure, because two of these people I've been asked of are slaves sleeping out. They didn't go by their masters' with the money from their work. I've prayed, and looked into the ink, and asked of other slaves and those who sell berries in the streets, and no one's quite sure when they last were seen."

January had heard of Mamzelle Marie's network of spies and informers, a gossamer cobweb of words and conversations and bits of intelligence that covered the town like a mist, funneling information back to her house on Rue St. Ann. *The voodoos know everything:* Who hated their husbands or were waiting for their fathers to die, who had come into money lately and whose menses had stopped, who had spent what at the market or the silk shops, and what curious things had been found in the trash or the gutter or the river. Those who didn't serve her from love did it from fear, bringing her sometimes the nails and hair of this person or that, and sometimes love letters extracted from their mistresses' desks.

It could have been Mamzelle Marie in the first place, he thought, who'd asked Olympe to ask him to look for Robois Roque at the hospital, weaving him into the web as well.

"They could have run," said January. Past her shoulder he, too, was watching the street—for Cora or for Shaw.

"Why?" Marie Laveau shook her head. "These men were saving for their freedom. They knew their masters here; they had work, on the levee or at the cotton press. Their friends were here. If a man's set free he has to leave the state. They had no call to run. It might be the sickness took them far from home, but . . . I don't like it. There is that about it that—" She made a gesture, like a woman testing the hand of silk for slubs, and she shook her head again. "Speak to me if you hear anything, M'sieu Janvier, if you would be so kind."

Cora was waiting for him in the Pellicots' yard. At first he didn't see her; then she emerged from behind the banana plants that grew around and behind the cistern, and her eyes were scared. "Who was that woman?" She whispered the words as if she feared they'd be heard from the street. "The one in the yellow tignon, that you were talking to?"

"That's Marie Laveau. She's the Queen of the Voodoos," he added, seeing the incomprehension in the girl's eyes.

She crossed herself quickly.

"She was at Black Oak," said Cora. "In the evening, when I went out there once to meet Gervase. She was waiting on the porch, in the twilight. I ran back and Gervase and I, we went elsewhere, but it was her."

"Marie Laveau? You're sure?"

"I saw her close. She had her tignon like that, in seven points. I never saw nobody wore it with so many before."

"They don't," said January. "That's something only the Queen Voodoo in New Orleans is allowed to do. Marie Laveau." His mind was racing. Not Olympe. Mamzelle Marie herself. "Did she see you?"

Cora nodded.

"Here, or there?"

"Both," the girl said, despair and panic in her voice. "I mean, she saw me when I came out of the woods—I didn't see her till I got right up close to the porch—then I turned and ran, since I wasn't supposed to be at Black Oak, ever. None of us was. And just now, I was crossing the street to come here, and she saw me, stopped to watch me pass. I didn't see it was her till I was close. She knows I'm in town."

"And probably doesn't think a thing of it," said January soothingly. "I don't think she'd even recognize you." He remembered how she'd looked back over her shoulder, scanning the street, and knew perfectly well that Mamzelle Marie recognized anything or anyone she'd seen once, however briefly, before. Most of the voodoos did.

"Then it wasn't me she spoke of?"

He shook his head. "She works with me at the Hospital. It's nothing to worry about. I spoke to Madame Lalaurie."

Cora's eyes, wide already, stretched farther with alarm.

He took from his pocket the little purse of silver and put it in her hand. "Madame Lalaurie sends you this," he told her.

Suspicion leapt into the girl's eyes, but her small hands closed tight on the little oval of plush. It was an expensive purse, with a line of jet beading along its bottom and a tassel, but someone had dripped grease on it. A tiny spot, and easily hidden if a woman carried it with the spot turned toward her skirts, but enough, evidently, for Madame Lalaurie to want it out of her house.

"Why? Why'd she do a thing like that?"

January sighed inwardly. "I think she's got a score to settle with Madame Redfern," he said, reflecting that it was a sorry state of affairs when a woman's good deed was more easily explained by spite than by generosity. "She's got to know Madame Redfern's hard up for cash and will be selling up her slaves soon. She gets you out of town, she's picking her enemy's pocket six hundred dollars' worth."

The thought, or perhaps the irony, made Cora grin, a quick smile quickly put away.

January continued, "My sister said for you to speak to a man named Natchez Jim, who has a firewood boat on the river. He'll take you out of town, after you've seen Gervase."

"Madame'll let me see Gervase?"

"She'll leave her gate open tonight," January said. "Her coachman will be watching, so don't try anything foolish, like getting Gervase to run away with you. That won't work. I promise you you'll be caught."

Her face went expressionless, and January felt a sinking in his heart.

"Don't go inside right away," he cautioned. "Wait down the street and look real close in case there's someone watching the gate. The police know about you and Gervase; they know that's where you're likely to go. And if you see someone waiting in the shadows, watching for you to go in, *walk away*."

Something changed in her expression. "All right," she said.

"But whatever you do, *don't try to get Gervase to leave with you.* If you get caught, I'll get in trouble, too, bad trouble." He didn't even want to think about what he was risking, and the sight of the defiance flickering in her eyes was enough to scare him badly. "You can't do it."

She said nothing, stubborn. Clinging to the dream of freedom for them both.

"At least you'll have seen him, Cora. Tell him I'll be in touch with him. When you reach New York, or Philadelphia, or wherever you choose to go, you can get in touch with me and earn money to buy him free. But don't try to get him to run away with you. Promise?"

The sullenness in her silence made his heart sink. There was a world of *You don't understand* and *I'll be quicker than that* in her averted face.

Dear God, what have I got myself into?

His silence made her look up at him, and for a moment their eyes met in understanding. She mumbled, "If I get caught I won't say who helped me."

"No. Not good enough." He wanted to shake her. "Promise you won't try."

"I promise."

She had no intention of keeping her word. He knew that as she slipped from him and fled up the passway to Rue Burgundy through the gathering dusk.

Damn it, he thought. *Damn it, damn it, damn it.*

The night was endless. For hours at a time the demands of the sick, the fear of the disease, the sweltering heat and sickening stenches, buried his mind in the immediate and hellish present. He sponged down exhausted bodies, carried out the dead, followed Dr. Soublet on his sanguinary rounds. A family was brought in, mother, sons, granddaughter all suffering the cholera; they were isolated in a stuffy little chamber as far from the other patients as possible, with the nearly twenty other sufferers of the disease. January worked vainly to keep them at least clean and keep them from going into convulsions. Fear of contracting the disease was enough to keep his mind from Cora Chouteau's defiant eyes, and the way she'd turned her face away as she'd said, "I promise." She was going to try to get Gervase to flee with her.

And they'd be caught.

He'd be caught.

I should never have helped her, he thought. *I should never have helped her.*

Then the image of that little boy on the gallery of the garçonnière would come back, the boy who waited for his father to come see him, the dream image of the man with the tribal scars on his face, pursued through the woods by dogs. And he didn't know what to think or feel.

I couldn't not.

Would Shaw accept that as an argument?

It would be like Shaw, he thought, *to watch Madame Lalaurie's house if he could get the men for it.*

His only hope lay in proving that Emily Redfern had poisoned her husband, had attempted or intended to poison Cora, or at least given the girl reason to believe she so intended. . . . And how could he do that?

Ask Mamzelle Marie?

He looked across the ward at her, remembering her on the street that day. Now she held the hands of a laborer who gasped, wept, flopped like a landed fish, his body voiding the wastes that were the sign that the fever had broken, the disease had run its course. Her face was calm and distant as it was when she danced, an Adamless dark Eve, with the great snake Damballah in Congo Square.

She'd seen Cora.

Here, and at Black Oak.

It didn't take a genius to guess that pasteboard coffins, black candles, and graveyard dust could be easily backed up with galerina mushroom or Christmas rose.

He'd confided everything in Olympe. *Sometimes we don't tell even each other what we know.* Would his sister put his confidence above the woman who was her sworn Queen?

His head ached with heat and worry and sheer fatigue by the time he left the Hospital, well after dawn. Shaw was not waiting for him outside. So far, he thought bitterly, so good.

He crossed Canal Street, with its usual rabble of drunken keel-boatmen, carters cursing as they hauled firewood and produce from the turning basin of the canal where they were unloaded. Dead dogs and garbage floated in the reeking gutters—gnats and mosquitoes whined about his ears. A few vendors moved along the streets by houses shuttered tight, or stopped to gossip at the rare doors that opened to them, hawking eggs or rat poison, asking after neighbors who were gone. His sister's house was shuttered but the plank lay welcomingly across the gutter, so he assumed that things were as they should be there. His hand fumbled for the rosary in his pocket and he whispered a prayer, *Dear God, not them.*

Lying awake in the breathless heat of his room, he wondered if they'd heard word yet of Alys Roque's missing husband. Wondered how Zizi-Marie and Gabriel had fared, packing up the indigent Perrets for their sojourn on Uncle Louis's floor.

Wondered if he had gotten Ayasha out of Paris—if they'd had the money to go anywhere else—if she would have survived.

That way lay madness, and he shoved the images from his mind.

Tried to think instead of Cora Chouteau. The thought was scarcely more comforting. He felt a little embarrassed as he groped for his rosary again—*Dear God, don't let her have got caught*—but he did it anyway. He remembered the night he'd spent in the Cabildo last spring, the prison hot as it was hot here, stinking of human waste and human fear. Remembered the voices of the jailers down in the courtyard in the morning, and the smack of the whip as slaves were disciplined.

Stupid, he thought. *Stupid, stupid, stupid, to have let yourself help her . . .*

Twenty years old, terrified, running away from a woman who would have killed her . . .

Presumably God knew whether he had done well or ill to help her.

Between fear and guilt he slid again into uneasy dreams, from which he was waked by the sound of footfalls on the gallery stairs.

Shaw. Panic grabbed his heart. He could probably make it to the far end of the gallery, drop the twelve feet or so down to the yard, make it through the passway and out to Rue Burgundy before the Lieutenant could follow. . . .

And then what? Hide in the swamp for the rest of your days?

Why don't you see who it is first before you decide to turn maroon at your time of life?

He got to his feet, put on his boots and a shirt. The room was still an oven, and another trail of ants had started along the wall, (*What, you boys like red pepper?*) but the light had changed. Long gold slats of it leaked through the jalousies before they were blotted by the shadow of a man.

"Hey inside?"

It wasn't Shaw's voice.

January shrugged his shirt straight and went to open the shutters.

The man who stood there wore the leather breeches of a groom, and a rough corduroy coat.

"Michie Janvier? Cyrus Viellard here, for Michie Henri Viellard." The man bobbed a little bow, and took off his hat. "Michie Henri, he say bring you out to Milneburgh, if you please, sir. Your sister, Mamzelle Dominique, took in labor, and she wants you there."

Milneburgh stood some four miles north of the city on the shores of
Lake Pontchartrain. The elegant hotels, modest boardinghouses, and
small wooden cottages sprinkled along the shallow beaches or shelter-
ing in the pines presented a soothing contrast to the shut houses,
reeking heat, and terrible silence of the city. The air here was sweet.

As January and Henri Viellard's groom rode up the white shell
road along the bayou, the sun was just setting, the golden peach of a
full moon low in the east. Doorways and windows stood open to the
fresh breezes. Lights from a thousand candles made glowing patchwork of the dove-colored gloam. Even the bathhouses of the two
main hotels were illuminated, floating topaz reflections gemming the
lake at the end of the long piers.

Impossible, thought January, that this could exist in the same
world as the stricken city he had left. He'd passed through a fairy gate
somewhere in the twilight swamps along the Bayou St. John and left
the earth of plague and loss and stench and grief behind.

"Henri is an old lady." Dominique held out her hands to him
from her bed as he entered the bedroom of the cottage Henri Viellard
had bought for her, three tiny rooms arranged one behind the other

in a little stand of red oak at the water's very edge. The rear gallery perched on stilts in the lake itself; two chairs of white-painted willow-work were just visible through the open doors, and a cage of finches, fluffing their feathers for the night.

"There's absolutely nothing to be worried about," added Catherine Clisson, friend to both Dominique and January's mother, still the plaçée of the protector who'd taken her under his wing twenty years ago. "We sent as soon as her water broke, but with first babies these things take time." As she spoke she brought extra candles from the dresser drawer. Nearly every candlestick and holder in the house stood on its marble top, a bright regiment of porcelain and silver drawn up for battle.

"Is my mother here?"

"Livia said she would be shortly, when she's finished her dinner."

Madame Clisson sounded like a woman carefully keeping her personal opinions out of her voice. But her statement didn't surprise January in the least. Having lavished on Dominique all the care and attention of which she scanted her two older—and darker-hued—children, Livia Levesque seemed to have lost interest in the girl once she'd negotiated a suitably cutthroat contract for her with the wealthiest white planter Livia could find. She herself owned a neat four-room cottage in the pines on the other side of the Washington Hotel, here in Milneburgh, but rented it out at an extortionate rate to a white sugar broker, and occupied a pleasant room at the Louisiana House, which catered to well-off merchants and landlords of color.

"I hope everything's well with your sister Olympe?" Madame Clisson handed him a towel, and folded back the wide lace cuffs of her sleeves. "We sent for her as well."

"She might be with Nicole Perret."

Dominique's friend Phlosine Seurat came in from the gallery in a froufrou of pink jaconet. "I don't think Nicole Perret—was she the one who's going to stay with M'sieu Louis Corbier?—I don't think she's come." She closed the shutters carefully behind her, for the night was coming on, and drew the curtains over it.

"Nonsense, darling." Dominique turned her head from the pillows. "I saw all their baggage carried into M'sieu Corbier's this afternoon."

January related his dinner at Olympe's while shedding his coat, then herded Phlosine and Iphègénie—Dominique's other bosom friend—from the room, keeping Clisson to help him with the examination. Quite a number of New Orleans planters and brokers paid to bring their plaçées as well as their white families out of the city, especially if there were children involved. Iphègénie Picard and Phlosine Seurat had walked over from their own painted cottages to support their friend through her confinement, bringing blancmanges, terrines, and lemonade.

Pretty women, all of them, beautifully turned out in their summery muslins and lawns, silk tignons folded and tied and trimmed for maximum allure. *And why not?* thought January, remembering the girls at Rose Vitrac's little school, and the different, harder road they were being shown.

Interesting a wealthy protector was a sure way to establish oneself, to acquire a little property, a little security in the world, without losing one's eyesight to dressmaking or one's youth to hard labor. Even the respectable wives of artisans, the free colored ladies who refused to let their daughters play with the daughters of the plaçées, envied the plaçées their ease and their wealth. He thought of Marie-Neige's older sisters, educated in the more womanly arts of music and conversation, as his sister Dominique had been. Powdered and painted and dressed in silk, they were already being escorted by their mother to the Blue Ribbon Balls.

And why not? He looked around him at the tiny room, the plain but gracefully expensive furnishings, the curtains of sprigged English chintz and the linen sheets starched and ironed by servants' hands. *Why not?*

Dominique would never have to fear for herself, or for the child she was now bringing into the world, thanks to his mother's hard-headed bargaining.

She was further in labor than Clisson had thought, further than she had shown while her friends were in the room. She lay back in the cushions of the cypress-wood bed while January examined her, and he saw her hand grip hard on the sheets. Once she whispered, "She'll be a little octoroon, my petite. So pretty . . ."

Hearing the wistfulness in her voice, January didn't ask, *Would you love her less were she darker?* Grief and questions were not what Minou needed now. Instead he jested, "What, you're not going to give Henri a boy? With spectacles like his and no chin?"

As he hoped, it made her smile. "Wicked one, Henri has too got a chin! In fact several," she added, and her burst of giggles dissolved into another whisper of pain.

"Where is Henri?" he asked Madame Clisson, as he and she left the bedroom a few minutes later. He'd examined Dominique two or three times in the past several months and had conferred with Olympe and anticipated no major problems with the labor itself. But the child had grown in the two weeks since he'd seen his sister last, and he guessed she'd have a difficult time.

"The Hotel St. Clair." Agnes Pellicot and her daughter Marie-Anne—a shy tall girl in her first year of plaçage to a planter's son—had joined Phlosine and Iphègénie in the parlor. With them were Dominique's maid Thèrése, and January and Dominique's mother, the redoubtable Widow Livia Levesque.

"That mother of his is giving a concert and ball." The Widow Levesque uncovered Phlosine's blancmange, regarded it with a single downturned corner of her mouth, and with her free hand rearranged the decorative sprig of leaves that crowned its smooth, ivory-colored dome. She replaced the bell-shaped glass cover with a sniff, as if to say, *Well, that's the best that can be expected of* that. "Like her, to pick the same night as the Musicale for the benefit of that heathen preacher the Americans are holding at the Washington, but there! The woman would have scheduled her own funeral rather than let the Americans have a sou for that vulgar heretic. I trust she will have her reward in heaven," she added dryly, contemplating the terrine. "You used chicken liver for this, Iphègénie? I thought as much."

The inflection of her voice was the same one with which she had turned every small triumph of January's childhood into a common-place. *Dr. Gomez says you will make a fine physician one day? I expect he would say that.* Slender and delicate in appearance, Livia Levesque had put off her mourning for her late husband as soon as the obligatory year was up on the grounds that black did not become her—few women of color looked really good in it—but still dressed soberly. To hear her talk, she had never been any white man's plaçée, let alone a slave and the wife of a slave. January could never remember hearing her speak of his father.

"Don't tell me the girl's going to give you problems?" Livia turned immense, wine brown eyes upon her son.

"I don't think so." January kept his voice low and glanced at the half-open bedroom door. "But she's in for a good deal of pain and struggle, I think."

"Hmph." There was a world of, *Not like* my *pain,* in the single expulsion of her breath. "Fine time for that other girl of mine to be lollygagging in town. Thérése, extinguish some of these candles! The waste that goes on in this house is shocking. And beeswax, too! I don't see how M'sieu Viellard puts up with it. I suppose you think you need to fetch him."

"Someone should," said January. "It should be . . ."

"I can manage here," his mother cut him off coolly. "How far along is she? Is that all? Phlosine"—She looked around, but the girl had vanished fairylike into her friend's bedroom—"Never there when you need them. No more sense than butterflies." She turned her cool gaze back to her son. "You can't suppose that any of those girls are going to be admitted anywhere near a ball at the St. Clair, do you?"

As if, he thought, *she hadn't been one of those girls herself.*

When he left she was ordering Madame Clisson and Thérése to bring in two dining-room chairs and a plank, to approximate a birthing-chair if Olympe didn't arrive in time.

The Hotel St. Clair stood amid lush plantations of banana, jasmine, willow, and oak some distance back from the lakefront; but its galleries opened to both the prospect and the breezes that came off the water. As he and the groom Cyrus approached the graceful block of brick and whitewashed stucco that was the main hotel, January saw that colored paper lanterns were suspended from the galleries and smudges of lemongrass and tobacco burned near all the windows against the ever-present mosquitoes. Though it was by this time nearly nine o'clock, well after the hour that entertainments began, as he came up the garden's white shell path he heard no music, only the dull muttering of voices, and an occasional woman's exclamation of anger and outrage.

The first-floor gallery was thronged with little knots of people, the men in black or gray or blue evening dress, the women in the pale-tinted silks of summer wear—and the looped, knotted, wired, and lace-trimmed hairstyles they favored these days that made January wonder despairingly if women had taken leave of their senses in the past ten years—sipping negus and lemonade from trays circulated by white-coated waiters.

"Honestly, the woman deserves to be horsewhipped!" wailed someone buried to her chin in a snowbank of lace, whom January vaguely recognized as an aunt (cousin?) of Phlosine Seurat's protector. Through his mother and Minou he was being reintroduced to the interlocking webs of Creole society gossip.

"Well, what can you expect of Americans?" returned her escort, as January skirted the shell path under the gallery. He sought the inevitable refreshment tables, whose colored waiters he could approach without violating anybody's sensibilities.

"Well, we know who's responsible, anyway," muttered another woman, patting the yellow roses in her hair under an extravagant Apollo knot. "And her husband only dead a week Wednesday!"

"I always said she was a cold hussy. . . ."

"I've heard she doesn't have shoes on her feet, poor thing. . . ."

"And well served, I say! I'm told she led the poor man a dreadful life. . . ."

". . . gambled away every sou . . ."

". . . no more than twenty-five cents on the dollar, they say!"

At the far end of the wide gallery that fronted the lake January spotted the buffet, framed in a glowing galaxy of hanging lanterns, candles, and potted ferns. As he approached, above the growl of the crowd he finally heard music, a wistful planxty spun like gold thread from a single violin. He followed it to its source. The violinist perched tailor-fashion on one of the tall stools set behind the buffet for the use of the waiters, a bottle of champagne within easy reach and a dreamy expression in his black-coffee eyes. The gallery wasn't particularly high at that point, and January was a tall man. He caught the balusters, put a foot on the edge of the gallery, and swung himself up. One of the waiters called out, "Well, here's an answer to M'am Viellard's prayer now. You bring your music with you, Maestro?"

"I'm looking for Monsieur Viellard." January stepped over the rail. "What's happening here?"

The violinist set aside his instrument and generously offered him the bottle of Madame Viellard's best champagne. "Departed in command of a force to rescue the captives," he reported. Hannibal Sefton's white face was a trifle haggard but he seemed in better health than when January had seen him a week ago. With his long brown hair tied back in a green velvet ribbon and his shabby, old-fashioned coat, the fiddler had the look of something strayed from a portrait painted half a century ago. "*He armed his trained servants, born in his house, three hundred and eighteen, and pursued them into Dan.* The guests turned up half an hour ago to discover that the Committee in charge of the Musicale for the Benefit of the Reverend Micajah Dunk had hired away every musician but me and Uncle Bichet. Madame Viellard's fit to burst a corset string and she's gone to the Washington Hotel—with Our Boy Henri in tow—to get them back."

January swore. "I'd have thought that at this time of year there were at least enough musicians in town for two concerts on the same evening. Even if one of them does have to feature Philippe de Coudreau on the claronet."

Hannibal winced at the mention of one of the worst musicians of the rather slender selection available, even at the best of times, in New Orleans, and shrugged. "You reckon without the necessity of showing up the Americans. Madame Viellard heard that the Committee to Buy a Church for Micajah Dunk was having a Musicale to raise money—and Dunk being a hellfire lunatic who believes the Devil is French makes it all worse—and moved her concert and ball up to the same evening, to make sure that anybody with any pretentions to society in Milneburgh came to *her* party and didn't drop money at the Musicale when the collection plate went around. That would have settled the Musicale's hash, except that the Committee that's running it is headed by a lady rejoicing in the name of Emily Redfern, who's damned if she's going to let herself get shown up by French heathens who keep the Sabbath the way people in Boston keep the Fourth of July. The result being that Mrs. Redfern upped her Musicale to include an orchestra that would shame the Paris Opera."

He poured out a glass of champagne for January; he drank his own from the bottle. "La Redfern offered me twice what Madame Viellard did—enough to keep me in opium for weeks. I strongly suspect old Reverend Hellfire isn't going to get a whole lot of money once expenses are met, but I also suspect that's no longer the point."

"Wonderful." January sighed, too used to the rivalries between Creole society and the lately come Americans to even attempt to argue the matter logically. Maybe Madame Lalaurie *had* been trying to pick her rival Redfern's pocket.

"So if you've got your music with you, Maestro," added Uncle Bichet, a thin old freedman who still bore on his face the tribal scarrings of the African village where he'd been born, "I opine you can make a good five dollar this evenin'—or ten, if you want to walk over by the Washington and play the piano there."

"Not this evening." January reflected ruefully that tonight was the only occasion in the past ten years on which he stood to make more from his medical skills than from his piano playing. "But I do need to go to the Washington, if that's where Monsieur Viellard's to be found. Hannibal, can I beg your assistance?" At a Creole society ball, January knew, a man of color could enter without problems, provided he knew his place and kept to it. But the matter would almost certainly be otherwise at a function given largely by Americans.

They collected Cyrus and the horses from the courtyard in the front of the hotel. As the three men walked the crushed-shell path along the lakefront toward the Washington Hotel, January asked, "What's Madame Redfern doing running the Committee? She's newly a widow and just over being sick, at that."

Hannibal shrugged. He had a fresh bottle of Madame Viellard's champagne in hand, but aside from a slight lilt to his well-bred, Anglo-Irish French he didn't show the wine's effect—not that he ever did unless well and truly in the wind. "If you know that much about her you'll know of her determination to figure in society—society as Americans understand it, that is. They're a repellently godly lot."

Away from the hotels the darkness lay warm and silken, thick with the smell of water and decaying foliage, and the drumming of cicadas in the trees.

"What else do you know about her?"

"Redfern's late lamented owned a plantation down the river from Twelve-Mile Point and, as you say, has just shuffled off this mortal coil. But since God has almost universally been known to make exceptions to social rules if you hand His Representatives enough money, I suppose it's perfectly acceptable for her to carry on whatever chicanery necessary for the good of the Church. You thinking of marrying La Redfern for her money? I toyed with the notion but gave it up."

January laughed. "Just curious. A friend of mine had a run-in with her." He wondered if there were any way of getting up to Spanish Bayou to have a look at the little house on Black Oak.

"Just as well." Hannibal sighed. "The Redfern plantation's on the block for about a quarter its worth, for debts—the man owed money to everyone in town except me—and she's selling off the slaves for whatever they'll fetch. They don't think her creditors are going to realize thirty cents on the dollar."

"Twenty-five," said January, mindful of the conversation he'd overheard.

"Ah. Well. There you have it. So much for cutting a figure in society." He took a long pull from the bottle, a dark silhouette against the gold-sprinkled lapis of the lake.

Cyrus Viellard, walking behind with both horses on lead, added, "I hear she still got that little place next by Spanish Bayou, that they can't sell for debt cos of some way her daddy tied it up." He spoke diffidently, as was his place. "Michie Fazende and Michie Calder, that was owed money, they're fit to spit. But it won't do her no good neither, cos it ain't a farm or anything like that."

Just a place where she could conceal poison from her husband, thought January, as they mounted the rear steps of the Washington Hotel and made their way through the kitchen quarters to where a waiter said they'd find "all them ladies havin' a to-do."

It was always difficult to get more than a general impression of a woman in the deep mourning of new widowhood. Entering the ballroom built behind the Washington Hotel, January had an impression of a stout little figure of about Cora Chouteau's height but approximately twice the girl's slight weight. Though the ballroom was illuminated as brilliantly as myriad oil lamps would permit, black crêpe and veils hid everything of her except the fact that she was on the verge of poverty: despite considerable making over to lower the waist and the addition of far more petticoats than the skirt had originally been designed to accommodate, Mrs. Redfern's weeds were about fifteen years out of fashion. As January approached—with a proper air of deference—he had a vague view of a pale, square face and fair hair under the veils, but his clearest impression of her was her voice, sharp as the rap of a hammer. She was speaking English to a purpling and indignant Madame Viellard.

"I'm sorry if you feel that way, Mrs. Viellard, but as I've explained to you before, the musicians signed a contract." Mrs. Redfern jerked her head to indicate a slender, gray-clothed man, like an anthropomorphized rat, hovering at her side. "Mr. Fraikes drew it up and it does specify that it is legally binding no matter what the date—"

"What is she saying?" All her chins aquiver, Madame Viellard turned to her son. Henri was a fat, fair, bespectacled man in his early thirties whose sheeplike countenance amply attested the relationship. "Does that woman *dare* tell me that the men I hired for my own party are *forbidden* by law to play?"

"It's the contract, Mother," explained Henri Viellard in French. "It invalidates even a prior agreement. I'm sure the men didn't read it before signing. It isn't usual—"

"Isn't usual! Who ever heard of musicians signing a contract! They should never have done so! I paid them to play, and play they shall!"

Ranged among the buffet tables, a group of ladies in mourning or half-mourning—the fever had as usual struck hardest in the American community—observed the scene with whispers and gestures concealed behind black lace fans. With the utmost air of artless coincidence, they jockeyed among themselves for a position next to the short, burly, rather bull-like man in their midst. His self-satisfied expression accorded ill with his ostentatiously plain black clothing: presumably the Reverend Micajah Dunk. On the other side of the buffet the musicians themselves were gathered, every violinist, cellist, coronetist, clarionetist, and flautist January had ever encountered in nearly a year of playing balls and recitals in the city since his return last November. They clutched their music satchels and looked profoundly uneasy, and who could blame them? They played for both Americans and Creoles, turn and turn about. If they fell seriously afoul of Madame Viellard they could lose half their income, and if of Mrs. Redfern, the other half.

Hannibal sidled over to an excessively turned-out American gentleman in a cutaway coat with a watch chain like a steamboat hawser. "Sharp practice," the fiddler commented in English. "Making them sign a contract."

The man spat a stream of tobacco juice in the general direction of the sandbox in the corner. "Got to be sharp to stay in business, friend." The ballroom was hazy, not only with the mosquito-smudges burning in the windows but with cigar smoke, and stank of both it and expectorated tobacco.

"Mrs. Redfern's a better businessman than poor Otis was, if you ask me," added another man, stepping close. He had a weaselly face and an extravagant mustache, and spoke with the accent of an Englishman. "Of course, the same could be said of my valet. Pity her father's no longer with us. Damn shame, her being sold out like that, but it would have happened anyway."

"Anyone know what's being done with her slaves?" asked somebody else. "She had a few right smart ones."

"Like the one ran off with the money Otis got from selling those six boys in town two weeks ago?" The American spat again.

"Damn fool, Otis, insisting that money be paid him cash, not a bank draft or credit—but that's the man for you! Hubert Granville tells me—"

"I hear she didn't get but four-five hundred for good cane hands. Damn shame." The American looked at January, and said to Hannibal, "That your boy? Looks like a prime hand. They're paying eleven, twelve hundred apiece for good niggers up in the Missouri Territory. I could give you a good price for him."

"My friend," said Hannibal gently, "is a free man. We're here with a message for Mr. Viellard."

"Oh." The American shrugged as if the matter were of little moment. "No offense meant." He was still looking at January as if calculating price. January had to lower his eyes, and his hand closed hard where it lay hidden in the pocket of his coat.

"None taken." The softness of his own voice astonished January, as if he listened to someone else and thought, *How can he be so docile? What kind of man is he?* Again he wondered why he had left Paris, except that to have remained there would have cost him his sanity from pain and grief.

Evidently some compromise was reached among Mrs. Redfern; her lawyer, Mr. Fraikes; and Madame Viellard. Henri Viellard escorted his mother in queenly dudgeon toward the ballroom door, and Mrs. Redfern bustled importantly back to relate the results, whatever they were, to the committee of widows basking in the radiance of the Reverend Dunk. January noticed how the Reverend clasped Mrs. Redfern's mitted hands and bent his head close down to hers as they spoke, like an old friend.

He guessed that money had changed hands somewhere.

Hannibal touched Henri Viellard's sleeve as he passed, and drew him aside in the carved square arch of the ballroom door. "Monsieur Viellard?" said January. "I've come from Mademoiselle Janvier's house."

He did not mention that he was Madamoiselle Janvier's brother. He'd met Viellard before but wasn't sure the man remembered him, or remembered that he was Minou's brother. It wasn't something a protector wanted to know about his plaçée.

But Viellard turned pale at his words, gray eyes behind the heavy slabs of spectacle lenses widening with alarm. "Is she all right? Has she . . . ? I mean . . ."

"She's started labor, yes," said January softly. "I don't anticipate there being real danger, but it's going to be difficult for her, and she's in a good deal of pain. I'm going back there as quickly as I can. And if something does go wrong, I think you should be there."

"Of course." The young planter propped his spectacles with one chubby forefinger—their lenses were nearly half an inch thick and the weight of them dragged them down the film of sweat on his nose. "It's . . . it's early, isn't it? Does she seem well? I'll be—"

"Henri." His mother's voice spoke from the hall. "Do come along. Our guests will be waiting."

Henri poised, frozen, lace-edged handkerchief clutched in hand, eyes flicking suddenly back to January, filled with indecision, grief, and fathoms-deep guilt. Then he looked back at his mother.

"Come along, Henri." Madame Viellard did not raise her voice, and though no woman of breeding would have held out hand or arm for any man, even her son, merely the gaze of those protruding, pewter-colored eyes was like the peremptory yank of a chain.

Viellard dabbed at his lips. "I'll be there when I can." His eyes, looking across at January's, begged for understanding. "You'll tell her?"

"I'll tell her."

Dominique was in hard labor all night. Weakening, exhausted, propped in the birthing-chair by her friends and her mother, she clung when she could to her brother's big hands. Only once, when she was laid back on her bed half-unconscious to rest between contractions, did she whisper Henri Viellard's name.

Shortly after dawn she gave birth to a son.

"I expect Henri will be along soon," remarked Hannibal. He had walked over from the Hotel St. Clair with a napkin full of crayfish patties left over from the buffet and a bottle and a half of champagne. "Having gotten at least some musicians back, the company was determined to make the most of them. The dancing broke up only a half hour ago."

"Throw those out." January regarded the patties with a dour eye. "They've been out all night and they're probably bad. It would serve Madame Viellard right if half her precious guests died of food poisoning. And drink to Charles-Henri." He uncorked one of the champagne bottles, drank from it, and handed it to his friend. "Poor little boy."

"With a father as wealthy as Henri Viellard he's a not-so-poor little boy." Hannibal followed January into the house, leaving the crayfish patties, napkin and all, on a corner of the porch for the cats. "He'll have an education—not that three years at Trinity ever did me noticeable good—and with luck a start in business. My beautiful Madame Levesque . . . my exquisite Phlosine. . . . Catherine, I kiss your hands and feet . . ." He made his way around the ladies in the room, pouring out champagne. "To Charles-Henri."

January crossed through the little dining room to his sister's bedroom, cleaned now of the smells of blood and childbirth. Sandalwood burned in a china brazier, to sweeten the air. Olympe had never come. There were a thousand plausible reasons, most probable of which being that others simply needed her care, but he felt the clutch of fear in his heart that he would return, and open her door, and find what he had found in Paris.

He pushed the thought away. Iphègénie and Madame Clisson had tidied the room, bathed Charles-Henri, made Dominique as comfortable as they could. She slept now, haloed in white lace and morning light, her son nestled against her side.

Poor little boy.

She had done by him the best she could, January reflected. She had borne him to a white man, and a wealthy one. Her son would, as Hannibal said, have an education, probably a good one. He would be fair-skinned—octoroon, according to the usage of the country, and with any luck featured more like his seven white great-grandparents than the single African woman who had been brought across the Atlantic in chains to be raped by her captors. That helped.

It helped, too, to be a boy, especially if one's father took care to see his son apprenticed to a trade or profession and not raised as a "gentleman" in the expectation of an inheritance that might never come. Hèlier the water seller was a plaçée's child, whose father had married a white lady and lost all interest in his Rampart Street mistress and her crippled son.

For girls it was another matter.

Too many among the respectable free colored looked askance at the daughters of the plaçées, assuming automatically they would be what their mothers had been. Rose Vitrac had told him about the pressure put on her pupil Geneviève by the girl's mother, for Geneviève—before the fever had wasted her—was a beautiful girl, seventeen and with the fair-skinned beauty so valued by the whites. Even for those girls who had the strength to battle their mothers' expectations, it was sometimes hard to marry among the free colored.

And if you wanted something different, something besides being a mistress or a wife?

An education is almost a guarantee of a solitary road, Rose Vitrac had said, propping her spectacles on her nose in the stifling dark of the attic room above the school she had fought so hard to establish. Yet there had been that bright triumph in her eye as she'd added, *I've made it thus far.*

On his way to the little railway station later that morning—accompanied by Hannibal, who was declaiming *The Rape of the Lock* to egrets, cattle, and passing market-women for reasons best known to himself—January turned his steps to the modest cottage on Music Street where Uncle Louis Corbier rented rooms to colored professionals for the season. The old man himself was still asleep, but January ascertained from a servant girl sweeping the porch of the boarding-house next door that no couple from town had arrived yesterday to sleep on the old man's floor and replace his departed servants in tending to his guests.

Something must have happened, he thought uneasily, and occupied his mind through the short train journey with appalling scenarios of what he would find when he reached Olympe's house.

What he found, of course, was young Gabriel competently making a roux in the kitchen for that evening's gumbo, while Ti-Paul gravely spun pots on the kitchen floor. "Mama, she's on her way out there now," the boy reported to January. "Juliette Gallier's son was took bad with fever yesterday, so Mama figured Aunt Minou would be all right, with all her friends there that've had babies, and you, and Grand-mère, even if a message didn't get to you in time. She left 'bout an hour ago."

January nodded. "Did Nicole Perret and her husband stay in town for some reason?"

The boy frowned. "I don't know," he said. "I know they were getting ready Thursday night—they sent their heavy stuff that Zizi-Marie and I packed—and they were going to go Friday morning first thing. I walked past there today and the place is all locked and the plank up." He set the skillet on the back of the stove and gathered the assortment of bowls from the table in which sausage, onion, celery, and peppers had already been neatly chopped. "You care to come back here for supper before you go on to the Hospital, Uncle Ben? I'm making *callas*."

"You got a deal there." Young as he was, Gabriel made the best deep-fried rice-balls January had ever tasted.

After checking on his brother-in-law's progress—scarcely necessary, since Paul Corbier had never developed the jaundice stage of the fever and was well on his way to recovery—exhausted as he was, January made his way down Rue Toulouse to the Cathedral to hear Mass and light candles for the safe recovery of Minou, and the safe passage of little Charles-Henri through the coming weeks. It was difficult to find a space unoccupied before the Virgin's altar to set the two new votives. You would need a forest fire of lights, he thought, gazing at the soft-glowing holocaust of yellow wax, to safeguard all who stand in need of it now.

He set up a candle for Cora Chouteau as well.

Returning home in the smoky glare of sunset he kept glancing behind him, certain that Shaw was watching the place, positive that he was again being followed. He checked the garçonnière thoroughly—or as thoroughly as his fatigue would let him—for signs that it had been entered, then lay for a long time listening to the distant rattle of drums from the direction of Congo Square. He wondered whether Cora had succeeded in getting herself caught for urging Gervase to escape and if she had given his name to the City Guards.

The worst of it was that he didn't know. He didn't know how he could find out, either.

He could only wait for the trap to close.

He slept, but not well.

The specter of arrest followed him through the streets to Olympe's house after dark, and from there to the Hospital, to be obliterated only by blind weariness, heat, and stench. Following Soublet with his leeches and his cupping-glasses among the bodies of the sick, still he felt a kind of weary anger at the bright silken figures sipping negus on the galleries of the Hotel St. Clair, in the ballroom of the Washington Hotel. *How dare they,* he thought, *fight their trivial battles over which musicians would play at whose ball, when four miles away men and women were struggling for their lives against an invisible slayer and the air dripped with the stink of corpses, smoke, and death?*

Unreasonable, he knew. If you have the money to flee, why picnic in the garden of the Angel of Death? His mother's presence in the city, or Minou's, or that horrible iron-voiced Madame Redfern's, wouldn't lessen the suffering of Hèlier or that poor Italian, since beyond doubt they would only lock themselves behind their shutters and smudges as everyone else in town was doing.

Except people like Olympe.

And Marie Laveau.

And Delphine Lalaurie.

And Rose Vitrac.

He returned to the house on the Rue Burgundy through morning heat that he knew was already too overwhelming to permit sleep. Gabriel had sent a jar of ginger-water home with him yesterday afternoon. He was sitting on the steps drinking the last of it—and reading an editorial in the *Gazette* that claimed all reports of fever in the city were the base falsifications of alarmists—when the gate to the yard opened, and Rose Vitrac stepped through.

She looked around the yard, shielding her eyes. January recalled telling her he lived in the garçonnière behind his mother's house, but didn't remember whether he'd described the house or said what street it was on. He must have, he thought, ducking back into his room to catch up his waistcoat and put it on. He was buttoning it—and his shirt—as he clattered down the wooden steps.

She looked up, tension and uncertainty leaving her face like shadow before light. "I'm sorry to trouble you like this, M'sieu Janvier."

"My fault." He led her into the shadows under the gallery, and brought up one of the wooden chairs there. "I meant to come check on your girls Saturday, but I was called out to Milneburgh to care for my sister. She's not ill," he added, seeing the flash of genuine concern on Rose Vitrac's face. "She was brought to bed, safely delivered of a son. I did see Marie-Neige's mother for just a moment—she's a friend of my mother—but with everything happening I wasn't able to speak to her."

Mademoiselle Vitrac shook her head. "It isn't the girls," she told him. "Though Antoinette is still a bad case; the others seem a little better. It's Cora Chouteau. She never came back Friday night, and I'm afraid some harm has befallen her."

SEVEN

He was so tired it took a moment for the pieces to drop into place in his mind. "Cora?"

A dusky flush bloomed under Mademoiselle Vitrac's freckles. "I didn't know it was you she'd gone to for help until after you left," she said. "She was helping me look after the girls. She saw you through the attic window and was afraid you'd tracked her to my school, and that I would get into trouble for harboring her."

January held her chair for her to sit, then dashed upstairs again and fetched a couple of lemons he'd set to ripen on the windowsill, a spare cup, and the pitcher of water. When he came down again she was sitting with her brow resting on the knuckle of her forefinger, her spectacles lying on the table beside her. The lids of her shut eyes were bruised looking.

"Are you all right?"

She raised her head quickly and retrieved the spectacles, settling the light frame of gold and glass into place as the brief smile flashed into life again. "Well enough. Nursing takes it out of one so." In contrast to her haggard face her frock of blue-and-white-striped cambric was clean and pressed, the wide white collar spotless and bright with starch.

"Where did you know Cora?" He set down the pitcher, drew his pocketknife, and cut and squeezed the lemons. "It's not very cool, I'm afraid."

"No, thank you, it's exactly what I needed. Only a little," she added, as he ducked through the kitchen doors and came out with Bella's blue pottery sugar jar. "I've never really liked sweet things." She drank gratefully, straightened her shoulders, and put on an expression of calm competence the way another woman would don a bonnet, because it was the proper thing to wear in the presence of a stranger.

"Cora is the daughter of my stepmother's maid. Mother died when I was very small, as I said, and Father brought me down to Chouteau to raise. Chouteau was his father-in-law's name, the original owner of the plantation. Father's wife treated me very well until she had her own child. Then things were different. Not through her intention, you understand," Rose Vitrac added quickly, "but because that's what happens when a woman has a child of her own."

Something altered in her eyes, though. A thought or memory intruded that she swiftly pushed aside. She took another sip of the lemonade. "For a long time Grand-père Chouteau's books were my only friends. Later, Cora and I were fast friends, though I was much older. We were like sisters, despite the fact that she never could understand why I wanted to know about people who were dead and what rocks are made of."

She smiled, as if she saw that scrappy dark slip of a girl again; perhaps seeing a gawky know-all bluestocking as well. "I remember trying to explain Plato's Cave to her, and she dragged me out into the woods and taught me how to set a trapline. She said the next time I was contemplating shadows thrown by a fire on a cave wall at least I'd have something to cook over that fire. When I was sick . . ." She paused, her mouth growing tight; and behind the spectacles her eyes flicked away again.

Silence lay on the sun-smitten yard; unsaid things hovered near enough to touch. Then, a little shakily, she went on, "In any case, Cora thought I was a lunatic. Well, everyone did. But she accepted that that was the way I was. That's important, when you're seven-teen."

"It is indeed." January remembered the Austrian music-master who had never questioned what drove him to seek perfection in his art but had only shown him the stony, solitary path to that perfection. "More important than anything else, maybe."

Mademoiselle Vitrac shook her head. "I thought so once." She passed a hand over her forehead. "But eating is more important. And having a safe place to sleep. But it's right up there with them, especially when the people around you—the only people you know—are all trying to get you to say you like taking care of children, and scouring pots until they shine, and sewing fine, straight seams and buttonholes so perfect they're the talk of the neighborhood." Her voice took on another inflection there, gently mocking other voices heard in her childhood and youth. She added reflectively, "I suppose there are people who really enjoy those things."

"There are." January smiled. "The seams and buttonholes part, anyway. I was married to her."

The cloudy-bright sunflash smile appeared again—vanished. "Well, I left Chouteau when I was twenty. Cora was almost thirteen. I didn't see her again until she knocked at my door a week ago Wednesday night. She told me about Gervase; told me she was afraid her mistress was going to try to poison her, because her master wouldn't let her be sold. She insisted she only wanted to see Gervase again, to see if there was something that could be worked out. She was . . . Cora was desperate, M'sieu Janvier. She was afraid the City Guards were after her—which is ridiculous on the face of it, with the epidemic going on—and she was terrified that her master would come after her."

"Was she?" asked January thoughtfully.

Mademoiselle Vitrac met his eyes with cool challenge in hers. "Yes. But that isn't the reason I believe she didn't put monkshood in his soup as a *congé*. Cora—Cora *wouldn't*, M'sieu Janvier. She has her faults, but she isn't vindictive."

"Not even to a man who raped her?"

Her eyes turned away from his, and he saw the generous square of her lower lip tuck a little, drawn between her teeth. After a long time she looked back at him, carefully covering what had flickered across her eyes. "I don't think so. Cora—Cora doesn't regard rape the way a . . . a free woman might. A woman who didn't—didn't expect it. I don't say she wouldn't have avenged it under certain circumstances, but . . . I don't think she did in this case."

She finished her lemonade quickly and turned the horn cup in both hands on the plank table, still avoiding his eyes. "Well, to make a long story short, she told me last Friday afternoon that she was going to Madame Lalaurie's that night—"

"That's all she said? Just that she was going?"

Mademoiselle Vitrac nodded.

"Nothing about the gate being left open? Or Madame Lalaurie giving her money?"

"Giving her money?" She looked up in surprise. "She did that? Then . . ." She thought again about what she was going to say, and stopped herself. "No. She didn't say anything about that."

"I don't know why it's easier for people to believe Madame Lalaurie would help Cora out of spite against Madame Redfern, rather than out of a desire to help her," he said. "And maybe it is only spite. Emily Redfern has certainly gone out of her way to make herself obnoxious to the Creole families in town. She's selling up her slaves to pay her husband's creditors—Madame Redfern is—and the loss of one of them is going to put her in an extremely embarrassing position."

Mademoiselle Vitrac chuckled, suddenly amused. "It's always nice if you can pay off an old score and get credit for being saintly while you're doing it: like finding a coin on the banquette. And I wouldn't put it past Madame Lalaurie. But she's a law unto herself, you know. That's why she stirs up so much envy. How much money did she give Cora, do you know?"

"Twelve dollars or so, mostly in Mexican silver."

"Oh," she said softly, and then sighed. "Oh, well." With a deep breath, steeling herself, she took from her belt a reticule of cardboard faced with blue silk and opened it. She withdrew a man's linen handkerchief knotted around a heavy mass of metal that clinked, a double-strand of slightly golden pearls, and Madame Lalaurie's small plush purse. This last she pushed toward him across the table. "That would be this, wouldn't it?"

January nodded. He looked inside, and saw that it still contained the ten Mexican dollars it had originally held. Then he undid the handkerchief and counted what was in it. There were a few English guinea pieces and a number of Bavarian thalers, four American double eagles, and the rest in Mexican dollars—a hundred and eighty dollars all told. Nowhere near the five thousand Madame Redfern claimed had been taken.

Levelly, expecting a fight, Mademoiselle Vitrac said, "I still refuse to believe that Cora harmed a hair of Otis Redfern's head."

"This was all you found?"

"Yes. When she didn't come back Friday night I looked in her room Saturday."

Silence returned to the yard, broken by the creak of a wheel in the Rue Burgundy and a woman's voice saying impatiently, "Hurry, would you?" to some unknown servant or child.

"Well," January mused, "if she'd spent four thousand eight hundred and twenty dollars between Twelve-Mile Point and the levee, she'd have been wearing something better than that red dress."

"I gave her the dress," said Mademoiselle Vitrac, but he saw her mouth relax and the strain ease from her shoulders, not so much at his jest itself as at the fact that he was joking instead of accusing. "And the shoes. They were Geneviève's when she came to the school, and she outgrew them. The thing is, M'sieu Janvier . . . if Cora fled, even if she got Gervase to flee with her, why didn't she come back for the money? The pearls I can understand, if she realized they were being looked for. But the money was the only thing that guaranteed her she wouldn't have to go back to Madame Redfern."

January turned the necklace over in his hands. He'd seen enough pearls close up, between his mother and her friends, and Ayasha's customers, to see that these were medium to high grade, lustrous, evenly sized and closely matched.

"What can I do?" Mademoiselle Vitrac asked.

He folded the necklace together into the palm of one big hand. "What we can't do," he replied, "is go to the police. You know that."

"I know that."

"I don't know what the penalty is for aiding and abetting a murder—even if you know and I know that it was Emily Redfern and not Cora who put that monkshood into Otis Redfern's soup—but at the very least I think we'd both be cleaning out the municipal gutters for a long time."

Her mouth twitched a little in a smile, in spite of herself, and she averted her face as if she had been punished as a child for laughing when adults thought she should be having the vapors.

He held out the pearls. "Get rid of these. Throw them in the river, but make sure nobody sees you do it." When he saw her hesitate—no woman throws pearls away lightly—he added, "If you're caught with them on you, I can guarantee you you'll lose everything you've worked for so hard."

"Yes." She took them from his hand. "Yes, I see that."

"We need to check the fever wards," said January. "Yellow Jack hits quick. If Cora started with a headache on her way home Friday night, with chills and pain and cramps, she might have been too disoriented to find her way up from Rue Royale to your school."

"I can do that," said Mademoiselle Vitrac. "There's an emergency fever ward at Davidson's Clinic on Circus Street and another one at Campbell's. *Damn* the newspapers for not publishing where these things are. Didn't the Ursulines set up a ward in their old convent? The one the legislature has been using now?"

January nodded. "I think so. Soublet has fever patients at his private clinic on Bourbon, though God help her if she was taken there. And the first thing to do," he added, rising as she rose, "is to talk to Madame Lalaurie herself."

"You don't have to—"

"I don't want you to be connected with Cora in any way." He handed her her reticule, and the plush purse. "Madame Lalaurie knows at least that I've spoken to her."

Her smile was rueful as she shook out her petticoats. She wore a little gold cross around her neck, and tiny gold studs, like beads, in her earlobes. "I see I wouldn't make a particularly good desperado."

"Want of practice." He returned her smile, and she laughed.

"Ah. So I can look forward to getting better at skulduggery with time. Cora would be proud of me."

"I'll let you know what I find out." He walked with her to the pass-through, opened the gate, and followed her to the street. The only movement there was a woman in a red headscarf selling kerchiefs and pins door to door and the flies that swarmed around a dead dog.

"But I think the first thing we need to do is ascertain whether Cora made it to Madame Lalaurie's house that night at all."

Shutters tight closed and latched, curtains drawn to exclude any possibility of fevered air, the small ward on the ground floor of the yellow stucco building on Rue Bourbon was like those ovens in which Persian monarchs had had their enemies immured to roast. But there was no flame here. Only darkness, and the bleared glare of the jaundiced lamps; the smell of human waste, medicine, and blood, solid enough to cut. For a few moments January only stood looking down the ward, with its double row of makeshift pine-pole beds, bare for the most part of any semblance of mosquito-bars—most without sheets as well. The air was a low thick mutter of delirium and panting breath.

No nurse was to be seen. January made his way between the beds—not more than twenty could be crammed into what was usually a shop selling coffee and tobacco—to the shut and curtained door at the rear. In the courtyard behind, the air grated with the smoke of burning gunpowder. The kitchen building was nearly invisible through its cinder gray screen. A wooden stairway ascended to a gallery, and as he put his foot to the lowest step, January heard a woman groan.

"That's good, that's good!" cried Dr. Soublet's voice, enthusiasm bordering on delight. "The ligaments and bones are accommodating themselves to the pressure of the apparatus!"

There were three rooms upstairs. One seemed to be a sort of office, tucked in a corner where the gallery ran around to join the slave quarters, and unoccupied. In the second, several beds had been set up in the shrouded gloom. These were farther apart than those in the shop, and equipped with mosquito-bars. Small tables between them bore slop-jars and bleeding-bowls. Their contents crept with flies. The candlelit darkness reeked of opium.

In each bed a sufferer lay, invisible behind white clouds of gauze and murmuring in narcotic dream. January stopped beside the first bed, put aside the netting, and looked down into the face of Hèlier the water seller. The young man was strapped into an iron apparatus like Torquemada's nightmare, over head, shoulders, and back. In spite of the netting, flies swarmed on the sores that the straps had worn in the flesh of his splayed-out arms, and crawled over his unprotected eyes and mouth.

Angrily, January leaned down and unbuckled the straps. *To hell with the "process of the cure,"* he thought. It was one thing to joke with Mademoiselle Vitrac about that obscene iron maiden in the school; this was quite another. In all his years of witnessing "infallible machines" invented by one physician or another, he'd never seen one with his own eyes that worked.

Could a man of color be arrested in this town for interfering with a white physician's patient?

These days it wouldn't surprise him.

"Get up," he said softly. "Get out of here while you can."

But the water seller only rolled his head and stared at him with drugged turquoise eyes. "Get out?" he asked, and giggled. "All this opium and you tell me, 'Get out'? Who're you to tell me anything, nigger man? Who're you to tell a white man—a white man . . ." He groped about for the end of his sentence.

January took him by the arm and sat him up. "You're not a white man," he said. "And if you stay here . . ."

Hèlier dragged his arm free, lips drawn back in an ugly rage. "Don't you tell me I'm not a white man, you black nigger." He crawled to his feet, and grabbed the end of the bed with a gasp of agony. "Don't you tell me *anything.* Why ain't I a white man, eh? *Why ain't I?* Look at that!" He held out his arm. "You ever see whiter?"

Then the drug sponged the anger from his face. He gestured around him at the ward, and giggled again. "I'm in a white man's hospital, ain't I? Serves me right, eh? Serves me right."

Hunched and crablike, Hèlier staggered away between the beds, as if his curved spine and the additional pain of what he had been through were burdens that bent him to the ground. From the gallery January watched him descend the stairs and disappear into the shadows of the carriageway, clinging to the pale stucco of the walls.

January drew a deep breath.

The third room was Dr. Soublet's clinic per se.

"Don't want it," muttered a woman's voice in German. *"Friedrich—wo ist Friedrich?* Hurts . . . God, it hurts!"

Soublet and a small, slender man of about thirty whom January vaguely recognized bent over a leather-topped table on which lay the German woman Soublet had been talking to at Charity only a few nights ago. She was nude but for a dirty shift pulled up to her belly. An enormous brace or bracket of iron and leather was strapped to her waist, thigh, knee, and down to the deformed foot. It was she whom January had heard groaning, as Soublet readjusted the straps. The slim little man held a spouted china cup to her lips, but his silent dark eyes watched Soublet's face with a disturbing cold intensity.

"It only hurts because it's improving," replied Soublet bracingly. "Nicolas, for God's sake if the woman won't take the laudanum, hold her nose as you pour! I can't have her jiggling about so. What do *you* want?" He looked up irritably as the light from the outside fell through upon them with January's lifting aside of the curtain over the door. "And close that door, man! This woman has recently recovered from the fever! Do you want to provoke a relapse?"

January stepped in and closed the door of the ward behind him. The woman, whose arms were strapped to the table, wriggled and began to cry. *"Hilf mir,"* she muttered, *"hilf mir* . . . Oh, Friedrich!"

"May I speak for a moment with Dr. Lalaurie?" January looked carefully aside so they would not see the sickened rage in his eyes.

The small man set down the cup and stepped forward. His pointed, waxy face was polite, but there was something in the way he looked at him that reminded January of the American businessman in the ballroom at the Washington Hotel: a calculation of value, an estimate of what he, Benjamin January, could be used for or sold for. "I am Dr. Lalaurie."

"Please excuse the familiarity of my seeking you out, sir." January bowed. "My name is Benjamin January; I work at the Charity Hospital."

"I know who you are," broke in Soublet. "You're one of the servants there."

"I'm a surgeon, actually, sir," said January, in his most neutral voice. He turned back to Lalaurie. "I'm looking for Madame Lalaurie, sir. I know she nurses. I thought I might find her here. I have a few questions I need to ask her about a mutual acquaintance who may have been taken ill with fever."

"My wife nurses at the ward set up in the old Convent of the Ursulines," Lalaurie said. About twenty years younger than his wife, he was slender and small and, January guessed, handsome in a sleek-haired, wiry way. The sleeves of his shirt were linen and very fine, his boots expensive kid, his silk waistcoat embroidered with red and golden birds, nearly hidden under the spotless white apron. His mustaches and the tiny arrowhead of a Vandyke lay on the pale face as precisely as if painted. "She should be there this afternoon."

"Really, Nicolas." January heard Soublet's voice as he lifted the heavy double-layer of curtain, stepped through the door to the opium of the ward again. "We can't allow these interruptions. Now bring me the lancets, and the clyster as well. This woman has far too much of the fiery humors in her to permit the submissive state required for proper mollification of the bones."

There were few Sisters in the ward set up in what had been the hospital operated by the Ursuline nuns, before the convent had been moved to larger quarters nine years ago. This building, a long, low room of many windows, had returned to its original use for a time, and that may have accounted for the uncrowded look of the room, the impression of air that could be breathed. The smell here was less foul, and daylight filtered through the windows looking onto the old convent's central courtyard. On pallets, on cots, on two or three old and battered cypress beds donated by the charitable, men and women gasped in the heat, or wept with pain.

From the doorway January saw Madame Lalaurie, clothed in

black as she had been Wednesday night and severely neat as ever. She held the hands of a man who was clearly dying, not of the fever but of the cholera: drawn, ghastly, his bedding sodden and stinking.

A priest stood by, reading the offices for the dying. January crossed himself as the Host was elevated and murmured his own prayer for the stranger's comfort and salvation. The priest, January noticed, stood at a safe distance, or as safe as one could be around the cholera. Madame Lalaurie, however, sat on the edge of the bed; and what arrested January again was the expression on her face, the intense, almost holy pain of a contemplative martyr, as if she herself were dying with her eyes upon the Cross. It was an unnerving sight, so at odds with her controlled strength, and shocking in its way, as intimate as if he watched her face while she submitted to the act of love. Her body swayed as the priest recited the words:

"May you never know the terror of darkness, the gnashing of teeth in the flames, the agonies of torment . . ."

The dying man retched. Madame Lalaurie quickly and competently turned him, reached down for a basin while he vomited, and held him as he went into convulsions; the priest backed hastily away. She wiped the man's face, and wiped it again when he vomited again, all with that expression of desperate longing, of pain shared and gladly absorbed into her heart. She had lost a child, January remembered; her only son. She lived daily with her crippled daughter's pain. Was that in some way the source of that glow, that expression almost of exultation?

Or was it only the relief of release from being forever in control, forever perfect?

She murmured something else, leaning close to the beard-stubbled face. From a safe distance the priest murmured, *"Remember not, O Lord, the sins of this man's youth and of his ignorance, but according to Thy great mercy, be mindful of him . . ."*

Be mindful of us all, thought January, his hand slipping into his pocket to the rosary that never left him. *Be mindful of us all.*

The young man sobbed weakly, and Madame Lalaurie gathered him to her, his head on her breast. It was there that he died.

She held him still for a long time, her head bowed over his. Her face was a marble angel's in the frame of her nunlike veil, her skirts and sleeves spotted with filth and slime. January saw in his mind Emily Redfern in her black widow's cap and veil, arguing about musicians with Madame Viellard in the refulgent gaslight of the Washington Hotel. He remembered, too, the plump, self-satisfied Reverend Dunk among his adoring Committee ladies. The priest at this bedside didn't look any too happy as he whispered the final prayers, January murmuring the responses in his heart. But at least the man was there.

When he had spoken the final blessing, the priest touched Madame Lalaurie on the arm. Like one waking from a trance, the woman laid the dead man back on the shabby straw. An Ursuline Sister approached, offering a bowl of water and a clean apron to cover her simple black dress, but Madame Lalaurie shook her head, said something too softly for January to hear. She rose and started to turn away. The Sister touched her sleeve again, pointed to January. Madame Lalaurie blinked, her eyes coming back into focus.

"M'sieu Janvier." She looked down at her dress. "Please excuse me." She seemed unruffled and unembarrassed, a woman whom no disarray or dishevelment could touch, not even a dress spattered with the vomitus of death. "I shall join you in the courtyard in a few moments." And she moved unhurriedly away through one of the doors leading toward the convent itself.

In fact, it was closer to twenty minutes before the courtyard door opened and the tall, slender figure emerged, attended by one of the nuns. From a bench under the hospital's gallery at the side of the cobbled yard, January saw her, stood, and bowed. She had not only completely changed her dress—though the new dress was also black, with touches of blue on bodice and sleeves—but had had someone comb out and redress her hair. In place of her veil she wore a bonnet, conservative by the day's standards but recognizably in the height of fashion, and gloves of black kid. As she came closer, he saw that she had also taken the time to apply fresh rouge. She looked, in fact, as she always looked: flawless.

She must have brought the fresh gown, the cosmetics, the bonnet with her when she came to nurse. Of course, the nuns would trample one another to give her a place to change.

"M'sieu Janvier, I hope you will excuse a woman's vanity. Sister

Jocelyn, would you have my other things sent around at your convenience? Thank you. Do you mind walking as we speak, M'sieu? I should have been home hours ago. That poor man. . . ." She looked back over her shoulder at the long, low gray bulk of the hospital, then gave her head a small shake. "I trust that your little girl reached her place of lodging in safety?"

"In fact she did not," said January, and those brilliant black eyes widened with surprise. "That's what I came to ask you, Madame. Whether she in fact met with Gervase."

"She did." She stepped through the gate before him, which he held open for her, and they walked together up the Rue des Ursulines. "Poor Gervase was quite distraught afterward. He said she spoke of 'taking the first boat up the river,' but naturally I assumed she would first go to her lodgings, wherever they were. Was this not the case?"

January shook his head. "No, Madame. The friend with whom Cora was staying said that she did not return that night. Moreover, as she left the money you gave her at the friend's lodgings, I don't see that she could have taken any boat anywhere."

January handed her across the gutters of the Rue Condé, like new-polished tin in the harsh sunlight. This near to the river the city had less of the dead aspect that made the rear portions of the French town so chilling, though Gallatin Street, with its unsavory taverns and brothels catering to the trash of the river and the wharves, was perhaps a little close for comfort. Under the haze of steamboat smoke an occasional market-woman walked the banquettes, a wicker tray of berries or peppers on her hip. The nasal voices of a gang of upriver keelboatmen, jostling along on the other side of the street on their way to Gallatin, rang shockingly against the shut and silent fronts of the houses; a dark-clothed Creole gentleman coming in the other direction hastily crossed to avoid an encounter.

"No," murmured Madame. "No, that's true. Unless she had money from some other source on her person, or someone else she could go to." She withdrew a fan from her reticule, and waved it gently as they walked.

"I understand from the newspaper that she stole quite a substantial sum from her master, and her mistress's pearl necklace—not that I'm inclined to believe a word that Redfern woman says, M'sieu. And

the newspapers will print anything. I would not be in the least surprised to hear that Emily Redfern was the one who poisoned her
husband, and faked the symptoms herself for the benefit of the coroner. It's quite easy to do with a little belladonna in one's eyes and a
weak elder-leaf tisane—or sticking a broomstraw down one's throat in
an emergency. In fact I wouldn't be surprised to hear that it was she
who made off with that five thousand dollars and pushed the blame
onto that poor girl."

"Did Emily Redfern hate her husband that much?"

"M'sieu Janvier," said Madame Lalaurie, with a slight tightening
of her beautiful mouth, "it was less a matter of *hating* M'sieu Redfern—whom I believe she liked tolerably well—than of *loving* his
money. And of resenting every sou he expended on purposes other
than her aggrandizement in the eyes of her admirers. Or it may be
that he uncovered something about the relationship between her and
that backwoods Antichrist, Dunk."

She shrugged, and clipped her fan shut, putting the matter from
her as if disgusted with herself even for the thoughts.

"Was M'sieu Redfern so much of a gambler, Madame?"

"No more so than other men, I believe. That's another thing the
Puritan daughters of Boston don't understand: that a person can
gamble, even for quite large sums, without being possessed of a devil.
But Emily Redfern has always believed that whoever causes her annoyance must be an emissary of Satan. Like that poor girl."

January said nothing for a time, but the red-and-gold candy tin
rose to his mind.

"Did Gervase say anything about where she might have gone?" he
asked.

"Only that she said she was 'getting on a boat' that night. He
is . . . quite desolate. He's a simple soul at heart, you know. I think
he thought that, having run away from the Redferns, the girl was
going to remain in the city and meet with him on a regular basis."
She frowned, dark brows pulling together over the brilliant eyes. "I
sent him into the country, upriver to my cousin's plantation. In a few
weeks I'm sure he'll be fine."

They turned along Rue Royale, passing an open lot and then a small, graceful town house plastered with rust-colored stucco, before reaching the pale green fortress on the corner.

"I never saw her very closely, you understand, M'sieu." Madame Lalaurie paused before the gorgeously carved front door. "Only as a shadow, passing along Rue de l'Hôpital in the darkness." She nodded up along the street, in the direction of the swamps. "But she seemed so . . . alone. A little colored girl, going out to brave the world. I hope no ill befell her."

The door opened at her back. "Madame, Madame," chided Bastien in his soft voice, "you should have sent for me."

She laughed. "What, to spare myself a walk of two streets? You should have been a nursemaid, my Bastien." Smiling, she held out her gloved hand to January. "Good luck with your search, M'sieu."

He bowed over her fingers. "Thank you, Madame."

The door closed. January looked up along Rue de l'Hôpital, in the direction of her nod. She'd been watching in a window, then: natural enough, if she had worries about Gervase fleeing with his lover. And Cora had gone back in the direction of town—in the direction of Mademoiselle Vitrac's school, where Madame Redfern's necklace and nearly two hundred dollars were cached.

And had never reached her goal.

"M'sieu!"

He turned his head. In the doorway of the little rust-colored town house stood the Creole gentleman in the dark coat, the one who had crossed the street to avoid an encounter with the Americans.

The man beckoned him, and January walked to where he stood.

"I beg your pardon," the gentleman said in a low voice. "I could not but overhear what passed between you and Madame. You have a friend, a young woman of color, who went to Madame's house by night?" He was stooped and thin, pointed of nose and graying of hair, rather like a harassed ferret.

"Not a friend," said January carefully. He and Madame had not spoken loudly, and the amount of information gleaned seemed rather a lot for a chance hearing. "A friend of a friend. Did you happen to see her? This would have been Friday night."

"I saw nothing," said the little man. "But the things that I hear . . ." He laid a crooked finger alongside his nose. "My name is Montreuil, Alphonse Montreuil. I live here, I and my good wife." He gestured to the town house behind him. He looked down-at-heels, though the main branch of the Montreuil family were fairly well-off.

"Like all sensible people I had my windows shuttered tight Friday night, in the hopes of evading this terrible pestilence." Montreuil crossed himself, and January did the same.

Then the man leaned close, his voice dropping conspiratorially. His teeth were bad and his breath like a day-old midden. "All the same, Monsieur, the things that I hear. . . . This young friend of yours. She went into that house. Are you certain she came out again?"

January stepped back, startled. "What?"

"Are you sure she emerged from the house of that woman?" Montreuil's dark eyes flickered back to the formidable walls of pale green stucco, the neat galleries and tightly closed black shutters. "I have heard terrible things, Monsieur, terrible things. In the dead of the night, when I am unable to sleep—and I have never slept well, even as a child, never. Groans and cries come from the attic of that house; the sound of whips, and the clanking of chains. That woman—I've heard she keeps her slaves chained, and tortures them nightly! No one will admit to it," he went on. "The woman is too powerful, her precious family too prominent—No, no, she can do no wrong, everyone says! But me . . . I know."

"I'll keep that in mind," said January, nodding gravely at the fierce little man and his feverish fancies. "Many thanks, Monsieur."

He backed away and returned to the corner of Rue de l'Hôpital, looking up it in the direction in which Madame Lalaurie had said Cora had gone. It was only a matter of five streets to the school, and at that hour of the night it was unlikely she would encounter any of the City Guard. Not with everyone in that less-than-valorous organization terrified of the fever that rode the night air.

Had Cora encountered someone else? Seen someone who caused her to turn her steps and flee to the river, to seek Olympe's friend Natchez Jim and the first boat out?

And abandon two hundred dollars? The pearl necklace might very well have been left, considered too dangerous, but for two hundred dollars one could probably purchase faked papers attesting one's freedom. He suspected Hannibal had eked out a living from time to time by producing them.

Or had she only encountered Bronze John, waiting in the darkness as he always waited?

Thoughtfully, January began to retrace the girl's probable route from the big green house on the corner of Rue Royale, to Rue St. Claude, looking for what he might find.

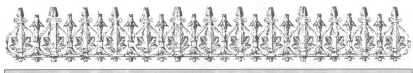

EIGHT

At any other time, it would have been ridiculous to suppose that an event that took place late Friday night could have left signs still readable on Monday afternoon. The sheer volume of foot traffic along the banquettes—market-women, flatboatmen from the nearby levee, children rolling hoops, ladies out for a stroll, sellers of everything from pralines to shoe pattens—precluded so much as a dropped cigar stub from remaining in the same place or state for more than ten minutes, much less the marks of some unspecified conflict, meeting, or event.

At any other time.

But as he walked along Rue de l'Hôpital to Rue St. Claude on the upriver side of the street, then back on the downriver side; as he repeated the process on Rue des Ursulines, up and back, then Rue St. Philippe, January saw only one market-woman in a tignon, hastening head-down in the direction of the river, and, on Rue St. Philippe, a drunken, bewhiskered American, staggering along the banquette, pounding on the shutters of the houses he passed and shouting, " 'Sa matter with this town? Can't a man find a hoor fr'is natural needs?"

Even such life as still beat in the town—the fashionable shops, the gambling houses that ran full-blast as if Death were not waiting like a coachman at the curb, the cafés and taverns along Bourbon and Chartres and Royale—were farther over toward the center of the old French town or closer to the river.

Here the tall town houses, the pink and green and yellow cottages were closed tight against the creeping advent of evening. The invisible plague rode the deepening twilight with the humming of the mosquitoes and the cemetery stink.

January quartered the streets between the Lalaurie house and Mademoiselle Vitrac's school until it grew too dark to see. He studied doorways, walls, the brick of the banquette underfoot and the very ooze of crap and vegetable-parings in the gutters. It had rained at least three times since Friday, and he wasn't even certain exactly what he sought, and in any case he didn't find anything particularly interesting: a certain amount of spat tobacco, indicating the recent passage of American males; crumpled newspapers; three dogs and four rats in advanced states of decay; innumerable roaches; celery leaves; garbage. No pools of blood conveniently sheltered from the rain. No knives driven into doorposts. No headscarves or golden rings or pulled-loose necklaces so beloved of sensational novelists, no half-scribbled letters of enigmatic names.

He passed the house of the Perret family on Rue St. Philippe, and wondered whether they had, in fact, taken refuge on the floor of Uncle Louis's porch within breathing distance of the lake or whether they might by some chance have remained home Friday night and seen something of Cora's disappearance. The house was the last of a line of artisans' cottages, backed up against the side of a modest town house; it, and about half the houses of the row, were shuttered and lightless. January hopped the gutter—for as Gabriel had said, their plank was taken up—and rapped sharply on the shutter.

But there was no sound within the Perret house, and no light gleamed out through the jalousies. He was late already to the Hospital. He made his way there through thick hot gathering twilight, trouble and defeat in his heart.

Early the following afternoon he told Rose Vitrac what he had heard, what he had sought, and what he had not found. "I picked up this morning's *Gazette*," he added. "Madame Redfern is still advertising for her recapture, so Cora hasn't been caught yet."

Mademoiselle Vitrac sat on the corner of Antoinette's bed, next to his hard wooden chair. She pushed her spectacles more firmly onto the bridge of her nose, and read past his shoulder the few lines printed next to the standard slug of a negress running:

Ran away—Cora—Aged about twenty-five, a skilled house servant and cook. Of medium height and very dark, with a black birthmark upon her left shoulder. Speaks both French and English, thought to be going to New Orleans. Stole $5000 upon her departure.

"If that's the best description of her Madame Redfern can come up with," remarked Mademoiselle Vitrac, "Cora's quite safe, wherever she is. 'Medium height?' "

"Have you seen La Redfern?" Hannibal Sefton emerged from the small door at the top of the steps. He carried a pitcher of lemonade, the result of a windfall heap of lemons on the levee, and his dark hair hung over his shoulders and down his back. "I could eat sandwiches off the top of her head."

January recalled that stout tiny figure in widow's black, and laughed. He'd been a little surprised to arrive at the school and find his friend there, but only a little. Hannibal had known Rose Vitrac, it transpired, since they'd been the only two patrons of a job-lot sale at the Customhouse to be looking at the books rather than bolts of silk or boxes of lace fans from Paris at fifty cents the dozen. In the ten months since then, she had occasionally bought books from him when he was particularly hard up for opium or medicine or had given him a place to sleep when he'd been turned out of whatever whorehouse attic he'd been occupying that week.

Now he set the pitcher down on the dresser and poured a cup for Victorine, who though weak and wasted sat propped among her pillows, and held it for her while she drank. Her fever had broken the previous night, Mademoiselle Vitrac had told January on his arrival.

A dozen years seemed to have been erased from the schoolmistress's face.

"Something clearly prevented Cora from coming back," January said thoughtfully. "Either physically, or she saw something or someone that frightened her so badly she fled. If she was arrested, Shaw would have spoken to me by this time. Was anything happening in town Friday night? Or has there been anything taking place at nights?"

The drunken American returned to his mind, staggering along the banquette, banging on the shutters. With Gallatin Street so close and every gaming hall in town open nearly all night it was possible that two or three such men might have encountered the frail, tiny woman walking alone. . . .

"I was out of town that night and I've been in the Hospital every night for weeks. Hannibal?"

"*Insensible of mortality, yet desperately mortal.* . . . Bar the occasional straying inebriate there's been nothing I've heard of. Though of course with so many people out of town there's always some who'll risk the night air, in order to help themselves to unguarded plate or trinkets—and it would take a fine, strong febrile miasma indeed to penetrate the alcoholic fog that surrounds some of our bold American boys. Have you thought that Cora might simply be living in one of the houses you passed?"

Mademoiselle Vitrac laughed, "That's ridiculous. Isn't it?" She looked hesitantly at January.

"What's ridiculous about it?" demanded Hannibal indignantly. "I've been living in the town house of one Eustace Dèlier and his family since July, which is cheaper than paying rent to Willie the Fish over on Perdidio Street. Quieter, too, and it isn't as if I'm taking anything from the family. How could anyone tell?"

How indeed? January remembered the shuttered doorways, the silent houses along every street in the town.

"Why?" he asked. "Why not come back for the money?"

Hannibal shrugged. "She may have thought she was being followed. She may have actually *been* followed—it happens, to women walking alone that time of night. Or she may have met some friend of

Otis Redfern's, someone who could peach on her. For all we know, her Gervase may have lied to Madame Lalaurie about what Cora told him. Cora may be hiding somewhere in town waiting her chance to get him away."

"Reasoning that he needed to be rescued at once from a woman who tortures her slaves to the sound of screams and clanking chains," finished January dryly.

Mademoiselle Vitrac, who had gone to the end of the empty bed where she'd left the armload of clean linen she'd brought up, straightened and turned as if burned. *"What?"*

"According to Madame Lalaurie's neighbor, cries and groans issue from the house on a regular basis."

"And I suppose according to this *man,*" and the twist of her voice made the word the most venomous of insults, "Madame Lalaurie also entertains a regiment of lovers, like the Empress Catherine of Russia? Or practices poisoning slaves for the entertainment of watching them die, like Cleopatra? Or threw that little girl off the roof last year, the way the Americans claimed she did? Or any of those other things that *men* put about concerning any woman who's competent in business, beautiful, wealthy, and socially more prominent than they are? Any woman who doesn't *need* a man around to run her life?"

She caught up the basket and strode from the attic, jaw set with rage. Hannibal and January exchanged a startled look; then January rose and straightened the sheet over Antoinette. He caught up with the schoolmistress in the yard, where she was running water from the cistern into a tin tub for the sheets to soak.

"I'm sorry." He bent to pick up the heavy tub. "I made you angry, and I didn't—"

"No, no." She shook her head, dried her hands on her apron— she continued the motion long after they were dry, her eyes avoiding his. "I'm sorry," she said at last. "That was uncalled for. It was a long time ago. . . ."

"What was?"

"Nothing." For a moment he thought she would walk away, into the kitchen or back to the main house, anywhere so long as it was away from him. But she remained where she stood, though she wouldn't face him. Her lips were set, as a man will hold still after he's

been hurt, knowing he'll hurt more if he moves. For all the strength of her firm mouth he saw how delicate the structure of her bones was, like a long-legged bird.

"It's nothing," she said again.

He didn't reply.

"I just got—very tired of having to defend loving learning above liking boys. Men. Boys. I don't know if you understand."

"I understand." He wanted to touch her hand in comfort but sensed that to do so would turn her from him, perhaps forever. "At least in part. My mama thought I was insane, wanting to do nothing but play the piano." Other boys hadn't been particularly forgiving about it, either.

Rose Vitrac nodded, but still didn't look at him. The rain that rolled in from the Gulf every afternoon was gathering fast overhead, the air thick with it, and with the whirring of cicadas in the trees that grew behind and around the kitchen.

"I didn't mind boys—men—when I was a girl. Around the plantation, I mean. I thought they were dull, was all. But they acted as if . . . as if my lack of interest in them made them furious. As if it were a deliberate insult, which it wasn't. I just wasn't stupid enough to think I could go away to school, and learn about what the world is, and how things are made, and about steam and metals and the mountains at the bottom of the sea, if I bore some man a child. And I wanted to go away, to learn, more than anything. More than life."

She raised her eyes then, smoky green, like leaves just before they turn in autumn, fierce and intent behind the heavy cut slabs of glass.

"It was so *disproportionate*," she said, wondering at it still, after all the years. "Not just the dirty names, but them lying in wait for me. I never understood why they couldn't just leave me alone."

Because they were boys, thought January, to whom the answer was obvious, if not explicable. He understood without being able to explain how it is with boys, who cannot endure being ignored by a woman, any woman. And he knew from his own dealings with the quadroon and octoroon boys in his own schooldays as the darkest boy in the little academy as well as the biggest—boys as fair as Hèlier and as proud of their fairness—that boys egg each other on.

No wonder Montreuil's rumormongering touched her on the raw.

But all he could say was, "I'm sorry." He carried the tin tub to the table by the kitchen's open door, where the inevitable gallery overhead would protect it from the coming downpour. "Did you sleep last night? Then lie down for a few hours now. I don't have to be at the Hospital until eight."

"You don't have to, Monsieur Janvier."

"No," he agreed, and smiled. "And you can make that Ben, if you want."

She hesitated a long time, looking up again into his face. Then she said, very softly, "Thank you. Monsieur Janvier."

She walked back to the house, and this time he did not follow, only waited until she had gone inside before he climbed the stairs to the attic himself.

January heard the violin as he climbed, entered that long, low room dense with heat. Hannibal was playing to the girls, frail airs from the west of Ireland, gentle and sad. When he came in, the fiddler reeled the music to its close, but January held up his hand and signed him to play on.

Geneviève murmured in her pain-racked sleep, nearly hidden behind the white gauze of the mosquito-bar around her bed; Victorine and Antoinette rested easily. Marie-Neige, who had come up with vinegar-water to help wash the girls, had lain down too on one of the other beds and slept as well, even her plumpness seeming somehow fragile in repose. Of Isabel there was as usual nothing to be seen.

January scratched a lucifer to light the candle under the veilleuse, and checked the round china pot for water. He dug from his satchel the red-and-gold tin of willow bark and borage, and stood for a moment holding it near the votive light, swamped with thoughts he did not care to think.

"How do they look?" Hannibal set his fiddle aside. He'd borrowed a couple of tortoiseshell combs from Geneviève, and knotted up his long hair like a woman's on his head.

"Better." January put the tin and his speculations aside. He looped back the mosquito-bar around Victorine's bed to feel her forehead, then her pulse. He was coming to know these girls a little, mostly from what Mademoiselle Vitrac said of them: Victorine's hot-headed stubbornness, Antoinette's day-long silences in which she'd raptly figure geometric proofs, the half-embarrassed streak of Geneviève's sensationalism that drew that deceptively lovely girl to the gorier chapters of Roman history and the fascinated study of poisons, explosives, catapults, and mummies.

Rose's pupils. Rose's life.

"We're holding them. The fever should run its course soon."

Hannibal turned away to cough. Strangely enough with the onset of the summer fever his own consumption had gone into one of its periodic abeyances: "Just my luck," he had remarked to January on Saturday night, "with everyone out of town and nobody hiring." Now he said, "I met her here once or twice. Cora. I didn't know who she was, of course."

"The damn thing is," said January, returning to the wooden chair, "that anything could have happened to her. The city's no Peaceable Kingdom at the best of times, and with the streets empty and the City Guards afraid to go outside at night themselves—and small blame to them—anything could have happened. A young girl like that, wandering the streets at that hour of the night. . . ."

He paused. He remembered Alphonse Montreuil's ferrety face and the way his thin white hands had picked and fidgeted with his cuffs. "What do you know about Montreuil?" he asked. Voodoos—and Marie Laveau—were not the only ones who knew everything in the town. "Alphonse Montreuil, Madame Lalaurie's neighbor? If he was up at that hour, watching her house . . ."

"You mean, is he dangerous?"

"Not dangerous, but . . ." January thought again. "Yes. Is he dangerous?"

Hannibal settled his back to the rail of the empty bed's footboard, folded small white hands, delicate as a woman's, around his bony knees. "I don't think so," he said, after long consideration. "But he's certainly cracked where Madame L is concerned. He's a cousin of sorts to the Montreuils who own that plantation downriver. It seems

Alphonse's brother married a woman named Manette McCarty, who's some kind of cousin to Madame. Now, when Alphonse and Albert's father died, he left his money, not to his deserving sons, but to his widow. She in turn, when she was gathered to the reward of all good Creole matrons, passed along the money and a substantial hunk of property to brother Albert's children by means of an unbreakably airtight will. Don't ask me why she bypassed Alphonse. Maybe she didn't like him very much."

"I can understand her sentiments."

Hannibal coughed, a brief line of pain appearing between his dark brows, and he fished in his pocket for the opium tincture that suppressed both coughing and pain. He took a tiny, judicious swig. "I suspect he's even more unpleasant on close contact. God knows how his wife . . . well. In any case, the brother's children, instead of sharing some of the proceeds with Uncle Alphonse, as he probably hoped they would, turned the real estate by an Act of Procuration over to their mother—who, as you recall, is Madame L's cousin, Creole society being stiff with McCartys. The Act of Procuration was handled by the Louisiana State Bank—Jean Blanque's old outfit— and since Madame is widely known to keep all her business affairs in her own hands rather than let Nicolas Lalaurie lay a finger on them, Montreuil assumed that she was behind the plot."

"Was she?" January got to his feet to light a pair of candles, for with the thunder of rain overhead the afternoon had gone pitchy dark.

"Who knows? Most of the McCartys go to her for business advice, or for money to float investments. She bankrolled this school, I know that. I don't know whether she advised Cousin Manette or not. But Montreuil's never forgiven her." Hannibal picked up his violin again, sketching threads and bones and shadows of airs while he spoke, as another man might have drawn boxes and diamonds on the margin of a paper while speaking, or made knots in string. "Then when the Ursuline Sisters put their land along Rue de l'Hôpital up for sale, Montreuil wanted to buy the lot next to his house, except he didn't have the cash—*videlicet* Act of Procuration, above. Madame bought the lot—and the unfinished house—out from under him.

"Since that time he's been telling everyone who'll listen that she's a monster. His wife claims she saw her chase a little Negro girl off the roof with a cowhide whip—though how she could have seen that I can't imagine, since the Montreuil house is a full story shorter than the Lalaurie—and reported her to the police for it. The girl had actually died of a fall, and Madame was fined, so it isn't really surprising that Madame is pretty careful these days to keep her servants behind walls and away from anyone who might talk to any of Montreuil's people. You grew up in this town. You know the kind of things that get printed in the papers, and talked around the markets, and believed."

January was silent for a time, listening to the rain and remembering the fury in Mademoiselle Vitrac's voice, the bitterness in her gray eyes. "I take it Mademoiselle Vitrac knows Madame Lalaurie? If Madame helped finance the school?"

"Rose knew the wife of one of Madame's McCarty cousins—she'd gone to school with her in New York. The banks were less than eager to lend Rose money once they found out there was no Monsieur Vitrac. I gather someone made the mistake of remarking to Madame Lalaurie how one couldn't really expect a mere woman to manage a business—some people have no sense of self-preservation."

The violin shaped a phrase of notes, as clear and mocking as the ironic lift of an eyebrow: were it not for consumption, and pain, and the twin nepenthes of alcohol and opium into which that pain had driven him, Hannibal would have been the greatest at his art. He was still one of the finest violinists January had encountered, in New Orleans or in Paris. As he played, his eyelids had a crumpled look, lined and discolored, but the dark eyes themselves were dreamy, lost in the music and the rain.

Every penny I own is tied up in this building. . . .

January thought of his sister, and of the child she had just borne. Of Agnes Pellicot, and of his mother. Men routinely gifted their plaçées with money or property as a *congé* when they put them aside; it was, he knew, one reason why many women of color crossed over the line of respectability and allowed white protectors to take them. With even a little money, it was possible to start a business, to buy a boardinghouse or rental property, to invest in steamship stocks or sugar futures. Men would start a plaçeé's son in business, but rarely her daughter.

"What do you think of Cora?" he asked. "You met her. Do you think she'd have done murder?"

Hannibal considered for a time, tatting his bits of Rossini and Vivaldi into a glittering lacework in the dimness. "I think she could have," he said at last. "She's hard—but then most women are harder than one thinks. Even our Athene." He nodded toward the house below them, where Rose Vitrac would be lying, sleeping, January hoped. Alone as she had always been alone. "Whether she *would* have is another question. The problem could have been solved fairly simply by her running away, if she hadn't decided to take the money and the pearls with her—and of course as a house servant she'd have known where to find them. Myself, I wouldn't have taken the whole five thousand dollars, let alone the pearls, because the theft would be a guarantee of pursuit. But it may be she wasn't thinking very clearly."

Beside him, the girl Geneviève turned in her sleep, and whispered something, despairing. Hannibal leaned close, but the girl fell silent again. The sound of the rain seemed very loud.

"I know Cora did tell Rose not to seek out or try to speak to Madame Lalaurie for her, not that Rose has more than a bowing acquaintance with Madame. It's hard to tell how people will react to things, and Cora didn't want to jeopardize her friend's position. Which doesn't mean she didn't dose Otis Redfern's soufflé for him: a woman can treat those she cares for with kindness and still be an ogre to her enemies, the same way a man can manumit a loved and loyal slave on the same day he whales the living tar out of another slave for putting too much sugar in his tea. People have surprisingly hermetic minds."

"Do you think Emily Redfern poisoned her husband? If the mistress was gone beforehand, the wife would have no cause to do it; if it was before Cora left, would she have done herself out of six or seven hundred dollars by poisoning her?"

"Don't ask me." Hannibal wrapped his fiddle in its holed and faded silk scarves, and stowed it carefully in its case. "It's hard to believe La Redfern would pass up a chance at the money, but one can't tell. Maybe not even the servants in the household could tell. In Dublin when I was growing up there was a woman who kept her two nieces chained in a cellar for five years so she could go on lending their inheritance money out at four and a half percent. One's always hearing about domestic tyrants who beat or mistreat their wives and children, and no one in the family dares speak of it because they know it'll do them no good. There may have been things going on in that household we'll never know about—which may be one reason why our Emily is trying so hard to retrieve her runaway property."

The rain was lightening. Pale daylight leaking through the cracks in the shutters struggled against the candle glow, then slowly bested it. Hannibal gathered up his fiddle case to go.

"One thing I do know, though," he added, pausing in the door. "And I think you know this, too, if you talked to her even for a short time. Cora isn't one to give up. I don't think she'd have left New Orleans without Gervase. And given her circumstances, I don't think she'd walk out either on that money, or on Rose."

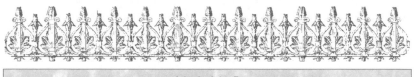

NINE

January was careful, upon approaching the Lalaurie house later that afternoon, to stay on the downstream side of Rue de l'Hôpital, crossing over only when directly opposite the gate rather than risk another encounter with Monsieur Montreuil. The rust-colored town house seemed shabby and sordid to him, and he imagined, as he studied it through the thin-falling rain, that the curtains in the upper-floor windows were half-parted, to afford a view of whoever might be passing in the street. The Montreuil house and the Lalaurie shared a party wall. There was no way that he could perceive for anyone in the Montreuil house to see if Madame Lalaurie hurled a dozen slaves from her own roof.

The bony servant entered with the inevitable glass of lemonade for Mademoiselle Blanque in the stifling heat, and vanished in well-trained silence. If nothing else, thought January, Jean Blanque's widow would have far too accurate a knowledge of what men and women cost to indulge in that kind of waste. When the lesson was over he asked one of the market-women selling berries in the street outside if she had seen or heard of anyone leaving the Lalaurie house the previous Friday night, but the woman only crossed herself quickly, and hurried on her way. January put up his oiled-silk umbrella and made his way riverward to the cafés that sheltered under the market's tile-roofed arcade.

Most of the market-women were gone, and the shadowy bays empty to the coming twilight. The air smelled thick of sewage, coffee, tobacco, and rain. A few crews still worked in the downpour, unloading cargoes from the steamboats at the levee. Others sheltered on the benches under the arcades, black and white and colored, joking among themselves and laughing. At the little tables set up on the brick flooring, brokers and pilots and supercargoes sipped coffee and dickered over the prices of flour and firewood, corn and pipes of wine. At other tables, upriver flatboatmen or the crews of the keelboats that still plied the river's jungly shores muttered in their barely comprehensible English; and under the arches on the river side a stocky, curly haired man in a somber black coat argued prices with the broker Dutillet over a little coffle of slaves standing, manacled, in the rain.

As he passed them January heard Dutillet say in English, "Nine-fifty is as high as I'll go; take it or leave it, sir." And the man protested, "Nine-fifty! Why, a good field hand's going for over eleven hundred in the Missouri Territory!"

January paused, recognizing the melodic organ-bass of the voice.

"Then take 'em up to Missouri and sell 'em there, by all means, Reverend," retorted the broker. "And considering what you paid that poor widow for 'em, you ought to take shame to yourself."

January realized the man in the black coat, whose face was vaguely familiar to him, was the Reverend Micajah Dunk, in whose honor Emily Redfern had gone to battle with the entire Creole community over the matter of musicians.

He passed on, shaking his head. A market-woman pointed out the man he sought, sitting alone at a table with a cup of coffee and beignets before him. January approached him, held out his hand: "Natchez Jim?"

"I was last time I looked." The boatman smiled, and clasped January's fingers in a grip like articulated oak logs. "You're the musician, Mamzelle Snakebones's brother."

"Last time I looked," replied January, and Natchez Jim gestured him to the other chair. The boatman was bearded, his hair a mass of braids like a pickaninny's, done up in string. His clothing had all started out different colors shortly after Noah's flood but had weathered to the hue of the river on a bleak day. He smelled of pipe tobacco and badly cured fur, but his French, except for an occasional Creole pronunciation, was the flawless French of Paris. "My sister told me you'd be willing to take someone upriver to Ohio."

"She told you that, did she?" Jim gestured, asking if January wanted some coffee, and January shook his head. He propped the dripping umbrella against the side of his chair; rain still thundered on the tiles overhead and veiled the cathedral, away across the Place d'Armes, in opaline curtains of moving gray. "It might so be. I owe her many favors, your sister."

He fished from the front of his shirt a grimy ribbon that had once been red, with a flannel juju bag on the end of it. "This has saved my life, not once but time and again. He's an angry man, the river. Sometimes all you can do is stay close in to the bank, that he see you not. Yes, I told her I'd take a passenger. Four days, five days it must have been. She spoke then as if it would be soon. Is your friend ready to travel?"

January shook his head. "She's disappeared. We can't find her. I sought you out to see if you had taken her already, Friday night."

"Not me." The boatman replaced his juju bag in his breast. "Have you checked the fever hospitals? The cholera wards? It takes one fast, the cholera."

"I work at Charity," said January. "I haven't seen her there, or at the Ursulines."

"There's a place that's opened near the turning basin, up in the Swamp where the keelboatmen stay: St. Gertrude's, I think. If she's a runaway she may be there."

"I'll check," said January. "But if this girl tried to leave the city another way—on a steamboat, perhaps—how carefully are they looking at people's papers?"

"People like us?" A glint of anger appeared in the boatman's eye. "People of color? Very closely indeed. People who might not have papers to prove they're truly people in the eyes of the law? A runaway is money out of someone's pocket. And maybe money *in* someone else's as well."

He sipped his coffee. His dark eyes moved to Dunk, deep in conversation now with stout Mr. Granville of the Bank of Louisiana, and to the men and women standing nearby, chained and dripping in the shelter of the eaves.

"There's not much by way of law up there," Jim continued. "I've been taken twice, up in Missouri, with not a sheriff or a lawman who'll even ask if I was or wasn't free in the eyes of the law. What's the use of having records here in Louisiana that you're a free man, if you're chained on some farm out in the territories? The second man who kidnapped me was the local magistrate. I was a week hiding in the bushes and the streams like an animal, until I reached the river again."

Natchez Jim shook his head. "I don't go up there anymore," he said softly. "Even here where there's law, they don't let many slip past."

No, thought January, looking back at the tall black masts of the steamboats, spewing slow rivers of smoke into the nigrous sky. *They don't let many slip past.*

From a woman selling bright-colored kerchiefs—and wearing one so brilliant and so elaborately tied as to put all of her stock to shame—he found out the direction of the place he wanted next to seek. "He's still abed, I hear, poor man," she told him. "For shame, those doctors turning him out of their clinic before his cure was done, because now, of course, he's more crooked than ever. You'd think if they'd started they'd have finished, and made him straight, wouldn't you?"

"They'd never have made him straight," said January, startled at this reading of the event.

"Silly! Of course they would," retorted the market-woman. "Rich people go to them all the time, they must know what they're doing. Here." She stepped over to her neighbor, who was just clearing up the last of her okra, her grapes, and her aubergines from her table. "Philomène, have you got something our friend here can take to poor Hèlier? And what do you think? This fellow says Dr. Soublet doesn't cure people after all with those machines of his."

"That a fact? But I hear he fixed this lady's clubfoot so she can dance just like a little girl. It was in the newspaper. . . ."

Carrying the basket of vegetables, January made his way down Gallatin Street, an unspeakable waterfront alley leading from the markets whose every rough wooden shack and grimy cottage seemed to house either a taproom or a bordello, though they all smelled like privies. Rain splashed in gutters that brimmed with raw sewage, and glimmered like fire in the dull orange bars of light issuing from shuttered windows and open doors. A dark-haired woman in a dress that had to have been bought from a fever victim—overly fashionable and too new to have been sold from a servant's ragbag—called out to him from a doorway, but he walked on.

Just why he was doing this, he could not have said. He would be late to the Hospital, and with almost no sleep—he had risen earlier than his habit, to walk to Mademoiselle Vitrac's school to see how her girls did and to tell her what he had found. Though he would never have mentioned it to Mademoiselle Vitrac, he still considered it a very real possibility that Cora Chouteau *had* poisoned Otis Redfern. He had encountered nothing yet that proved she hadn't.

Because of his father, he thought. Because of a half-recalled dream of hounds baying in the swamp. Because of the little boy sitting on the gallery, waiting for someone to come who cared for him, who would tell him that he wasn't alone.

Maybe because he knew that Rose Vitrac would be doing what he was doing, did she not have the girls who were her charge. Because she had once been alone and desperate, and Cora had stood by her.

Amid the darkness and the fever-heat and the stinks of death, everyone needed friends.

Even if those friends still called you "Monsieur Janvier."

Hèlier Lapatie lived in a bare little one-room shed in the rear yard behind what was officially termed a "grocery" but was in fact a groghouse, owned by a man who'd been manumitted years ago by one of the Lafrènniére family. The place was a sort of gathering-place or clubhouse—illegal, of course—for the free colored stevedores of the levee and the slaves who "slept out." The crowd in the groghouse whistled and called out comments when January came in, for he still wore the black long-tailed coat and sober waistcoat of a music teacher and carried an umbrella, but the owner behind his plank bar asked good-naturedly, "Get you somethin', sir?" and directed him out the back to Hèlier's little shack.

As he went through the door January thought he recognized by lantern-light the woman Nanié, sitting on a flour-barrel talking earnestly with another woman and a man—light-skinned, so he could not have been the Virgil whom she'd sought through the fever wards. But in the flickering gloom he could not be sure. Had Nanié found her man or was this his replacement?

He found Hèlier out of bed, stubbornly dragging himself back and forth across the dirty boards of the shed's floor with the aid of two sticks. The water seller turned his head sharply as January came up the few plank steps: "Is that you?" he called out in English.

"It's me," replied January in French. "Benjamin January." He wanted to add, *the big black nigger,* but didn't, knowing the man had been under opium when he'd said it. Long dealings with Hannibal Sefton had taught him to let what was said under the influence of the drug slide like water off his back.

"Ah." Hèlier dragged himself to the door of the shed. The young man's face was bathed in sweat, his blue eyes sunk in new webs of pain. "The surgeon no one will hire. I'm sorry," he added quickly, stepping back to let January into the shack. "It's the pain—and the opium, a little." He was very much more bent than he had been before, the spinal muscles that had been stretched and torn contracting, hunching him further, the damaged ligaments restricting the movement of his right shoulder and leg. "Wonderful stuff, opium. Twenty-five drops for a penny, old Lafrènniére charges, which is fine if you've got a penny. My father would be proud."

"Your father?"

"Giles Lapatie, of Beau Rivage plantation. A gentleman of the belief that children should be neither seen nor heard nor acknowledged, if they're not as comely as they might be. Educated, yes. Given promises, yes—promises are cheap. Provided for, no. But I'm sure you're familiar with the type. What's that?"

"Philomène, at the vegetable market, sent them along."

"Leavings from my betters? Wrap them up for the helpless? How very kind of her." Hèlier knocked the basket aside with his stick. For a moment there was no sound but the mice-feet of the rain. "And what about yourself? Come with a few pennies for opium? Maybe make a little music to cheer up the sufferer, since music after all is free?" His voice slurred just a little; January guessed he'd been dosing himself on whatever he could come by.

In a different tone, he went on, "I seem to remember it was you that unlatched me from that hell pit. Thank you. Soublet seemed to think if they unjointed every bone of my body they could straighten me out, the fool. Lalaurie just stood by rubbing his hands, watching like a schoolgirl when they put the stallion to the mare."

"One of my pupils in Paris had her hands crippled by a 'patented finger-stretcher' her parents were convinced would improve her playing," said January. "It's the fashion, these days."

"Oh, well, I'm so glad to be in fashion." The darkness in the shed was almost complete, but January saw the twisted man's mouth quirk into an ironic grin. "I suppose the priests would say I deserved it. And maybe I did. What can I do for you, my friend?"

"I'm looking for information," said January. "You know everyone in town; hear everything. A friend of mine disappeared off the street last Friday night. It was while you were in Soublet's, but since then you might have heard something."

Hèlier tilted his head a little, peering up at January like a turtle under the weight of its shell. His back was to the fluttering rush-dips; impossible to read either his face or his voice. "Disappeared, did she? What sort of friend?"

"A young girl, maybe twenty or twenty-one. Very thin, dark but not Congo black. I think she was wearing a red dress and red-and-black shoes. She would have been coming along Rue de l'Hôpital, sometime around midnight."

Hèlier considered for a time, then shook his head, or made a motion that had once been a headshake but now involved his shoulders and upper back as well. "Have you checked in the Swamp? Along the levee? She might have met a personable gentleman—maybe even a wealthy white man who promised to look after her and her son."

"She had no son," said January, aware that the last remark did not concern any event of Friday night. "And she was just coming away from seeing a lover for whom she had made considerable sacrifice."

"The sacrifices of women, pah. They're like cats. They'll park their bottoms on the warmest chair."

January wondered what had been the reaction of Hèlier's mother, when Giles Lapatie had refused further support of their son because of his deformity.

"What about Marie Laveau?" he asked. "To what length would she go, if she thought someone were a threat to her; if she thought someone knew something about her? Had seen her, perhaps, where she wasn't supposed to be?"

She was waiting on the porch, in the twilight. . . .

The water seller giggled. "The whore-bitch poisoner who blackmails half the town? Mustn't say anything against *her*." He put a finger to his lips in owlish malice. "You'll wake up one morning to find a cross of salt on your back step and no one in the town willing to talk to you, for fear of her. If your friend ran foul of that heathen bawd she'd best cover her tracks; Laveau's hand is everywhere."

Had it been Mamzelle Marie whom Cora had met that night on the street?

He watched her that night, through a lead-tinged curtain of exhaustion: sponging off the bodies of the sick, holding the hands or heads of the dying. Her face was impassive as she bent down to listen to the broken ravings of a young Irishman—gathering secrets? *Not much of importance in this place,* January reflected bitterly. Charity Hospital was the final refuge of the poor, those without families to care for them, with only their hopes of making a fortune in Louisiana. And most would leave their bones in its soggy, heaving earth.

She saw me, stopped to watch me pass. . . .

And he saw again how the voodooienne's head had turned, dark eyes taking in every detail of the street.

Marie Laveau at Black Oak. Of course Emily Redfern couldn't come into town without occasioning comment.

January closed his eyes, his head throbbing like a drum.

By three in the morning he knew himself to be too exhausted to continue. He'd helped Barnard carry a woman down to the courtyard for the dead-cart and climbed back up the gallery stairs, but instead of going in again, only stood outside the door, leaning his head against the doorframe, feeling as if he were slowly sinking into the earth. A wonderful feeling, he thought. Maybe he could fall asleep like this and not have to go to the trouble of walking home and lying down.

"You had a tiring day, M'sieu," the soft soot-and-honey voice said at his side. Turning his head he wondered how Mamzelle Marie knew this. She stood at his elbow, and even the bottom edge of that fantastic seven-pointed tignon was dark with wet in the oil lamp's dirty glare. "Best for all maybe that you go on home."

She fetched him his hat and coat, and walked with him to the courtyard gate, standing in the torchlight for a time, watching him as he went.

He made his way along Rue Villere, in the district of the vast, stinking charnel-houses of the two cemeteries, toward Rue Douane, which would lead him back to the relative safety of the French town. At this hour the town was silent, save for the scuttling of rats in the alleyways leading toward the burial grounds, the incessant whine of mosquitoes, and the roaring of the great reddish roaches and palmetto bugs around the iron lamps suspended above the intersections of the streets.

From the direction of Rue Royale and Canal Street drifted the far-off jingle of piano and coronet, where the lamps burned bright in gambling parlors. *Insensible of mortality,* Hannibal had quoted. . . . What was the rest of it? *Careless, reckless, fearless of what's past, present, or to come. . . .*

Boccacio's revelers—or was the story in Chaucer?—stumbling over the rotting corpses of the plague's dead.

In the windows of the pharmacy across the street, huge ornamental retorts glowed like rubies with the candles set behind them, all red, a warning to travelers of what the newspapers still denied. The day's rain had left the streets mucky, breathing with the stinks of wet and decay. Everything had a glitter to it, like the sheen of sweat on a dying man's brow.

In the silence it was easy to believe the disease roved the streets like the angel of death. Easy to half-expect the skeletal white shape of

Baron Cemetery, the voodoo lord of the dead, coming around a corner in his top hat and his spectacles.

What *was* disease, anyway? The cholera that had squeezed the life out of Ayasha like a wet doll, the yellow fever that left him every day wondering if Olympe, or Gabriel, or Hannibal would vanish the way the Perrets or Robois Roque had vanished, struck down in their tracks so swiftly that they could not call for help. . . .

The hair prickled on his neck.

He was being followed.

This time by more than one person.

He quickened his pace, hopped over the gutter, and waded down the dragging muck in the middle of Rue Douane, keeping clear of the rough shacks and stucco cottages on either side.

Behind him nothing moved. Only a fleeting impression of something in the already wavering darkness away from the hanging lamps. His first superstitious dread—of the dark stalker Bronze John, the softly clattering bones of the bespectacled Baron—switched immediately to the more real dread of those bearded, whiskered Kaintucks, river pirates and killers who roved the streets looking for drink, or a woman, or a black man to beat up.

Ahead of him a man stepped out of the shadows. Then another, sticks in their hands. Every house between the Rue Marais behind him and the Rue Trémé before was locked, empty, their inhabitants enjoying the breezes of the lake in Milneburgh or Mandeville or Spanish Fort. January doubled on his tracks and bolted for the dark mouth of the Rue Marais. As he did so, another man appeared in the street behind him, running toward him, as all of them were running now.

It was like flight in a dream, the horrible slow movement with the primordial ooze gripping his feet. Grimly he wondered where the City Guards were, who were supposed to be enforcing a curfew against colored and slaves. He reached the corner of the Rue Marais moments before they did and slithered into the long pass-through which led between two houses to the yard behind. It was a dead end, a cul-de-sac, knee-deep in garbage and night soil, and this house, unlike Agnes Pellicot's, had no convenient window to force. But one of the few advantages January had ever found in looking like a field hand was that he was tremendously strong.

He drove his foot through the jalousies that covered one of the rickety doors, plunged through in a tangle of curtain, in the dark stumbling into and knocking over unseen articles of furniture. He crashed and thrust his way into the front parlor, hearing the men behind him as they broke through into the rear, groped along the wall. He forced himself to slow down, to move carefully, to feel his way until he touched the door that led into the front bedroom.

He shut it behind him, big fingers shaking as they found the key that such rooms nearly always had, turned it in the lock with a click that made him wince. His pursuers were making far too much noise tripping over furniture themselves to hear. "The curse of Cromwell be after ye, ya stupid pillock!" "Where the Sam Hill'd he go?" "Ye got no more sense than to leave the lantern in the alley. . . ."

Silent, silent, desperately silent he followed the wall around the room, thrust open the casement window that looked onto the pass-through to the next house and opened the shutters, the reddish reflections of lamplight falling through to show him the door into the rear bedroom, the rough, battered-looking chifforobe with its broken mirror, and the big wooden bed, the mosquito-bar tied neatly back above it.

He slithered through, pulling shut the casements and pushing closed the shutters behind him. As he'd suspected, there was another man waiting in the street, but he was watching the front of the house. January slipped along the pass-through to the rear of the next house. He used one of the scalpels from his bag to slip the latches on the jalousies, then ducked inside.

It didn't buy him much time, but enough to move through that house, and the next, cursing every time he fell over a chair or a table, knowing they could hear, they would follow. Thank God it was, on the whole, too dark for them to trace his foot tracks of garbage and muck. He came out a final window on Rue Bienville, and moved along the walls, his heart in his throat, toward the high stucco wall at the end of the street, behind which sulfurous yellow light flared like the glare of hell.

He heard them running behind him, the slop and suck of mud under their boots, and the slither and splosh as one of them fell. Four men, he saw, glancing back again, three of them with clubs, one with what looked like a rope. Bearded faces half-unseen under slouch hats, but their hands were white. He had half the length of the street on them now and was of a height to reach the top of the wall with his hands at a jump, dragging himself up and over.

The stench of the place was like liquid muck in his lungs, but at this point he cared nothing about that. The cemetery of St. Louis lay before him, a horror of gaping pits and standing water. The little white houses of marble and stucco and stone clustered beyond the darkness, like the huts in a village of the dead.

The dead lay along the wall, wrapped roughly in sheets of cheap osnaburg or canvas, the fabric moving with rats. January dropped down onto the piled corpses, sending forth the rats in a shrieking horde, and fled, stumbling, sickened, across the pitted ooze and into the black-and-white jumble of shadow that was the tombs.

The disease isn't contagious, he told himself, slipping from tomb to tomb. He dodged behind one, then another, working his way through the dense-packed mazes. *I've worked among the dying for three months now and I haven't contracted it yet.*

He was gasping, shaking in every limb, nauseated with horror and disgust. Roaches the length of his finger crept through the cracks of marble boxes. A rat perched on the head of a bricked-up sepulcher marked DESLORMES; eating something, January couldn't see what. In a spot of open ground, water had worked and thrust arms and hands and legs and shards of coffin wood up through the earth, as if Bronze John's victims were trying to climb back out of the ground again, and the surfaces of the pools crept and shivered with feeding crawfish.

There were lights by the graveyard gate, and men moving around, slinging sheeted forms, or emaciated and livid bodies picked off the streets, into piles along the wall. Torches stuck in the ground added their grimy light to the glare of pots of burning hide and hair and gunpowder. The men swung around, startled, when January emerged from among the tombs.

"Where you come from, brother?" called out one, and the other grinned and said, "Hey, Joseph, look like we bury this one alive by mistake. We begs your pardon, sir." They bowed mockingly, cheerful themselves to be wielding the shovels instead of waiting for them.

But their leader, standing naked to the waist on the carload of corpses, like Bronze John himself with the torchlight reflected in his eyes, asked, "Where you come from, sir?"

"Over the wall." January gestured back behind him. "I was coming back from the Hospital. I was followed by a gang of white men with clubs."

"I seen them," said the man on the dead-cart. "Pickin' up the dead, I sometimes seen them. Three men, sometimes four, just shapes in the darkness, but they're carryin' clubs. Never stop me, though." And he smiled. "Can I take you somewheres, friend?"

January started to say, "Take me to the Rue Burgundy," but another thought came to his mind. He thought of his brother-in-law, asking him to look out for a friend's missing husband; of a woman in a ragged yellow dress, searching through the charity ward for her man. Of his niece and nephew saying, "We packed 'em up. . . ."

"Take me over to Rue St. Philippe, if you would." He had no stomach for moving about the dark streets of the French town alone.

The man on the dead-cart smiled again. "Hop right on," he said.

TEN

Eustace Dèlier, being a moderately well off advocate of color, owned a snug little town house on Rue St. Philippe, stuccoed dark rose in color and sporting shutters painted blue. The house was dark and boarded shut, when Bronze John the dead-cart man dropped January off in front of it: "Look like nobody here." In the heat, beneath the swaying oil lamp's flare, he was no more than a sheathing of gold over blackness, and the gleam of eyes.

"Somebody's here," said January. "If you listen you can hear his violin."

The music, though stronger in the rear yard, was still muted and difficult to locate, as if, like the harps of faerie, the soft sad planxty issued from beneath the ground. January listened at the shutters of first one side of the house, then the other, but the sound grew no clearer. At length he walked backward until he could see the gables in the roof. From the soft bricks of the kitchen loggia he selected a suitable chip—in Paris there were always pebbles for tossing at windows, but Louisiana was founded on silt, and if there was a pebble in the length and breadth of New Orleans it had probably been imported from New York—and threw it at the blue shutters that over-looked the yard.

The violin did not stop. To do so would be an admission that there was a trespasser in the house.

Knowing the houses on both sides of the Dèliers' were vacant, he called out softly, "Hannibal!"

He tossed another chip of brick, and called the fiddler's name again. This time the shutter opened. Long dark hair hanging down over his shoulders, the fiddler's face was a pale blur in the hot blackness. "But soft—What light through yonder window breaks? Or attempts to break. . . . Bear you the essences of immortal grape or poppy flower? Good God, Benjamin," Hannibal added in a more normal voice, "what happened at that Hospital of yours? You smell like you've just come out of a common grave."

"I have," replied January somberly. "Come down and let me in. I'm not so comfortable, standing outside in the night."

He pulled off his coat and boots on the open loggia at the house's rear, and ran water from the rain cistern to wash his hands and face and hair. While he was doing this the shutters that led from the loggia into one of the *cabinets* opened, and Hannibal stood there, resplendent in his usual shabby white linen shirt—he disdained calico—and dark trousers that hung on his too-thin frame like laundry over a fence. "Mind the bath," he said, holding aloft the cheap tallow candle he carried. It was typical of the fiddler, thought January, that he would purchase candles rather than use the household stores, just as he was sleeping in the attics rather than occupying his unwitting hosts' beds. The bath of which he spoke was an enormous one, copper and expensive, established in its own alcove under the stairs, with a cupboard for towels wedged in behind. "They store the extra chairs here, too, if you'd care to carry one up. We can return it later."

"I'll sit on the floor," said January. "You're right. I came out of a shallow grave tonight, and it's made me wonder about some things that have been happening, since the fever season began."

Hannibal had brought in a cot from the slave quarters across the yard and a table. Half a loaf of bread and some cheese occupied a tin box, beside a jug of water, his violin, and the inevitable stacks of books and newspapers. A bottle of whisky and another of Black

Drop—triple-strength tincture of opium—stood, both corked, on a small packing box next to the cot, near a candleholder of pink-and-blue porcelain hung with Austrian glass lusters. He'd collected all the mosquito-bars in the house and rigged them as a sort of tent over the entire bed, including the packing box. At his gesture, both he and January crawled up under the clouds of white gauze, to sit on the worn, patched sheets while the insects hummed fitfully in the darkness outside. As January had suspected, there was a packet of tallow lights inside the packing box, with a Latin copy of *Metamorphosis,* a stack of old copies of the *Bee* and the *Courier,* and a couple of volumes of Goethe.

"When did the Perrets leave?" he asked the fiddler. "The folk next door?"

Hannibal thought about it a moment, not at all surprised by the question, counting back days in his mind. "Must have been the night of the twenty-sixth. Thursday night. They were packing up on Thursday and sent the carters away with the heavy baggage that afternoon. I saw lights in the house and heard voices when I went out Thursday evening, and they were gone the next morning when I came back."

"How'd you know they were gone?" Thursday night, the twenty-sixth, was the night Rose Vitrac had come to find him at the clinic, the night Zizi-Marie and Gabriel had helped the Perrets pack.

"The house was locked up," said Hannibal. "The plank was up. I'm out most nights—I can still get money playing at Davis's gambling palace on Rue Royale—but it's been still as death in the days. If they'd taken sick with the fever," he added with a wry practicality, "there would have been some sign—flies, and smell, and rats when I come in between midnight and dawn. It's one thing I worry about here—that I'll be taken sick, and present my poor hosts with a most unpleasant surprise on their return. I would feel bad about that."

January shivered, both at the thought that it could happen to the fiddler, or to himself, alone in the garçonnière. His mother wouldn't even inquire as to why she wasn't receiving letters from him anymore. She never answered in any case. Olympe would check, he thought, and tried to put from his mind the memory of his own steps ascending the narrow stairs, his own hand on the handle of the door of that Paris apartment. . . .

"Would you like to move into Bella's rooms at my mother's house?" he asked the fiddler. "My mother will be in Milneburgh until the fifteenth. At least you wouldn't be alone. Or wondering if you're going to wake up in the morning to find the Dèlier servants getting the place ready for Monsieur and Madame to come back."

"There is much in what you say," agreed Hannibal gravely. "Why ask about the Perrets?"

"Because they never reached Milneburgh," answered January. "Nor have they appeared in any of the clinics—I've been asking. They're the poorest people in this street, you know, and since Jacques's brothers died last year they have no other family in town. Everyone else has just enough money to leave: the Dèliers, and the Dugues on the other side; I think the Widow Kircher across the street and her daughter have gone as well, if I remember what Olympe's told me. Get some candles," he said, sliding carefully out from beneath the mosquito-bar again. "There's some things I'd like to have a look at over there."

The latch on the rear door of the Perrets' small house had been broken, and by the stains and mildew on the floor just within the doorway this had been done not quite a week ago. "Robbed right after they left," murmured Hannibal, holding aloft half a dozen bees-wax candles in the Dèlier's best dining-room candelabra. January had left money for the candles in the store cupboard they'd broken into, reckoning they would need the stronger light.

"Were they? I wonder." The house consisted of two rooms only. This, their bedroom, looked out onto the yard with its tiny kitchen. There were no slave quarters, no garçonnière over the kitchen: a young couple, the Perrets had been childless so far and certainly too poor to afford a slave. "They didn't have much to steal. Just looking at the outside of the house, any thief would know that." He touched his friend's wrist, raising the lights. They showed the white gauze of the mosquito-bar hanging down free, not tied back out of the way.

January had hunted enough mosquitoes within the tents of mosquito-bar—trying to singe them to death with a bedroom candle where they clung to the gauze without immolating the house—to know that nobody in Louisiana would leave the bar untied.

He led the way to the narrow cypress bed. Unlike those at the Dèlier house next door, there were sheets still on the mattress, the top sheet simply flung back.

It could mean only that Nicole Perret was an untidy housekeeper, but the spic-and-span neatness of the rest of the room put a lie to that. In the armoire that was one of the room's very few pieces of furniture he found a smock—such as a harness-and-wheel mender like Jacques Perret would wear to work—folded on a shelf, along with two calico shirts and two pairs of breeches. In the drawers were two petticoats, some stockings, a few chemises and tignons, and two corsets.

Folded up and put away upon retiring?

Two pairs of shoes, a man's and a woman's, were under the bed.

Brushes and combs still lay on the small vanity table, though the drawers of that table had clearly been opened and gone through for earrings, bracelets, whatever could be found. A cheap French Bible lay on the floor.

"No sign of violence." Hannibal pushed open the door that led through into the parlor. Shadows reeled as he put the candelabra through to look. "Though I suppose if one woke in the middle of the night with a man pointing a shotgun at one, one's impulse to violence would be limited." He came back into the bedroom, stroking at his graying mustache.

"No," said January softly. "No sign of violence. No smell of fever or sign of disease. A band of men," he said. "A band of men roving the streets, carrying clubs—probably carrying guns—breaking into houses where the neighbors are gone, where the inhabitants would not be missed."

"That means they were watching the place."

"Maybe," said January. "You can make a fortune in a year, in the new Indian lands, planting cotton—if you have the hands." He touched the small porcelain bowl of hairpins on the little dresser, something no woman would have gone to the lake—or anywhere else—without. "It would be worth putting a little time in, to learn who has no family to miss them and no neighbors to be able to say exactly when they vanished. Marie Laveau isn't the only one to employ spies. And in the fever season, no one would look. Everyone would assume they simply died and were buried. By the time anyone who knew them came back to town, they couldn't even identify a body."

He shivered, the fear he had felt that night turning to anger, a deep and burning rage. Remembered the boatman's dark eyes gazing out from string-wrapped pickaninny braids: *I don't go up there anymore. . . .* "As they would have assumed of me."

Hannibal set the candles down and trimmed the wicks. What person leaving town for a few weeks wouldn't have taken the candle scissors from the corner of the dresser? What woman, who couldn't afford more than two corsets, would have left both behind?

Very softly, January went on, "Americans coming into town complain about our people sticking together. They make jokes how everybody knows everybody's cousins and sisters and friends and business: how you need an introduction to so much as have dinner. But there's a reason for it."

He stepped back through the shutters to the yard, drew them closed behind him and worked a wedge of the splintered wood between them to hold them shut. Hannibal blew out the candles, plunging the tiny yard from shadow to Erebean darkness.

"It's so we can prove who we are," said January. "So none of us is out there alone."

He slept the remainder of the night at the Dèlier town house, unwilling to walk the streets of the French town until daylight. In the morning he and Hannibal made their way back to Gallatin Street, to the shabby groggery operated by the freedman Lafrènniére. Lafrènniére told them the woman Nanié usually could be found there around noon—"Before she starts her work," he put it—and as it was already well past ten, January paid a couple of picayunes for two bowls of beans and rice, and asked if Nanié had ever found her friend.

"Who—Virgil?" Lafrènniére winked. "Nanié, she got lots of friends. Virgil, I think Bronze John must have got him."

"He wouldn't have run away?"

Two or three children peeked in through the back door, staring at the unprecedented spectacle of a white man consuming beans and rice in their father's grocery. Hannibal, who abhorred children whatever their race, ignored them.

"Run away? Why?" The barman shrugged. "Virgil had four hundred dollars saved up in the Bank of Louisiana, to buy his freedom with. He paid his wages at the cotton press over to Michie Bringier, and Michie Bringier gave his word not to sell him. And why should he, when he's bringin' in five dollars a week? Michie Bringier, he has six, seven men that sleep out—two of 'em livin' in the attic just down the street. Why'd Virgil want to run away? Where'd he go, that he'd have it this good?"

Nanié, when she came in, confirmed this. "I think it have to be fever," she said, a worried frown on her gap-toothed face. "It musta took him away from home. I keep hopin' I'll find him in one of the hospitals, but this was a week ago now that Virgil didn't come visit me like he said he would. Widow Puy, what own the shed in back of her place that he slept in, rented it out yesterday to somebody else."

"And there was no sign that he'd been taken sick at his shed?" January asked.

"No, sir." The 'sir' was a tribute to his well-bred French and black coat.

January was silent, thinking. The woman was raggedly dressed, but the colors of her thirdhand gown were sufficiently bright, coupled with the overabundance of cheap glass jewelry, to indicate her trade. She wasn't wearing a tignon, either, her pecan-colored hair wound up in elaborate ringlets and cupid knots on her head; she was stout, and shopworn, and not very clean.

At last he said, "Has this happened to anyone else you know? Someone who lived alone, and had no family, that disappeared out of where they live? Or off the street?"

She nodded immediately. "Stephan Gaulois's pal 'Poly and his wife. They didn't live alone—I mean they live with each other—but their neighbors been took with the fever, both sides, and they ain't been on St. Louis Street long enough that anybody know 'em. Stephan say he thought the fever took them, too, so he broke in their house to find 'em, but they gone. 'Poly's wife, Lu, just got her freedom, and they took that house not seven months ago."

January said softly, "Show me."

There was not that much to see. 'Poly and Lu had occupied a two-room shack in the sloppy gaggle of buildings that backed the canal and the turning basin, close behind the St. Louis Cemetery. It was a neighborhood, like the Swamp and Gallatin Street, given over largely to Kaintuck keelboatmen, cheapjack gamblers, purveyors of nameless drinkables, and bravos and whores of assorted hues and nationalities. The lot on one side was still vacant, knee-deep in hackberry and weeds, where pigs rooted among stagnant ponds. On the other side stood a house and a sort of shed. Both were boarded tight.

They entered through the back door, whose bolt had been broken off in the socket. "That was done when I got here," explained Nanié's friend Stephan, who joined the party on the way up from Gallatin Street. He was the light-skinned man who'd been at the table with her last night.

"Was there mud on the floor here when you came in?"

The man frowned, trying to think back. The mud tracked from the door to the bed. The mosquito-bar, untied, was thrown sloppily aside. Half a dozen of the insects clung like the brown grains of wild rice to the exposed inner surface of the gauze.

"I don't remember," he said, and January nodded. It was pretty clear which tracks were Stephan's. They led from the door through to the front room, the outlines of his bare feet in all places overlying the muddle of boot-prints that had been there before. He was barefoot still, like most workers on the levee, and his feet even shod would have been broader and longer than any others represented by the pale ghost shapes on the bare plank floor.

"Only one pair of shoes here," remarked Hannibal, kneeling to look under the bed.

January brushed his fingers over the dried mud of the tracks. Two or three days old, at a guess. It had rained daily for weeks.

"Lu only had the one pair," provided Nanié, twisting her necklace of cheap red beads around her fingers. "Lu only just bought her freedom, over to Mobile, and come to town; 'Poly got his papers not so many months back. They didn't have much, and that's a fact."

"What happened to them?" Stephan, who had gone to look in the front room again, now returned, his face troubled and angry. "I thought they might have been took by the fever when they was away from home, but now you show me them tracks. Who'd come in here and take 'em away? And where'd they take 'em?"

"At a guess," said Hannibal quietly, "to the Missouri Territory, to pick cotton."

January and Hannibal parted in the weedy little yard before Lu and 'Poly's humble shack, Hannibal to make his way back to Mademoiselle Vitrac's school to offer what assistance he could and perhaps to cadge a meal. January intended to return to Gallatin Street and ask Hèlier what he knew about 'Poly, Lu, and Nanié's Virgil, but something else Natchez Jim had said to him came back to mind. So, instead, with a certain amount of misgivings, he made his way upstream to where the turning basin lay at the end of the brown stretch of the Carondolet Canal.

The area around the basin was known, quite descriptively, as the Swamp. Even the City Guards didn't go there often. This time of the afternoon it was getting lively, and January moved with silent circumspection among the rough-built shacks and sheds that housed the bordellos, saloons, and gambling dens that made up nine-tenths of the businesses thereabouts. Once, he was stopped by a trio of hairy and verminous keelboatmen who demanded his business—it took all the diplomacy of self-abasement he could muster to get out of the confrontation with no more than tobacco on his shirt—and as he passed the two-room plank shed owned and operated by a woman known as Kentucky Williams, that harridan and the ladies of her employ, sitting uncorseted in their shabby petticoats on the sills of their open French doors, rained him with orange-peels, cigar-butts, and some of the most scatalogical language he had ever heard in his life.

"Sure makes me proud to be an American," remarked Lieutenant Shaw, slouching down the single log that served as a step before an establishment called the Turkey-Buzzard, then wading over to January through the ankle-deep swill of the street. The gutters that surrounded every square of buildings in the French town and gave them the name of "islands" did not extend across Rue des Ramparts, nor had the municipality bothered to lay down stepping-stones across the streets in this district. *And why should they?* thought January dryly. *No wealthy cousins of the largely Creole City Council are likely to cross* these *streets.*

"Not your part of town, Maestro."

"Nor yours, sir," observed January, falling into step with Shaw. Out of long habit he kept to the outside, as men of color were expected to, leaving the higher, marginally drier weeds along the buildings for his chromatic better. "If I may say so."

"You may," replied Shaw gravely. "You may indeed." Behind them Miss Williams, a strapping harpy with a long snaggle of ditchwater blond hair and a pockmarked face like the sole of somebody's boot, screamed a final insult and flung half a brick. It hit Shaw's shoulder with the force of a cannon-shot, but he caught his balance and walked on, merely rubbing the place with one bony hand. "And they say women ain't strong enough to go into the army. You know, if you're despondent and all that an' really want to die, Maestro, probably settin' out all night and lettin' the fever get you would be more comfortable than comin' down here. Not that these folks ain't dyin' like flies in every attic an' back room an' alley," he added somberly.

A corpse, puff-bellied already in the heat, lay just outside the door of the Tom and Jerry saloon on the other side of the street. January wondered whether that was Bronze John or a statement of management policy concerning winners at the gaming tables.

"I've been out all night already," he replied quietly. "And I must say it nearly worked." And he recounted to Shaw the events of last night, and what he had found in the houses of Nicole Perret, and 'Poly and Lu. "Over the past week or ten days, people have been coming into the clinic, or coming to my sister Olympe, or to others, and asking us to look through the fever wards for people who have disappeared, but don't seem to have come down with fever. Always people of color or blacks."

The lieutenant stopped, his slantindicular glance suddenly sharp and hard.

"Always people without families, people whose neighbors have left town or been taken sick themselves," January continued. "Always people no one would miss for days. I don't know how long this has been going on. Longer than ten days, I think. The man who drives the dead-cart says he's seen men moving through the streets, in the slack-end of the night. They've taken seven I know about. Maybe more. Maybe a lot more."

Shaw scratched his head thoughtfully. "Now, it's funny you should mention that, Maestro." Sleeplessness and overwork had thinned his already narrow face; his long jaw wore stubble like a brownish mold. January thought suddenly of all those houses standing locked and empty, and of the fear that fueled drinking, and the drinking that fueled violence in an already violent town. "We had two queries so far about runaways that don't listen right, men that worked the cotton press or the levee, men that slept out, and only went to their owners every night with what they made. Only in this case the owners was out by the lake, one in Spanish Fort and one acrost the lake in Mandeville, so the men only went and paid 'em their take once a week. Steady men, they said. In fact their owners was more inclined to think their men had took sick of the fever. 'My boy wouldn't run away,' they said."

"And did each of these men," asked January, "rent a place to sleep by himself?"

"Well, as it happens," said Shaw, "they did. They was good men, but not with any particular skill. And it's the slow season on the levee. They worked here and there, so nobody really missed 'em at a job for some several days. At least so far as I can tell, since it's sort of hard to find people who'll admit to rentin' sleeping room to some other man's slaves, let alone find them that sleep out to talk about the matter theirselves. And there's dozens dyin' every day."

"There are," agreed January quietly. It had begun to rain again. The two men paused under the wooden awning before the doors of a grimy barrelhouse scarcely larger than the shed 'Poly and Lu had shared. Steam heat rose from the marshy street. Through the open doorway a slatternly woman was visible behind a plank set on a couple of kegs, dispensing what might charitably be termed whisky to a barefoot white man in the togs and tarred pigtail of a British sailor, a keelboatman whose clothing and body could be smelled from the door, and a couple of the weariest, grubbiest whores January had ever seen in his life. Even after growing up in the city it still mildly surprised him that such places, within a stone's throw of the cemeteries with their piles of corpses, could find customers willing to pay for anything within their walls.

"That's why whoever is doing this considers himself safe."

Shaw propped one bony shoulder against the porch post, chewing ruminatively. He made no comment about the discrepancy between those six, and January's earlier count of seven, and only spit a long stream of tobacco juice onto the boards of the porch.

"You didn't happen to get the name of this dead-cart man, did you?"

January shook his head. "Just that he was almost as big as me, and as dark. Heavy in the shoulders and arms. His head was shaved."

"I'll ask around amongst 'em," said the lieutenant. "I just come down here to inquire after a little amateur surgery over a faro game. I will never in my life understand a gamblin' man."

He shook his head marvelingly. "Bank's gonna foreclose, man's gonna lose his plantation, he comes into town with a draft for eight thousand dollars in his pocket to replace a grinder that'll keep his family's home for 'em and what's he do?" He jerked his head back in the direction of the Turkey-Buzzard. "He really think he's gonna *win* in a place like that? You understand it, Maestro?"

"I don't understand the fever." January stepped aside from the stream of water that had begun to drip down from the awning above. "I just see men dying of it every day."

Across the street a man in a formal black coat and tall hat emerged from a ramshackle conglomeration of buildings. He walked with the careful deliberation of a drunk, rain sluicing down his hat and off the shoulders of his coat, the dozen yards to the Jolly Boatman Saloon. Other than that the street was still, though a man's voice, harsh and flat with an American accent, roared out that he was a riproarer from Salt River and wore a hornet's nest for a hat decorated with wolves' tails.

Shaw nodded across the street at the dirty, rambling warehouses from which the man had come. "I take it you done checked the clinics? Even places like that?"

The crudely lettered sign over the door proclaimed the place to be St. Gertrude's. God knew, thought January, the Swamp needed a clinic—most of the dying in Charity were Americans—but the existence of the place surprised him.

"If these people took sick in the street, or in a strange part of town, they might have been took anywhere," Shaw went on. "I'll ask around the Exchanges, and amongst the dealers, and at the steamboat offices. I don't doubt for a minute that any black man who goes to the new cotton lands runs the risk of bein' kidnapped, no matter what kind of proof he's got of his freedom either on him or back here in town. But in the town itself—it's different. Iff'n these folks is kidnappin' people of color, they gotta be movin' 'em out of town somehow. Even quiet as things are on the levee these days, I'd feel right conscientious, myself, tryin' to get a coffle of folks that didn't want to go acrost the wharf and onto a boat."

"You think any of those folks wants to go?"

January met Shaw's eyes, aware of the anger in his own. There was silence between them for a time.

Then Shaw said quietly, "You know what I mean, Maestro."

"I know what you mean. Sir."

It was Shaw who turned his eyes away. "We'll find 'em." He spit out into the brown lake of the rain-pocked street. "I warn you, even if we do, it'll be hard to prove. There been too many slaves smuggled in and out of this town since the African trade was outlawed for folks to want to admit somethin' like this is goin' on. But they'll slip up somewheres, and we'll be waiting for 'em when they do. Coming?"

The rain was letting up. It was tempting to simply walk with the Lieutenant back to the relative safety of the French town. There, if he was regarded as something less than a man, he was at least not in peril of life and limb.

January shook his head. "There's something I have to take care of," he replied.

"Suit yourself. Mind how you go, though." Shaw touched his hat—something not many white men would have done in the circumstances—and made his way down the sodden slop of the street in the direction of the French town and the Cabildo, shoulders hunched, like a soaked scarecrow in the rain.

January took a deep breath, glanced around him for further warning of trouble, then mucked his way across the street to the shabby walls of St. Gertrude's.

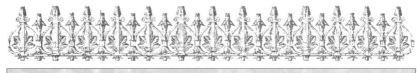

E L E V E N

St. Gertrude's Clinic was completely unattended. A ramshackle building or collection of buildings that had once been a warehouse, it was
nearly windowless, its roof leaked in a dozen places, and the smell
would have nauseated Satan. As his eyes struggled to adapt to the
grimy light admitted by a few high-up squares of oiled linen, January
heard the scuttle and swish of rats in the darkness around the walls,
and the hard whirring flight of a palmetto bug. Somewhere a man
sobbed. When his eyes did adjust, he saw some twenty men and
women lying on the floor on straw mattresses, tossing and shuddering
with fever.

None of them was anyone that he knew. Seven were dead, three
clearly dying. Along the wall two corpses, wrapped roughly for the
dead-cart man, were already the target of long ribbons of ants. January steeled himself to pull the sheets from their faces.

Both were naked, and had been harvested of their teeth, the white
man of his hair. The other, either a slave mulatto or a man of color,
was far older than any of the men who had disappeared. January
would have scrupulously avoided most of the sick men in the clinic
had he encountered them on the streets: sailors, vagrants, upriver

Kaintucks or Irish laborers, bewhiskered, gasping obscenities in barely comprehensible English.

But seeing them lying in a thin soup of rainwater and their own filth, January felt a blaze of anger go through him. Even Soublet's hellish premises didn't enrage him like this. At least the man had a dedication, and kept the place reasonably clean. People might be objects to Soublet, but he had the decency not to relieve them of their teeth when they died.

He left the clinic, and sloshed through the mire to the doors of the Jolly Boatman.

The black-coated, top-hatted man who'd emerged from the Clinic sat on one of the rude benches that flanked both sides of the big room, consuming a plate of crawfish and rice with a brown bottle of whisky at his side. Rather unusually for the district the place had a floor, wrought of used flatboat planks like the walls. With every other saloon in the Swamp awash in seepage the investment must pay off on rainy days.

Two tables stood in the center of the room, under soot-blackened lamps suspended from the low ceiling; at one of them a broad-shouldered, fair-haired man in a tobacco-colored coat played solitaire. Behind a plank bar another man, heavily mustachioed and with one pale blue eye bearing all the signs of an old gouging—it tended out, the torn muscles having never recovered—dipped a brownish liquor from a barrel on the floor beside him into a tin funnel, refilling the bottles of his stock. Past him two doors sported tattered curtains. A couple of men leaned on the bar itself, hard-bitten roughnecks of the sort who frequently ended up joining the crack-brained military adventures launched from New Orleans from time to time against the Spanish or the French. It was one of them who looked up as January's shadow darkened the door.

"Don't you know better than to come in here, boy?" He shoved himself away from the bar and crossed to January, rapidly, to block his way.

"Is there something you're after, my friend?" The card-player rose from the table with no appearance of hurry, but he was between them with surprising quickness nevertheless.

January recognized him as the fair-haired Irishman who'd

searched through the ward of the Charity Hospital the night Mademoiselle Vitrac had come to ask his help for her girls.

"I'm looking for the man in charge of St. Gertrude's Clinic." It was an effort to keep his voice steady, let alone affect the soft-spoken subservience white men expected of those darker than themselves. January had no clear idea of what he was going to say, or how he would phrase it. His one desire was to drive his fist into the jaw of the man who slouched on the bench, sucking his bottle when men wept and pleaded for water next door.

"Furness," the gambler called out gently. And, to the mercenary beside him, "That'll do, Hog-Nose, thank'ee." The black-coated man took another pull on his whisky, and sulkily came to the door, bottle still in hand. "This bhoy has a word for you."

"What you want, boy?" Close up, Dr. Furness's face was unshaven, mouth embedded in a brown smear of tobacco stains, nose and eyes alike red veined. His breath was a lifetime of alcohol and uncleanness.

"I just wanted to let you know you've got about seven dead in your clinic, sir, and water coming in through the roof so they're lying in puddles on the floor."

The doctor stared at him open-mouthed. "Who the hell you think you are, boy, coming here telling me how to run my business? You get the hell outa here! Goddam uppity . . ."

January inclined his head and stepped back, trembling with rage. Everything he would have said to the man had he been in France— *How* dare *you set yourself up as a healer, you incompetent drunkard? Who put you in charge of a clinic, even in times such as these?* died in his mouth, with the knowledge that to speak—even to raise his eyes— would only earn him a beating from the military filibusters and maybe the gambler as well. But he was so angry that all he could see were the toes of his own boots, and the tips of Dr. Furness's, mudsoaked and dripping on the dirty boards of the floor.

Thus he didn't even see the blow Furness aimed at him, until the gambler moved and caught the drunken man's arm. January looked up and saw the cane in the doctor's hand.

"Leave it," warned the gambler softly. Furness made an effort to jerk his arm free for another strike. The cane was teak with a head of brass, and by the way Furness handled it, he'd used it as a weapon before.

"Boy got no goddamn business telling me how to run my hospital!" he screamed, angry-drunk. He wrenched his arm again but the gambler's grip was strong.

"The bhoy has a point, Gerald." The mellow voice was as mild as that of a governess. But in the tanned face the blue eyes were pale steel. " 'Tis true ye've no business bein' away from the place, and anyone walkin' in off the street. I think it best ye'd be gettin' back."

"I'm not going back because no buck nigger comes here all high and mighty and tells me—"

"You're not. You're goin' because Liam Roarke's tellin' you."

Furness's jaw jutted so far he seemed in danger of dislocating it, but his bloodshot gaze couldn't endure the cold pale blue. He yanked his arm a third time, and this time the gambler released him, making him stagger.

"I'll have Trudi send one of the girls over with your breakfast."

Cursing, the doctor pushed through the door, jostling January as he passed, so heavily that January was thrown up against the framing. January watched him stomp through the mud, pausing to finish his bottle with another long pull, then send it spinning away above the barrelhouse roof.

"Ye'll have to excuse him." Liam Roarke guided January out into the doubtful shelter of the porch that ran around three sides of the building. "Settin' up a fever hospital in that old warehouse of his was the one decent act the man's ever done, and widthout help nor even a relief that can be counted on, the rage of it and the helplessness get to him. And he's bone weary."

As he had been even in the dead of night in the Charity Hospital, Roarke's chin was cleanly shaven between the golden wings of his side-whiskers and his linen was spotless, his coat pressed. "As who is not?" January said. "Did you find your friend?"

Roarke hesitated, some thought passing fast behind the pale eyes. Then he said, "That I did not. I fear the fever's took him, poor fellow. And yoursel', sir? You're one of the surgeons at the Hospital, are you not? And no man's bhoy?"

"That's true, yes, sir," said January. "I looked in, searching for a friend who's taken ill, no one knows where. I suppose I should only be glad this part of town has someone willing to run a hospital, with the Charity and the regular clinics overflowing."

"He's a good man in his heart, you know." Roarke gazed sadly in the direction of the shambling labyrinth that was St. Gertrude's. "I've never been one as has a spark in his throat, as they say, but I can pity a man who has. You say you're after searchin' for a friend? It's turn and turn about, then. Come over there wi' me. I'll make him take you round, never fear."

"I've had a look already. I'd best be on my way." The rain had ceased, the day's heat redoubled. January, still in the black coat and white shirt of his medical office, felt himself more and more acutely a target in a hostile land. Exhaustion descended on him, the endless night and the day that had gone before it crushing him like seven hundredweight of chain.

"Come back, then, when you've a chance." Roarke smiled in the shadows of the porch. "The fact is, Gerald needs a surgeon in the place, and it might so be he'd pay you better than the Charity folk do."

And what makes you think I can get to the clinic and back alive? Even if I didn't mind being belabored with a cane if I should happen to forget to call that drunken lout "sir"?

Nevertheless January thanked him and left, to make his way along Rue des Ramparts. At St. Anthony's Chapel he stopped, and in its silent dimness knelt for a time, glad only for the silence and the peace, telling over the prayers of the rosary in the dark.

Praying that he would survive the fever season.

Praying that he would not come one day to Olympe's house to find her, and Paul, and the children dead with blackened faces in puddles of their own bile.

Praying that he would not receive today, or tomorrow, a letter from Milneburgh informing him that his mother, or Dominique, or her child, had succumbed.

Praying that he would not be left to face the remainder of his life utterly alone.

It was the second of October. Only a few weeks, he thought, until the summer broke. Until the fever broke.

When he emerged from the chapel, he knew that he ought to go to Mademoiselle Vitrac's, to relieve her for a time of her nursing duties, as Hannibal had done. But he went home instead. He stripped and bathed in tepid rainwater from the cistern and for a long time lay on his bed, the heat of the day on him like a soaked blanket. Remembering Ayasha. Trying to remember his father's face. Seeing in his mind the straight slim figure of Cora Chouteau, walking up Rue de l'Hôpital in the dark.

Through the open windows he smelled the smoke of burning, and he slept at last in the terrible silence of Bronze John's domination of the town.

He reached the school a few hours before sunset the following day and related to Mademoiselle Vitrac all that had befallen him since leaving Charity Hospital and all he had learned or guessed. "Not that the Guards will do a thing about it," he concluded bitterly. He tilted the veilleuse, carried the cup of tisane to Geneviève's bed.

The girl was dying. January could see it in her face. There was little more to her than a skeleton, her exquisite complexion livid orange with the mask of fever. Yesterday Mademoiselle Vitrac had cropped the girl's long black hair, which tangled and knotted with Geneviève's helpless thrashing. January had suggested it, a few days ago; now he was sorry, knowing she would be buried thus. She looked like one of the dried Indian mummies that trappers found sometimes in the mounds and caves upriver.

"I can't believe they could be just—just selling them." Mademoiselle Vitrac's voice was shaky, as she bent over Victorine, sponging the girl's thin body. "I mean, the first time this Madame Perret, or the woman Lu, could slip away, couldn't they go to—Well, not the local magistrate, but someone . . . and say, *I was kidnapped*? Their free status is on public record here. . . ."

"And who's going to check?" said January softly, when she failed to finish her sentence. "These are people who have no family in town. People who mostly don't even speak English. And what white man is going to run the risk of alienating all his neighbors, whose help he depends on, for the sake of a man or a woman who's probably lying?

On the frontier, where people must have each other's help at picking time and planting? Men don't need to be evil, Mademoiselle. They just have to be bad enough to say, *There's nothing I can do.*" He straightened up. "How well is this place locked and bolted at night?"

"Pretty well." She picked up her bowl of vinegar-water and brought it to the dying girl's bed. "And Madame Deslormes at the grocery on the corner and the Widow Lyons across the way both see me every day."

January nodded. Still he felt uneasy, but knew a part of that uneasiness was less for her than for Olympe and her husband, for young Gabriel and Zizi-Marie. These marauders did not content themselves with taking people whom no one would miss from their homes or from the tiny rooms they'd rented in the back streets of the town. *Three or four of them, wandering the streets with clubs.* The men who'd tried to abduct him.

The men who'd taken Cora Chouteau off the banquette.

Mademoiselle Vitrac bent over Geneviève's bed and sponged the girl's heat-blotched face and body. "She was the most beautiful of them, you know," she said, keeping her voice matter-of-fact; a line of concentration marked her fine-drawn brows, as if she were doing accounts or grinding up mineral salts for a chemical experiment. "Her mother was just waiting for her to finish 'this nonsense' as she called it, and start going to the Blue Ribbon Balls. She seemed to take it as a personal insult that Geneviève wouldn't consent to be the most beautiful girl there, so that *she* could be the mother of the most beautiful girl." She shook her head. "We—Geneviève and I—had one quarrel with her already, at the beginning of this year. She was so afraid of it," she added softly. "Geneviève."

I'm not very good at this, she had said to him once, and she still wasn't. Spilled water blotted her dress and soaked her sleeves, dribbling black patterns on the floor all around. She'd pulled off her tignon in the heat, and her dark hair, drawn back in a clumsy knot, was beaded with sweat, long curly tendrils of it escaping to drift around her face. Her hands were blistered with the unaccustomed work, and January saw how achingly she moved.

"It's funny," she went on, more softly. "Because when it came to chemical experiments, to fire and explosions, she was—not even *brave* is the word, she simply didn't think about fear. She even learned how to make bombs, stuffing gunpowder in the bottom of a clay jar and packing it in with cotton, and sawdust to take fire in the explosion and make the explosion seem bigger—I remember her timing how long it took a fuse to burn. The other girls were terrified."

Her mouth curved, cherishing the memory, bright as a stand of daffodils that catches sunlight before the engulfing shadow of storm.

In time Geneviève's feeble movements ceased and she lay with shut eyes, beaten. Mademoiselle Vitrac got quickly to her feet and went from the room, leaving the vinegar-water where it was. Leadenly weary, January finished dosing Antoinette and went to Geneviève, but the girl still breathed, though barely. He wrung out the sponge, finished neatly the job Mademoiselle Vitrac had abandoned, and dressed the girl again—it was like dressing a stick-puppet—in one of the nightgowns that he, or Hannibal, or Mademoiselle Vitrac endlessly boiled and washed.

Some said the clothing and bedding of fever victims ought to be burned. With only a few paying pupils, Rose Vitrac could barely afford to put food on the table, much less buy new sheets and nightclothes, or even pay a laundress to do them. More than anything in the world he wanted to go down after her, to comfort her in the face of the approaching death of the girl who had been her pupil and her friend.

But all he could see in his mind was Ayasha with her lifeless fingers stretched toward the water pitcher, and there were no words in his mind to say. And in any case he would not leave the dying girl alone.

He was still sitting by Geneviève's bed, holding her burning hand, when he heard the stairs creak, and the rustle of skirts.

"I'm sorry. That was inexcusable of me."

In the dimness of the attic he could see that she'd slopped water on her face to take down the swelling of tears.

"I was here. And she wouldn't have known."

"They do know." She crossed from the door and sat on the bed next to Geneviève's pillow, stroked the hacked bristle of hair. "At least I did."

"Did you have the fever?"

She shook her head. "I . . ." She hesitated for a long time. Then, very carefully, "I was sick. Eight, nine years ago, just before I went away to school in New York. Father told me later I didn't know one person from another, but that isn't how I remember it. Cora . . ."

She broke off again, wrapped her arms around herself, though the attic was sweltering. Looked down into the face of the dying girl.

Her words came slowly: "I don't know whether this really happened or not. But I remember one night when Cora heard my father pass the door. She went out into the hall and told him, 'The least you could do is go in there and hold on to her hand.' "

"Did he?" He saw it in his mind, as he saw Cora's small straight shadow disappearing in the darkness of the street: the shadow of the dark girl on the wall, tiny before the tall white man. Arms folded, looking up at him the way she'd looked up at January under the shadows of the Pellicots' kitchen gallery.

"His wife told him not to." Mademoiselle Vitrac sounded resigned about it, accepting that such was how things were.

"Were you contagious?"

It's not bad if you don't fight. . . .

He knew Rose had not been contagious.

She was silent for perhaps a minute. Then, "I wasn't an easy child to have in the house." She touched Geneviève's hand, her own cut and bandaged fingers rendered exquisite and alien, like intricately jointed bamboo, by the knife of sunlight that fell across them. "Like Geneviève. And Victorine, and Isabel, and some of the others. The ones who can't be what their mothers were, or want them to be. The ones who see too clearly, and speak too frankly. The ones who . . . who damage themselves and their position in the house every time they open their mouths, but can't keep from doing so."

He saw in the long oval bones of her face the face of a proud, gawky child: erudite, stuck-up, above herself and everyone around her. As she would have been to him, he realized, had they not met as they had.

A shudder went through her, tears suppressed as they had always been suppressed. "She never had a chance."

January gathered her against him as he would have gathered one of his sisters, had she been in pain, and felt the woman's body stiffen like wood. He released her, stepped back the instant before she wrenched herself from him. . . .

"Don't . . ."

He stood back helplessly, his hands at his sides.

She was trembling, looking away from him. "I . . ."

There wasn't a thing she could say without saying everything. He could feel the knot of it, wringing tighter and tighter, like a noose of pain.

To sever it he said, "She had what no one else could have given her: the assurance that there was a path for her, even if it was narrow and lonely." What he wanted to say was not that: what he wanted to say was, *Don't turn away! I wasn't the one who hurt you!* But he knew that did not matter, against the touch and the strength of a man's hands, and the smell of a man's sweat. Some women never recovered.

If you don't struggle it's not so bad.

He forced himself to speak of this dying girl, whom he had never truly known, instead of to the bitter, struggling adolescent trapped within the schoolmistress's brittle calm.

"At least she knew someone else had walked that way before her."

The schoolmistress fought for a moment more to steady her breath, to regain her composure. To pretend she hadn't cried out, and pulled herself from what she knew was offered only in comfort and in love. Then she turned her face toward him again, and said, "I'm sorry. It's . . . she was the oldest of them, and the closest to me."

She looked down at Geneviève's face again, and from being, a moment ago, a shield against him, the girl became again a friend in her own right, a loved friend with one foot in Charon's boat.

"I tried. I did try. If she hadn't been so bright—if she hadn't been so cutting about everything she saw and heard—her mother would have been gladder to have her with her in Mandeville."

"We can't know that," said January steadily, his eyes meeting hers. Her trembling ceased, and there was only grief, and no more vile memory, in her face. "We can't know what would or would not have befallen her, if she'd gone with her mother out of town. I suspect she was happier here, without her mother on her to put up her hair and go to the balls."

The sensitive mouth flinched. He saw old memory flit across the back of her eyes, trailing a silvery wake of pain. "That's true," Rose Vitrac said. "Her mother . . ." She made a small gesture, and ceased.

"If we start to make up those stories in our heads, about would-have and might-have and if-only-we-hadn't, we'll go mad," said January softly. "You know that."

"I know. . . . You're seeing me at a bad time, M'sieu Janvier. I'm not usually this . . . this ticklish."

He met the green-gray eyes again, and smiled. "Well, Mademoiselle Vitrac, since you're the only woman of my entire acquaintance to ever be brought down by the death of those she loves, the fear of the plague, and the sheer exhaustion of a hero's work in nursing, I'll have to give it some thought before I forgive you."

She gave a swift, tiny spurt of laughter, clapped behind her hand again before sheer fatigue could turn it into tears, and her eyes sparkled quick gratitude into his. "*Dum spiro spero;* where there's life there's hope."

"And as a doctor I can tell you," he replied, "that where there's hope, there's often life."

"And where there's a will," added Hannibal, climbing up the last few boards of the stairway with his arms full of rough-dried sheets, "there's a relative, and I've found a most curious thing in the newspaper."

"What?" January turned, grateful for the diversion. "An admission there's an epidemic on?"

Mademoiselle Vitrac flung up her hands like a comic servant in a play. "An epidemic? Really?"

"Heaven forfend. Nothing so custard-livered and contrary to the principles upon which Our Great Nation was founded, whatever those are." Hannibal dumped the sheets on one of the unoccupied beds, and from the rear pocket of his trousers produced a folded page of the *New Orleans Abeille.* He was in shirtsleeves, the shirt itself stained with soap and blotched with water, his long brown hair wound up in a knot on the top of his head scarcely dissimilar to Mademoiselle Vitrac's makeshift coiffure. Like hers, his small, pale hands were blistered and burned.

Perching tailor-fashion on the end of the bed beside the sheets, he unfolded the paper.

"This is Wednesday's," he announced. "The eighteenth of September. *Runaway—Cora—Age about twenty-one, housemaid. Small, mulatto, well set up, speaks both French and English. Stole $250 and a necklace of pearls from Mrs. Emily Redfern, thought to be going to New Orleans. Reward.*"

"Two hundred and fifty dollars?" said January, baffled. "What happened to the five thousand in cash Redfern got from Madame Lalaurie and the Bank of Louisiana? What happened to the birthmark on her shoulder?"

"Cora didn't have a birthmark on her shoulder." Mademoiselle Vitrac sat back down on the edge of Geneviève's bed, and took the wasted hand in hers. "At least not one that I ever saw, and we washed each other's hair a thousand times."

"The two hundred and fifty would be the original sum of that hundred and eighty you found, Rose," said Hannibal. "What did you do with that money, by the way?"

"It's in my desk." She looked slightly embarrassed. "I know it's stolen money, but . . . I'm keeping it for now, in case things get worse before the fever season ends. There's a hidden compartment, a false back behind the left-hand upper drawer. And I'd say it's fairly clear why the five thousand isn't mentioned. The advertisement must have been placed Tuesday. When did Otis Redfern come down sick, M'sieu Janvier? Tuesday? Wednesday?"

"Wednesday night." January leaned over to take the paper from Hannibal. "When did Cora come to you?"

"Wednesday night, after the girls were asleep. It must have been ten or ten thirty."

"This would have been placed Tuesday. Cora told me she slept out in the Swamp the night before coming down here. Obviously whoever placed this didn't know yet that the five thousand dollars were missing."

"Do you think she took it?" asked Hannibal.

Rose Vitrac sighed again and sat for a time with folded arms, hands on shoulders as if instinctively protecting her breasts. Not wanting to be disloyal, thought January. But she knew Cora.

At length she sighed, surrendering one bastion of the fortress she could no longer defend. "I think she would have, if she'd known it was in the house," she admitted. "If both the Redferns were ill, and she saw her chance to get away in the confusion. But she didn't have it when she came to me. I know she didn't. And if she'd taken it . . ." She had clearly been about to say, *She would have told me,* but the discovery of the hundred and eighty dollars, and the necklace of pearls, had proven that trust untrue.

"In any case," she finished, after that sentence had died untouched, "I know she wouldn't have done murder."

"She may not have," said January. He sorted two sheets from the pile and went over to one of the stripped beds; Hannibal went to help him. "But you're going to have a hard time proving she didn't. What I'm trying to figure out is why the money was in cash instead of a draft."

"Easy," said Hannibal. "If you were a gambling man yourself, Benjamin, you wouldn't be asking a silly question like that. No, stay where you are, Athene, we don't want your help."

Rose smiled a little at the nickname and settled back on the edge of Geneviève's bed gathering the girl's hand again in hers. Grateful, January thought, to be still.

"It takes only an hour to come downriver from Twelve-Mile Point," said January thoughtfully. "Cora could have slipped back into the house Wednesday evening sometime. . . ."

"Wouldn't she have known the Redferns were sick, then?"

He shook his head. "According to Shaw, at least, that didn't take place until after dinner." He didn't add that if Cora had slipped back into the Redfern house Wednesday evening she would have had access to the food, but he saw the searching look Mademoiselle Vitrac gave him. "Monkshood acts fast. The coroner would know what time, exactly, they started to show signs of illness. And he's the only one, now that the servants have all been sold off."

He spread the clean sheet over the bed, and gently lifted the girl Victorine from her soiled, sweaty, wrinkled sheets to the clean ones, the endless, brutal labor of sick nursing.

After a time he went on, "If Cora took the five thousand dollars, it might explain why she left the hundred and eighty dollars here—a hundred and ninety, counting Madame Lalaurie's money—and the pearls. If she had the five thousand with her, in a pocket or a reticule, she might not feel she needed what was here. I certainly would think twice about trying to bribe Madame Lalaurie's coachman. But if the five thousand was on her when she was taken, it'll show up somewhere. And given human nature, I suspect I know where."

I will never in my life, Abishag Shaw had said, *understand a gamblin' man.*

But at least, thought January, if you did happen to want one you knew where he'd be.

Naturally, no man of color was permitted through the front doors of John Davis's casino on the corner of Rues Bourbon and d'Orleans. From the small service courtyard in the building's rear, January could look through the windows to the salons within. The flickering glow of gas lent a curious cast to the faces of the men grouped so intently around the roulette wheels, to the polished tabletops scattered with the garish reds and golds of the cards.

Maybe it was just the heavy buzzing of sleeplessness in his head, the too-recent memory of that stifling dormitory bedchamber he had just left, but there was something weirdly disjointed about that sight.

Money lay on the tables, too, green or orange or brown banknotes, gold American cartwheels and eagles, silver Spanish dollars. Folded papers—deeds to houses, papers for slaves, letters of credit for crops or cargoes. Men who had only their six-reale daily wage to gamble away didn't come to Davis's. The croupiers—fair-haired Germans, quick, small Frenchmen or Mexicans, mustachioed Italians—scooped up cards and money impassively, deft and expert. Did they realize that newcomers to the city were the first to die in the epidemics?

Maybe the management didn't beat up greenhorns or rob winners the minute they cleared the door, as was the procedure in the hells of the Swamp or Gallatin Street, but the net result was usually the same. As Shaw had asked, did those men around the tables think they were actually going to win money here?

Did they think the fever, or the cholera, would not get them, if they remained long enough in this town?

The rear door to the service wing stood open. A waiter in shirtsleeves was washing glasses in the tiny kitchen, his crimson coat hung on a peg on the wall behind him. Another arranged oysters on a tray. No gaslight burned in these rear purlieux; the gluey heat of the evening curdled with the smells of the tallow candles, with the tang of spicy sauce and the garbage in the gutters outside. The man in shirtsleeves saw January and grinned. "How you keepin' yourself, Maestro?"

One of his mother's greatest objections to January's musical calling was that it put him on the same standing with servants.

"Getting by." January accepted the lemonade that the man poured out for him. In the heat, after the hours spent caring for the sick girls on Rue St. Claude, the liquid was mouth-wringingly sweet. "Yourself?"

"Can't complain. We're stayin' well, is all that counts." Like January, the man was sufficiently dark to stand a fighting chance against the fever. His mother denied there was a difference, of course. But January suspected his mother would cheerfully succumb to the fever if by doing so it would prove her to be more white than her neighbors.

"Would you mind taking this in to Monsieur Davis?" January fished one of his cards from the breast pocket of his black wool coat. On the back he'd already written his request for a few minutes of the entrepreneur's time. Though he couldn't really afford it, he held out, along with the card, a two-reale bit as well. The waiter straightened his sleeves, resumed his coat, and returned a few minutes later to lead

January up a narrow flight of service stairs to a smother-box of an office on the upper floor.

"Ben." John Davis rose from his desk, held out his hand.

"M'sieu Davis."

"Get Ben some champagne, would you, Placide? Unless you'd like something a little stronger?"

"Only lemonade, if that's all right, sir," answered January. "I'm going straight on to Charity Hospital tonight. To tell you the truth I've been so short of rest that if I had anything stronger you'd probably have to carry me out of here."

Davis shook his head with a chuckle. "Don't have enough men for that, Ben." With a gesture he invited January to sit, then peered at him closely in the candlelight. "You don't look well, and that's a fact." January reflected that the entrepreneur didn't look any too well himself: stouter than when he'd seen him last and with far more white in the grizzle of his hair.

"Well, it can't last—it never does." Davis's French carried an echo of the Caribbean islands, after all these years. "I'll have something for you come November, when people start coming back to town. What can I do for you?"

"I'm not sure how to put this, sir." January turned in his hands the cool glass of lemonade the waiter Placide had brought him. "I know you have the confidence of your clients here, and I wouldn't ask you to violate it. I'm only asking if you feel you can help me."

He paused for a moment, as if marshaling his thoughts, though in fact he'd rehearsed his story with Hannibal several times. "A friend of my mother's was robbed of three thousand dollars," he said at last. "We have no idea who took it—the house was broken into while the woman was visiting her daughter. I know that most of those who gamble here are, of course, not the men who would do such a thing, sir, but if a petty criminal should suddenly find himself possessed of that sum of money—particularly unexpectedly—he might very well come here."

"And paint the town bright red, eh?" Davis chuckled richly. "We get them coming in all the time. These—what do they call themselves?—these mercenaries, these filibusters, these Kaintucks from the levee, they often 'hit it rich,' as they say. Three thousand dollars." His eyes, dark as café noir, sharpened, speculative, as he regarded January across the rim of the bourbon glass Placide had brought on the same tray with the lemonade. Under that keen gaze January was very thankful he hadn't named five thousand as the sum. "Lot of money. Why didn't your mother's friend have credit on the bank?"

"She didn't say, sir. She'd just sold her cook and her coachman that afternoon, a private sale. She was leaving town and needed the money pretty badly."

Davis grimaced. "And lost it that same day? What a damn shame. This town just isn't safe. Some people don't trust banks. I don't, myself, but I trust my fellow man even less." He chuckled again, and gestured with his glass. "But fifteen hundred apiece—that's damn good bargaining, even with prices as high as they are now. Who'd she sell to, do you know?"

January appeared to think hard, frowning. Then he shook his head. "I don't . . . Redfield? Redman? Redfern? Maybe Otis Redfern?"

Davis's eyes widened. "Otis Redfern?"

"I might be thinking of someone else."

"I'd say you are, my friend." Davis shook his head. "Otis Redfern, God rest his soul, couldn't raise three thousand dollars to pay his debts here, let alone buy a coachman and a cook. He had a cook, anyway, the best in town; that wife of his saw to that. She asked around for months, and nothing was good enough for her; in the end she paid twice what he was worth for that stuck-up yellow fussbudget who used to cook for Bernard Marigny. And for all that the man ended up sold to that church fellow for six hundred dollars—money he probably took straight out of the profits of that silly Musicale those American ladies held for him out in Milneburgh last week. Now, that's gratitude for you!" he concluded sarcastically. "At least he could have paid her a decent price."

January remembered the Reverend Micajah Dunk bargaining in the Exchange: nine hundred, nine hundred fifty dollars for men who would be sold for over a thousand in Missouri next week. He wondered if one of them had been the Marigny cook.

He said, "Tcha!" and related, with libellous embellishments, the tale of the musicians' contracts for the Musicale, something Davis had heard secondhand or thirdhand already, but listened to avidly again.

"Well, for all her airs she's having the plantation sold out from under her," Davis remarked, after a fairly derogatory discussion of Emily Redfern's pretensions. "It went under seal by the bank today; Granville's going to auction it at Maspero's Monday. I never knew the lady well, but a harder, more grasping woman I have yet to meet. It must have driven her insane, the way that poor man let the ready slide through his fingers—and he was about the most inept gambler I've seen," he added, shaking his head. "Otis Redfern was one of those poor souls who couldn't let it alone, not even against plain common sense. He'd bet on anything, for the thrill of it. Last week— Wednesday, it would have been—when everyone in town knew he was over his ears in debt, he came in here playing roulette. . . . *Roulette,* like a fool!"

"Wednesday?" said January, startled.

Davis's gray brows raised politely; January said, "A friend of mine tried to reach him Wednesday and was told he was indisposed."

Davis shook his head. "The small hours of Wednesday morning it was—Redfern came in here around midnight or one, and gambled until just after sunrise. God knows what he said to his wife when he reached home."

He gestured with his glass toward the door and the gambling room beyond. "Liam Roarke, that slick Irishman who runs some dive by the Basin, came in at four with a couple of his bravos, and braced the man over money he'd lost to *them,* five thousand dollars two days before. *Two days before,* with Fazende and Calder ready to go to law over what Redfern owed them from last year's crop coming in poorly because of the cholera, and him selling up his slaves to cover the debt. And after they left, what does the poor fool do but go back to the tables."

He sipped his whisky and shook his head again at the marvel of human conduct. Through the floor January heard voices rise in sudden fury, the stamp of feet and shouting: a fight downstairs, inevitable in gatherings of Creoles and Americans. He heard something that sounded like "species of American!" and "Consarn if I'll take that from any man!" Davis tilted his head a little, ready to rise, but the noises died away.

The entrepreneur sighed, and his stout shoulders eased in their bottle green superfine. "I've been a player all my life, you know, Ben. I've seen enough money won and lost, here and in Paris and in Haiti, probably to buy back all of the Mississippi Valley from the Americans, with this city thrown in for lagniappe. I know these men who gamble everything, who can't stop gaming any more than a drunkard can stop drinking; who ruin themselves at the tables—I understand what they'll do, how they'll react, how they'll lay their bets. I can read these men like books. But I don't understand them. I don't understand why."

The door behind January opened upon a gentle knock. Placide looked in, caught Davis's eye: "I think they need you downstairs, sir."

"Ah." Davis sighed and stood. "My apologies, Ben . . ."

"None needed, sir. It's your job."

"For my sins." He gave a wry grin.

"Perhaps for your virtues." January picked up his hat.

"About your mother's friend's money." Davis waited until the waiter was gone. "I haven't seen anyone in here. . . . How to say this? Spending money it doesn't appear they should have. It's been quiet. Mostly what you have here these days are the local men, the ones who come in all the time—the ones who stay in town, like fools, to gamble. And here I am like a fool catering to them, but there! In a year or two I'll open that place in Spanish Fort that I've been looking at, and then you'll see something like!"

January nodded. He hadn't noticed any diminution of the establishment's clientele, but then, Davis's was not a place where he performed regularly. Maybe it *was* quiet.

"You'll have better luck asking in the Swamp, and near the Basin, or down on Tchoupitoulas Street by the levee. But frankly, Ben, I wouldn't advise you to go down there. Slaves are very high this year. I wouldn't want to see you come to harm."

So Otis Redfern had been in town all Tuesday night.

January turned the matter over in his mind as he walked to the Hospital, carefully choosing the most populated and best-lit streets.

Redfern would have ridden in Tuesday to post the runaway notice in the *Bee*—presumably before the loss of his five thousand dollars was discovered. And despite the debts that had forced the sale of Gervase and the others, he'd stayed on, his gambler's logic telling him that this was the way to recoup his loss.

If Emily Redfern hadn't already been planning to include her husband, as well as his mistress, in her plans for murder, thought January, shaking his head, that would have decided her.

Too little remained of his dwindling funds to hire a horse, so when he forced himself to wake next day in the heat of noon, he bathed and dressed and walked the six or seven streets to the levee. The *Missourian* had left that morning, bound on its usual run to St. Louis; the *Bonnets O'Blue* was just in and off-loading cotton and tobacco. The *Philadelphia* would leave sometime that afternoon for Natchez—"Or this evenin', more like," said its engineer, with whom January managed to get a quiet word in the arcades of the market, while the small white ship sat idle on its wharf and its crew of stevedores played monte in the shade. "That big mess of brandy that came in on the *Caledonia* yesterday ain't yet been brought over here, and it'll be four hours loadin' at the least. Mr. Graham—that's our pilot—says we can make as far as Red Church, 'fore we'll have to tie up for the night. You'll be fine."

So January booked deck passage as far as Twelve-Mile Point, all he could afford, and returning home, packed a small grip with a change of linen, a blue-and-red calico shirt, rough trousers, and a corduroy jacket. While he was doing so he heard sounds, first in the little room next door to which Hannibal had moved his books and clothing the previous afternoon, then out on the gallery. He deduced that his friend was at least out of bed, if not precisely awake.

He found him being thoroughly sick over the gallery railing. Considering the hour at which the fiddler had come in last night— well after January's predawn return from the Hospital—he suspected this illness was the usual result of Hannibal's drinking, but went to him nevertheless, and while steadying him, unobtrusively checked for fever.

"Non vinum virus moderari," whispered Hannibal at last, draped like a wet rag doll over the railing. *"Sed viri vino solent.* Have I died of the fever yet?" He was panting as if he had run a long distance.

"No," replied January unfeelingly. Given the present possible fates of free colored who lived alone with no one in the houses on either side, he felt safer knowing there was another person on the premises, and he was genuinely fond of the fiddler, but sharing quarters with Hannibal Sefton did have its disadvantages. "It isn't Bronze John—just your old friend John Barleycorn. And if you'd *moderari* your intake of *vinum* you wouldn't be having this problem."

"Ah, but think of the others that would be caused by worry in its place." He wavered back into the dark little chamber that had from time immemorial been occupied by the Widow Levesque's cook Bella and, unequal to the task of fighting his way back through the mosquito-bar, simply collapsed on the floor with his back against the foot of the bed. "I'll sleep here, thanks."

January went into his own room and brought in the tub of water he'd drawn to sluice his head and arms before getting dressed for the Blanque girls' piano lessons. Hannibal thrust his head into it as if he expected there to be a twenty-dollar gold piece on the bottom that he could pick up only with his teeth. He came up dripping and gasping, like a drowned elf.

"Thank you," he said.

"Thank *you,*" replied January seriously. "The two young ladies who brought you home this morning told me you'd been making enquiries among their friends about people spending more money than is their wont to have. Did you learn anything?" *Anything you can remember?* he wanted to add, but didn't. Hannibal was having enough problems this morning.

"Ah. The lovely Bridgit and the equally lovely Thalia. They did say that nobody's showed up with five thousand all in a lump, but, of course, if Cora were abducted by a group the money would have been split. No one seems to have even been throwing around as much as a thousand. They did say that Roarke, the proprietor of the Jolly Boatman, had been expecting such a sum, that he'd won from one Otis

Redfern, but nothing came of it: Roarke's *inamorata du jour,* one Miss Trudi, abused the other girls for a week on the strength of the disappointment."

"That sounds genuine," murmured January. He thought that one of the girls who'd greeted him in the yard in the small hours—an incapable Hannibal in tow—had looked vaguely familiar. She'd been dishing the crawfish and rice yesterday, behind the gotch-eyed bartender's back.

"Are you off to Mademoiselle Vitrac's, when you're feeling better? Then let her know I've gone up to Spanish Bayou, to have a look at the Redfern place. They're auctioning it Monday. The slaves are gone; Madame Redfern herself is in Milneburgh; this is our last chance to see anything there that is to be seen. I should be back tomorrow, when the *Lancaster* makes her usual run down from Natchez. Copies of my papers are in my desk."

Hannibal nodded. January scooped aside the mosquito-bar and helped him back into bed, exasperation and pity in his heart. January knew better than to remonstrate with a man whose illness and pain had led him into addiction. The road that led away from opium would lead only back to pain, and both had given Hannibal an uneradicable taste for oblivion. So he said only, "Will you be all right?"

"*Eripere vitam nemo non homini potest, at nemo mortem; mille ad hanc aditus patent.* I'll look after Athene of the Bright Eyes. You watch yourself, upriver."

There wasn't time to walk to the levee and check on the progress of the *Philadelphia's* cargo; January could only hope it was delayed. Most steamboats left before noon, and with the waning moon rising late he guessed the captain of the vessel would be pressing the pilot and the engineer to be off as soon as could be. The next upriver boat was the *Lancaster,* early Sunday morning, and January did not like to count on the house at Spanish Bayou remaining empty for that long. As he walked the length of Rue Burgundy, and down Rue de l'Hôpital, he found himself listening for the groan of steamboat whistles that would tell him he was too late and had lost his passage money; within the high walls of the Lalaurie house he strained his ears, and grudged the thick curtains that masked all noise from the streets.

The heavily decorated, ostentatious parlor was nearly dark, as usual; oven-hot, as usual; and neither Pauline nor Louise Marie had practiced, as usual. Pauline was peevish, caustic, and spiteful; Louise Marie sniveling with an exquisitely calculated appearance of martyrdom: "It's only that my silly pain has made it so difficult for me to practice. The pain, and the heat, and one of my dizzy spells." She raised a wraithlike hand to her forehead. "I have told you of my spells, have I not, M'sieu Janvier?"

January thought of Hannibal, weaving exquisite beauty through pain to earn enough to sleep under a roof. Of Rose Vitrac, sponging off the bodies of the dying in the heat.

"The heat?" Pauline laughed with a sound like breaking glass. "We're like to die in the heat. It isn't as if we didn't have a house at the lake."

"Oh, but you can't expect Dr. Lalaurie to give up his work with Dr. Soublet, just for us." Louise Marie lifted sunken eyes to meet her sister's. January recalled what the market-women had said, when he'd asked them about Madame Lalaurie: *"She's had enough to bear, with that poor girl of hers in and out of that clinic, but she never would have no truck with laudanum. . . ."*

Soublet's? Was that where Madame had met the suavely dandified Lalaurie?

"No more than she deserved," had grumbled another. *"I heard how she throwed a little pickaninny of hers off'n the roof. . . ."*

"I heard it was down a flight of stairs," had said someone else, and the discussion dissolved into an exchange of rumor that would, January reflected angrily, have made Monsieur Montreuil proud.

"And with a doctor in the house, and Mama, you know we must be perfectly safe." Louise Marie's plaintive tones tugged back his thoughts. "We can survive the heat." She sighed as she said it, to let everyone know she did not expect to. "I'm just so sorry, Monsieur Janvier, that I haven't been able to learn my pieces better. I did try."

Pauline's mouth twisted, her sharp nostrils flaring with an unmade comment. Was this, January wondered, one of those girls of whom Mademoiselle Vitrac had spoken? The ones who were too bright, too sharp, for their own good? Delphine Lalaurie was the pinnacle of Creole womanhood: hostess, businesswoman, mother, manager of a household of twenty or more persons. What recourse had a daughter of this house, if that daughter's goals and needs did not include a husband and children, Creole tradition, and Creole society?

Halfway through Pauline's careful but unpracticed recital of a Haydn contredanse the door opened. He saw the thin back of the girl at the piano grow rigid. The sticklike hands fumbled on the keys. Louise Marie, in the midst of a complaint about her ankles, fell silent and seemed to shrink into the hard golden upholstery of the divan.

A gleam of silk, dark peacock blue veiled with the shadows of the lightless hall, flickered in the doorway. A pale face crowned by a glory of dark hair.

"Pauline," chided that lovely contralto in a tone like level steel, "after all Monsieur Janvier's work, that is as well as you can do? From the beginning again, please."

They'd be finishing the loading of the brandy onto the boat at the wharf, but something in the tone of her voice stilled January's protest in his throat. It was the voice of a woman who has never been contradicted, a woman who will tolerate no less than the perfect.

Pauline played as if a gun were pressed to her back.

"Pauline," said her mother, still unseen within the rectangle of gloom, "from the beginning again, please. You know that no one appreciates mistakes in a piece of music, any more than they appreciate food spots on a silk dress."

"Yes, Mama." Sweat stood out in a crystalline wash on Pauline's forehead; January thought he had never seen such rage, such hatred, in a girl's downcast eyes. The spindly fingers trembled as they lurched through the first three bars.

"From the beginning again, please."

The voice was a whalebone lash.

"From the beginning again, please."

"From the beginning again, please."

Pauline was crying without a sound. Her body was a wooden doll's in her overlacy pink gown; and her hands fumbled, groped, struck note after note awry. In the doorway, her mother's face remained in shadow, the strong, white, black-laced hands moveless where they rested among the folds of her dress: "From the beginning again, please."

It was nothing January would have put anyone through, even in private, much less before a music-master and a colored man to boot. For a white girl the humiliation would have been excruciating. In her chair Louise Marie made neither sound nor movement, her hands locked around the lemonade she had sent for, as if she believed that by keeping very still she could avoid some terrible fate. Somewhere outside January thought he heard a steamboat whistle. But he would no more have spoken than he would have spoken to a madman with a knife.

At last Pauline broke down completely. She sat at the keyboard, fighting the dry, racking sobs with all that was in her and shuddering like a beaten racehorse. From the doorway that exquisite golden contralto said, "I see we're only wasting Monsieur Janvier's time, Pauline. You may go to your room."

Pauline flinched and caught her breath as if struck, then fought herself to stillness again. She rose like an automaton, not even daring to wipe the tears from her face and the snot trickling from her nose, and made her way to the door. Petticoats rustled as her mother stepped aside to let her pass, a thin harsh sound like flakes of steel. A good Creole daughter, Pauline curtsied to her mother, then vanished into the bake-oven shadows of the hall.

Louise Marie's eyes flickered, showing white all around the rim— *Does she think after thirty minutes of that, her mother's going to put her through it, too?*

"You may go to your room as well, Louise Marie."

"Yes, Mother." The words came out like paper scraping as it is crushed. She rose quickly and without the ostentatious demonstrations of pain and bravery—the bitten lower lip, the tiny gasps, the hand on the hip—so characteristic of her every move. She still limped, and badly, but not nearly to the usual extent; she had almost reached the door when her mother said in that same whip-cut voice:

"Is this a sty or a garbage bin, Louise Marie, that you leave your dirty crockery all over the house?"

The young woman turned quickly back and collected her lemonade glass.

"I'm very sorry, Monsieur Janvier," said Madame Lalaurie, as Louise Marie's halting rustle of petticoats retreated down the hall. No anger inflected her voice, and no contrition. Only pleasant calm, as if reducing her children to tears of terror and exhaustion were a daily commonplace. It occurred to him suddenly to wonder what being "sent to one's room" entailed. "I assure you, both girls will be able to demonstrate the proper proficiency at Tuesday's lesson. Of course, Bastien will compensate you for the extra time today."

She melted into the gloom of the hallway with barely a whisper of silk. At no time during the previous forty minutes had January seen her face.

"M'sieu Janvier?"

He turned to find Bastien at his elbow, urbanely gesturing him out.

On the docks there were still two wagonloads of brandy to unload. Passengers loitered grumpily along the railing of the upper decks; on the lower, uneven gaggles of slaves and poor and keelboat Kaintucks jockeyed for places in the shade.

At the steamboat offices January sent in his card and asked for the lading lists for Wednesday, September 18: the *Missourian* and the *Vermillion* had docked in the morning, if the clerk recalled aright, the *New Brunswick* had been in by afternoon for certain, the *Walter Scott* and the *Silver Moon* sometime between four and eight o'clock, he thought. But, he said, he might be wrong.

During the lesson, January had left his grip in the charge of a woman at a silk shop a few houses down Rue Royale from the Lalauries, and now he changed clothes in a sheltered corner of the *Philadelphia*'s deck. Once out of the formal disguise of black coat and linen shirt, he wandered over to the engine room, watching a mixed crew of black and Irish stevedores carrying barrels and packages aboard and stowing them on deck.

"You made it," remarked the engineer, coming out beside him in time.

"And I feel like a prize fool for hurrying." January grinned, and the stout, heavily muscled little man grinned back up at him.

"Oh, I seen 'em do this a thousand times." He spoke rough English, like an American; January guessed him a freedman from one of the American enterprises in the town. "Rushing around like somebody took and lit they tails on fire, and then we end up waitin' all the same." He wiped his hands on a rag.

"Think we'll make Twelve-Mile Point by dark?"

"Oh, sure. Once the old *Philly* get goin', she goes, and Mr. Graham, he can work her up the banks close enough you can pick daisies off the levee. We'll make Red Church by dark, easy, never mind Twelve-Mile Point."

January personally didn't think so—Red Church landing was a good twenty-five miles upriver—but nodded and looked impressed. He lowered his voice, and leaned down a little to the engineer. "Look, sir, this's my first time out of New Orleans. I got all my papers just fine, and notarized at the Cabildo, but I been hearing rumors and talk. How safe is it, going up to Twelve-Mile Point? I'm going to see my sister, that still works for Mr. Bailey up there, and I'm . . . well, I'm a little worried. About river pirates and slave stealers and such."

All humor vanished from the engineer's eyes. "Where you staying, brother?"

January hefted his grip. "I thought I'd sleep out in the woods."

"You should be safe. But watch your back, you know? You don't have to sleep in the woods, neither. The big house up at Spanish Bayou, 'bout two miles down from the Point, is empty now, they're sellin' it up. You can probably sleep on the gallery or in one of the cabins. There'll be water in the well and everything. Just be a little careful who you talk to, and don't get yourself anywhere where you can't run. How you gettin' home?"

"I thought if nobody's around the plantation I'd put out a flag on the landing when the *Lancaster* comes by tomorrow."

"Just what I was going to tell you. Bailey's a good man—county magistrate in St. Charles Parish, as you probably know. Go to him if you can, if you get in any kind of trouble. His place is about three miles above the point. Skylark Hill, he calls it, but most people still call it the Old Marmillon Place."

"I know I sound like a timid old maid," said January deprecatingly. "I hear most people can travel pretty safe—I hear even Marie Laveau went upriver for a bit, last month."

The engineer chuckled. "That she did. Took a cabin on the *Lancaster,* bold as paint, is what Guidry on the *Lancaster* told me, and put a gris-gris on his engine room into the bargain, for them lettin' her off at the old Black Oak landing like she asked, and tellin' off the *Jefferson* to pick her up there again on their way down. I'd sure like to see some slave stealer try to mess with *that* lady." He threw back his head and laughed richly, relishing the picture of the slave stealers' discomfiture. "Now that I truly would."

It was five thirty, and close to sunset, when the *Philadelphia* finally backed out of the wharf. From among a group of black freedmen and free colored laborers on the bottom deck, January nervously watched the banks slide by, wondering how from the height of the texas deck Mr. Graham could possibly navigate among the slanting shadows, the hot, hard glare of brazen sun on the water and then the fast-falling twilight that changed every snag, every bar, every line of ripples from moment to moment as he watched.

The engineer hadn't lied about the pilot's skill. Once clear of what had been the Hurst plantation, now divided up into house lots, the river's banks deteriorated. Hugging them close, out of the heavy strength of the main channel that swept the downstream-bound boats so quickly by, was a matter of avoiding fallen trees; submerged mud spits; hidden obstacles; and, January reflected uneasily, the corpses of other boats that had come to grief on similar debris.

How the pilots did it January didn't know, but in a very short time he saw the lights of the Carrollton wharf twinkling primrose through just-gathering dusk. They stopped there and went through what seemed to him to be an endless, fiddling rigmarole of offloading cargo, taking on passengers, holding the boat while the passengers went hunting for the youngest member of their family who had wandered away; no, wait, Mr. Slow-Toad and his worthless wife and family want to get off here after all. *Luggage? Good heavens, sir, we did have luggage! Let's send the slowest waiter onboard to look for it while we all stand here and talk. . . .*

Between Carrollton and Twelve-Mile Point lay about three miles of fickle shadows and dark water inhabited by every snag, bar, and submerged tree in Louisiana—*sea-serpents, too, belike,* thought January gloomily, watching the matte, dark cutouts of the trees glide by.

Alligators, anyway.

Sixteen years ago, when he'd left Louisiana for France, nothing but cane and *cipriere* lay between Girod Street and Baton Rouge. Even then, the plantation of Bellefleur where he had been born had been sold and subdivided. He knew the names of the streets between which it had lain, but was not able to pick out where they were, behind the levee. In time Bellefleur and all who had dwelt there would be forgotten.

In his mind it still stood, and presumably in Olympe's, and his mother's: the whitewashed brick house, and the quarters; the cypress swamp through which his father was pursued, endlessly, by red-eyed hounds in dreams.

His elbows on the railing, January closed his eyes. The heavy churning of the water only a few feet below him, the throb of the engine, shuddered in his bones, but not enough to shake out those memories of innocence and love and pain.

You were born in the country, in thick hot rain and the smell of burnt sugar, the silence and the cicadas and the frogs. You waited on the gallery in the dark for your father to come, and he never did. Where do you go now?

Ayasha.

Rose.

She'd flinched from his touch. . . . *Don't* . . .

Did he think if he found Cora for her—rescued her friend from the men who'd taken her, cleared her name so that she could come back without being hanged for the murder of the man who'd raped her every day for the past who knew how many years—always supposing that she *was* innocent—that Rose would fall into his arms?

But he didn't want her to fall into his arms.

We all need friends, he thought. Although it was not wholly friendship in his mind when he saw again the cocoa brown tendrils of Rose's hair lying soft over her cheeks, the thin angular shape of her shoulders in her blue-and-yellow dress.

Ayasha rose to his mind, the way her hot black eyes flamed when he admired another woman, the desert-witch smile. *Oh, a friend is what you want, is it, malik?*

Yes, he whispered. *Yes. I am lonely, and I want a friend.*

Under his feet he felt the engines change their note. From somewhere above a man yelled, "Back her! Back her! Bring her around!"

The twilight was still luminously clear, delicate as the heart of a blue topaz, like water through which all things seemed perfect, without shadow or light. He saw the cluster of cypress on the batture, the floating wooden platform of the landing at Twelve-Mile Point.

When he climbed the levee, his grip in his hand, the world was an identical patchwork, long thin strips of new-growing cane, rustling corn black in the twilight, trees like clouds sleeping on the ground where they guarded the houses of the whites.

The lacy ghost of the *Philadelphia* floated away into the gloom around Twelve-Mile Point, but he could see its lights twinkle for some time. Lights burned, too, in the houses among the trees, until from the top of the levee he saw a big white house in the circle of its gallery and its trees that showed no lights, and whose fields, when he walked down through them, were already rank with the quick-growing weeds of these tropical lands.

There was no smell of human habitation; not around the privies of the big house or around the cabins of the slaves. No cattle in the barns or horses in the stables. January wondered if the Reverend Dunk had convinced Madame Redfern to sell these, too, to him for half what they were worth. The woman seemed clever, sharp, and hard as a horseshoe nail. But January had seen her simper like a girl as the man of God kissed her hands.

People would be here Monday, to look over the house before buying it. Maybe sooner.

Among the slave cabins he took candle and lucifers from his grip and made enough of a light to look into one or two, to make sure they weren't inhabited by anything or anyone else. The sight of them jabbed something inside him, as if he'd closed his hand on cloth with a needle still in it: the single big pine-pole bed each family shared— two beds if it was a large cabin and two families shared it. Pegs where clothing had hung, where pots had been removed. In one cabin someone had left a banjo, a five-stringed instrument of a skin stretched over a gourd.

January went back up to the big house, and drew himself water from the well. Returning to the cabin where the banjo was, he shook up the straw tick and tightened the bed-ropes, then for the first time since childhood lay down under a slave-cabin roof. He thought the place would trouble him, or the fear of discovery, of being kidnapped as Cora had been kidnapped. At least the ghosts who'd died there, of pneumonia or overwork, would whisper in the corners.

But he prayed for them, those nameless ones, with his battered blue rosary, asking God's rest for their souls. The deep silence of the country, the whirring of the cicadas and the peeping of the frogs in the swamp, was a sound of comfort to him, a song from his childhood. He realized that this was the first night since July that he had not worked among the sick, the dying, and the dead.

He slept, and no one visited him in his dreams.

THIRTEEN

The Redfern house at Spanish Bayou was fairly new, built in the American style probably not more than a decade before. Square, brick, it had a pillared porch and galleries front and back instead of all around, as was the French or Spanish way. It was painted blue instead of whitewashed or stuccoed, the shutters of the windows painted yellow, an astonishing piece of ostentation, considering the price of coloring agents in paint. Instead of all the rooms opening onto the gallery they opened inward, into a central hall. *They'll never believe I'm not here to rob the place,* January thought, as he flipped loose the catch of a ground-floor window.

His mother would disown him.

Inside there was the same elaboration, the same display, that he recognized from the Lalaurie house, though without Madame Lalaurie's exquisite taste. Where Madame Lalaurie's parlor might boast a marble-topped bureau touched up with gilt handles and hinges, here were tables of black marble crusted with ormolu, jewelers' work rather than cabinetmakers', and a bad jeweler at that. Thick-stuffed brocade furniture in the German style instead of the spare, cool French; four sets of china laden with curlicues and scroll-work instead of the single, elegant Limoges.

It was the house of a woman frantic to have the best.

And it would all be sold.

No wonder Emily Redfern was angry enough to do murder.

Twilight, Shaw had said. Presumably just before the windows—American casements, far less easy to trip from the outside—were closed up for the night. If Cora had come here Tuesday it would have been simpler: into the study, take the pearls and the money, then out the same way. And there was the chance that if another servant saw her, they wouldn't realize yet that she'd run away.

If it had been Wednesday—how soon before the arrival of the boat at the Spanish Bayou wharf? How fast could a slim young girl run, when she heard the hoot of the boat whistle?—it would be more difficult by far, if she'd slipped from the study, down the central hall to the warming-pantry where she'd have had access to supper. If it had been earlier yet, before supper was finished cooking, it became more complicated. She'd have had to cross the open yard to the kitchen, where the cook would certainly have seen her. Would she have risked that, twenty-four hours after she'd gone missing, with no possibility of a shrug and a lie? *Oh, I was just off in the woods for a little, I wasn't going to run away. Sir.*

It grated on January's nerves to go upstairs. Should anyone come in, he'd be cut off from escape, but he knew he had no choice. The Redferns had slept in separate rooms: his plainly furnished, the pieces new but not extravagant, hers a fantasia of ruffles, lace, silk, carving, and gilt. It was hers that he searched. She'd put the red-and-gold candy tin up inside the fireplace, in a sort of ledge on the inside of the mantel. It was the fourth place January checked.

Foolish, he thought, opening the tin. At least she'd had the sense to dump out the rest of the monkshood, leaving only fragments and powder in the seams of the tin itself. But then, the slaves' children probably checked the rubbish heap regularly for broken china and bits of scraps, and if she was supposed to be so sick from the poison-ing that she couldn't leave her bed she'd hardly have been able to throw it down the outhouse.

He wrapped the tin carefully in two handkerchiefs, so as not to confuse whatever marks might still be on it, and stowed it in his grip.

In the warming-pantry at the back of the house he searched drawers until he found what he guessed would be there: Emily Redfern's menu for the week of the fifteenth. Of course Bernard Marigny's stuck-up yellow fussbudget cook would do things the French way. He'd consult his mistress over a written menu, which would be amended in her hand.

And there it was. On the eighteenth of September the fare had consisted of turtle soup, sautéed shrimp and mushrooms, grilled tournedos of beef, roasted guinea hen, rice and gravy, fresh green beans, with jam crêpes and berry cobbler for dessert. Breakfast, he was interested to note, had originally been omelettes and creamed gizzards with waffles and jam, but had been augmented—apparently at the last minute—with apple tarts, ham, and crêpes.

Company for breakfast? Michie Otis returning in a foul mood after being threatened by Roarke and his bravos in full view of Monsieur Davis's gambling hall?

It was still early morning, barely eight by the sun. The *Lancaster* would not be coming down the reach above Twelve-Mile Point until three at the earliest. Cora Chouteau had spoken of Black Oak, as lying next to Spanish Bayou. Coming along the top of the levee last night he had seen that on the upriver side of the Redfern property there was only cultivated land. Downstream, however, lay a long tangle of woodlot and swamp, through which the bayou meandered in a couple of lazy curves.

January drew another pail of well water and ate some of the bread and cheese he'd packed and added to this apples from the small orchard behind the house, or what passed in Louisiana for apples anyway. It was a walk of about two miles, on the narrow paths between the canes, to the silent woods of black oak and ash, the suffocating green gloom of the slip of property that had been Madame Redfern's own.

The house here was much older than her husband's, and smaller, an old Creole dwelling from a time when Black Oak had been a proper, if minor, plantation. Like Mademoiselle Vitrac's school, the building was three rooms raised above three low storage chambers, with a couple of *cabinets* tacked onto the back for good measure. The kitchen and the quarters beyond had long ago crumbled to nothing, swallowed up in thickets of hackberry and elder when the fields had been bought up by the bigger planters on either side. Stripped of its whitewash by the weather, the house itself bore signs within of leakage, storm damage, and vermin.

January found the candle cupboard in the side of the fireplace where Cora had discovered the tin of poison. The small, square hollow had a lock, but had been opened, and was empty. In another room a pile of old leaves and branches was spread with a couple of blankets. Here Cora and Gervase had shared the only privacy, the only happiness, permitted those whose bodies and lives and service belong to other people.

He looked through the rest of the house, opening cupboards, looking in fireplaces, not sure what he was seeking or what he thought he might find. People had been in and out, that much was clear from the way the dirt on the floor was scuffed up, but who they might have been he could not tell. He went out on the gallery, where Cora said she had seen Mamzelle Marie waiting in the twilight. But beyond ascertaining that the path back to Spanish Bayou did emerge from the oleander bushes at a point where someone on the porch *could* easily see someone approaching the old house unawares, he found nothing.

There was a well between the house and where the kitchen had been, and the water in it was still good. He drank, and washed himself, and changed back into his white shirt, bettermost trousers, sober waistcoat, and black coat and hat; and so attired, made his way the three-quarters of a mile or so through a frog-peeping hush of red oak, hickory, palmetto, and vine to the levee once again, and so upstream to the plantation called Skylark Hill.

From the top of the levee he saw that there was, in fact, an old landing sheltered behind a tree-grown bar at Black Oak, as well as the one at Spanish Bayou. Easy to come there, to walk up to the house, to wait . . . or simply to leave a small red-and-gold candy tin, and walk down to the landing again. And later, easy for a small, stout woman to walk down from the Big House—for instance, on the day when her husband had gone into town to advertise for his runaway mistress—to collect the tin. Particularly when the hours stretched out into a familiar absence that meant the gambling tables yet again.

If that was in fact what had happened.

January was very interested to see what the actual death certificate—and the parish magistrate-cum-coroner—would have to say.

He settled his official-looking beaver hat more firmly on his head, and turned his steps inland once again at the tidy, oyster-shell road that bore the sign SKYLARK HILL.

"Mr. Bailey, sir?" The butler at Skylark Hill spoke the English of one raised among the Americans. There were more and more in Louisiana who spoke no French at all.

He handed January his card back and made his bow, but not as much of a bow as if the caller had been white. "Mr. Bailey's gone to Milneburgh, sir. He should be back on Monday, if you'd care to come then."

January thanked the man, but something of his thoughts must have showed in his eyes, for the butler added, "If you wish to go on back to the kitchen, I'm sure Polly can get you something to eat, to set you on your way."

It was slaves' fare, but not bad for all that: black-eyed peas with a little ham, rice and ginger-water, for the day was hot. After a little thought January changed clothes again in the back room of the Skylark Hill kitchens—the old Creole-style house had been pulled down and replaced by a moderate American dwelling, but the original Marmillon kitchen survived—and set off walking, first along the top of the levee as far as Carrollton, then inland till he reached Bayou Metairie, and so along the shell road through the dense green shade of the swamps toward the lake.

Where the McCarty lands ran into those of the Allard and Judge Martin plantations, the bayou joined the greater Bayou St. John. January crossed at Judge Martin's stone bridge there and continued along the Bayou Road. He felt a little safer, this close to New Orleans, but never ceased to listen before him and behind. Each time he heard the crunch of hooves approaching from either direction he quickly left the oyster-shell pathway and waited in the woods until whoever was passing him had vanished from sight.

Stopping to rest frequently, for the day's heat was savage, he reached Milneburgh shortly after three in the afternoon. The first place he sought was Catherine Clisson's little house, on London Avenue near the lake. As he expected, he found his mother on the porch with her cronies, fanning herself with a painted silk fan and systematically destroying every reputation they could lay tongue to. While still some distance away, hidden by the scattering of pines, he heard Agnes Pellicot's voice: ". . . heartless as a cat. And positively helping herself to the funds . . ."

"Well, you could tell *that* just to look at her." The sweet, throbbing tones belonged to Euphrasie Dreuze, who fancied herself the victim of the world. "If you ask me, Agnes, you really were too trusting to let your daughter . . ."

"Is that you, Ben?" Catherine Clisson rose from her chair and shaded her eyes, slim and straight and lovely as the night in her gown of simple white lawn. "Nothing's happened, has it? To Olympe? Or the children?"

"Not that I've heard," January replied. "I've been out of town since yesterday afternoon. I'm looking for a man named Bailey, a white man, magistrate of St. Charles Parish. He's supposed to be in town."

The women looked at one another, frowning and shaking their heads. Even January's mother was stumped, but she raised her nose loftily and said, "What would you want with some white magistrate, Ben? An American, too, he sounds like. They all are, these days." She had a way of pronouncing the word *American* that implied a world of lice and tobacco stains.

"Binta!" Madame Clisson rose, and called back into the house. When her maid appeared—considerably lighter-skinned than she, January noted—she asked, "Have you heard of a magistrate from St. Charles Parish in town? A M'sieu Bailey?"

As January had observed before, everybody always knew everything. Half an hour later he was being ushered by a hotel servant onto the rear veranda of the Hotel Pontchartrain, where Mr. Bailey rose politely from a wicker chair and held out his hand.

"Mr. Rillieux?" he said—Rillieux being the name on the business card January had sent in, one of several from Hannibal's extensive collection. "You asked to see me?"

"I did indeed, sir." He'd changed at Madame Clisson's back into the black coat, white shirt, and high-crowned hat again. "Please forgive the imposition, Mr. Bailey, but I'm a physician, doing research on the pathologies of various types of poisons, particularly those in use among the Negro slaves." What the original Monsieur Rillieux did for a living he had no idea, since the cards Hannibal collected were generally those bearing only a name. He used his best English, silently thanking the schoolmasters who'd drubbed it into him. It worked far better than any business card could have. "I understand that you've recently had a case of poisoning in your own parish."

"Ah!" Bailey's face darkened with genuine sorrow. The magistrate was a much younger man than January had expected, the breadth and strength of his shoulders according oddly with a build that was in fact rather slight. "A very sad case, that; quite tragic. Personal friends of mine . . ."

"I'm terribly sorry, sir. If you'd rather not speak of it . . ."

"No, no." Bailey shook his head, black hair shiny with pomade. "No, it's one of the griefs of my office to attend at the deaths of people I know. From the description it was quite clearly a case of some sort of vegetable poison. Monkshood was my guess, from the dryness and paralysis of the vocal cords—"

" 'From the description?' " asked January, startled. "You weren't there?"

"No, as it happens. I had gone to town the previous day on business, and stayed to oversee the delivery of a team of my carriage-horses. Due to a mixup I didn't receive word of the death until the day of the funeral. I suppose I should count myself fortunate, since I dined there the evening before my departure, but I can't convince myself I was in any danger. The attack—the intent of her attack— was all too clear." His neat fingers smoothed the slip of mustache.

"From Mrs. Redfern's descriptions of her own symptoms, and the accounts of the servants, it was almost certainly aconite, or wolfsbane: monkshood is the common name for it in this country."

January nodded and sat patiently through a catalog of symptoms with which he was already familiar: burning and tingling of the tongue and face, vomiting, difficulty in drawing breath, a sensation of bitter cold. Monsieur Montalban, back in Paris, had displayed them all. Bailey, thank God, seemed a reliable witness, relating what he had heard with a minimum of speculation, aware of the significance of details. "The first symptoms appeared, according to Mrs. Redfern, shortly after dinner on Wednesday evening. The servants said the master complained of a burning in his mouth first, and within a quarter hour the mistress did as well. Either she had eaten more of the untainted food than he, or the alcohol remaining in his system—I understand he had been in town all the previous night—accelerated the effects of the poison, as well as rendering them more severe. He died later that same night; and though poor Mrs. Redfern was extremely ill throughout the night and the following day, she survived."

His lips pursed, and he shook his head. "It was a sad business, Mr. Rillieux, a sad business indeed, for he left her deeply in debt."

And with the Reverend Micajah Dunk buying her slaves and her cattle at the lowest possible prices, January thought dryly, as he thanked the magistrate and descended the gallery steps once more, it was unlikely that she'd get out of debt any time soon.

"And the girl herself?" he asked. "I understand one of the servants said he saw her about the house?"

Bailey looked surprised. "I'd heard nothing about that," he said.

The day was hot. The city would be wretched, thought January, taking off his hat as he walked back toward Madame Clisson's house along the level, sandy beach. The breeze from the lake flowed over his face, exquisite in his sweat-damp, close-cropped hair. The temptation was overwhelming to leave the dying in Charity Hospital to their own devices—*let the dead bury their own dead*—and remain here tonight. Clisson, at least, would give him space to sleep above the kitchen of the little cottage on London Street.

He walked as far as the long wharf of the Washington Hotel's bathhouse, nearly a thousand feet out in the warm shallow waters of the lake, then ascended the gentle slope to the grounds of the hotel itself.

He wondered what Emily Redfern would have to say about the time and circumstances of her husband's death to an enquirer about poisons in use by those of African descent, but when he sent up his card—or more properly the card of one Hilaire Brun—a servant informed him that Mrs. Redfern had gone into town. "She got this letter, see," the boy said, when January handed him a half-reale. "She sent for that Reverend Dunk that's staying here, and they both went off for town in his gig, 'cause she don't have no carriage no more."

"Did you see who the letter was from?" January held out another half-reale.

The boy nodded, though he seemed a little puzzled at the obviousness of the question. "It was from a letter-carrier, sir."

January wondered whether it was worth his while to try again in the morning.

When he reached Madame Clisson's cottage, only his mother and Euphrasie Dreuze still occupied the porch. Madame Dreuze was saying, ". . . wouldn't be at all surprised if she was feathering her own nest all along! I'm sure she didn't feed those poor girls enough to—"

They broke off as January came up to the porch.

"Your sister's sick," said the Widow Levesque bluntly, snapping shut the crimson silk fan. "The baby, too. I told that maid of Dominique's when she came over here I'd send you on to have a look, but in heat like this I don't see what the good of it is."

January felt the cold clutch of terror in his heart. Not Minou . . .

"I'll be there," he said.

That night he wrote to Hannibal Sefton, care of his mother's house, that he would be delayed in Milneburgh for as many as three or four days. He asked Hannibal, if at all possible, to check the barracoons of Dutuillet or Hewlett's or the St. Charles Exchange to see if any of the former house servants of Emily Redfern still remained in the city.

Of Abishag Shaw, he asked the same, adding in his note that though the local magistrate of St. Charles Parish had signed the death certificate of Otis Redfern, no investigation of the death had been performed and only the widow's word existed as to her husband's symptoms or her own.

And in between mixing saline draughts for Dominique, and sponging Charles-Henri's tiny, brittle frame with vinegar-water and cream of tartar, he would sometimes unwrap the red-and-gold candy tin from his grip, and wonder where, and when, he ought to confess to Lieutenant Shaw that he had spoken to Cora Chouteau and was an accessory after the fact to the murder that she had not done.

What use to find Cora, if she would only be returned to be hanged?

Yet he could not leave her where she was—wherever that was.

Head aching, he would return to Dominique's feverish murmurings, and the patient, endless, agonizing work of dripping saline draught thinned with a little milk into Charles-Henri's tiny mouth.

On the second night he understood that he was going to lose the child.

It happens, he thought, while the pain of the realization sank through him slowly, like a stone dropped in a bog's peaty waters. His mother had lost her first two babies by St. Denis Janvier—not that his mother had cared more than a cat cares about one drowned kitten more or less. Not many weeks ago Catherine Clisson had spoken to him of a child she'd lost, a boy of four, and he knew Olympe had had at least one still-birth. New Orleans was an unhealthy place at best, and it was dangerous to birth a child in the time of plague.

Still, he thought, looking from the white wicker cradle across at the white-draped bed where his sister lay, it was a grief he would have spared her. Life held grief enough.

Coming out of the bedroom he found Henri Viellard, dressed for a party in a coat of prune-colored superfine and a vest the hue of new lettuces, sitting on the cypress-wood divan. The fat man stood up quickly—January had not been completely aware before this of how tall he was, easily six feet. "Will she be all right?" he asked.

"I don't know." It was the middle of the evening, not midnight. Phlosine Seurat, when she had brought a blancmange for Minou and some étouffée for January, said there would be a danceable at the St.

Clair to which everyone who was anyone in Creole society was going. He wondered what this man had told his mother.

"May I see her?"

January stepped out of the doorway. "She's sleeping," he warned.

Henri paused beside him, gray eyes anxious behind the thick rounds of glass. "That's good, isn't it? I understand that with . . . with the fever . . . sleep is healing. Normal sleep, that is."

January nodded. "But it isn't the fever," he said. "It's milk sickness, which is just as serious."

A look of surprise flickered behind the spectacles, followed by relief. "Oh," said Henri, a little foolishly. "Oh, I was told . . ." He turned quickly to go on into the room, then hesitated and turned back. "Is there anything I can do? For you, I mean. You must be done up. If you need to rest I can sit with her. Do whatever you tell me to do. It's what I came for."

Even though you thought she had yellow fever, thought January. *Even though your mama probably told you to stay at whatever ball she's giving tonight.*

The anger he had felt at this man melted, and he smiled. "In that case, yes, I could use a little rest. I thank you, sir."

The shutters were fastened and the muslin curtains drawn, but plague or no plague, January felt he must breathe clean air, or die. Smudges of lemongrass and gunpowder burned on the gallery over the water, keeping at bay the mosquitoes which, though fewer than in town, could be found even along the lakeshore. Legs dangling over the water, arms draped on the gallery's cypress rail, January gazed at the constellations of rose and citrine light burning through the trees far along the shoreline. On the heavy air, Haydn and Mozart drifted like the smoke of some far-off battle.

Henri fell asleep shortly before dawn, on the daybed in Minou's room; his infant son died about an hour later, in January's arms. January wrapped the wasted little fragment of flesh and bone in a clean towel, and set it aside in the *cabinet* at the back of the house, where neither of the baby's parents would see. Then he went back to sponging Dominique's flushed, burning face and body with cool water, trying to bring her fever down. As he worked he whispered the prayers of the Rosary, not counting decades, but simply repeating them over and over again: *Hail, Mary, full of grace. The Lord is with thee.*

It kept him from thinking. Kept him from wondering if this fate would have overtaken Ayasha, had she borne him the child she had been almost certain she carried the week before her death. Kept him from wondering what point there was in carrying on.

Pray for us sinners, now and at the hour of our death.

Not, *Keep us from dying,* as Olympe would petition the *loa* to do, with colored candles and the blood of chickens and mice. *Pray for us at the hour of our death. Hold our hands in the dark. Get us across that wide water safely.*

He looked down at his sister's face, and felt a great weariness inside.

He wanted Rose. Wanted to talk to her, about Minou's child, and death; about a dozen other things. It might be months, it might be years, and it might be never, before he could lie with her, talking in the night as he and Ayasha used to talk of matters that do not enter daytime conversation. But in the meantime—or even if not—he wanted Rose as a friend in this smoky world of injustice and contagion and deceit.

Feet vibrated on the gallery. January rose from Dominique's bedside and dried his hands, thankful there was someone he could send for the undertaker, for it was clear that Minou could not be left. Opening the door, he saw Agnes Pellicot, a fashionably decorated straw bonnet on over her tignon and a porcelain crock of something warm and spicy wrapped in a towel in her hands. Behind her, shy and awkward in sprigged white muslin with a long blue sash, was Marie-Neige.

"Marie-Neige," said January, startled, even before he bowed and took Agnes Pellicot's hand in greeting. "Madame Pellicot, I . . . I thought Marie-Neige was in school in town. There hasn't been a problem . . . ?"

"Problem?" She sniffed, and at his gesture of invitation crossed the threshold in a swish of crinoline. "I don't know how much you know about that stuck-up hussy Vitrac, but I never trusted her from the very start. And the thought that I'd leave my poor little one at some school in town at this time, like some other women I could mention . . ."

"What happened?" He took the crock of jambalaya without being aware of it, stood stupid in the middle of the room with it in his hands.

"What happened? The lazy slut let three of those poor little girls die—*three of them!* What their mothers can have been thinking of to leave them there with her . . ."

Like you did all summer?

"Mama . . ."

"Hush, darling, about things you know nothing of." Madame Pellicot turned back to January, bristling with indignation. "Well, I should have known, but of course she was sly, and I wanted my dearest Marie-Neige to have all the very best. But I never felt comfortable with it. I always felt uneasy. I—"

"What happened?"

"Really, Ben, you don't need to take that tone. And set that jambalaya down. It's hot and you're like to drop it." She unpinned her hat from her tignon, straightened the neck-ruffle of her dress. "I took Marie-Neige out of that dreadful place yesterday. The woman was a complete fraud, I knew it from the first."

"Mama . . ."

"Hush, darling, you know that I'm right. And don't pick at your glove buttons; those gloves cost seventy-five cents. And I *was* right," she added, pausing on her way to the bedchamber. "Not enough that she was harboring a runaway—"

"That's a lie! Where did you hear that?" Cold congealed in him, like steel shot behind his breastbone.

"A lie, is it?" Pellicot planted her hands on her ample hips. "A lot you know of it, out here, M'sieu! The police came and got her yesterday, and a good thing it was that I'd been warned to take my dearest Marie-Neige out in time. *And* the things they found out about her, once they turned that school of hers inside out. Stealing her investors' money, shorting the girls on food. . . . No wonder the poor things couldn't survive the fever! I only wonder my poor little darling didn't starve, although really, dear," she lifted an admonitory finger to her poor little darling, "now that you're back with your mama you'll have to do something about your weight. Gentlemen are not attracted to young ladies whose waists are above eighteen inches, and a round face is never kissed, you know. . . ."

"That's a lie," said January softly. "It isn't true. Rose—Mademoiselle Vitrac—she does the best she can with what she has, but she would never steal money."

Pellicot's eyes narrowed. "And how well do *you* know Mademoiselle Vitrac, pray? Marie-Neige," she added sharply, as the girl began to speak again, "maybe it's best that you run along to the cottage, if you can't learn to be seen and not heard. And don't let me find you've eaten so much as a morsel until I get there! Really, you've simply turned into a little piglet since you were at that school.

"It will take me months to undo the damage that *vache* has done," she continued, as Marie-Neige obediently stepped through the front door and retreated down the shell path toward New York Street. "And I refuse to argue the matter with you, Ben." She took off her lace mitts. Her hands, though fine, were large and competent looking, with nails polished like jewelers' work. She disposed of her reticule, picked up Henri Viellard's dark plush coat and settled it over the back of a chair, and passed into the bedroom as she spoke, checking the water in the pitcher and moving Henri's spectacles to a safer place as she went.

She paused for a moment, looking down at the empty wicker cradle, and her eyes met January's over it. He saw in them the shine of tears. Then she turned away again and stood beside Dominique's bed, folding back her pink voile sleeves.

"Be so good as to go down to Decker's store for ice, would you, Ben? There's some come in on the boat from town, at twenty-five cents a pound. Take some money out of that *cochon*'s purse for it." She nodded down at the sleeping Henri. "Left word for his mother at the ball last night he had a migraine, I've heard, and she's fit to be tied this morning, for, of course, she wasn't fooled a moment—he slipped away when she was in the cloakroom."

She shook her head, and leaning down, touched Minou's cheeks with the backs of her fingers. "And speak to Mr. Bailey at the Pontchartrain—the magistrate, you know," she added. "Poor Minou. We'll pull her through." And then, as though ashamed of being caught in sympathy, she went on briskly, "Run along now. And if you see your mother, tell her I'm here."

It was another thirty-six hours before January could leave Milneburgh. During that time, unable to leave Minou's side, he was forced to listen to Agnes Pellicot discuss the shutting-down of Rose Vitrac's school with his mother, with Catherine Clisson, and with any of Dominique's friends who came to offer help and support. By the time his sister's fever broke, shortly after noon on Tuesday, January could be in no doubt that Rose Vitrac's school had been searched by the police, though rumors varied as to whether Rose herself had been arrested. But everyone who had heard anything of the matter seemed to agree that Mademoiselle Vitrac had harbored a runaway slave, and that three girls in the school had died, just as if, thought January furiously, people weren't dying in every street and building of the town.

As darkness was falling he boarded the steam-train for town, jostling along in the rear carriage listening to the whine of mosquitoes in the dimness of the swamps.

The raised Spanish house on Rue St. Claude was closed like a fist, lightless on the moonless street. The stenches of burning hooves, of sickness, of privies clotted the damp air like glue. The bell on the cathedral was chiming nine. Somewhere a man called, "Bring out your dead." January walked on, regardless of the curfew, down Rue St. Philippe and along Rue Chartres, past mute dark houses with the planks propped up beside their doors, past pharmacies whose windows glowed with plague-red jars and bottles, his shadow monstrous on the walls.

"What you doin' out this time o' night, boy?" demanded the sergeant at the desk, looking up as January came through the Cabildo's great double doors.

Before leaving Minou's he had changed again into his black coat, his waistcoat and beaver hat, knowing he'd need to be perceived as a free man of color despite the blackness of his skin, which said "slave." Now he took his papers from his pocket and said in his most Parisian French, "My name is January, sir. I'm one of the surgeons working at Charity." *And I'm not your goddamned boy.* "I've been in Milneburgh with a sick woman and child. I've just returned to learn that three of my patients at Mademoiselle Vitrac's school on Rue St. Claude have died, and I'm trying to learn something of the matter. I understand that I might find Mademoiselle Vitrac here?"

Not in the Cabildo, he prayed, sickened at the image of Rose in those filthy cells that flanked the gallery, among the madwomen and prostitutes. *Not here.* He had spent a night once in the oven-hot, verminous cells: he would not have wished such a thing on his worst foe.

But he kept his voice impersonal, his demeanor respectful of the two or three blue-clothed Guards who lounged on the stone benches of the corner office. The sergeant at the desk—a square-faced, square-handed American—shuffled around in his papers. Outside in the Place d'Armes, voices lifted in angry shouts:

"You're a fool, and can't dance!"

"Consarn if I don't make daylight shine through your gizzard quicker'n lightnin' can run around a potato patch!"

"Is Lieutenant Shaw available, sir? He'll vouch for me. Please tell him Benjamin January is asking after him, if you would, please."

"Benjamin January?" The sergeant raised his head again. He looked sweaty and worn, piggy eyes sunk in bruises of sleeplessness and jaw scrummed with two days' growth of beard. "Got a note here for you. Mademoiselle Vitrac was released yesterday morning. I don't know the right of it, but charges against her were dropped."

"What was she charged with?"

But the man only shook his head, and held out to him a folded sheet of paper between stubby fingers. "She left this. Seemed to think you'd come here lookin' for her. Looks like she was right."

His eyes followed January suspiciously as January carried the paper to one of the oil lamps that burned in brackets around the walls. They did little to illumine the murk, but holding the paper close, January was able to read.

The letter was written in Latin.

Of course, thought January, fingering the much-thumbed edges of the page. *They'd try to read it.* No wonder the sergeant was suspicious. He wondered if someone like Monsieur Tremouille, the Chief of Police, had succeeded.

Monsieur Janvier—

If you receive this you will have heard something of what has befallen. The police came yesterday, and found hidden in the building a string of pearls and a quantity of money that they claim links me to a runaway slave, whom they likewise claim was a girl I knew in my youth.

[*Why didn't you get rid of the pearls?* thought January furiously. *I told you to throw them in the river!* At least she'd taken into account the possibility that they'd show the note to someone who had been to a proper school.]

The day before their arrival, Antoinette, Victorine, and Geneviève all succumbed, at last, to the fever. I sent word to you, but you had already left for Milneburgh, and later events prevented me from writing you there. Occupied as I was with them I could not give my full mind to matters when Madame Pellicot and Madame Moine came to remove their daughters from the school, though I understand that rumors have begun that I speculated with the school's money. These rumors are untrue, and I am at a loss to understand how or why they began.

The fact remains that I am ruined. I understand people are even blaming me for the deaths of my poor girls. I know it will be impossible for me to open the school again, even should I find pupils. At the moment I have no idea where I will or can go, or what I can do.

I may have little experience with the ways of the world, but I do know that calumny is a contagion far more to be dreaded than our friend Bronze John, and even your slight association with me in caring for the girls might be held against you by the malicious. Therefore I ask your indulgence. I know that I owe you the money we agreed upon for the girls' care . . .

[*What money?* A moment later he realized that the sentence was for the benefit of those who might read the letter, and wonder why else he would wish to seek her out.]

194

. . . but please, for your own sake, do not attempt to locate me. I will send the money to you in good time. I do not forget all the kindnesses you have done.

Thank you for the help you gave me with the girls. Without your timely assistance, matters would be far worse than they were. I am sorry that I cannot thank you in person, but you must see, as I do, that it is better we never meet again.

The letter was signed, not in Latin, but in Greek: more difficult for January to read, but impossible, he thought, for others to spy out.

He recognized it as a quote from Euripides.

Ουδεισ αλαστορ τοισ πηιλοισ εκ τον πηιλον.

It took him a few moments to translate:

Nothing can come between true friends.
Rose

"Obviously, someone talked."

Hannibal folded up his copy of *Emma* and leaned over to trim the tallow lights that transformed his little tent of mosquito-bar into a glowing amber box. Returning to his mother's house, with the dense, hot smell of storms brewing over the Gulf, January saw the thread of light beneath the door of Bella's room; even on those nights when he was sober and not working, Hannibal seldom slept before three.

"My guess is Isabel Moine, who never wanted to be at that school and hated learning of any sort. I know she'd written her parents two or three times asking for them to come and get her, and they wouldn't—Victorine told me this, one night when she couldn't get to sleep."

His brow pinched with compassion at the memory of the three girls. "They took a turn for the worse—well, Antoinette was losing ground all the way along—and they went quickly, in spite of everything Rose and I could do. Rose took it hard."

"Do you know where she is?"

Hannibal shook his head. "I went down there Sunday afternoon, and they said they'd released her, in spite of the evidence being pretty damning. Shaw wasn't there, and nobody would tell me anything. I don't know what happened to change everybody's mind."

He reached down to the pottery jug beside the bed and offered some to January, who was sitting on the end of the bed. It was ginger-beer, lukewarm but not unpleasant. Far off to the north above the lake thunder growled. Flares of sheet lightning outlined the shutters of the room's single French window.

"How long was she in the Calabozo?" Part of him didn't want to hear.

"Just the one night. Shaw did what he could for her—not that there's much one *can* do for someone in the circumstances."

January shut his eyes at the memory of the crawling mattresses, the stinking heat. At the thought of the fever, should it break out in those tiny, filthy cells.

Not Rose. Not Rose.

"The first night they took her, she wrote out a paper giving me quitclaim to her books—backdated to a week before her arrest, so they can't be seized in payment of her debts when they foreclose on the building. I've brought some of them over here already." Hannibal nodded. January had been vaguely aware of what, in the dense dark-ness, he had taken for packing boxes in the corners of the little room. Peering through the gloom, he saw now that they were stacks of books, piled crazily on top of one another.

"There's more in your room. And all the science texts and atlases yet to bring over. I've tried to find her," Hannibal added. "It was a long night, Friday. Geneviève must have died a little before sunset, but neither of us knew it at the time. Victorine and Antoinette both went just before dawn. As I said, Rose took it hard. I didn't like to leave her but she insisted, saying she needed to sleep. I went over there as soon as I was awake Saturday afternoon and found the place locked tight, with police seals on it. So I went to the Cabildo and she asked me to bring her some things like clean clothing and a comb and brush, and some paper and ink—that's when she gave me the books—and she told me what happened. The police evidently walked straight in and went to the compartment in her desk where she had the pearls. . . ."

"Why didn't she get rid of them?" moaned January. Somehow, it was all he could think of to say.

"Well," said Hannibal, "I did ask her that. She had some kind of idea of faking Cora's death to get pursuit off her and using the pearls as evidence of identity. Only, of course, the girls' illness intervened. She wouldn't write to you, and made me promise not to do so either. She said she had a note from you that morning saying that your sister was ill. Is Minou better?"

January nodded wearily. "Her baby died."

"Her first." The fiddler closed his eyes, as if seeing again the three girls in the stifling attic. "I'm sorry."

"It happens." January spoke without bitterness. His mind was full of disjointed pictures, reaching back and back through the previous days: Henri Viellard, asleep in the chair beside Minou's bed, clasping the hand of the sleeping woman. The soft chatter of the women in Minou's front room, and how they would come to keep him and Minou and one another company.

Whores, white society would call them, or those who didn't understand. But they looked after one another.

"Her friends are with her. I couldn't leave before this evening. Maybe it's best that neither of you wrote."

The pain in him was a hot weight, a fever he could not shake. A slow roll of thunder shuddered the air.

"I don't know," he whispered. He felt helpless, battered. Madame Clisson and Marie-Anne and Iphègénie had been there for Minou. Who had been there for Rose? "I don't know. Was she all right in the jail?"

"Well, she was pretty stunned," said Hannibal. "She said she kept thinking she was dreaming, or that this was all happening to someone else. This was after she started hearing the rumors about the money, too."

"What happened about that?" January looked up angrily. *I was warned,* Agnes Pellicot had said. "Who says that?"

Hannibal shook his head. "I only know it's being said. They locked up the school the day she was arrested—her creditors, and her backers, I mean, demanding it as an asset. Their agents, really, because, of course, all the Forstalls and Bringiers and McCartys are still at the lake. Hence the backdated quitclaim on the books. I've been sneaking them out a few at a time for the past three nights. Most of them are her personal possessions, anyway, not the school's. She's got a wonderful volume of the Lyric Poets in the original—I haven't seen this edition since I left Dublin.

> *Half-gone the night, and youth going—*
> *I lie alone.*

"She hasn't even been able to get in and get her own clothing; I looked. I've asked around the Swamp. . . ."

"She'd never go there." January hadn't meant the words to come out so harshly. He closed his fist against the urge to strike his friend across the face.

The fiddler's coffee black eyes were weary within the bruised erosion of lines. "No woman *goes* there," he said quietly. "But a lot of them end up there all the same. As it happens," he went on, as January opened his mouth again to protest, "she didn't, or hasn't yet. Myself, I think she's left the town completely."

January was silent. *I am ruined,* the note had said. *Every penny I own is tied up in this building. . . .*

And after all he felt for her—after running off to try to clear Cora for her—he hadn't been there when she most needed him. Only came in to view the wreckage, like the horrified survivor of a Euripides play. As he had come in on Ayasha, too late.

"Where?" January meant to speak a sentence. Only a word came out.

"Baton Rouge," guessed Hannibal promptly. "Though that's a little close to New Orleans, if she was planning on opening another school. Maybe Charleston. Maybe New York."

"Where would she get the money?"

And Hannibal only shook his head.

"There has to be some way to find her."

"And what?" Hannibal asked. Lightning flashed again, white and cold on his thin, lined face, overwhelming the small warmth of the candle.

January had no reply.

"She wouldn't come back, you know. Not to a town where she's been accused of harboring a murderess, or even a runaway slave, for that matter."

Still January said nothing. The thunder rolled over the town, far off and dim, like the breathing of some unknowable monstrosity in the distance.

Hannibal reached beneath his pillow, and brought out a sheet of creamy paper, on which Rose's penmanship lay like Italianate lace. "We have her books," he said logically. "If I know our Athene, it means we'll see her again."

In the breathless smolder of storm-weather, January made his way down the silent streets to the Cabildo the following morning. He found Abishag Shaw laboriously composing the report of the arrest of seven or eight men "of French and American extraction" for a brawl the previous evening that had begun outside the Ripsnorter Saloon on Gravier Street and had ended with a sordid biting, gouging, and hair-pulling match encompassing most of Canal Street. "Duellin', they swears it was." The Kentuckian sighed, shoving a greasy forelock out of his eyes. "With three or four so-called seconds per side takin' swings at each other an' everyone fallin' in and out of the gutters an' cussin' fit to break a parson's heart. We got the lot of 'em in the cells now, every man jack of 'em swearin' cross-eyed as how the others busted the 'Code' an' deserved the whalin' they got."

He leaned his bony elbows on the desk, arms extended flat on the plank surface like a resting cat, and blinked up at January with deceptively mild gray eyes. "I take it you come about Mademoiselle Vitrac?"

"Who told you Cora Chouteau took refuge with her?" January was far too angry to pretend he knew nothing of the matter now, and Shaw showed no surprise at the question. The letter January had sent asking for him to question Mrs. Redfern's servants lay between them on his desk.

"That Isabel girl," replied Shaw promptly. "Isabel Moine." Any other American would have pronounced it 'Moyne' instead of opening the vowel like a Frenchman. "I got to admit, Maestro, considerin' your friendship with the lady, and them inquiries you was makin' at Madame Lalaurie's, I wasn't tetotaciously astonished. And them pearls, and that sack of money, they was right where that girl said they was in the desk."

"Eavesdropping little bitch." Isabel's sulky dark face returned to him, flushed with sleep. The way Rose had brushed a strand of hair from the girl's lips. The affection in Rose's eyes, even for her. *Don't you rip up at her. . . .*

"Emily Redfern poisoned her husband. Cora found the poison the day before and fled, thinking it was intended for her. Maybe it was. She came to town on the *New Brunswick* Wednesday afternoon; half a dozen stevedores on the wharf can attest it was there by four, probably earlier than that. If the cook Leonide told you he saw Cora entering the house at twilight—"

"It was Mrs. Redfern that told me," said Shaw mildly, and spat in the direction of the sandbox. The brown expectorant fell short of its target by at least a yard. Fifteen or sixteen previous efforts marked the stone floor between box and desk. "The cook was gone by the time I spoke with her."

"The same way she told the magistrate about her own symptoms?" January produced the menus from his pocket, laid them on the desk. "That's what they ate for supper that night. Bring in any cook in the city and ask him; there isn't a thing there that takes over an hour to prepare. Cora Chouteau couldn't have poisoned the supper before she left."

Shaw turned the papers over with fingers like jointed oak sticks. "And you got these where?"

January met his eyes coldly. "The rubbish bins outside the house at Spanish Bayou." He opened his mouth to add, *This was in Emily Redfern's chimney,* but knew even as the words came to his lips that Shaw—and any lawyer—would only ask, Did Cora Chouteau have access to that chimney? And, of course, she had. So he waited, silent, while Shaw scratched his stubbled jaw.

"This is all very interestin', Maestro. And believe me, with your permission I'll sort of set it aside in a safe place to kind of ferment a spell, and see what else I can find. But I do think I should point out to you that even if Miss Chouteau gets cleared of Borgialatin' the soup herself, it ain't gonna win her freedom."

The lieutenant folded up the menus and secreted them in his desk. Scraps and shards of quill lay all over its tobacco-stained and scarified surface; the report he'd been working on looked as if a lizard had escaped from the inkwell and run madly about on the page.

At most, January thought, if Emily Redfern were hanged, Cora Chouteau would become the property of her estate. And he knew as he formed the words in his mind that Emily Redfern would never hang.

"I would suggest that you speak to Mademoiselle Vitrac about why Emily Redfern would want to shift the blame for the murder onto Cora," he said, more quietly. "Except that Emily Redfern seems to have taken pains to have her driven out of town in disgrace."

"Well, it's a funny thing about that." Shaw dug in the back of his desk drawer, and withdrew a double-strand of softly golden miniature moons. "Miz Redfern says these ain't her pearls. And that hundred and ninety dollars we found at the school—Miz Redfern says the money that feller Granville from the Bank of Louisiana paid her Tuesday was all in banknotes. Not a coin in the lot."

He trailed the pearls from one big hand to the other, as if admiring the smoothness of them, the organic satiny texture, like flower petals, so different from the jewels of the earth.

"What?"

"Well, them was my very sentiments, Maestro. You ever have the privilege of meetin' the lady?"

January nodded. He had, he realized, only the dim vision of blurred whiteness behind crêpe veils, and the sharp hard voice biting out orders to the obsequious Fraikes. But he'd seen Emily Redfern in action. That was enough.

"She strike you as a lady who'd forbear to recover a necklace worth five hundred dollars out of consideration for a schoolmarm's reputation? Or who'd pass up a hundred and ninety dollars which could be hers for the sayin' of, 'Yes, it's mine?' 'Specially now, with her not able to even pay the rent where she's stayin'?"

January opened his mouth, then shut it again. Someone came over behind Shaw's desk and lit one of the oil lamps; with the thickening of the storm clouds the big room was fast becoming dark as evening, though it was barely ten. "Have you investigated?"

"Investigate what? Why a lady chooses not to prosecute or pursue the gal she claims killed her husband? Iff'n she says these ain't her pearls I can't shove 'em in her pocket for her, nor," Shaw added shrewdly, "would you want me to."

January was silent, trying to fit pieces together that would not fit.

"Now as for them servants," Shaw went on after a moment. "I checked every exchange and barracoon from here to Carrollton. I got a passel of directions." He delved into the drawer once more to produce a sheaf of unreadable notes. "But I can't go traipsin' to the Missouri frontier lookin' for 'em to ask. 'Specially when you know and I know the case would be just as likely to go against her as for her, with the evidence we got."

Shaw cached the notes back in his drawer, and dumped the pearls unceremoniously in after them. "That whole business about havin' only Miz Redfern's word about her symptoms, and all the servants bein' gone now, kind of itches me, too, Maestro. But if we took it to court there'd only be one person hurt. . . . And she's gone missin' anyway."

Two people, thought January. *Two.*

"And what about Mademoiselle Vitrac?" he asked, after Shaw's words had lain silent on the air for a time. "Do you know where she went?"

"Once the charge against her was dropped," pointed out Shaw, "it ain't our lookout where she goes nor what she does. Miz Redfern sayin' those pearls wasn't hers, and that money wasn't the banknotes that Cora girl stole, means we got no case against Miss Vitrac for harborin' a fugitive—nor you, neither. Given what they's sayin' about her school, I'd say she left town."

A blue-uniformed City Guard came through, leading a line of chained men with buckets and shovels. A city street-cleaning contractor ambled dispiritedly in their wake. Shaw smiled and saluted them as they went past; the contractor mouthed something, but didn't make an audible noise.

"Who," asked January, slowly and coldly, "is saying about Rose's—Mademoiselle Vitrac's—school?"

"Well, everybody, now. Chief Tremouille's been asked to investigate the finances of the place. Armand d'Anouy's one of the backers; he's close as a louse with Mayor Prieur. They all say one of the other backers tipped 'em, but they won't say who. And if you think I can ask 'em," Shaw added, scratching his long hair, "you don't know as much about this town as I thought you did, Maestro."

Another Guard pushed through the doors from the Place d'Armes, called out, "Lieutenant? Trouble at Kentucky Williams's." Blood streamed from the man's nose, mixing with the sweat on his face to accomplish a truly sanguinary effect.

"Lordy, those girls of hers got energy." Shaw got to his feet, and fished his disreputable hat from the floor. "I'm purely sorry, Maestro. I know what you're thinkin'—that this Redfern bissom started them rumors to run Miss Vitrac out of town to punish her for harborin' Miss Chouteau and shut her up into the bargain. But it don't fit. If Miz Redfern wanted to punish Miss Vitrac, she had her in her hand Sunday, and she let her go."

"And made it impossible for her to remain in New Orleans."

"We don't know that." He studied the inside of the battered hat for a moment, then retrieved a flea and crushed it between his thumbnails. "If so be I hear anythin', you know I'll tell you, first thing."

"I know."

From the stone arcade before the Cabildo's doors, January watched the tall Kentuckian and his little escort of Guards disappear around the corner into Rue St. Pierre.

No, he thought. *No.* There seemed to be nothing in his heart but a kind of strange stunned disbelieving blankness. *No.*

She has to have gone somewhere.

And he went out into the streets to search.

Throughout the day, under the sickly blanket of the growing storm heat, he paced the streets of the town. At the grocery on the corner opposite the boarded-up Spanish building on Rue St. Claude, he spoke to the woman behind the counter.

"It's a crime," she said, shaking her head. "A crime. Never will I believe Mademoiselle Vitrac stole that money. After I've seen her work so hard to make that school, coming down here after she had to

let her cook-woman go—I cooked for her many nights, you know."
The woman nodded, a withered walnut face within the startlingly
gaudy blue-and-yellow tignon's folds. "I never thought it right, her
teaching all that Latin and Greek and silliness, but she was a good
sort, once you got to know her, for all her top-lofty airs. She could
have come here. I'd have got my man to let her have a bed in the
attic."

"But she didn't."

The woman shook her head again and ran her dustrag over the
already spotless planks.

"Did she have family? Any other friends?"

But Rose was not the sort of woman who easily makes friends.
The woman did not even know where Rose's home had been.

Even in the dead, ghastly stillness of the fever season, it was
surprising how many people could be found in a neighborhood, once
January started to look. Unobtrusive people, little more than the
furniture of the street. A woman selling soap from a willow basket. A
man hawking pokers. Women peddling pralines and needles. A phar-
macist's assistant, fishing for leeches in the gutter. Hèlier the water
seller, far out of his own territory but willing to gossip as always. The
boy who worked at the livery stable around the corner. The cook and
the housemaid for a lawyer named Guttman in the yellow cottage
that backed onto the school.

"It is a terrible shame. . . ."

"No, Mademoiselle had no family that I heard of."

"Imagine, her taking all that money and living like a pauper—
and making those poor girls live that way, too."

"Stuck-up yellow bitch." Hèlier's voice was bitter. He was clearly
struggling to balance his yoke and buckets at the new angle across his
shoulders necessitated by the damage Soublet's "mollification of the
bones" had done to his back. His fair, handsome face was drawn with
exhaustion and pain. "Like all the colored, thinks herself better than
everyone around her."

Including you, my friend, thought January, remembering the water
seller's drugged tirade in the clinic. *And all the white fathers in the
world won't make you white.*

Or straight-backed, he thought, suddenly ashamed.

He thanked him, and walked on, turning back to see the twisted form staggering crablike along the banquette with his yoke and his cane, water slopping from the buckets and dribbling around his feet.

"I never held with education for girls," declared an Italian woman who kept a shop down the street. "Look what it led to, eh?"

"Is it true she starved them to death?"

Calumny, Beaumarchais had written sixty years ago. *You don't know what you are disdaining when you disdain that. . . . There is no false report however crude, no abomination, no ridiculous falsehood which the idlers in a great city cannot, if they take the trouble, make universally believed.*

And Rose's education, her reserve, her strength had made her a target. No wonder she'd lashed out at him when he'd mentioned Alphonse Montreuil's jealous fantasies about Madame Lalaurie torturing her slaves. In her own way, Rose, like that beautiful Creole matriarch, was everything a woman should not be.

And she was gone.

He was obsessed with the thought that, returning from the Cabildo, she had been snatched from the sidewalk by the same men who had tried to kidnap him, who had abducted Cora on the threshold of her freedom. Remembering Hannibal's earlier living arrangements, he slipped through the pass-throughs along the sides of houses shuttered tight, looking for signs of occupation.

He found none. But he did find, in two other houses, broken hasps on the rear shutters, bedclothes rumpled, the signs of swift and unwilling departure. In neither house—and in a shed where he found a little heap of clothes and the tin badge of a slave who earned his own keep—was there evidence of children. In all three cases, the houses on either side were closed and empty.

Rain began to fall, wild and blowing and bathwater warm. Lightning cut the darkness, not bolts and spears but sheets of whiteness, prodigal and terrible, leaving denser dark behind. January, who by three in the afternoon had made a circuit of every cheap lodging house in the city, took the steam-cars to Milneburgh again, to be greeted by the news that the Widow Redfern had departed for the remainder of the fever season. Stopping at Minou's house cost him more time; and the returning train was overtaken by the storm, the branches lashing frenziedly in the gloom of the swampy woods on either side of the tracks and the dark, near-empty cars shaking with the blasts of the wind.

By the time he walked back from the terminus to his mother's house it was nearly ten, lightless as the Pit save where the wildly swaying street lamps flung ragged flares of red across the intersections, the blowing rain transformed to bloody jewels.

He made his way across the yard by memory in the dark, groped for the rail of the stairs. No light shone from behind Bella's shutters. It was logical that were Hannibal making a little money playing in a tavern somewhere, he would stay rather than soak himself walking home. Still, January felt his way along between wall and gallery railing, and passed his hands over the latch of the shutters.

They were bolted from the outside. Hannibal had not returned. January was turning back to the door of his own room when a white flare of lightning illuminated the length of the gallery. It showed him two men just clambering up the stairway, knives in their hands.

Blindness returned the next second, but January had seen in their faces their surprise that he hadn't gone into his own room. With the noise of the storm, he'd never have heard them till it was too late. Even the thunder of their boots on the gallery, running toward him, was drowned. He caught the railing in both hands, swung himself over, felt their bodies blunder and slam against the rail as he let go and dropped.

He heard one say "Tarnation!" in a heavy Irish brogue, as he ducked through the kitchen door and by touch in the dark found where Bella kept the iron spits, and the woodbox with its short, heavy logs. There was no time to search for anything more—Bella's knives were in a drawer someplace, but the building was already shaking with the descending boots, and he knew he had to take them when they came off the stairs, when they'd still be single file.

He made it, barely, driving the spit in pure darkness out of the abyssal night beneath the gallery, hearing and smelling the assassin as he reached the bottom of the stairs and knowing by touch, because he had ascended those stairs himself a thousand thousand times, where the man had to be. He felt the sharpened end of the iron plow into meat; he heard the man scream, a dreadful animal sound.

Feet blundered, then more shrieking as the second man fell over the first. January swung his makeshift club like Samson smiting the Philistines and felt it connect with something, but a hand grabbed his arm, and he twisted out of the way of the foot-long knife he'd glimpsed on the gallery. The blade opened his sleeve and the arm beneath in a long mouth of shocking pain. He grabbed where he guessed the man's head had to be and drove his knee up hard. Metal rattled on the brick underfoot, then the two of them fell outward, landing in the oozing muck and sluicing rain of the yard.

Hands groped and fumbled at his throat. He saw the silvery flash of eyes. With his forearm he smashed away the man's hands, grabbed for him again and dragged him bodily up to slam him into one of the gallery posts, but the marauder slithered free. An instant later, above the hammering of the rain, January heard the yard-gate rumble as heavy weight clambered over it.

He turned back, flung himself into the kitchen again and grabbed another spit, then, when there was no pursuit, groped, shivering and dripping, for the tinderbox and striker always kept in a tin holder above it, Bella not holding with new-fangled stinking lucifers in *her* kitchen.

Wedged into a corner, listening with what felt like his entire body and unable to hear a thing over the rain, January kindled the tinder. By the flickery light, he found candles and a lamp.

The man he'd stabbed with the spit lay facedown in the mud of the yard. The metal had pierced the thorax just under the rib cage. January suspected, by the strong smell of the blood as he dragged him back under the shelter of the gallery, that he'd gone into shock and subsequently drowned and suffocated in ooze. In addition to the skinning knife he found at the foot of the steps—and the one the second man had dropped in the gallery—the first man had a slung-shot—a lump of lead on the end of a leather thong—at his belt, and a pistol wrapped in greased leather under his shirt.

January brought the lamp close, and dipped a cup of rainwater from the nearby barrel to wash off the man's face.

It was the gotch-eyed bartender from the Jolly Boatman Saloon.

FIFTEEN

The Jolly Boatman's lights burned through the rain like a scattering of rusty jackstraws. From the weed-grown alley January listened. The bass rumble of men's voices carried easily through the thin plank walls. The shutters were closed against the storm, and here in the Swamp no street lamps burned. In his rough corduroy jacket and dark trousers, January blended with the night.

Curiously, though it was past curfew, he felt safe. The City Guards avoided the Swamp. Should he be attacked or murdered himself, he could look for neither protection nor vengeance, but he was too angry now for that to matter, and in any case he was coming to understand that the Swamp was not the only place where that was true. In his belt, against every law of the state of Louisiana, he wore both knives he'd taken from his would-be killers. He carried the dead man's slungshot rolled up in his pocket. The only reason he hadn't added the pistol to his arsenal was because the lock had been drenched in the puddles of his mother's yard, and there was no time to dry it. The weapon and its attendant powder-bottle now reposed under his mattress.

Ten, maybe eleven buildings backed up against the turning basin—it was difficult to tell where St. Gertrude's Clinic started and ended. January memorized rooflines as well as he could against the pitchy dark of the sky, then moved along the wall through the weeds and muck.

Listening. Listening.

"Hell with 'er, I ain't goin' out in this," said a man's voice, so close January nearly jumped. Jaundiced lantern-light sprayed the rain around a door in the shack on the Boatman's riverward side. Forms jostled in the opening. By daylight January would have been visible. He doubted he was so now, even had the two men emerging into the weedy yard been sober.

They weren't, however. A narrow strip of yard backed the shack, and the grimy waters of the canal lay beyond, the view broken by a small and mangy outhouse.

Both men turned their backs on the canal, and urinated against the wall of the house. Rain running down his hair and under the collar band of his calico shirt, January had to agree with their sentiments.

When the men had gone in again he continued his wary circuit of the building. He'd brought a small bull's-eye lantern, and with the slide closed nearly completely and the dark side of the lantern turned toward the building, he doubted he could be seen even had anyone next door taken his attention from his cards long enough to look. The Jolly Boatman ran down almost to the waters of the canal, separated only by a sodden yard that quite obviously doubled as a general privy.

He'd already observed that the building itself was large for the Swamp, though it held at most three rooms. The barroom occupied most of the floor space, orange light blearing through the shutters; table legs scraped on the floorboards, barely audible under the steady roar of the rain. A man's voice rambled on, low and conspiratorial, about how a hundred Americans properly armed could easily seize the harbor at Cartagena, march overland to Bogotá. . . .

January moved on. What he estimated to be a storeroom lay behind the bar, silent and dark but far too close to the scene of commerce to house kidnapped men and women. Not that the men who patronized the saloon would care if the Perrets, Robois Roque, Virgil and Cora and a hundred others were chained in a corner of the barroom weeping, he reflected with a queer cold detachment. But word would get out if someone thought there was a reward to be had. Next to the storeroom lay another chamber, dark also and probably also originally another storeroom, or perhaps the late barkeep's boudoir. There was certainly a bed in there, anyway. He could hear the ropes creak rhythmically, and the knock-knock-knock of the frame against the outer wall. The lovely Bridgit and the equally lovely Thalia? Roarke's lady friend Mistress Trudi? There was no other sound.

So where the hell were they keeping them?

He couldn't be wrong. He knew he couldn't.

It was possible that the kidnappings had been planned with an eye to handing the victims straight to the brokers. January settled his wide shoulders into the corner where the Boatman's rough kitchen thrust out toward the canal. But turning the victims over immediately would only raise problems for the brokers, the kinds of problems they looked to an outfit like Roarke's to solve for them.

The heated tin of the lantern made a localized radiance against his thigh. He slipped the cover enough to show him where to tread. At the kitchen's end, only feet from the choppy black of the turning basin, he widened the chink still farther and scanned the ground, though he didn't expect to find much, after hours of hammering rain.

Keelboats rocked at the wharves of warehouses built around the Basin, squat craft with low cargo boxes, long steering oars knocking in their locks. No wharf lay behind the Jolly Boatman itself. He'd half-expected there would be, given the difficulties of forcing men and women down a rope or ladder to a keelboat's deck without a fuss.

Rain sluiced down his face. St. Gertrude's loomed above him like a lightless mountain, but the stink of it flowed over him, even in the downpour.

Turning back, January studied the saloon again. The kitchen shed was barely taller than his own head at its lower side; though like most "quarters" buildings, its roof rose at an angle of more than forty-five degrees to the outside of the yard. Unlike most of the flat-roofed shacks thereabouts, the saloon itself was easily tall enough to accommodate an attic. The ceiling of the barroom, January recalled, was low.

There was a window up there, within easy reach of the kitchen roof.

Stepping back a few paces, January found that one of the lightless service wings of the clinic backed straight onto the rear of the kitchen, so closely that they shared a party wall. Its inner side was lower still. It was a quick scramble to the roof of the one, then up the steep slope and over the ridge to the roof of the other, and so along to the window under the Boatman's eaves. From there it was an easy matter to flip the catch of the shutter with the back of a knife blade—the shutters fit sufficiently ill they would have admitted a finger. Slatternly light trickled through gapped floorboards and showed him a big room, low pitched, uninhabited, and ostensibly safe. He hoisted himself over the sill, closed the shutter, and flipped shut the catch again, lest the heavy wooden leaf bang in the wind.

Carefully he held the lantern up for a better look.

The room was hot and stank. Astonishingly, the roof didn't leak, like the plank floor another tribute to Roarke's business acumen. Smoke rose through the ill-fitting boards as well as light, shifting wraiths that collected thick under the ridgepole. The stench of it and of tobacco spit rose, too, nauseating: filthy clothes, spilt liquor, dirty bodies, dirty hair. The sweetish, pissy odor of rats.

And none of it masked the all-encompassing sticky reek of opium.

Boxes of it were stacked on a couple of boards, laid across the floor joists above the ceiling's more fragile planking. January edged out along the joists; the crates were marked BRITISH EAST INDIA COMPANY and heaped nearly to the rafters. Rats had gnawed one corner, and lay dead or stuporous, surrounded by trails of ants.

Kaintucks as a rule preferred to pickle their brains in alcohol. It was January's experience that flatboatmen so sodden with forty-rod that they could barely speak would still spit on an opium-eater with contempt.

But there was more opium here than he'd seen in the back room of Soublet's clinic.

Soublet's clinic.

Cautiously, January began to make his way toward the attic's north wall. Away from the noisier plotting of the filibusters (*And what do they think the Spanish government's going to be doing during all this? Or the French? Or the British Navy?*) other voices came clear, soft though they were, nearly under his feet. A grunting Kaintuck nasal. Roarke's honeyed Liffey drawl. And a well-bred Creole accent, a mellow tenor that it took him a moment to place:

". . . watched the place all yesterday, but he never came near it."

"Doesn't the man ever sleep?" That was Roarke's voice, speaking, as Hèlier spoke, in French. "Gotch and Hog-Nose should have been back by this time."

"I still say it's a shame to make away with him. His size, he'd fetch eleven, twelve hundred. . . ."

January felt the hair of his nape prickle. They were talking about him. Roarke, and Hèlier Lapatie.

Is that you? Hèlier had called out to him once, in English. It hadn't occurred to him then to wonder to whom the water seller spoke.

"Not that kind, he wouldn't," said Roarke. "His English is too good and there's too many as would miss him. . . ."

"And what would they do?" demanded Hèlier's voice. "Go up to the Missouri Territory looking for the man?"

"Now, my friend, you know what they say about simplest plans being best." Roarke's voice, musical at any time, became purringly conciliatory. "And your first plan was the dandy. Only those as we know have nobody to go askin' after 'em. That was the brilliance of your idea."

"Well . . ." muttered Hèlier, sulky like a sulky child, eating up praise.

"You saw what happened when you were laid up, and Gotch and Hog-Nose got greedy and brought our big black bhoy-o askin' after questions in the first place."

"Hog-Nose is a cretin!" snapped Hèlier sharply. "I was very specific when I said *only* those I'd marked for capture. . . ."

Hèlier.

The cripple selling water in the streets.

The man who stopped to chat and gossip with every housewife, every other peddler. The man who knew everyone's business almost as thoroughly as Marie Laveau.

January felt a rush of furious heat and crept silently on.

Mamzelle Marie wasn't the only person in town to have her spies. Almost certainly she paid Hèlier for information, little guessing what the water seller made of the knowledge he collected himself or to whom else he sold it.

I should have guessed. Their informant as to who was safe, who had family, whose neighbors were gone, would almost have to be black or colored. Servants wouldn't gossip with a white man.

He was trembling with anger, though whether at Hèlier or at himself he did not know.

Why did that make it worse? Men are men and make their livings how best they can.

He should have suspected Hèlier, with his spite against those whose lives were more comfortable than his own. He could hear it now in the water seller's voice, and in Roarke's as the Irishman coaxed and praised his accomplice: praise that might, January thought, be as treasured as the money. Even if Hèlier himself were ill or missing, those he worked for would still know the names and houses of those he'd chosen, like a farmer choosing lambs for the pot.

It was his pity for the man's infirmity that had blinded him. *Pity?* he wondered. Or the assumption that as a cripple he was helpless—in itself the contempt Hèlier despised.

Along the attic's swamp-side wall January found half a dozen cardboard boxes that scuttered at his approach with a stinking confusion of fleeing gray bodies. He crouched for a better look, and slipped back the lantern slide. The boxes contained nothing very remarkable. It was the implication of what he saw, rather than the objects themselves, that made his hair prickle with a renewed fever-wash of rage.

What they held were only rough trousers of osnaburg cloth, new and stiff as boards, unworn, the kind made cheaply for laborers or slaves; and the cheapest calico dresses and headscarves available.

"Consarn!" exclaimed a voice in Kaintuck English almost directly beneath his feet. "I never seen sech a place for water! Ever' damn buildin' leakin' like Noah's flood!"

"Shut up." Roarke's voice, deadly soft. January felt their silence.

Silence in which the thunder of the rain seemed overwhelming, but not loud enough to cover the slow drip of his soaked clothing on the ceiling boards.

He could almost feel them looking up, and froze like a deer: *It's only a leak. It's only a leak.* But the flimsy walls vibrated with even the stealthy opening of the door that led to the attic stairs, and at the first shudder of ascending feet, he bolted. His own thundering footfalls along the joist brought the men below pounding up the stairs with no further thought for surprise; January flung open the window shutter as someone yelled behind him; the crash of a gun filled the attic's hollow as he dove through.

Rain streamed in his face, slicked the shakes of the kitchen roof as he scrabbled for his balance on the steep slant. A second shot barked. To his right and down he saw men in the yard, Roarke's height and white coat and fair hair plastered straight, rendering the Irishman visible through the rainy murk and dark jostle of bodies. January flipped himself over the top of the roof-ridge and fell three or four feet to the slanted roof of the service wing on the other side, ran along it, keeping low, headed for the basin. A moment later Roarke's voice roared, "There he goes, lads!" and another shot cracked. The ball sliced a burning track across the muscles of his thigh.

Roarke and three men were now on his left, behind St. Gertrude's—*Cut through the kitchen,* thought January. *The two buildings are connected.*

He reached the end of the service wing, the men clamoring beneath him like possum hounds, a glister of eyes and teeth in the sudden flare of lightning. When he leapt up onto the kitchen building again he was skylighted against the rainy blackness, and another ball passed close enough over his head that he could hear it whistle. There were men on that side, how many he couldn't tell.

From the end of the kitchen, if he remembered rightly, it was about four feet to the cutting of the basin's bank. No wharf, no steps, no boat.

He reached the kitchen end two strides ahead of his pursuers. There was no time to think, almost none to feel fear, and in any case fear was beside the point. He knew he was a dead man. As he flung himself outward into blackness something passed across the flesh of his back like a red-hot whip—the thought went through his mind with weird leisureliness that many of the riverboatmen could shoot the eye out of a squirrel on a branch. Then he hit the water like Lucifer falling: blackness, suffocation, cold.

At the downstream end of the American faubourg of St. Mary, even the more respectable of the rooming houses jumbled among the brickyards, warehouses, and mercantile establishments along Magazine and Tchoupitoulas Streets didn't have much over the buildings in the Swamp. They were slightly taller and rather sturdier, and fewer of them were devoted to the active pursuit of alcohol sales or prostitution, but that—January could almost hear his mother's smoky voice saying the words—was about all that could be said.

The rain-swamped yard around the privy of the tall, raw-looking whitewashed building on Gravier Street smelled just as bad. And it was just as easy to scramble to the top of the shed at the end of the kitchen building, up to the kitchen roof—two stories high, this time, with slave quarters above the kitchen—and along the high ridge to flip back the shutter of a rear window overlooking the odoriferous yard. January was making an educated guess about which of the boardinghouse rooms was the one he sought. It would probably be the farthest back in the building on the highest inhabited floor, with a grand view of the slave quarters and the kitchen with their attendant smells and heat.

He pulled the shutter open and snaked through fast. He'd lost the lantern—either in the turning basin or in the attic of the Jolly Boatman, he couldn't remember—and was almost certain the lucifers in his pocket were too soaked to function. As soon as he stepped clear of the window's problematical light he whispered, "Lieutenant Shaw?"

"Right behind you, friend," replied a voice from nowhere near the likely location of the bed. "You got any especial reason for callin' informally like this?"

"It's Benjamin January." He'd never seen Shaw anything but lazy and slouching and spitting tobacco with an appalling lack of accuracy, but he'd also never been fooled by the man. "I thought I might have been followed or they might be watching for me in the street out front." All the way here through the lightless, foul warren of shacks and fences near the basin, and along the oozing lanes that paralleled Canal Street, he had dared not leave the shadows. The strain of listening behind him, of watching in every direction through the obscuring sheets of black rain, had left him as exhausted as if he'd run for miles.

Lightning flared outside. It showed him, as he'd suspected, the bed empty, mosquito-bar bundled carelessly to the side. The light was gone before he could turn or see anything else, and the dark deeper than before. He heard not the slightest whisper of scuff or footfall. Nevertheless, the next moment a scratch of sulfurous matchlight holed the darkness beside the bed. The slow-widening glow showed him the Kaintuck lieutenant hunkered naked on the floor by the bedside chair—the room didn't boast a table—holding lucifer to candlewick with one hand while the other kept a grip on the biggest skinning knife January had ever seen. Under a lank curtain of pale-brown hair Shaw's gray eyes were like an animal's, cold and watchful, ascertaining that his visitor was in fact alone.

Only after he'd satisfied himself of this did he stand, knobby as an old horse and scarred across pelvis, ribs, and arms with the ragged pale gouges of old wounds, and reach for his pants, hung neatly over the back of the chair. "I take it you found the fellas who's been kidnappin' yore sister's friends?"

One never needed to explain much to Shaw.

"Roarke," answered January. "The Jolly Boatman's connected at the back with St. Gertrude's Clinic. The attic's full of opium to keep them quiet, and clothes to put on them when they take them out of there on keelboats up to the bayou and out across the lake."

"You see this?"

"I saw the opium and the clothes, and the connection between the clinic and the Boatman's kitchen."

"They see you?"

"I had to swim for it."

"You're lucky." Shaw was dressing while he spoke: trousers,

boots, shirt, and coat, moving with the silent speed of a snake. "They'll be clearin' 'em out. Boechter and LaBranche—two of my men—sleep in the attic here. You shuck whatever weaponry you're packin' whilst I fetch 'em down." He caught the room's single thread-bare towel from the bar on the back of the door as he passed it, flung it back to January out of the hall's blackness. He didn't take the candle. January guessed Abishag Shaw was the kind of man who would have found the kitchen knife–drawer in the dark.

Shaw was back in minutes, accompanied by Constable Boechter, a swart little Bavarian still rubbing sleep from his eyes. January had toweled dry his hair and face—not that it would make a particle of difference in ten minutes—and had set the slungshot and one of the two knives on top of the neat, shoulder-high arrangement of packing-cases that occupied the whole of the room's riverward wall. The cases held an assortment of tidily folded calico shirts, another pair of clean but sorry trousers, and a dozen or more books. The tops of them were strewn with weapons—pistols, knives, brass powder-flasks and sacks of balls; a braided leather sap, an iron knuckle-duster. A six-and-a-half-foot-long rifle with a dozen crosses cut neatly in its stock hung on pegs above the bed. When Shaw and Boechter returned to the room Shaw began gathering these weapons and distributing them about his angular person—he'd acquired another plug of tobacco from somewhere as well—and January felt a flash of anger, that by the law of the state he could only follow this man like an unarmed valet.

"LaBranche went for reinforcements," the Kaintuck remarked as he checked the pistols' loads. "We been watchin' Roarke some little time, over one thing and another. Not havin' a fancy to break my neck or drown'd, I'd say we got no choice but to follow up the shell road on foot. With luck we'll catch 'em 'fore they make the lake— God knows, in rain like this they won't be makin' much time. You got any idea how many are in it, Maestro?"

January shook his head. "Five, maybe ten."

"We'll catch 'em, then." Shaw spat on the floor. The whole place was stained and sticky with old expectorations, the smell of the to-bacco a faint, sweet queasiness in the heat. "Even haulin' on the canal they won't be making but a few rods an hour, an' when they hit the

Bayou it'll get worse. Roarke'll never make it across the lake in this weather, but he's got a place up along the shore just over the border into Jefferson Parish. If so be he reaches it, we're in for some trouble."

It wasn't likely, after all this time, that they'd be there, January thought, as he strode through the darkness along Canal Street, head down in the sheeting rain. Not Cora.

Rose?

His heart beat hard and heavy. She'd been missing only three days. Three days since she'd walked away from the Cabildo into the gathering dusk, with nowhere to go and no one to know if she vanished.

No one except Hèlier Lapatie.

How long did they keep them before shipping them out?

They skirted the shacks and slums that lay between Rampart Street and Basin, passed the dark trees of Congo Square, silent in the rain. The smell of the burying-grounds hung thick on the gluey night, and January wondered if the dark form he saw under those trees was Bronze John himself, or just one of the dead-cart men taking refuge from the storm. His clothes stuck to his body in the wet, and the exertions of the night whispered to him from exhausted muscles; but he moved on, following Shaw's scraggy pale form and followed in turn by Boechter—hustling hard to keep up with the two taller men—fueled by the fury in his heart.

Under the shallow embankment of mud and tree roots, the canal rattled with the rain, a hollow roaring, like tons of deer-shot being emptied into the sea. What scattered lights there were—here and there lanterns in sheds and bordellos—gave place to the shapeless dark of the city pastures, then the thunder of rain in the trees of the night-drowned swamps. Lightning flashed faroff over the lake now and then, and showed up the fidgeting trees, the desolation that the French called the "desert." After each purple glare the dark was like blindness, through which the shell road shone like a bone, and the sound of water running off the back of Shaw's hat-brim was a constant, a localized spatter in a world of deluge.

After almost half an hour they reached the Bayou, turned right along it and crossed over Judge Martin's stone bridge. The road ran a little wider along the murky watercourse. Somewhere to their left lay the oak trees that constituted the favorite dueling ground outside the city, and the dark buildings of Monsieur Allard's plantation beyond those. Across the Bayou, January thought he could make out the glistening track of the towpath, hugging the water's edge and slippery with rain.

Shaw was right. They wouldn't be making much time. Even with well over an hour's start, they'd be skidding and falling in the mud, unable to get a footing against the weight of the keelboat, blind with the hammering water. It said a great deal for Roarke's command over his men that they hadn't abandoned their task thus far.

"There." January pointed.

"I see 'em." Shaw squinted through the flooded darkness at the firefly twinkle of lights. "Though where the hell LaBranche and his boys got to—"

Under the rain the snap of a shot sounded like a breaking twig, then another and a third.

"Damnation!" Shaw started to run, startlingly graceful and astonishingly fast. "I told that idjit not to brace 'em!"

January ran, too, knowing what Roarke was bound to do if attacked.

Hooded lanterns bobbed under the dripping canopy of overhanging trees. LaBranche and his reinforcements ranged along the Bayou Road, firing down at the keelboat in the narrow confines of the channel. By the single light fixed on the boat's prow January glimpsed two or three forms moving back and forth along the towpath on the other side, though now and then a belch of flame showed up a gun muzzle in the blackness. Over the rain he thought he heard a ball tear into the tupelo thickets between the shell road and the water's edge. One such flare from the top of the keelboat showed him Hèlier's face, and the red splash like blood that was his shirt; by the lantern light January saw the water seller throw down his pistol, unable to reload, and tug another from his belt. Men ran back and forth along the catwalks of the gunnels, dodging and shooting; January saw the jitter and sway of lantern light in the cargo box below and heard a muffled voice yell, "Hold 'em off, boys!"

January plunged down from the road, hearing the tear and whistle of bullets but knowing himself nearly invisible in the rain. Shaw was somewhere to his right. The Bayou was deep hereabouts, twelve feet or more. He flung himself in, black water and the black loom of the boat above him, and men in the lantern light, firing down.

Someone grappled him as he scrambled up onto the gunwale catwalk and they rocked and struggled, a hand digging at his forehead and eyes. He seized the man's wrist and wrenched it over, driving his whole weight against the arm—heard the man scream. He flung him into the canal, then plunged and fought his way toward the doorway of the cabin, hearing as he did so the sodden crack of an ax.

Someone grabbed him, dragging at him. He wrenched and twisted, knowing there had to be a knife in play and saw by the flare of the lantern light the crippled Hèlier's handsome, boyish face. He pulled the knife free of Hèlier's hand—the man had no more strength to his grip than a young lad—and pushed him aside. Later he thought he should have held him. But he knew what Roarke was doing in the cabin and knew, too, that he had to get there first.

One of the City Guards made a grab for the water seller. Hèlier sprang, scrambling, staggering, to the catwalk at the nose of the boat. Afterward January didn't know whether the sheer weight of struggling men on the keelboat was responsible, jerking and bobbing the vessel so that the cripple could not keep his balance, or whether Hèlier flung himself into the water with some notion of swimming ashore.

If the latter, he should have known better. If the former, he never had a chance. January saw one arm thrash wildly above the surface of the water as Hèlier tried to bring his twisted body around to some position that would permit swimming, but it was hopeless.

Below him, January heard again the strike of an ax on wood.

In panic fury he kicked his way through the cabin door and ducked as Roarke swung around on him, ax in hand. Had Roarke dropped the weapon and gone for the pistol in his belt then he'd have had January cold. As it was his hands were both full and the cabin, with its two tiny bunks occupied by the slumped bodies of three naked, mumbling men and women in the lantern's jerking light, pinned his big body, smothering his stroke. January dodged the first ax blow, which buried the weapon's head in the doorjamb beside his shoulder. He ripped with the skinning knife, a deliberate blow, meaning to gut, meaning to kill.

Roarke seized his arm, thrust him off. Water splashed up through the split bottom of the keelboat, around their knees and rising. January came at him fast, and Roarke fumbled in his belt, belatedly pulled out the pistol; January flinched aside and slapped water, hard, hurling it into the man's eyes. The shot went wild, like the clap of doom in the tiny cabin, and then Shaw said, "That'll be enough of that, Mr. Roarke," quietly, as if reprimanding a not-very-obstreperous drunk.

He was aiming a pistol; another was in his belt.

Roarke flung himself at Shaw, dodging aside as the pistol roared, and bearing him down, his own knife leaping to his hand. January dragged him back and with a single hard blow to the jaw sent him spinning against the bulkhead. The last expression in Roarke's eyes, before he slumped unconscious, was furious, indignant surprise.

"Send for my lawyer," was all that Roarke would say.

Gray light leaked through the breaking clouds outside as the little party returned to the Cabildo. For the first time in what seemed like years cool air breathed through the open double-doors onto the Place d'Armes.

While Roarke was led out to the courtyard and up to the cells, the two elderly men and their middle-aged sister, whom January had barely been able to drag out of the sinking keelboat, were taken into a rear room, to be wrapped in blankets and plied with coffee. "They'll live," said January, drawing back the older man's eyelids and holding a candle close to the contracted pupil, then pressing the man's nails, and listening to his breath. "Barring pneumonia, they should take no hurt from it. Is there anything to tell us who they are?"

Shaw, who had come in behind him drying his hair, shook his head. "Couple of the boys went and had a look at St. Gertrude's, whilst we was fishin' in the Bayou. We been, as I said, interested in Mr. Roarkes doin's for some little while, though slave stealin's a new lay for him. Since most of them poor folk that disappeared was taken out of their houses in their nightshirts there wasn't much to find—

not even the nightshirts, mostly, and sure enough not a pin or a shoe or a piece of jewelry."

"Manon?" mumbled one of the men they'd rescued. "Manon?"

"Manon's here," said January reassuringly. "She's safe." He looked over at the woman. Her features were so similar to those of both men: emaciated, exhausted, her skin ashy gray with cold and fatigue. "Lousy, probably," he added, remembering conditions at St. Gertrude's, "but safe."

"Well," said Shaw, and spit into the corner. "They's worse things than lice."

January was silent for a moment. Then he said, "Did your men find a red dress at St. Gertrude's? Or a pair of black-and-red shoes with white laces?"

Shaw shook his head.

"And nothing of . . . nothing of the dress that Mademoiselle Vitrac had on when she left here Sunday evening?"

"Nuthin'." There was a curious gentleness in the policeman's voice as he added, "We're lookin'."

They came out to find a thin, black-mustachioed little man with coal-dark eyes waiting by Shaw's desk; Shaw stopped in his tracks, as a man does who sees a snake in his path. "And what you doin' here this hour of the mornin', Loudermilk? All the debtors you chase asleep?"

"I understand you have my client illegally detained in your cells." The dark eyes flicked from Shaw to January, calculating.

"I don't know about that illegally," replied Shaw, and spit a few inches from the man's foot. "Kidnappin' or slave stealin', they's both crimes in this state."

"To be sure they are. But my client is a businessman, with dealings among other members of the business community here in this city. I don't think I need emphasize that any breath of allegation of either of those heinous crimes—of which he is entirely innocent—will result, not only in civil action against you and your Chief, but in all probability in a spontaneous demonstration of support from other businessmen along the levee and Tchapitoulas Street. May I speak to my client, please?"

Shaw slouched a little farther against his desk, like a pole of beans improperly tied up, and looked down at the smaller man. "Come back at eight."

Loudermilk's mouth widened just a fraction at the corners, showing rotted teeth. "I'll wait."

From the arcade outside a woman entered, the breeze off the river curling her cloak about her, the seven points of her tignon like unholy sun around her dark, expressionless face. She paused for a moment, regarding January, and Shaw, and the lawyer Loudermilk with enigmatic serpent eyes, then passed, silent, to the desk.

"I'm here to see Mademoiselle Jouvert, Sergeant deMezieres."

Ordinarily a request to visit a drunken Gallatin Street whore like Elsie Jouvert would have drawn a jocular remark from the sergeant, but the man only nodded. He was Creole, not the American who'd been here the night before last. "I'll take you up, Mamzelle."

"I'll find my own way," said Marie Laveau. "Thank you." She glanced again at the group near Shaw's desk, thoughtfully, and disappeared through the double-doorway that led through the courtyard, her cloak billowing gently, to show and then conceal the blue of her calico skirts.

Loudermilk rose to his feet and made to follow. Shaw interposed himself.

"Eight, I said." The lieutenant had the tone in his voice January recognized, of officialdom being obstructive because it could.

"You have one rule for Negroes, and another for white men?"

"Madame Laveau comes pretty regular to visit the prisoners," said Shaw. "She nurses them that's sick. Iff'n you've a mind to do the same, we got a couple jail-fever cases up on the higher gallery been pukin' all night and need a little cleanin' up."

If looks could flay, thought January, Shaw's hide would have been stretched on the Cabildo doors.

"I'll wait."

Cut, aching, limping, and a little queasy from the exertions of the night, January stepped from the Cabildo into the puddled morning in the Place d'Armes. A wagon rumbled away from the levee, laden with trunks, silverware, furniture; a gentleman in a dove-colored coat followed it, a woman leaning on his arm and two young boys dashing and shouting around them, delighted to be back home.

People were coming back to town.

January returned to the Rue Burgundy to find Hannibal gray-faced and deathly ill. He checked for fever, of which there was none, and fetched him coffee from the kitchen. "I suppose I'm lucky they didn't kill me," said the fiddler later, at intervals in vomiting. "It would have been cheaper than buying me drink after drink—if those friendly gentlemen were indeed dispatched by Mr. Roarke to make sure I wouldn't come in and rescue or warn you at an awkward moment."

He slumped back against the gallery wall, too exhausted to crawl back into Bella's room to his bed. January wondered if there'd been more than liquor in those glasses, though God knew the drink dispensed along Tchapitoulas Street was lethal enough.

"Maybe they just liked your music."

After making sure that his friend was resting easier, January went to bed and slept. But in his dreams he was back on the keelboat, struggling with Roarke in the flooding cabin; and in his dreams there was someone he knew, someone he loved, trapped behind a bulkhead with the water pouring in. He woke in panic two or three times from this dream, and the last time, found that the sun was setting, and cooler air breathing in from the river across the town.

He and Hannibal were having supper outside the open doors of the kitchen when Shaw appeared in the passway and loafed across the yard to them, spitting tobacco as he came. "Not meanin' to intrude, Maestro," he said, and January shook his head and gestured to him, a little ironically, to take a chair and share the coffee and jambalaya.

"Not at all—sir."

Shaw remained standing. "Thank you all the same. I just thought you ought to know, Maestro, they pulled Hèlier Lapatie's body outen the Bayou this afternoon. We went through his rooms, too. He had a bankbook on the Louisiana State Bank for nigh onto four thousand dollars, but nuthin' by way of records or notes."

"He wouldn't have," said January softly. "He kept it all in his head. My mother does, too, and my sisters." He could have added Mamzelle Marie's name to that list. "It's just things everyone knows."

"Him havin' no heirs, nor no family, nor nuthin', I'm tryin' to get that money released to the police force to pay for a search for those folks what disappeared, but it's hard goin'. That Loudermilk, Roarke's lawyer, filed a plea at the arraignment to have the whole case throwed out."

"Thrown out?" Hannibal set down his cup, disbelief scraping in his voice. "I know I was never cut out for a lawyer, but could you explain that piece of legal reasoning to me?"

"And does he have an explanation for why he was chopping a hole in the bottom of that keelboat?" demanded January. "Letting in a little fresh air? He didn't know those three people were sodden-drunk on opium in the hold? It never occurred to him that if they drowned he'd get off without a stitch of evidence against him, thank you very much? Or doesn't he think anyone else noticed?"

"Well now, Maestro, that's another matter." Shaw spit again on the bricks, and scratched absentmindedly. "Fact is, Roarke's claimin' he ran down to check on those poor unfortunates he was carryin' out of the town for their own good, when you came crashin' down into the hold, grabbed the ax, and started hackin' through the floor of the boat. When he tried to stop you, you attacked him with a knife."

Hannibal let out a yelp of laughter, instantly stifled behind his hand, "Sorry," he said. "Sorry. *There's ne'er a villain dwelling in all Denmark but he's an arrant knave!*"

"Shut up," said January, cold and soft, and returned his eyes to Shaw. He kept his words level, almost conversational. "And what does Chief Tremouille say about this version of events?"

"Not anythin' yet. 'Ceptin' that the Chief called me on the carpet for lettin' you have a weapon, which is a clear violation of the city's code. Roarke's countersuin' you—and the City Guards—and havin' me prosecuted personally for conspiracy to cause a slave uprisin'."

For a moment January could only sit, openmouthed with disbelief, while Shaw scratched under his shirt again. "Tremouille," the policeman added, "is not real pleased." The man's long, almost lipless mouth was relaxed as if he spoke of the antics of somebody else's rogue horse, but January could see the queer chilly light that burned far back in the gray eyes. "Whatever Tremouille thinks about Roarke's storytellin' abilities, the fact remains that when I came in it was to see *you* chargin' *him* with a knife, and the ax stuck in the wall. And there's also the fact that we don't know the names of most of the victims—and those whose names we do know of course Roarke's claimin' he couldn't tell from Adam's off-ox and they was never within a thousand yards of the Jolly Boatman or St. Gertrude's Clinic or Mr. Liam Roarke, so there. We don't have one flyspeck of evidence of any specific person bein' there."

Slow flame started in January's belly. "What about the people on the boat?"

Shaw reached thoughtfully down to the table, to turn the blue porcelain bowl of jambalaya a quarter-turn. "They say they'd rather not testify."

The flame condensed to a core, cold now, like a fist of lead under his breastbone. "Just like that?"

"Just like that." The gray eyes met his. Under the water-colored mildness he saw the distant, steely glint of anger to match his own. "I just come from seein' 'em. There's a good deal of feelin' down along the levee—some was even talkin' of marchin' on the Cabildo an' organizin' a jail delivery. Not that Mr. Loudermilk had anything to do with that. He's a Christian and he thought it'd be right Christian to buy all them filibusters free liquor. And I'm sure he had legitimate business earlier this afternoon up on Marais Street, where the Grilles live. . . . The Grilles bein' the folk that can't remember now whether they were ever on that keelboat or not. Edouard and his brother, Robert, and their sister, Manon. A gal sellin' berries off'n a tray saw him, she thinks."

"And have you," asked January, surprised a little at the cold conversational tone of his voice, "told Monsieur Tremouille about this yet?"

"No." Shaw turned the bowl another quarter-turn. "No need for the Chief to know about it 'fore the trial. If there's a trial." He shrugged. "Seems Roarke's feelin' poorly, with all the to-do last night. I'm thinkin' it might so be he needs to be bled."

You could have dropped a picayune bit into the silence, thought January, and heard the splash it made in Paris. The stillness went on, as much of the heart as of the air. He was aware of Hannibal's eyebrows going up, considering the idea; of the anger still alive in his breast, but cold now, like poison; of Shaw watching him beneath those straight colorless lashes, not speculative now, but only waiting.

Waiting for what he would say.

He didn't know what he was going to say until the words came out. "I can't."

Shaw neither replied nor moved.

The words stuck in his throat, as if he were trying to dislodge individual lumps of broken stone with every syllable.

"I may make my living as a piano player, but I did take an oath. And that oath says, 'Do no harm.' I can't. . . ." He paused, oddly aware of his own breath in his lungs: Gabriel and Zizi-Marie going to help the Perrets pack; the woman Nanié searching through the charity ward, night after night. Someone saying, *They just bought their freedom.*

Cora walking away into the darkness of Rue de l'Hôpital.

The weather was cooling; by the feel of the evening air there would be frost that night. Fever season was done. People would be coming back to town.

And there would be holes, in the fabric of people's lives.

There were men and women, confused, terrified, somewhere in the frontier territories of Missouri or the west of Georgia, begging and insisting they were free to men who did not speak their language, whose reply to their clumsy pleas would be a laugh and a blow. Men and women who were going to spend the rest of their lives at back-breaking agricultural work. *The second man who kidnapped me was the local magistrate. . . . I don't go up there no more.* Men and women who were going to die of pneumonia and malnutrition and exhaustion in thin-walled shacks like the one in which he'd slept at Spanish Bayou less than a week ago.

He closed his eyes.

Do no harm.

The anger pounded in his head like the hammer of a migraine. "I can't."

"Just thought I'd ask."

Get Soublet.

He closed his mouth hard on the words. *If you won't do it, don't tell him who will.* "Is Roarke really poorly?"

Shaw nodded. "Happens, in jail. Likely it's the food. I'll find someone."

For some reason January remembered Mamzelle Marie, passing through the big downstairs room of the Cabildo, cloak flickering like a conjure of invisibility around her. Her eyes touching his.

She'd set the man up for this. Without knowing how he knew, he knew.

He rested his forehead on his fist, and listened to Shaw's footfalls, barely audible, retreat across the yard and blend with the waking noises of the street.

Only one case of the cholera was brought into Charity Hospital that night. Soublet did not appear at all, and neither Emil Barnard nor Mamzelle Marie came in, nor were they needed. There was frost on the ground in the morning. At six, January made his way to St. Anthony's Chapel, to make his confession and hear early Mass. He prayed for guidance, and for Rose Vitrac's safety, wherever she was. When he came out the air was crisp, stinking of the usual city stink of sewage but unfouled by the smudges of the plague fires. Carriages jingled by, coachmen saluting with their whips to friends on the banquette, men and women within nodding or touching their hats. A child dodged around him, clutching her doll. Street-vendors cried gingerbread and umbrellas and chairs to mend.

The following Sunday, after Mass, he met Shaw by chance in the Place d'Armes. The policeman informed him laconically that Dr. Soublet had been called to the Cabildo. After being bled eight times in two days and dosed with "heroic" quantities of salts of mercury and turpentine, Liam Roarke had died in his cell.

Of those men and women who had been stolen from their

homes, or dragged off the banquettes on their way to their friends' houses or to doctors' late in the night, nothing further was ever heard.

Through October and November, and on into the fogs and bonfires of Christmastime, Abishag Shaw made inquiries, patiently writing to slave dealers in Natchez, in St. Louis, in Jackson, none of whom, of course, knew anything about the Perrets, Robois Roque, or any of the other dozen or half-dozen or score or however many it had been. Hog-Nose Billy, when he confessed to kidnapping people off the street as a sideline during Hèlier's illness, didn't know how many it was, as he'd been more or less drunk half the time. (*It serves me right,* Hèlier had said, giggling, gesturing around him at the opium-dazed patients of Soublet's clinic—and indeed, thought January, it did.) Nor had the drunken Dr. Furness any better idea. "Hell, we didn't keep track or nuthin'," he said, when Shaw and January spoke to him in his jail cell. "Bring 'em in and get 'em out, that was Liam's way, and didn't we just have our hands full keepin' 'em from gettin' sick while they was there. I do recall as we lost two or three." And he shrugged.

January wrote, too, over Shaw's signature when Shaw was too taken up with his other duties to have time; and kept writing, to newspapers, to clergy, to anyone who might know anything. It was early established that no New Orleans dealer had purchased slaves from Roarke—"None who'll admit of it, anyways," remarked Shaw sourly.

He did not hear from Rose.

It was a bad winter for January. Whether due to loss of income during the fever season or to the general slump in sugar prices, many of his pupils' parents elected not to send their children to piano lessons when they returned to town: "It isn't anything personal, you understand, Monsieur Janvier." Lettice Sarasse fanned herself with a delicate circle of stiffened yellow silk. "Only times are a little difficult now, you understand."

"I understand." The class he held in his mother's parlor shrank to two—Catherine Clisson's eight-year-old daughter, Isabel, and little Narcisse Brize—and he lost every one of his white pupils.

"Nothing to do with your teaching, M'sieu," explained Madame

Lalaurie, slender and queenly in the hot sunlight of her parlor, Bastien in his jam-colored uniform lingering behind her in the door. "It's just that I've come to the conclusion that the lessons aren't doing the girls any good. But I shall certainly recommend you to those of my friends who seek instruction for their children, and to my good Monsieur Huny at the Opera."

But November turned to December, and Christmas drew on, and there was little money for coffee at the market or to attend the Opera himself. It was Hannibal, who had gone back to his make-and-scrape existence with the return of Livia Levesque and her cook to New Orleans on the fifteenth of October, who first suggested that there might be something more to the matter than simply "hard times."

"You haven't actually been going around saying you're going back to medicine, have you?" he asked, perched on Livia's sofa rosining the bow of his violin after January's two pupils had departed one afternoon. "I had the impression you didn't think you'd do well at it, but if Ker or one of the *beaux sabreurs* of the local medical community decided to become your patron . . ."

"Ker couldn't do a thing for me." Puzzled, January turned from the piano keys. "He said I was welcome to work at Charity anytime, but I know what that work pays a junior surgeon. The only offer I had," he added wryly, "was from Roarke, as a means of getting me into the clinic to murder. Who said I was going back to medicine?"

"Froissart." Hannibal named the manager of the Orleans Ballroom, and tightened a peg. Beside him on the sofa, Les Mesdames—Livia's two stout, butter-colored cats—slept with their paws over their noses just as if they hadn't finished their daily round of hissing and posturing at one another fifteen minutes ago. The December afternoon was a misty one and the slow chilling of the light made January tired and depressed, a holdover from childhood memories of the grinding season. "I asked him why he'd hired Rich Maissie to play the St. Stephen's Day ball next week, instead of you."

"Maissie?" January had read of the ball in the newspapers, and had been expecting a note from Leon Froissart any day. He'd only thought the fussy little Parisian late with his arrangements.

"Well, he hemmed and hawed and wouldn't look me in the eye and said something about that he'd heard you'd gone back to medicine and weren't playing anymore, and anyway he'd already spoken to Maissie about the rest of the season. . . ."

"The *rest of the season?*" Nobody contracted, save by the night.

The white man's dark eyes met his, worried and questioning. January had the odd feeling of having been punched beneath the sternum; the sense of seeing the first sores of something incurable on his own skin.

"No," he said slowly. "No, I haven't spoken to him at all." It was childish to feel hurt; to remember the quadroon boys calling him *sambo* from a safe distance away.

"I thought it was strange, myself." Hannibal angled his fiddle a little toward the glass panes of the door. January got to his feet, lit a spill from the fireplace, and touched it to the branches of tallow work-candles on the piano, the table, the sconces on the wall. His mother would fuss—it was barely four—but the room was genuinely dark. "And I thought he was lying, but I couldn't imagine why. Still can't."

"Could you ask around?" said January worriedly, shaking out the spill. "Find out?" He'd been back in New Orleans now exactly thirteen months. It had been his impression that balls and parties began earlier than Christmastime, at least among the town dwellers, though the big families didn't come in from the plantations until after the grinding was done. But with no notes or requests coming in he'd thought that perhaps the fever—or maybe the summer's "hard times"—had affected the Creoles' enthusiasm for holding dances whenever and wherever they could.

But Uncle Bichet, who played the violoncello, shook his head when January had asked him about the matter in the shadowy vaults of the market one afternoon: "I thought you managed to make some remark about Ma'am Soniat that got repeated back to her, that she didn't hire you for her little ball last week—either your or that mama of yours." The old man shook his head again and dusted the powdered sugar of a beignet from his fingers.

"You know you got to be careful, Ben." Bichet eased himself back on the brick of the bench where he sat. "These Creole ladies, they take against a man, they tell all their friends. You not talkin' out of turn, since you came back from Paris, are you?"

"I didn't think Creole ladies even knew one musician from the next," replied January bitterly. "Let alone paid attention to what we say—and no, I haven't had any particular opinion about Solange Soniat. And my mother slanders everyone in town, and I've never been blackballed because of it. Have times changed that much?"

"Ben," sighed the old man, "times changin' now so that I don't know what to expect." Steamboats whistled sadly, invisible through fog gritty with soot and thick with the burnt-sweet smell of a thousand sugar vats. "All I know is you wasn't playing at the Soniats' last week, or the Bringiers' Wednesday, and that Richard Maissie that can't find his way through a country dance with a compass and a Chickasaw guide just been hired to play the Opera when they open with *Euryanthe* next month. You got somebody real mad, and that's for sure."

Xavier Peralta? January wondered. It was true that he'd run afoul of that haughty old planter last winter, when it had appeared that either he or the Peralta's son was going to hang for the murder of an octoroon beauty at a ball. But in clearing himself, he had cleared Peralta's son as well; and though at one point Peralta had attempted to kidnap him and put him on a boat out of the country, he'd gotten the impression that the planter now considered the matter closed.

In any case a few enquiries among the market-women satisfied him that Peralta père was still on his chief plantation at Alhambra, where he had been since May. And certainly a man who owned five plantations and nearly four hundred slaves had better things to think about at grinding time than scuppering the career of a piano player.

But whoever had declared himself—or herself—his enemy, thought January, he or she was almost certainly white. He was asked to play at the Blue Ribbon Balls at the Orleans Ballroom—not so frequently as last winter, to be sure—and Monsieur Froissart showed no embarrassment in dealing with him on those terms. Nor did the ballroom manager make mention of passing him over for the St. Stephen's Day subscription dance. January, hoping the matter would be forgotten, said nothing.

Still, after speaking to Uncle Bichet he began to feel uneasy whenever he passed through the brick carriageway into the courtyard behind the ballroom building, or climbed the service stairs to the ballroom itself above the gambling halls on the lower floor. From childhood he'd never liked the sense of people talking of him behind his back.

At a Mardi Gras Ball early in February he asked Dominique about it, Dominique masked and radiant in a rose silk Court-dress of sixty years ago: panniered, powdered, and patched, clinging close to Henri's side. Henri for his part did not speak to January or acknowledge that anything had ever passed between them in that little cottage in Milneburgh: but that was only the custom of the country. It wasn't done to admit that one's mistress had a brother who was a black man, whether or not that brother had saved her life. January didn't grudge it exactly. He was in fact moderately gratified to see how assiduous the fat man was of his mistress's comfort, fetching her pastries and lemonade and making sure she always had a seat in one of the olive velvet chairs around the three sides of the dance floor.

When Minou finally came over to the ivy-swagged dais, January explained what Hannibal and Uncle Bichet had told him. "You heard anything about that?" he asked his sister, under the soft strains of a Haydn air played to cover the between-dance gabble of flirting and champagne. "About someone wanting to have me blackballed? Starting rumors? Though God knows what they'd be about."

What were the rumors of Rose Vitrac about? The thought made him shiver.

"God knows what any rumor is ever about, p'tit." Minou tapped his wrist with her lacy fan, concern for him in her eyes. After four months she'd put back a little of the flesh her illness had cost her, and though she still looked tired and brittle, her smile was just as lovely. "It will blow over, cher. I've heard nothing from Mama, and of course Henri wouldn't know—I'm not sure Henri knows Jackson was re-elected. Or was elected the first time, for that matter," she added thoughtfully, though the corners of her mouth tucked up, as they always did when she spoke of her lover, and her eyes sought out the enormous pink-and-blue satin shape by the buffet, like an omnivorous pillow devouring oysters with the other Creole gentlemen. "I'm not sure it would be best to ask him, for fear of making the situation worse. All one can do is . . . well!"

January didn't know how she did it, since she wasn't looking in the direction of the triple doorway into the ballroom's vestibule at the top of the stairway from below, but she caught sight of a mother and daughter entering, and turned her head. "She must want that poor little thing out of the house! I'd have said Marie-Neige was too young to come to balls for a year yet."

It was Agnes Pellicot, with Marie-Neige.

The poor girl looked painfully shy in her grown-up gown, green-striped satin cut low over small, lush breasts. Her face peeked shyly from an explosion of fluffy dark curls beneath a Circassian turban and pearls. Her two older sisters—the eldest of the four, Marie-Anne, was with her own protector in the cluster around the buffet tables—walked behind her. Marie-Louise wore an expression of miffed suspicion, but Marie-Thérése seemed serene in the knowledge that no prospective suitor of hers—or Marie-Louise's, for that matter—was going to find the chubby fourteen-year-old any competition for the elder two. January knew better than to catch the girl's eye, though he suspected she'd be grateful to see a familiar face.

But he did say, "If you get a chance, Minou, would you ask Marie-Neige if she's heard from her schoolmistress, Mademoiselle Vitrac? Or if she knows where Mademoiselle might be found? I'd appreciate it."

"Mademoiselle Vitrac?" Minou's forehead wrinkled under the snailshell curls of her powdered wig. "That woman who stole all that money and let those poor girls all die of the fever?"

"That's a lie!" said January, shocked that the story had worked itself down to the plaçée demimonde. "Who told you . . . ?"

"Hey, Maestro." Uncle Bichet set aside the champagne he'd been sharing with Hannibal during this exchange, and picked up his viol's beribboned bow. "Old Froissart squintin' this way. Looks like those folks out there startin' to die of no dancin'. Can't let that happen."

"Will you play a Basket Quadrille for the next dance?" urged Minou. "Hercule Lafrènniére promised me one. . . ."

"I'll play one at the end of the set if you get Henri to dance with Marie-Neige." January felt a pang of pity for the girl. "She can't possibly be afraid of him."

"Well." Minou flirted her fan at him. "I'll see what I can do. But if Henri runs away with her I'll have you to blame."

January sank his concentration back into the music—a waltz-cotillion and a delicate Mozart country dance—but his eyes returned a dozen times to the dancers, seeking out the shell hue of his sister's gown, or the multifarious greens and whites of Marie-Neige's. It was hard not to think about Rose; hard not to imagine her stumbling along the banquettes after her release from the Cabildo, frightened and wondering desperately what would become of her. Hard not to picture the men he'd seen in the darkness of the Bayou step from an alleyway in front of her—then behind her as she turned in panic—clubs and rope in hand.

Not Rose, he thought, as he had prayed daily for months now. *Not Rose.*

Shouts cracked like gunshots from the vestibule, breaking the music's flow. "You, sir, are a lying lackey of an Orleanniste whoreson!" "Better the lackey of true kings than a half-caste Radical murderer!"

January broke off his playing as a woman screamed. Beside him, Hannibal murmured resignedly, "Here we go again."

Since everyone in the ballroom was rushing to the vestibule doors, the musicians rose and followed, at a more leisurely pace, Hannibal carefully stowing his violin on top of the piano and scooping up a bottle of champagne from the buffet table in passing. "Brinvilliers and DuPage, over that Conti Street brickyard lawsuit?" he guessed, naming two lawyers who, not content with an enlivening exchange of personalities in court ten days ago, had continued their insults of one another's ancestry, ethics, and personal habits in the *New Orleans Bee*'s ever-libellous letter columns. January's mother read them aloud over breakfast, with obvious relish—there was never any shortage of such altercations in the press, and they almost invariably ended in violence.

The fight in progress in the upstairs vestibule was hardly the first—or the thousandth—such event January had witnessed in two-thirds of a lifetime playing at New Orleans public entertainments. Both men were armed with small swords—fatally, the employees of the ballroom had hesitated to confiscate weapons that were part of their fancy-dress costumes—and the taller lawyer, younger and fiercely mustachioed, with a Romantic's crop of long black hair, was lunging and striking at the shorter, a military-looking little man in more-or-less Turkish garb who'd already taken a cut on his temple and was bleeding freely. The shorter man was shouting, "Cur! Coward! Having refused to meet me like a gentleman . . . !"

"Refused! When you set your thugs to ambush me and prevent me from reducing your carcass to the bleeding hash God intended that I should?"

"Brinvilliers used that sentence already in his letter about DuPage to the *Bee* last week," remarked Hannibal, worming his way to the forefront and taking a long pull at the champagne from the neck of the bottle.

"I thought it sounded familiar."

"Messieurs! Messieurs!" Froissart was bleating and circling but kept a wary distance from the fray.

The tall Brinvilliers lunged in in a whirl of lace collar and bucket-top boots. But his shorter opponent sidestepped, knocking the blade on the forte so that it spun from Brinvilliers' hand. Nothing discomposed, Brinvilliers seized the nearest chair and heaved it at DuPage, impaling the cushion and breaking DuPage's blade. With the older man thrust back and off balance, the taller proceeded to kick and bludgeon him when he fell to the floor. Everyone in the vestibule was shouting. A stout American in truly appalling Indian buckskins, whom January recognized as the banker Hubert Granville, lunged in to try to drag Brinvilliers off. He was himself seized by two of, presumably, the taller lawyer's friends; a second fight erupted, all participants of which staggered too far back and fell down the stairs, turkey feathers flying in all directions.

Brinvilliers half-turned his head to see what the commotion might be; and DuPage lunged up from the floor, a knife every bit as long and deadly as any Kaintuck's in his hand. Someone yelled a warning, which was the only reason Brinvilliers wasn't gutted. As it was, he took the blade in the left chest; and amid curses, screams, and fountains of arterial blood, the combatants were finally separated, all the women scurrying back, clutching at their skirts.

January was already striding forward, pulling his handkerchief from his pocket and calling out, "Handkerchiefs—quickly—anything . . ."

Hannibal, with surprising speed considering the amount of alcohol he had consumed, thrust at least two of the buffet towels into his hands; January wadded them into a pad and pressed them hard on Brinvilliers' chest. "Knife," he said. "Scissors, anything . . ."

A lady's lace-gloved hand passed a pair of reticule-sized German scissors over his shoulder. Hannibal was kneeling beside him. "Hold this," January told him. The towels were already a warm crimson wad under his hands. "I'll cut away the shirt. . . ."

Someone seized his shoulder, thrust him roughly aside. "*If* you please, sir . . . !"

It was Emil Barnard.

Emil Barnard in the new black swallowtail coat and tall hat of a prosperous doctor. Emil Barnard with a four-guinea pearl stickpin in his cravat and expensively scented macassar oil on his slick snuff-colored hair.

January was shocked, but not so shocked that he didn't make a grab for the pressure pad Barnard had dislodged from the pouring wound. Barnard pushed his hand away, "Keep your hands off him," he commanded ringingly. "I am a doctor. The man's constitution needs to be lowered before any further medical attention can be of the slightest avail."

"That man is bleeding to death!"

"Don't give way to panic at the sight of a little blood," said Barnard. "What kind of a surgeon are you?" He removed his glove, and pushed the sodden towel just slightly to one side, so that the blood would not spurt. "Indeed, I may have to bleed the man again tomorrow, should his sanguine humors remain elevated." He took the scissors from January's hand, snipped Brinvilliers's shirt free, and proceeded to extract a pad of clean bandages from his own medical bag, which someone had brought him double-time from the cloak-room below.

"Now this," he said, holding up a phial from his bag, filled with something that looked like rusty water to the view of the crowd, "is a formula of my own making, a compound of calomel and opium, to further depress the patient's humors and—"

"The man is bleeding to death," January interrupted grimly,

pressing forward and pulling another towel from the nerveless grip of one of the waiters. He started to slide it under Brinvilliers' body, to tighten the dressing; again, Barnard thrust him aside.

"Will someone please remove this man? He is interfering with me when Monsieur Brinvilliers's life may be at stake!"

Someone took January's arm. "The man knows what he's doing, son," said a firm but kindly voice.

January stared at the speaker, a Creole businessman probably ten years his junior. "He does *not* know what he's doing," he said, surprised at how level his own voice was. "Less than five months ago he was stealing clothes off the dead at the Charity Hospital! He—"

"You're speaking of a partner of one of the foremost physicians in the city, boy," snapped someone else, and Froissart hurried between, catching January's arm. Exasperated at being handled, January pulled free, but Froissart was already herding him to the back of the crowd.

"It's all right," the manager was saying in a mollifying tone, "he's only upset at the sight of the blood. . . ."

"Monsieur Froissart," said January in a low voice, as the manager pushed him toward the little hallway that led from the vestibule to the supper rooms—closed during the Blue Ribbon Balls—and a sort of retiring parlor where women could fix their hems and flounces and hair. "Monsieur Froissart, I was a surgeon at the Hôtel Dieu in Paris for six years! When a man is bleeding—"

"Yes, yes, but Monsieur Couret is right, you know," said Froissart. "Emil Barnard is one of the rising doctors of the city, one of the best of the new young men. Surely he knows what he's doing. I hope he didn't hear your remarks about him. . . ."

"I don't give a . . . it doesn't concern me if he did! Sir," added January. "If Brinvilliers were conscious enough to choose his own treatment it would be one thing, but—"

"You're upset," said Froissart. "I understand. Perhaps it would be better if you went home now. The others can manage without you, and I'm afraid after all this unpleasantness you probably wouldn't be able to perform."

That was all I needed, thought January, swiftly descending the service stairs to the courtyard a few minutes later, his bloodied coat and gloves folded carefully into his music satchel and his shirtsleeves damp from the wash water in the upstairs parlor in which he'd wrung them out. *What may be my only work this season—the quadroon balls—and now Froissart's worried about what his clients will think of me.*

The night was mild and thickly foggy, permeated with the haunting burnt smell of the sugar houses across the river. Each paper lantern on the courtyard trees was ringed in its own muzzy moondog of light. By their glow January saw a pale figure beneath the trees: the round little face, the explosion of pomaded curls beneath turban and jewels. "It's only me, Mademoiselle Marie-Neige, Monsieur Janvier. It's all right." He nodded back toward the ballroom. "You can go back in. The trouble's over."

"Thank you." The girl's voice was small and shaky. For all her pushiness, Agnes Pellicot kept her daughters fairly sheltered. It would have been Marie-Neige's first encounter with the violence of the city in which she lived. She started to hurry away, then turned back. "I'm sorry I didn't say hello. M'sieu Janvier. Mama told me . . ."

"And your mama was right," said January gently. "A young lady can't let the young white gentlemen see her talking to the musicians. We can talk other times."

"Minou told me you were asking about Mademoiselle Rose," the girl said softly. She stepped closer to him, but must have smelled the blood still on his clothes, for he saw her hesitate and saw the startled movement of her white-gloved hands. Under the rouge she looked quite young and very lost. She had, January remembered, only a few months ago nursed three of her friends through a terrible illness, only to lose them—and a place where she'd been happy—in the end.

"I don't know where Mademoiselle's gone," Marie-Neige went on. "She might have changed her name, you know, and gone back to New York where she went to school. She could teach school in New York, couldn't she? It makes me angry, when I hear people talk about Mademoiselle not taking care of us or stealing money."

Behind them in the ballroom, music rose again, violinless and with a fey, swooping rhythm, as if the heart and spine of the music had been taken over by Dionysus instead of Apollo.

"I know you liked her," the girl added, her voice now very quiet.

"She liked you. When you were gone, looking after Minou, Mademoiselle Rose was like . . . like a ship without a sail, she said she felt. I'm sorry you weren't there to help her."

"I'm sorry I wasn't, too."

"I was so happy with her."

Marie-Neige turned, and hurried back to the lamps under the gallery, to the broad double-stair that led up toward her mother and her sisters and all her potential suitors; toward the more-trodden and safer road.

January sighed. "I was, too, p'tit," he said. "I was, too."

As if to mock January's conviction that he would never work in New Orleans again, the following week brought a note in English from a Mr. Wallace Fraikes, business manager for Mrs. Emily Redfern. Mr. Fraikes requested his services as a musician at a St. Valentine's Day ball to be given that Friday in Mrs. Redfern's new home.

"Ruling her out, I suppose, as the source of the libels against you," remarked Hannibal, who was the first person January saw when shown into the tiny and barren chamber where the musicians were given leave to rest for precisely five minutes every other hour through the evening.

"I don't see how she could have been the source of the campaign against me in any case." January spoke quietly, though the footfalls of the polite, livery-clad majordomo were fading down the two flights of rear stairs up which January had been shown. The room lay at the back of the enormous yellow house in the American faubourg, overlooking the yard. "Madame Redfern left town before the campaign against me started." The penitential chamber had probably been designed for a governess, its wallpaper cheap and faded, its minuscule pine table chipped and battered. A shabby screen concealed a chamber pot. From the single tiny window January could just see down into the yard, where household slaves carried dishes across from the kitchen building: he counted two men, two women, and a young boy. The males all wore what looked like new livery.

"Never underestimate the power of the truly vindictive. I had a London aunt—Lady Elliswrode, her name was—who could slaughter, joint, dress, and smoke a reputation in a week from a hundred miles away. She had a truly vicious turn of phrase, and you could float a ship of the line in her inkwell. I thought you said La Redfern was destitute."

"She was." January poured a little of the liquid from the pottery jug on the table. It was beer—watered. There was bread, thin as a communion wafer and nearly as flavorless. "Although she can't have been that destitute," he added thoughtfully, "if she was willing to whistle a pearl necklace and a hundred and ninety dollars down the wind."

"And you're sure that was her necklace?"

"What other one would Cora have?"

A man came into the yard through the tradesman's gate, and spoke to the majordomo who came out to meet him. January winced. "Wonderful. It's our privilege to have Philippe deCoudreau and his clarionet confusing people all evening about what tune we're playing. Who do we get on viol—Pylade Vassage? The Deaf Fiddler of the Faubourg Trèmé?"

"Don't laugh." Hannibal took a careful swig of opium from one hip-flask and followed it with a sip of rum from another. "That's exactly who we have to work with. *And* Laurent Lamartine on flute. It may be coincidence, but I doubt it. The moment La Redfern set the date for tonight's entertainment, Delphine Lalaurie moved up *her* ball . . ."

"Not again!"

"And this time, Madame managed to bag the best musicians—*all* the best musicians. She must have ten of them tonight, everybody who wasn't already playing at Caldwell's Theatre. The only reason I'm not there too is because one of Big Annie's girls—did I tell you I'm living in the shed behind Big Annie's these days?—cut up her note and used it for curling-papers before I got it. God knows how many others have gone the same way this month." He coughed and took another sip of the opium tincture. "At least they don't steal my violin."

January stood still, hearing the far-off pressure of the door opening, closing; the muffled voice of the worst musician in Louisiana trying to cadge supper off Madame Redfern's majordomo. *For all the good that's likely to do him.*

He hurt inside, like a child left out of a party, and knew that his hurt was childish. "Hannibal, what's going on? What *is* this? I'm better than that. I know I am. Who could get to Madame Lalaurie? Tell her not to hire me? She's above pettiness like that, she does what she pleases and be damned. I taught her daughters . . ."

He hesitated, the ugliness of that hellish session returning to him. *From the beginning again, please. . . .* And the hatred and terror in Pauline Blanque's eyes.

There was a woman who kept her two nieces chained in a cellar. . . .

One's always hearing about domestic tyrants. . . . No one dares speak of it. . . . They know it'll do them no good.

Was this all because he'd seen her do that to her daughters?

"Damn it, the woman gave me money to help a runaway slave!"

Hannibal gave up looking around for another lamp—the one on the table gave barely more light than a candle—and opened his violin case. "They wouldn't have to tell her not to hire you," he pointed out. "Just tell her that you were an atheist, or a bigamist. Or that you helped Rose kill those three girls so she wouldn't have to feed them."

January felt his skin prickle with rage. "Is that what they're saying?"

"Ben, I don't know what they're saying. I don't move in those circles. Madame Lalaurie—or any of them—doesn't even have to believe you actually did anything. Just that your presence will offend someone who'll be there. They're all connected: the Prieurs, the Mc-Cartys, the Forstalls, the Blanques, the d'Aunoys. . . . They've all got daughters to marry off."

The door opened. Philippe deCoudreau entered, laughing and

shaking his head, a slim young dandy with skin as fair as Hèlier Lapatie's had been and a marvelous and unfounded conceit of himself.

"You know as well as I do they can't take risks about not being invited to the right parties."

"And isn't it just the right party tonight?" deCoudreau laughed, picking up the beer pitcher and sniffing it. "For a woman paying off her creditors at a shilling on the pound five months ago, Our Hostess sure found some money someplace." He nudged January in the ribs. "Think Madame Redfern found a wealthy widower to set her up? Did you take a look at that buffet she's laying down? Boeuf à la mode and wine jellies—we're in for some of that I *don't* think."

DeCoudreau laughed again. He had bright blue eyes and the sort of laugh described by popular novelists as "infectious," though January personally considered it in the same category with some of the other infectious complaints available in New Orleans. The thought of trying to play the piano under and around and through the man's aberrant sense of timing all night made his teeth ache.

As he descended to the ballroom January thought, *I'm doing it, too. Accepting that the Lalaurie party is the only place to be seen tonight. That everything else is second rate.*

No wonder the McCartys and the Bringiers and the Lafrènniéres found it so easy to manipulate those around them.

Unfortunately, all the evening's events bore out that judgment. The only Creoles present were the minor, on-the-make skirmishers on the fringes of society and political power. Everyone with money or influence was at the Lalaurie ball. As the evening progressed, these quarreled repeatedly and violently with the American lawyers, brokers, and real-estate speculators present. January recognized at least two of the slave brokers who had been at Madame Redfern's Washington Hotel affair that summer, and could not rid himself of the sensation of being priced by the pound: Americans always made him uneasy. If nothing else, the volume of tobacco expectorated was enough to pollute the room with its stench. Madame Redfern, still in deep mourning, circulated among her guests with the vulpine Fraikes in attendance, and January could not but note the fashionable lines of her dress and the quantities of black lace and jet jewelry festooning her stubby person.

"It's a terrible city, terrible city," he heard a man say in English, over the general babble of talk between sets of polka and waltz. "Did you hear about poor Yates and his family? Found them all together in his wife's bedroom, all dead of the cholera. . . . But opportunities?" The man, a thick-set Philadelphian—at least January thought the accent was Philadelphian—kissed his hand. "Speaking of opportunities, Gallagher, I've been meaning to ask you about renting slaves for the mill. . . ."

"I think you have been very, very brave," a woman was saying, taking Emily Redfern's black-mitted hands in her own. A number of women, January noted, were still in mourning, but fewer than he'd seen at Creole functions last winter. The Americans tended to have more money, and to flee earlier; their relatives were in New York or Washington or Boston, not in New Orleans itself.

"I was lucky." Madame Redfern was not veiled now, and her square face assumed an expression of pious martyrdom. "My poor Otis! I will always blame myself for not being more insistent that he get rid of that wicked girl! Because, of course, I saw from the beginning what she was. But he never would." She sighed, a world of carefully manipulated wistfulness in her eyes, as if it was her belief that the lamented Otis had been too good-hearted to think ill of anyone.

"Did they ever catch her?"

The widow shook her head. "Poor soul. I can only pray that she will one day realize the error of her ways." She still had a voice like scale weights clacking in a pan: *A measure of wheat for a penny, and three measures of barley for a penny. . . .* "I suppose I should hire men to pursue her wherever she flees, for, of course, her theft left me destitute; but I don't do badly now. Because of the way Papa tied it up in trust, at least they weren't able to distrain Black Oak. And the sale of the other slaves let me discharge Otis's debts at some percentage of their value. And Mr. Fraikes assures me that . . ."

They moved off, Madame Redfern relating yet again how Mr. Fraikes had made sure she would be no longer liable for the remaining seventy-five percent of her late husband's debt. January wondered how many people she had told this to. Still, given the quality of the chicken croquettes, quiche lorraine, bombe glacée, and éclairs ranged along the buffet table, and the obvious promise of money in the new red velvet side chairs and heavily gilded picture frames, everyone seemed more than willing to listen a second or third (or sixth) time.

". . . wicked girl, to do that to poor Emily, who had been so good to her. . . ."

". . . died in absolute agony. . . ."

". . . Mr. Fraikes simply told Fazende that he'd signed the paper expressing complete satisfaction with the discharge at the time. . . ."

". . . a trust fund in perpetuity, and not actually hers—and therefore not his to sell for debt, thank God—at all."

Mr. Bailey walked by, deep in conversation with a planter's son. The Magistrate glanced curiously at January, as if trying to recall his face, but failed and walked on.

A polka. A schottische. Flouncing laces and swirling silk. The memory of that small determined face under the red headscarf: *You know how they do.*

Why hadn't Redfern claimed the pearls?

When the Reverend Micajah Dunk made his appearance he was surrounded at once by nearly every woman in the room, and for some thirty minutes held a species of court under the skeptical eyes of the disgruntled men. Served them right, thought January, with a wry inner grin. He'd seen too many of these men sneak away to the quadroon balls, leaving their wives, their fiancées, to "make a tapestry," as the saying went. About time they found themselves with their noses out of joint.

And the Reverend Dunk, he had to admit, had a good deal of the messianic magnetism that frequently clings to preachers, particularly when they are physically powerful men in their prime. Dunk had the gift of grave and complete attention, a way of looking at any woman with those curiously long-lashed brown eyes, that, January knew, drew women. Hannibal had it as well.

A surrogate lover? A cicisbeo, such as well-born Italian ladies kept about them, safe but titillating?

And clearly, though he gave every woman present the impression that she was the most important person in his life—or certainly the most important contributor toward the building of his new church— Dunk favored Mrs. Redfern. As she walked with him down the length of the double-parlor toward the door that led to hall and supper room, January saw the minister's gestures take in the new velvet furniture, the carved mantelpiece and the Austrian lusters of the gasolier overhead, congratulating and admonishing, but admonishing with a twinkle in his eyes.

"Now don't let me hear this new wealth has gone to your head, Madame." He had a voice trained to fill a church, and the conclusion of the contredanse "Tartan Plaid"—in which scarcely a handful of couples had participated due to the desertion of all the women—left a space of relative silence in which he could clearly be heard. "Would you believe it, ladies," he turned to take in the dozen or so who clustered at his heels, "when I came down to the city last summer, at the very landing where I boarded they loaded a matched team of white horses whose cost alone could have provided a dozen beds for those wretched sufferers dying in the alleys of this city during the pestilence? It isn't God who sent the fever to punish mankind, ladies; it is Man who brought it upon himself, with sheer, greedy neglect of his fellow man."

"And I suppose," murmured Hannibal, plucking experimentally at a string, "that his idea of doing God's work was buying those slaves of La Redfern's at four hundred apiece and selling them the following day for nine fifty? She doesn't seem to notice that he scraped her for close to seven thousand dollars, 'doing God's work.'"

"I wonder." January blotted his forehead with a handkerchief. Though the windows to one side of the room stood open—American casements, not the French glazed doors—the place was stuffily hot, and in the hall outside he could hear voices raised:

"Sir, no man speaks ill of His Majesty while there is breath left in my body to defend him!"

Not again.

"You wonder if your services are going to be snubbed again in favor of a nice dose of calomel and citrus juice?"

"No." January turned to the next piece, a Mozart march, the last one of this set. His head ached. He felt slightly sick from the stench of tobacco soaking into wool carpets, from concentrating on the tempo above deCoudreau's constant efforts to speed it up, from remembering Cora and wondering where Rose might have gone.

"I wonder what Micajah Dunk was doing at Spanish Bayou the day before Otis Redfern's death."

The men down on the engine deck pulled me up and hid me in the hay bales. . . .

From his mother January had heard all about the white carriage team Laurence Jumon had bought, their cost to the penny, and the names of the other men who'd bid.

The horses at least stood a good chance of surviving the month of September, he thought, as he crossed the Place d'Armes in the pre-dawn silence of bone-eating fog. Which was probably more than could have been said of the thick-crowded gaggle of Irish and Germans coming down from Ohio on the *New Brunswick* that Wednesday, to make their fortunes in New Orleans.

But opportunities? the Philadelphia guest had said—broker or banker or one of those blackleg-lawyer-cum-slave-dealers who haunted the saloons of Bourbon Street plotting the conquest of Mexico—and had kissed his hand like a connoisseur.

For some.

Micajah Dunk had been at Spanish Bayou on the morning before Otis Redfern died. It was in *his* honor, not Redfern's, that the ham and apple tarts had been laid on. It fit. Dunk looked like a man who had never missed a meal in his life.

Through the fog, the Cathedral was a blur of white, gradually resolving into twin, pointed towers, round window black as a watching eye. Men's voices chimed from the levee behind him, as they loaded wood onto the steamboat decks: the *Amulet,* the *Missourian,* the *Boonslick,* bound upriver for Natchez and St. Louis as soon as the fog burned off and it got light enough, with cargoes of scythes and compasses, perfumes and coffee, and slaves for the plantations of the Missouri Territory. The smell of their smoke rasped in the cold air.

The party had ended at two. Late for Americans, but as January and Hannibal and DeCoudreau (who had invited himself along to late supper at one of the cafés in the Market) had made their way up Rue Chartres they'd passed half a dozen lighted windows where the Creoles still danced, gambled, gossiped, the custom of the country in Carnival season, January's second since his return from Paris.

Madame Redfern's provision for the comfort of her musicians had been decidedly lacking, and by the time the three musicians (Laurent Lamartine of the tin ear and squeaky flute said his wife would worry if he stayed out) had finished oysters, crawfish jambalaya, coffee, and beignets, the black river fog had rinsed to opal gray.

Micajah Dunk at Spanish Bayou. Micajah Dunk kissing Emily Redfern's hands. It was quite clear to January that the five thousand dollars Cora was supposed to have stolen had left the Redfern plantation somehow: the creditors had searched the place fairly thoroughly, and Emily Redfern had been flat on her back in bed. In bed, and loudly proclaiming in that clanking voice that she had been poisoned and robbed. And the minute they were out the door she had taken steps to close off her husband's debts for whatever the creditors would take.

It explained, he thought, why she hadn't claimed the pearls.

To do so would have led to the questioning of someone who had actually spoken to Cora. Someone who might cause Cora to be found. True, a slave could not testify against her mistress, but there were those who would listen to Cora and ask questions of their own.

January shivered and glanced over his shoulder at the dew-netted grass, the sleeping dark of the trees. He had never gotten over his uneasiness, born in the fever season, about being followed, had never lost the fear of being watched and stalked. Hèlier Lapatie and Liam Roarke were both in their graves, but the knowledge that anyone else could work a kidnapping—and get away with it—lay like a chip of metal embedded in the back of his brain. It was too easy for a free man of color—a free woman of color—merely to drop out of sight.

Easier still, for an escaping slave.

No one would ask.

Had Rose guessed? Had Cora told Rose things she hadn't mentioned to him, things that Rose hadn't even recalled until she saw the Redfern woman at the Cabildo? Things that would cause her to guess why Madame Redfern could not afford to have Cora found. It returned to him that Madame Redfern had left Milneburgh within a day or two of seeing, perhaps speaking to, Rose.

The thought tormented him as he edged down the narrow walkway between his mother's house and the cottage next door, as he crossed the silent yard to the garçonnière stairs. Hannibal slept once again among the bravos and whores of Girod Street. Rose's books— Anacreon, Plato, and Kant, Dalton's *New System of Chemical Philosophy,* and Agnesi's *Analytical Institutions*—still stacked the wall of January's room and the attic above it like bricks.

He passed his hand over them as he entered, the way he had touched the silks and wools folded everywhere in the Paris rooms once upon a time, seeking to feel in them the warmth of the woman whose hands had made them magic.

We have her books, Hannibal had said. *We'll be seeing her again.*

Rose had no fear. Rose would have gone to speak with La Redfern.

He glanced outside as he shut the door, his heart beating slow but uncomfortably heavy in his chest.

Just light. Too early to amble over to Nyades Street and ask casual questions of the Redfern cook on her way to the market. An hour, he decided and lay down, fully clothed, on the bed.

He had plenty of time. With the epidemics over, he no longer served at the Hospital, but neither was his schedule overburdened with pupils. Did Madame Redfern know of his connection with Rose Vitrac? Had someone at the Cabildo told her something that had caused her to guess? Was she, in fact, behind the effort to put him out of business, run him out of town, as she had run Rose?

But in that case, why hire him to play?

He seemed to be standing at the gateway of the cemetery on Rue des Ramparts, watching a man lead two women away among the tombs. For a moment he thought it was Reverend Dunk and his little court of females, but he realized in the next moment that the man was enormous and powerful and black: Bronze John the dead-cart man. January could see only the women's backs, but he saw that one of them walked like a jockey or a dancer, her witch-black hair unbound to her hips, and the other wore a neat white tignon, a simple green wool skirt. The women held hands, like sisters or friends. He cried out their names, and the shock of trying to do so, trying to run to catch up with them, was like falling.

It was fully light. Someone was knocking at the door.

January stumbled across and opened the shutters.

"I purely hate to be always comin' up on you this way." Abishag Shaw shoved aside his disreputable hat to finger-comb his long hair. His thin, rather creaky tenor was carefully neutral. "But I got orders to put you under arrest."

"Arrest?" January glanced past him toward the house. The rear door was shuttered fast. If his mother knew of Shaw's presence, which she surely must, she was having nothing to do with it.

All he could think of was Mrs. Redfern.

"Arrest for what?"

Shaw spit a line of tobacco to the gallery boards by his feet. "Murder."

"This is ridiculous." Judge J. F. Canonge slapped the warrant on his desk. "Who swore this out? Who's behind this?"

January opened his mouth to remark that he had wondered about that himself, but decided against it. He folded his manacled hands and forced himself to look at the floor until he had his face under control.

He knew he should be afraid, but all he felt was the trapped, blind rage of a baited bull and an overwhelming desire to break somebody's neck.

"Louis Brinvilliers is the brother of Jean Brinvilliers," said Shaw, in his mild voice, "who—"

"I know who Jean Brinvilliers was," snapped Canonge. His craggy face was that of a man who has packed life with everything that it will hold, in great careless handfuls: burnt brown, deep-lined, dark eyes impatient and intolerant of fools. There was a story that he'd once sworn out a warrant on all five State Supreme Court Justices rather than change his conduct of a case. Looking at him now January believed it. The Judge's English was pure as an upper-class Londoner's, his deep voice wrought gold. "The whole concept of a medical man's being held liable for a patient's death in these circumstances is absurd. That's like hanging me along with a thief if I failed to get him acquitted."

It was dark outside. Saturday night; Canonge was probably the only justice of the Criminal Court who'd have come in late rather than let a man spend the night in a cell, waiting for the Recorders' Court to reopen. With the part of him that wasn't seething with rage January felt grateful. The day had been a profoundly awful one.

Canonge turned the warrant over, looking for signatures. "Whose idea was this? Louis Brinvilliers doesn't have the brains to read a contract. Jonchere signed the warrant." He glared across at January, eyes piercing under graying brows. "You run yourself foul of one of Brinvilliers's friends, boy?"

"I don't know," answered January, and remembered to add, "sir." His knuckles smarted from an altercation with another prisoner—Tuesday would be Mardi Gras and every drunken keelboat hand, every argumentative Napoleoniste, every filibuster in the city, it seemed, had been in the jail cheek-by-jowl and looking for a fight. January's head ached from the constant thump and howl of brass bands and revelers in the street, and from the yammering of a madman in the cell next door. One of the men in his own cell had been far gone in delirium tremens. January felt like he'd never be clean again.

"I wouldn't know Jean Brinvilliers from President Jackson, sir. He was bleeding, he needed a doctor. I was a surgeon for six years at the Hôtel Dieu in Paris. Next time I see a man bleeding—" He bit the words off. One had to be careful with whites.

The first time he'd been locked in the Cabildo, almost exactly a year ago, he had been consumed by fear that he'd be sold into slavery by venal officials or simply from carelessness. Now he was sufficiently sure of his own position in the free colored community—and sufficiently confident that people, including Lieutenant Shaw, would vouch for him as a free man—that he had not suffered the same sleepless anxiety through the day, but still the experience had not been pleasant. All morning he'd listened to the whippings being administered in the courtyard, some to thieves and prostitutes for petty crimes, others to slaves sent in by their owners, at twenty-five cents a stroke.

Once he thought he'd seen Mamzelle Marie pass the door of the cell, on her way to comfort some other prisoner or perhaps for some other reason.

In a calmer voice, he went on, "For about two months it's been clear to me—and my friends will bear me out—that someone has been spreading rumors about me, trying to ruin me, for reasons of which I am ignorant. I don't know whether this is connected to those efforts or not."

Canonge tossed the warrant down among the neat stacks of papers that almost solidly covered his desk: dockets, journals, correspondence in English, Spanish, and French. In addition to being a Judge of the Criminal Court, Canonge and his law partner still handled the affairs and estates of half a dozen of the most prominent Creole families in town, disposed of estates and executed escrows and wills. The whole of his book-lined office on the Cabildo's upper floor smelled of beeswax and stale coffee—like most Creoles, Canonge seemed to prefer candles to lamps—and those from the clerk's empty desk had been transferred to his own when the man had gone home at six.

"It says the warrant was sworn out on the advice of a Dr. Emil Barnard." Canonge tapped with a skeletal forefinger at the notes written on the back of the warrant. "Barnard was the fellow took over from you at the ballroom that night, wasn't he? Took over the case. A regular doctor, not a surgeon. He seems to think—or he's gotten Brinvilliers to think—that your delaying of his treatment was what cost Brinvilliers's brother his life."

"Emil Barnard . . ." January began, then closed his mouth again. White men as a rule did not like to hear other white men insulted by colored.

"I hear tell," said Shaw mildly, "sir, that this Emil Barnard is a charlatan. He don't have a regular license, mostly got his doctorin' out of books. Ker over to Charity'll tell you. Somehow Barnard got took as a junior partner by Dr. Lalaurie. He works with Dr. Soublet at that clinic he's got on Bourbon Street."

"Hmph." Canonge scribbled a note to himself, then raised a dark impatient eye. "And Lalaurie will tell you Ker is a charlatan, and Sanchez over on Poydras Street will tell you Lalaurie doesn't know a clavicle from a clavichord, and Lemonier on Royal Street got into a duel a month ago with Sanchez over the use of lunar caustic and Velno's Vegetable Syrup. Have you ever read the letters Soublet exchanged with Dr. Connaud, on St. Louis Street, about 'stretching bones and reaccommodating the ligaments of the body'? It's enough to make you lock your doors and die. Take those things off that man."

Without comment, Shaw produced a key and removed the manacles from January's wrists. The iron had galled the flesh even in the short walk from his cell down to the courtyard and up the stairs; January made a mental resolve to douse the raw flesh with alcohol the minute he could. After being in the cell since nine that morning he was convinced his clothing harbored quarts of roaches and maggots, and he knew excruciatingly well that it harbored fleas.

"I'll deal with Jonchere when I see him. I'm surprised at him for even signing this. You, boy." Canonge jabbed a quill at January. "You be more careful whose bad side you get on, you hear? We can't afford to waste our time on foolery like this. Not at Carnival, with half the population trying to kill the other half in gambling brawls. Stick to what you know best."

Eyes on his boot toes again, January replied, "I will, sir. Thank you, sir."

"Give him his papers back and get him out of here." Canonge had already pulled another page of notes from the several neat piles on his desk. "Town's swarming with murderers and they pull in some damfool Good Samaritan. . . ."

In the main booking room downstairs, the Guards had just brought in Kentucky Williams, drunk, screaming, and fighting like a netted tigress against the four men it took to contain her. In this the whore was ably assisted by her sisters-in-crime, a trio of harridans known as Railspike, Maggie Fury, and Kate the Gouger. Shaw muttered, "Lordy," as Railspike produced a slungshot from her ample and unfettered bosom and began cracking heads: "You bide a spell, Maestro, if you would. If they kill me don't tell nobody how it happened. It ain't somethin' I want on my tombstone."

Shaw waded into the maelstrom of bare legs, thrashing breasts, yellowed petticoats and blue uniforms, dodging a swat with the slung-shot that cracked audibly on the point of his shoulder, and assisted Boechter—who was about half Williams's weight—and the others in dragging the Girod Street Harpies away from their manacled partner and thrusting them, screeching and cursing, out the door. January remained against the wall until the fighting was over, then came forward without a word and helped bandage up LaBranche, who'd taken a bad cut on the forearm from somebody's knife: "Don't let anyone arrest me if he dies," he remarked sourly, when Shaw came over to hand the hurt man a tin cup of whisky.

"Jesus, Mary, and Joseph, Lieutenant, I'll sooner fight one of their men anytime!" The man gulped it down.

"She's a she-steamboat and no mistake." Shaw helped him to his feet and supported him into the little infirmary cupboard where, four months previously, January had examined the Grille brothers after the fight on Bayou St. John.

"Now, that warrant was the silliest damn thing I ever heard of," said the Kentuckian when he returned, still rubbing his shoulder. "I thought Canonge ought to hear about it. He's a sensible fella."

"Thank you." January sighed, knowing that, even with the long day in the cells taken into account, things could have been far worse. "Thank you very much. I take it none of my family came to make my bail?" As he'd been led out of the yard past his mother's house she hadn't even so much as opened the shutters. Nothing to do with *her.* January didn't know whether to be bitter or amused.

"Your sister came by." Shaw pulled a kerchief from his pocket and wiped the last stray drops and smears of blood from the bench where January had made the injured LaBranche sit. "Mrs. Corbier, that is. Said Mamzelle Marie mentioned to her as how you was here. She asked if there was anything she could do, but seein' as the charge was murder, silly or not, there wasn't no bail." He fished January's papers from his desk and handed them over, official recognition that he was a free man.

January checked them and slid them into his jacket pocket. They were actually a copy of the original papers, the signatures carefully forged. He had six or seven such copies cached in his room and at the houses of both his sisters, just in case of mishap. It cost him an effort to say, "Thank you." Not to think about the fact that he had not needed such things in France. "And please thank Judge Canonge again for coming in and saving me two nights in the cells. I am very grateful for his trouble."

When Shaw returned to his desk January followed, hands behind his back. "What became of Mrs. Redfern's pearls?"

The Kentuckian didn't look up from trimming the candles. "Mrs. Redfern's pearls that allegedly ain't really her pearls?"

"Those very pearls," January said. "Because if you've still got them, I'd like to take them out to Milneburgh tomorrow, as bait to get me in to speak to Reverend Dunk." And he told Shaw about Laurence Jumon's carriage team of white horses.

"Now that is most interestin'." The gray cold eyes narrowed as Shaw settled into his battered chair. "Because I been a little curious about this particular Prophet of the Lord. Seems instead of buildin' this Church out to Milneburgh with the money he made out of resellin' Mrs. R's slaves, Reverend Hellfire turned around and *bought* slaves, to the tune of about eighty-five hundred dollars . . . which if you calculate the amount of Church money he used to buy them slaves from her, exactly half the profit he made, plus five thousand dollars, it all works out to just about that very figure."

There was a time when January would have been surprised that a Kaintuck could accomplish such mathematics. Now he only said, "Dunk's fronting for her."

"Either that, or he's doin' a damn good job of makin' it look that way." Shaw opened one of the desk's lower drawers, withdrew a tied packet of papers, then, rising, put a hand on January's shoulder as if to murmur a confidence, and drew him to the Cabildo's outer doors. With their backs to the lamplit room he tilted the papers. Pearls slid into January's hand.

In front of them, the Place d'Armes was a swaying sea of colors and flambeaux. Masked men and costumed women rioted among the cafés set up along the edges of the square. The music of a half-dozen bands cacophonized in the lamp-sprinkled lapis dark. Every steamboat on the levee was an illuminated palace, and somewhere a couple of clarionets and a bugle hooted out what was apparently supposed to be "Greenland's Icy Mountains."

"Well, them slaves he bought with the money are bringin' in a passel, rented out to Tom Jenkins's new sawmill," Shaw went on mildly. "And by all I can see Dunk ain't gettin' rich. And then there's Mrs. R out to Nyades Street in a nice new house with spang new mournin' dresses and no visible means of support. You be careful when you go out to Milneburgh, now, Maestro."

"His eyelids flutter. His breath gags in his throat. Sweat, the sweat of death, stands out on his face and brow. Oh, have you ever smelt the sweat of death, the stink of fear as a man approaches the horrible gate from which only one has ever returned? He gasps, fighting for air, for just one more mouthful of the blessed air of mortal life!"

On the bench at the front of the hall—the ballroom of the Washington Hotel, rented for the purpose by ladies of the Church Committee—a woman cried out, and buried her face in her hands. Two girls clung to one another, desperately fighting sobs; another turned her face aside, her breath in staggering hiccups of terror, tears and mucus running down her face. Throughout the room, close-packed, rustling, thick with the scents of verbena and lamp oil and pomade, the undercurrent of sobs and groans floated, a soft soprano humming like mosquitoes above swamp waters.

Reverend Dunk flung up his hands. "I see them!" he cried, and his brown eyes stretched, gazing into distance, the riveted horror in them the rival of a Kean or a Kemble. His finger stabbed out, trembling, his voice fell to a hoarse whisper that could be heard into the back of the room. "I see them even now. They writhe in the flames, flesh shriveling from their bones. They beg, they plead, they stretch out their hands for the touch, just the tiniest touch, of water." His fingers curled into a despairing fist. "But there is no water there. Only fire, and more fire . . ."

A woman in the middle of the room screamed, jerked to her feet as if electrified; stood panting, gasping, head lolling back. One of the several soberly clothed young men who had been moving up and down the two aisles between the chairs went to her, spoke soothing words, led her down the aisle to the front bench.

The better to hear Dunk's excrutiatingly detailed catalog of the pains of hell? wondered January, from the back of the room.

His mind went back to the Cathedral that morning, the deep still peace—even on the threshhold of Mardi Gras. Sunlight touching the priest's violet vestments, the sweet mustiness of incense, the gentle murmur of voices. *Esto mihi in Deum protectorem, et in locum refugii. . . . Be thou unto me a God, a protector, and a place of refuge to save me. . . .*

"I see worms, and rats, and ants, and all the vermin of the Devil's creation, gnawing on the flesh of those who lie in chains. Oh my brothers and sisters, do you imagine that your flesh will cease to feel when the last breath chokes from your heaving lungs? In the fires of hell, *there* your flesh will be as sensible, as tender, as shrinking as ever it was upon the earth. . . ."

One of the young ushers came soft-footed up to January and gestured invitingly toward the last four ranks of the room, where slaves and free colored occupied benches rather than the chairs set for their so-called betters. In the Cathedral, and St. Anthony's on Rue des Ramparts, no such distinction was made.

January shook his head, smiled polite thanks ("I've already had some salvation today, thank you"), and handed the usher another card from Hannibal's collection. "If Reverend Dunk might spare me a few minutes of his time. . . ."

"I'll tell him," murmured the young man. "You realize, though, sir, that the exertions of the Spirit take a terrible toll upon our brother, and he will need rest."

"I'll wait."

Milneburgh was quiet in the winter season. From the gallery at the hotel's rear, January looked out over the lake, beaten lead under colorless sky, silent save for an occasional stirring of wind. A servant swept the gallery. The air smelled of coffee and scorched toast.

Periodically January returned to the ballroom, though for the most part he could follow the progress of the meeting by the muffled howls and singing audible even through the hotel's walls. Dunk himself went on in Boschian detail with his vision of hell for nearly an

hour—*The man must have lungs of leather and a bladder to match—*
after which, hair and shirt soaked with sweat, the preacher collapsed
onto a chair on the podium. His soft-voiced assistants immediately
took up the exhortation, one of them urging the congregation to
"Come to Jesus; come to dear, sweet, tender Jesus; Jesus will save you;
Jesus will rescue you . . ." while the other moved about the room,
leading half-hysterical women and girls up to the benches in the
front. The third time he entered, January saw that several of these
front-benchers had fallen, twitching and writhing, to the floor. Dunk
had one of them in his arms, whispering passionate comfort, his face
so close to hers that the sweat that dripped from his hair fell to her
lips; she clung to him, sobbing out a confession that was probably just
as well drowned by the howling and the hymns.

Even after the sounds died away, and the scattering of slaves,
freedwomen, and free colored came out onto the veranda to revive
themselves on coffee and biscuits, it was another three-quarters of an
hour until Dunk could extricate himself from his white admirers and
gesture January into a small parlor where they would not be dis-
turbed.

"Where had you these?" Offstage, as it were, Dunk's voice was
quiet, but still beautiful, its natural depth and cadence making his
words a pleasure. He didn't appear either startled or put out when
January produced the pearls, only frowned with concern.

"A colored girl gave them to me, sir," answered January. "I
promised her I wouldn't say anything of her, and she's left town by
this time. . . ." He glanced at the angle of sunlight on the curtains,
as if confirming a time, and made a very slight nod to himself. "But
she said they belong to Mrs. Redfern, whom I gather is a friend of
yours. Do you recognize them?"

Dunk nodded, running the pearls through his fingers: sausage-
like, but clean and with a surprisingly delicate touch. "I believe I do,
though I saw her wear them only the once, two or three years ago.
Would this be the unfortunate girl who made off with them last
summer?" The warm sienna eyes grew wary under the long lashes.

Any Frenchman—or any actor—would have changed his shirt
and combed his hair after a three-hour performance of that intensity.
Dunk apparently regarded the saturated linen and matted mane as

badges of an honorable tussle with Satan. By the admiring gazes of the women who peeped through the panes at them, it was an opinion he did not hold alone.

"I don't know, sir," replied January. "I understand you've visited the Redfern plantation and might be going there soon? I thought you might . . ."

"Spanish Bayou has been sold." Dunk shook his head. "The girl who stole these pearls made off with the money that might have gone to the saving of it, poor wretch."

"I understand the bulk of the damage was done long before that, sir," said January quietly. "Though I've never had the fever of gambling myself, and so I can't pass judgment on those who do. . . ."

"Can't you?" Under the Assyrian luxury of his beard, Dunk's mouth hardened. "You have the generosity of one who hasn't seen a good woman's life ruined through the vice, my friend."

January assumed an expression of slightly startled enlightenment, as if the matter had never been presented to him or anyone else with such cogence before, and the Reverend's jaw came forward, a militant glint sparkling in his eyes.

"You can't pass judgment, you say. That does you credit as a Christian. But I happen to know that only five days before his death, Otis Redfern was obliged to sell six of his slaves—with no way of redeeming the labor force of the plantation before harvest time, you understand—in order to pay debts incurred by that pernicious vice. Upon taking those slaves to the city, he entered into gambling again, like a dog returning to his vomit, and lost the entire sum he had made by that sale, so that he had to return to his unfortunate wife the following morning and tell her that the money must immediately be paid over to his new creditors, and that they were ruined."

His brows plunged to shadow those deep-set eyes, and his voice subtly shifted, the voice of a preacher determined to convince his audience.

"Surely not!" January injected just enough doubt into his voice to bring Dunk up like a ruffling owl.

"I was there myself and heard them, my friend. And if Mrs. Redfern recriminated against him, who could blame her? Redfern was preparing to sell even her dowery land, a parcel too small to be of use to anyone, whose deeds the wretched woman asked me to remove from the house lest they become entangled in the ensuing settlement. Now, what kind of a man would rob his wife to that extent?"

"You shock me, sir!" January looked shocked.

"Gambling is a fearful curse, sir. It deteriorates the character. Until the man spoke to his wife in such a way that I promise you, neither Mr. Granville, who was breakfasting with me, nor I knew where to look."

Hubert Granville? thought January, enlightened. Granville was at Spanish Bayou that Wednesday morning? To render over the money from the previous day's sale of the six slaves, almost certainly. Arriving for breakfast, before Otis Redfern's return from town. And that being the case . . .

"And you took the deeds for this dower land away with you that day?"

"I considered it my obligation," replied Dunk. "The land was not the husband's to sell, but under the law he would have been able to do so."

Not if it was tied up in a trust, it wasn't, thought January wryly. But Emily seemed to have convinced her hellfire *cicisbeo* otherwise. And almost certainly, the deed to Black Oak had not been the only thing in that envelope.

"I was terribly shocked," Dunk went on slowly, "to hear of the unhappy man's death, but I cannot admit to much sorrow at it." He shook his massive head. "Still, to part from a man at the wharf after breakfast and to hear he has succumbed by midnight . . . It gives one thought for one's own mortality."

He let the pearls trail from one hand to the other, gazing down reflectively at the satiny spheres. "Did this unfortunate girl express contrition for what she did? Or speak about the money she had stolen? That was a sad business."

January shook his head. His mind raced, time and events fitting together like the cogs of a gear. "I had the impression this was not the girl who took them, sir. She spoke of having received them 'from a friend,' though of course that might have been only a story to cover her own guilt. The girl who took them: what did she look like?"

"I never saw her—only heard Mrs. Redfern's description. A mulatress, she said, with a thin little face and a snub nose. Did the girl who gave you these look so?"

"No, sir. She was bright, quadroon or octoroon, with freckles on her nose."

"Hmn," rumbled Dunk, deep in thought. "Hmn. And this girl made no mention of the money her friend had taken?"

"None, sir."

The Reverend sighed, gave himself a little shake, and made a sketch of a bow. "Thank you very much for bringing me these," he said. "Mrs. Redfern will be most grateful to have them back. As for the girl, we seem to be obliged, as the Bard says, to 'leave her to Heaven,' perhaps the best course in any case." He produced a clean handkerchief from his pocket, and wrapped the pearls carefully. "Thank you, Mr. . . . ?"

"Dordogne," said January, bowing in his turn. He'd memorized the name on Hannibal's card before sending it in. "Marcus Dordogne. Thank you for your time, sir. And you've given me much to think about." *More than you know, in fact.* "I understand you'll be setting up a regular Church here in Milneburgh?"

"If God is good to me, yes." Dunk's voice had returned to normal tones; he extended a meaty hand to shake. "May I hope to see you there, when the dream of it becomes reality?"

"You may well, sir." January resumed his hat, straightened his black coat, and with a final bow, made his way down the steps of the gallery, past windows where the white ladies of the congregation and Dunk's two assistants—were regaling themselves on beef sandwiches and punch.

It was all he could do to keep from jumping up and clicking his heels.

No wonder Emily Redfern had been at such pains to imply that Cora had returned to the plantation Wednesday evening. No wonder the woman had been so eager to ruin Rose Vitrac, and drive her out of town. No wonder she was willing to sacrifice her pearls and a hundred and ninety dollars cash money, to avoid Rose remaining in custody where she might be questioned by others. Granville had brought the money out to Spanish Bayou Wednesday morning; the money had departed with Dunk "after breakfast"—and, therefore, far too early for Cora to have had the slightest thing to do with the administration of the poison—and Otis Redfern had come down sick Wednesday night.

It only remained to be seen what, if anything, Dunk would do now.

Since the Reverend almost certainly had an evening performance as well as a matinee, January made his way through the pine copses to Catherine Clisson's locked-up cottage on London Street. There, settling himself on the gallery, he produced a spyglass from his pocket. Through this he watched the hotel, especially the white shell path that ran between the main block and the stables, until it grew too dark to see.

More women arrived; those on the gallery returned inside for another session. Lights blossomed behind the curtains with the evening's approach. Now and then, when the wind set right, he could hear the faint echo of wailing, the only enjoyment, he reflected, that the majority of the American women allowed themselves.

The moon was in its first quarter, already westering; not a night, he thought, that would permit carriages to be abroad late. At the dinner hour the building disgorged women again, some of them to carriages drawn up before the steps, others onto the galleries, where they talked and ate sandwiches and eventually moved off in twos and threes into the thickening dark.

But if the Reverend Micajah Dunk were discomposed or startled by the return of the Redfern pearls, or the news that someone might have spoken to Cora Chouteau, he did not hasten to break the news to Emily Redfern.

January took the last steam rail-car into town. The only other occupant of the colored car was a single elderly woman who cradled a small dog in her arms, and crooned it lullabies all the way back:

Go to sleep, my son, crab is in the shell,
Go to sleep, my son, crab is in the shell,
Papa has gone to the river,
Mama has gone to catch crab.
Go to sleep, my son, crab is in the shell.
Go to sleep, my son, crab is in the shell.

It was one of the few lullabies January could recall his mother singing to him, her body silhouetted against the lighter darkness of the slave-cabin's door. He tried to recall whether his father had been there then, but had no memory one way or the other. Only the rocking of the steam-train, and the creaking of the spring's first frogs, and the disembodied murmur of those nonsense words, like a voice from some other world speaking to him in the falling dusk.

TWENTY

To the Editors of the New Orleans Bee, *and to all concerned citizens of this town:*

To say that justice has been miscarried would be too feeble, too passive, too weak-kneed a description of the vile horror perpetrated yesterday on the bludgeoned sensibilities of a bereaved family and on the populace and good name of our fair city. Saturday night Judge J. F. Canonge permitted a murderer to walk free, a charlatan as black of heart as of hide. A week ago Wednesday, at the Orleans Ballroom, this self-styled doctor, Benjamin Janvier, in reality a voodoo practitioner and pander to the lusts of his fellow Ethiopes, prevented me by invective and threats of violence from bringing aid and succor to M. Jean Brinvilliers, who had been slightly wounded in an affair of honor in the lobby. When I attempted to remonstrate with Janvier he thrust me bodily back from his victim, and only after he had been forcibly removed from the scene by M. Froissart, the ballroom's manager, was I able to bring the light of medical science to bear.

Alas, too late! As the result of the delay in treatment, M. Brinvilliers succumbed, not so much to his wounds, as to the rough and superstitious treatment meted out to him by this Janvier.

It has come to my knowledge today, from the distraught Brinvilliers family, that this murderer was allowed to walk free.

Shame on you, Judge Canonge! This Janvier is a man well known for his libertinage, most recently and notoriously for the intolerable insult he has offered to a lady of quality. Not content with making the most indecent possible remarks to her very face, he has shamelessly spread lies and calumny about her through the coarsest strata of society.

It has lately been remarked that everything that we, the inhabitants of this beautiful city, hold dear is in danger from the sewage of depravity being dumped in upon us from outside forces. How much more disgrace is there in those officials who, for their own profit, foster and coddle the degenerates against whom we look to them for protection.

—Dr. Emil Barnard

January set down the paper, his hand shaking, and met his mother's eyes.

Livia Levesque was an early riser. The *Bee* had been lying, folded open to Barnard's letter, beside his coffee cup when her son entered her small dining parlor.

Her deep, smoky voice was dry. "I'd like to know what that's about, Ben," she said.

Anger rose in him, a fever-scald of rage. He wasn't even sure for a moment whether it was directed at Barnard or at her. "So would I."

"Well, everyone's going to be asking me about it," she said. "I have to tell them something. Really, Ben, I knew you'd gotten too free in your speech when you went to Paris. . . ."

"You really think I'm stupid enough to—to 'offer intolerable insult to a lady of quality'? To make 'indecent remarks' to her face? Excuse me, her *very* face, as he puts it."

"You changed in Paris." Livia's great, dark eyes were calmly cold.

"I didn't change that much! You raised me better than to do any such thing!" He saw her mouth soften, just a bit, and added, "I'm surprised you believe what a rag like this prints." In fact, the *Bee*'s stories were as a rule accurate, if overheated; but his mother never could let pass a chance to attack anything.

"Well, you're certainly right about that," she agreed. "They'll print any damn lie that's sent them, and that's for certain. Madame," she added, raising her voice without turning her head, "I hope you're not looking at the top of that table?"

The fatter of the two yellow cats sat down where she was and began to wash in an elaborate display of innocence.

"But Ben," Livia added, and there was now real concern in her eyes, "who was she?"

"I don't know!" He slapped the paper down on the table, feeling as if he were about to explode. "Aside from the stupidity of the thing, you know I'm not that rude. Have you *ever* heard me be rude to a lady?"

"Well." Her mouth primed tight again. "You certainly could watch your speech a little more around gentlemen. Especially those who stand in a position to do you good. I always told Monsieur Janvier that it was a mistake to send you to Paris."

As far as January remembered, she had told St. Denis Janvier nothing of the kind. In fact she'd been all for getting him away from New Orleans and out of the public view, if he was going to be something as low-class as a hired musician. But he wasn't about to be drawn into a discussion of his mother's version of the past. Instead he got to his feet, picked up the scarf of green silk Catherine Clisson had knitted him for Christmas—for the morning was bitterly cold—and shoved the folded sheets of the *Bee* into the pocket of his rough corduroy jacket.

"And you're not going out dressed like that," Livia added sharply, tonguing a chunk of brown sugar into her coffee. "You look like a street sweeper. People see you dressed like that, of course they'll think anything that paper says of you is true."

"All right, Mother," said January patiently. "I'll go change."

She nodded to herself and went back to her perusal of the *Louisiana Gazette*—January didn't even want to ask if Barnard's letter had been printed there as well. He stepped through the French doors back into the yard, turned immediately left, secure in the knowledge that she had ceased to notice him the moment he'd agreed with her, and made his way down the pass-through to Rue Burgundy, in quest of whatever Madame Redfern's servants had to tell.

Unlike the walled compounds of the old French town, the houses of the American faubourgs north of Canal Street were set, for the most part, in wide yards and scattered outbuildings and, in consequence, were easy to approach. Clothed in his shabby brown corduroy and a soft hat, January fell into step with Madame Redfern's housemaid—Claire, he had heard her called on the night of the ball—by the simple expedient of putting two or three reales in an old purse of Bella's, and calling out, "Miss Claire, Miss Claire, you drop this?"

They walked down Felicity Street and to the grocery-stalls by the batture at the foot of Market Street, together. Miss Claire was probably in her late thirties and had three children, a calm and matter-of-fact woman without inclination to flirt, but January didn't try to flirt with her: only talked, of this and that, mostly of her children—whom Emily Redfern had refused to purchase along with her—and the places she'd been.

"I understand what that Mr. Fraikes of hers says, that she can't afford to buy nor raise no little ones," said the slave, shifting her market basket on her hip as she moved from stand to stand of winter fruit. There were blood oranges from Mexico, and early strawberries; new lettuces now, and asparagus from Jefferson Parish; a glory of greens and flame-bright colors against the gray of the morning. "But rice is only a couple reales a peck, and you can buy three oranges for an English shilling—how much would it have cost her, to feed two little boys and a girl? She's a mighty hard woman, Mr. Levesque. . . ." She shook her head—January had taken some care never to use the same name twice among these people. "A mighty hard woman."

So it did not take much to learn whether Rose Vitrac had come to the Redfern home making awkward enquiries as to the possible fate of Cora Chouteau.

If she had, Claire Brunet knew nothing of the matter.

And what, precisely, he wondered, as he made his way back along Tchapitoulas Street toward the Cabildo once more, *did* he think had become of Cora? What did he think Emily Redfern's reaction would have been, had Rose Vitrac appeared one morning on her doorstep saying, *I have proof that you poisoned your husband for five thousand dollars, and cast the blame on his unwilling mistress?*

What proof could Rose have had?

Emily Redfern had certainly murdered her husband. No matter who had stowed the monkshood up Emily Redfern's bedroom chimney, if the boat that had brought her—along with Reverend Dunk and Mr. Bailey's white horses—to New Orleans had departed from the landing at Spanish Bayou "after breakfast," there was no way Cora Chouteau could have placed so fast-acting a substance as monkshood in her master's food.

Emily Redfern had certainly tricked the Reverend Dunk—if Dunk had been tricked—into taking the five thousand dollars Hubert Granville had brought out to the house so it would not be found by her husband's creditors. She had tricked her creditors as well, selling her slaves to the Reverend Dunk at half their value with the proceeds of the Musicale, so that she could pay off her creditors at a fraction of the debt, while he resold them and invested the profit.

But all that being so, what did he think Madame Redfern had done to Rose? Struck her over the head with slung-shot?

When? Where? For all her slim gawkiness Rose Vitrac was strong, and it was unthinkable that a colored woman would have been seated in the presence of a white woman who was not. Given Emily Redfern's lack of inches, the physical logistics of a blow over the head—or any sort of violence—became laughable.

And where did that leave him?

With a perfectly worked-out case clearing a woman who had vanished into thin air. Clearing a woman who had only slavery to return to, acquitted or not. Whose life was forfeit, not to the hangman but to the auctioneer's gavel.

And Cora could have met anyone as she left Madame Lalaurie's house that night, from the enigmatic Mamzelle Marie to Hog-Nose Billy to the vindictive and slightly cracked Monsieur Montreuil to Bronze John himself.

The fact was that she was gone, as Rose was gone.

January had the sense of having read down to the bottom of a sheet of paper, reaching the same conclusion, the same result, each time.

Cora was gone.

Rose was gone.

Weaving his way among the traffic of whores and roustabouts, of cotton bales and hogsheads of sugar, of pigs and pianos and oysters and silk, it occurred to him that Madame Redfern, had she dealt with Rose at all, would have been far likelier to settle the matter financially. Having ruined her, La Redfern would not need any such melodramatic expedient of a blow over the head and unceremonious burial in the nearest well. A five-dollar ticket on the next New York packet would do the trick as well.

Better, in fact.

She'd have taken her books.

A vision of hope, of Rose teaching at some comfortable girls' school in New York, somewhere that would properly value her erudition, crumbled like a sugar palace in rain. The image of Rose sharpening a quill in the bar of cold pale New York sunlight. . . .

Monsieur Janvier, I take pen in hand at last. . . .

Nothing can come between true friends.

But according to Miss Claire, Rose never went to Redfern's at all.

She has no one in New York. No one anywhere. At least when my life fell to pieces in my hand I could come home. I could come here.

Even in defeat, Rose Vitrac had a kind of clear, cool courage that could go to an unfamiliar city and start anew. But she had no money to get there. If she hadn't gotten passage-money from La Redfern. . . .

Memory touched him as he walked on toward the brick-arcaded shadows of the market, the tall iron-crowned towers of the steamboat stacks: the memory of a dream, of shadows on a hallway wall. A tall man's and a tiny, slender girl's. *You're her father,* the girl was saying. *You're her father. . . .*

Rose had never spoken of her home.

But once, on their first meeting, Cora had.

It was three days' voyage to Grand Isle in the Barataria country. Froissart having canceled January's engagement to play at the Orleans Ballroom's Mardi Gras Ball, January would have left that day, had any boat been departing on the eve of the feast. As it was, he fumed and fretted and cursed the revelers who jammed every street and filled the endless night hours with riot. The moment *"Ite missa est"* was out of the priest's mouth at the first Ash Wednesday Mass, January was out the Cathedral door and on his way to the levee.

Natchez Jim followed the still, green reaches of Bayou Dauphine to Lake Catahouatehe, motionless in fringes of cypress and reed, rowing or poling where there wasn't wind to fill the lugger's sail. January, helping on the oars or leaning on the long oak poles, watched the few houses on the banks grow more primitive with distance from the city, until they were little more than a couple of post-and-daub rooms circled by a gallery, presiding over a few arpents of indigo or rice. Now and then they'd pass the shack of a trapper or fisherman, perched on sandbars and *chênières,* but even these grew far between. They both slept with knives and pistols beneath the wadded-up jackets that served them for pillows, and never at the same time, for the Barataria had been the sole province of slave smugglers and outlaws until very recently. There was no telling who or what might lurk in the spiderweb mazes of bayou and marsh. Still, the green-gray aisles of water hickory and tupelo, bald cypress and palmetto were hushed, save for the slap of the water on the lugger's sides. Wind murmured among the endless reeds, and once, somewhere far off, they heard the rattle of African drums.

From Catahouatehe they entered Lake Salvator, and after that the world known as the *prairie tremblant,* the quaking lands: salt marsh, reeds, birds, February sky. Natchez Jim pointed out the salt grass that would tell a man where solid ground lay, the cattails that spoke of mud too soft to carry weight: "Even those who are born in these lands sometimes make mistakes about the walking prairie and are never seen again." An alligator slid down the trunk of a dying cypress, gray as the fading roots left out in sun and wind.

They came ashore on Grand Isle in midmorning, at a sort of settlement of oyster fishers and trappers on the landward side of the island. The night's fog still hung on, cottony and tasting of salt. The silence that had seemed menacing in the bayou country was calming here. Though the world slept its winter sleep still, all was lush with green.

"I'll be here two days, maybe three." Natchez Jim unshipped the packages he'd brought from town, tossed them on the crude plank wharf: calico, needles, coffee, a little nest of iron pans. Black-eyed women, swart-skinned men emerged from the straggle of huts and cottages among the stands of palmetto and Spanish dagger, and hastened down the path. Children darted around them like birds. From one of these January learned that the plantation of Aramis Vitrac lay on the other side of the island, "just down that road there." Their French was better than he'd feared it might be, though old-fashioned and strangely pronounced: *ch'min* for *chemin; l'* for *le.* Grimy, exhausted, aching in every bone and limb, he climbed the low hogback of tawny sand, through palmetto, fern, and creeper, cypress and oleander already putting forth the whites and crimsons of tropic glory. Green flats of rice bent to salt wind. On the other side of the path a work gang hacked at the ditches for next month's sugar crop. From the top of the path he heard the surf.

He half-expected to find Rose sitting on the gallery of the three-room, post-and-daub plantation house, reading Babbage's *Reflections on the Decline of Science in England.* Part of him, the part that had died in Paris, half-expected not to find her at all.

In fact she was working in the garden behind the house, a half-wild riot of dark-leaved azaleas, spinaches, and young peas. The rabbitty young woman who came out onto the gallery, led by what January guessed to be the single house servant, pointed her out to him. "This isn't about that school in the city, is it? Truly, what happened there was not her fault. I know my husband's sister, M'sieu. She is impetuous, but her heart is pure, like glass, like steel. She would give everything she owns to those she loves, or those in her care." Her quick grin showed two teeth lost to childbearing, and she added, "Except perhaps her books."

"I'm not from the school." January looked gently down into the narrow, anxious face. "I'm only a friend."

Rose sat back on her heels at the sound of the voices on the gallery. So she was watching him as he came down the gallery steps and through the neat dirt paths of the rambling garden. She pushed her spectacles straight on her nose, and he knew by the attitude of her back, by the angle of her straight square shoulders, that she recognized him instantly. She settled back, her hands folded in her lap, until he came near.

"Ben." She was trying to hide it, but there was deep joy in her face, her voice.

"Rose."

Joy sprang to her face, but when he helped her to her feet she took her hand out of his at once, closing it up on itself—her lips closed, too. He saw her at war with old hurts and old fears, thinking about what she ought to say.

"I'm not here to ask anything of you," he said. "I just wanted to see if you were all right."

Three days' journey down the bayous? He could almost hear the words as they went through her mind, and he smiled at the absurdity of his own assertion.

"Well, from what you told me of your brother I knew I couldn't write."

It surprised her into laughter, like sunlight on the waning sea.

"I brought you some books." He held out to her the parcel he'd carried down from town: a volume of Sappho he'd found at a Customshouse sale; Hamilton's *Theory of Systems and Rays* from the same source; Lyell's *Principles of Geology;* and a wonderfully hair-raising English novel by the poet Shelley's wife. "If you weren't here, at least I could have asked your family of you. Your sister-in-law seems a nice woman."

"Alice is a darling. Of course Aramis—my brother—half-brother—is a complete illiterate and she's not much better—why is it Creoles never educate their daughters?—but Alice is like Cora: willing to accept that that's the way I am." Her face lost the sparkle of her smile. "Did you ever find out what happened to Cora?"

January shook his head. "We caught the men who were taking people off the streets. They'd been kidnapping them out of their homes, too, some of them, and out of the sheds in the Swamp where slaves sleep out if their masters let them. Hèlier the water seller was trading the information to a tavern-keeper for a cut of the profits, when they sold them to cotton planters in the Missouri Territory."

He saw the fragile jaw set hard and wished there were an easier way to say it, or something better to say. "I've been writing to brokers and authorities in Arkansas and Missouri and anywhere else we can trace the ring's contacts. But, of course, no one's going to admit they were buying kidnapped free men."

She drew in breath, hard. For a time she looked genuinely sick. But all she said was, "I never thought it would be Hèlier. He was always so friendly."

"It surprised me, too. And, of course, it was to his profit to be friendly. Maybe I should have seen it. I would have thought . . ." He shook his head. "He had a grievance against the entire world, larger than anything he could have felt for any individual's rights." He was silent for a time, plucking a long stem of the jasmine that grew up the nearby fence and turning the small gold blossoms over in his hand. Then he said, "For a time I was afraid you'd been kidnapped, too."

"I'm sorry about that." She answered the thought that he did not speak aloud: *Why didn't you let me know?* "It wasn't completely shame—well, not after the first day or two. I know how rumors operate. I've seen how vicious they can be, especially about women. You've seen it, too. Half the women in the market seem to believe Delphine Lalaurie is the Devil's sister."

(*From the beginning again, please . . .)* January shook the thought away.

Rose's mouth tightened. "People believe what they want to believe. And I . . . it seemed to me so deliberate. So planned. Aimed, like a gun. And like me, you're a teacher. You depend on the goodwill of those around you for your daily bread."

January said nothing, looking down into her eyes. Even here on the island, the old laws against women of color uncovering their hair seemed to hold, or maybe it was just the habit she'd had in the city. Like the women of color he'd seen by the wharf, she wore a tignon, white and soft and clean as it had been in the city. Her complexion had darkened with the sun of the island sunlight, matte velvet the color of cocoa.

She saw his thought, the way he'd seen hers, and her eyes fell. He felt her move away from him, not physically, but in thought. Her fingers caressed the leather of the books. "I'm sorry," she murmured.

"I meant it when I said I didn't come here to ask you anything, only to see that you were well. Sometimes friends do that. I've missed you, Rose."

He hadn't known how badly, until they sat on the gallery after supper—which they ate with the house girl and the cook—watching the last color stain the clouds over the Gulf and talking about Mardi Gras, and the ending of the fever, and the spectacular change in the fortunes of Emily Redfern.

"Good for her," said Rose bluntly. And then, "I shouldn't say that, because she sounds like a horrible woman. But Monsieur Redfern sounded like a horrible man. And in fact I wondered once or twice about whether Madame Redfern really wanted Cora found."

She sat forward in her rough-made chair of bent willow, leaned bare forearms on the gallery rail, and frowned in the direction of the darkening sea. "When I read that second advertisement in the paper, the one that spoke of the five thousand dollars . . . The name was the same, but the description was all wrong. Madame Redfern had to advertise for Cora's capture, to look good to her creditors, but she did it in such a way that Cora would have every chance of escape.

"I think . . ." She drew in her breath again, and let it out, trying to speak calmly of the ruin of her dreams. "I think she must have been behind the rumors about the school somehow, trying to drive me out of town. She must have been horrified when I was actually arrested, and might be questioned. But I don't see . . . she doesn't have influence with those people. Certainly not with my investors."

"Who were your investors?"

"Armand d'Aunoy, Placide Forstall, Edmond Dufossat, Pierre Tricou, and the Lalauries," replied Rose promptly. "All of them old Creoles, you see. It was through Delphine Lalaurie's kindness that the loan was forthcoming at all. Emily Redfern's pretensions would be anathema to them."

January nodded. "True. Even after Lieutenant Shaw mentioned that it was one of your investors—who could have been given the hint by anybody, of course—I thought it still might be Madame Redfern. But she was the only person to hire me for a private ball in all of the Mardi Gras season." He withdrew Monday's *Bee* from his coat, and laid it, folded to the place, on the railing of the gallery.

" 'Murderer?' " Rose took off her spectacles, held the newspaper close to the window, where the light from inside could fall on it, peering with her shortsighted eyes. " 'Intolerable insult offered to a lady of quality . . .'? *What* lady of quality? 'Spread lies and calumny . . .'? This person"—she glanced at the bottom of the letter—"This Dr. Barnard has his nerve, talking of lies and calumny. What *is* this?"

"This," said January, "is the reason the trip down here left me penniless—and in debt to Hannibal, which has to be the greatest joke of the decade. I have exactly two pupils left and have barely worked all winter. It's the same person," he said, "spreading the rumors. I know it."

She sank down in her chair with a whisper of heavy skirts. Like countrywomen or servants, she had dispensed with the multiple petticoats of fashionable wear. The dark, thick twill, dusty from the garden's earth, became her. In the open neck of her countrywoman's waist a small gold cross glinted, fire on the dusky skin.

"Emil Barnard," she said. "That's a French name."

"He's a Thompsonian charlatan who worked around the Charity Hospital during the epidemic," said January. "By his accent he's from Pau or the Languedoc, coincidentally the same part of France Nicolas Lalaurie comes from. Lalaurie's recently taken him on as a partner."

"I don't . . ." Rose left her sentence unfinished, sat for a time running the folded paper through her fingers, as he'd seen her run the ribbons with which she'd tied back the sick girls' hair. Then her eyes met his.

"Why?"

January slowly shook his head.

"Placide Forstall is Delphine Lalaurie's son-in-law, you see," Rose went on, speaking as if to herself, trying to fit pieces together. Trying to align the woman whose reputation she'd so furiously defended with the one who would so casually and so thoroughly destroy all she, Rose, had worked to create. "D'Aunoy's her cousin. Jean Blanque was on the board of the Louisiana State Bank; Madame knew everyone there. That's how she influenced them to lend me the money to start the school. It has to be her. But I don't understand why."

"I'm only guessing," said January. The shadow in the doorway returned to him again, the voice like a golden whip, the silvery rustle of petticoats. The absolute fear in Pauline Blanque's eyes. "And I can't know, not knowing Madame. I'm beginning to wonder if anyone really knows her."

He frowned, as the woman's face came back to him, the desperate, yearning expression in her beautiful eyes as she sponged the bodies of the dying. "I think now that Cora must have tried to get Gervase to run away with her. And either Madame overheard them, or quite possibly Gervase actually made the attempt to leave, later that night or the following day. I never actually saw Gervase; Madame sent him out of town very soon thereafter. But I'm almost certain she'd see the attempt as betrayal, after all she did, for whatever reasons of her own, to make things easy for Cora. And that she would not forgive."

In the silence, the boom of the surf sounded very loud.

"I can't believe that she'd be that vindictive." Rose's hand sketched a gesture of denial in the air, but turned, folding in on itself with the refusal only half made. Her profile was only a shape of darkness now against the fading light. "To do this to me only for harboring Cora, to you for helping her . . ."

"I think it made it worse," said January. "She helped you, and you conspired to betray her, too."

"How would she know? I can't imagine her eavesdropping. But, of course, Bastien would have. Or even Dr. Lalaurie. I never liked him." She shivered. "He *crept* so, and was always asking if he could do 'tests' on the girls. He was the one who invented those postural contraptions I showed you. I never understood how a woman of her—her excellence—could love a man so *wormy.*"

"One thing I've learned," January said with a smile, "love is beyond comprehension. Anyone can love anyone. It's like the cholera."

Rose laughed, spectacles flashing in the reflected lamplight. "*Very* like the cholera," she agreed, and he heard the jest in her voice, and laughed too, at himself, and the ridiculousness of his love.

"But just saying that," said Rose at length, "makes me realize: it's true. I don't know that much about Madame Lalaurie. She might be an habitual eavesdropper, for all I know. I was thinking, 'She isn't a vindictive woman,' but I don't know that. I've never seen her be vindictive. I don't want a woman I've looked up to, as I've looked up to her, to be vindictive. But I don't know. How vindictive is she?"

"I don't know either." January rose, and took her hand to bid farewell before seeking the room alotted him above the kitchen. "I think I'm going to find out."

He remained on Grand Isle another day, going to Mass in the island's tiny wooden Church. Later, despite the fact that it was Lent, he tuned up and played the old guitar owned by Aramis Vitrac— there wasn't a piano on the island—and sang ballads and arias from the operas popular in Paris two seasons ago, to the delight of his hosts and the dozen or so neighbors who walked that night from all over the island to dinner. Alice Vitrac joined in gamely on a flute while Natchez Jim rattled spoons and bones and tambourine. "It's George Washington's birthday," reasoned the island's black-eyed priest. "Well, near enough, anyway."

The women brought cakes and scuppernong wine, the men brandy from the smuggler boats that still plied the Gulf.

By day he walked with Rose on the beaches, both bundled alike in rough jackets, the sand chilly between his toes above the tangled *chevaux-de-frise* of driftwood along the shore. It was difficult not to reach across and touch her hand, her face. Yet in some ways it was easier than he had feared it would be. If a friend was all she could bring herself to be, he thought, he would accept her on those terms; on any terms that would let him continue the quick-sparkle entertainment of her conversation, the rare chance to speak of other things besides the day-to-day commonplaces of life in a small French provincial town.

Early on Monday morning January walked to the beach alone, to watch the waves roll in from the Gulf. Coming back he encountered Alice Vitrac, with oysters she'd bought from one of the fisher-families, and took from her the rush basket to carry to the house.

"You're good for her," said Madame Vitrac. She looked up at him with her pale, lashless eyes, myopic as Rose, and smiled a little. "I'm glad you've come. I was worried for her. I'm sorry you weren't able to bring her any word of Cora. . . ."

"Did you know Cora?"

"Oh, yes." Her voice grew less shy. "I grew up just over on P'tit Chênière. I've known Rose most of my life. Cora, too. They were inseparable."

January thought of those two girls, growing up in this world of driftwood and tawny sand.

"Cora told me she nursed Rose when she was sick."

Alice glanced up at him, quickly, looking to see what and how much he might have guessed. They stood still for a moment, sea wind blowing cold over them and rippling the long grass; then she said, "Well, I've always thought Papa Vitrac . . . I think he was only trying to do right by Rose. By his own lights. The man who—who hurt her—was a neighbor of ours, a planter, a man of color like yourself. Much lighter than you, but big like you. He tried for years to get Rose to marry him, you see. I think he thought that by doing what he did, he would force her hand. Force her father's hand."

January said softly, "I see."

Something of his anger must have shown in his eyes, for Madame Vitrac went on, "Papa Vitrac wasn't the only one who thought it would be the thing. You know that generally if a man *does* ruin a girl, the first thing everyone thinks of is to have him marry her. So I suppose Mathieu can be excused for thinking it was a good idea." She shrugged. Her own opinion on the subject was plain in the sudden set of that soft mouth.

"And I take it," said January, resuming his way toward the house, "that Monsieur Vitrac thought so, too."

Madame Vitrac put up her hand to brush the fair strings of her hair out of her face, where the wind took them. "He told Rose that she would have to marry this man. I think he was only trying to get her established creditably and didn't want to have to look very far or very hard. The man did have quite a nice little plantation, over on Isle Dernière, though they said he was hard on his slaves. He later sold up and moved to the mainland, up in the Cane River country; Cora must have told Rose that, or she never would have returned. Because he—he came around. Trying to force her into saying yes. Afterward, I mean. That's when she became so ill."

January frowned. "You mean as a ruse? To get him to go away?"

"No." Madame Vitrac took back the rush basket from him with a brief smile of thanks as they reached the steps of the house. "I mean she went into the woods and ate nightshade. Cora and my mother were the ones who found her. I don't know, but I think that Cora—and my mother—were the ones who talked Papa Vitrac into giving her the money to go to New York to school."

Rose herself never spoke of the matter, and in her eyes January could see—or thought he could see—that whatever had happened in this place, she had made peace of a kind with it, and was content to be here.

They spoke of music, and the Opera in Paris and Rome; of Pakenham's invasion and the Chalmette battle; of steam engines and bombs and mummies and nesting birds. They built a fire of drift-wood, bought oysters from the fisher-boys and ate them raw with the juice of limes, while the waves curled on the sand and a line of brown pelicans emerged silent as ghosts from the mists and, as silent, vanished.

They spoke of the epidemic, and of why the fever might come in the summertimes and not the winters, and why not every summer; of why sometimes cures seemed to work—even onions under the bed—and why sometimes they did not; of the white ghost-crabs that scurried in the retreating scrum of the surf, and of pirate treasure and hurricanes. "I've watched the winds and the clouds here," said Rose, "and the winds and air in the marsh. It feels different there, but I can't say *why* it's different, what is different about it. There has to be some way of identifying what it is. Everyone talks about the miasma of sickness, but it's only a guess, you know. There has to be a way of making it visible, like a chemical stain turning the color of water."

"Will you come back?" he asked her at last, when on the second evening it grew too dark and too damp to sit on the gallery longer. "This will blow past, like a hurricane. It always does."

"And like a hurricane," said Rose softly, "it will leave wreckage, and that long tedious season of rebuilding. But you're right," she added. "I can't stay here forever, with nothing to read but newspapers a year old, and no one but Alice to speak to. I don't know." She shook her head, and reached out, very quickly, to touch his hand in parting for the night. "I don't know."

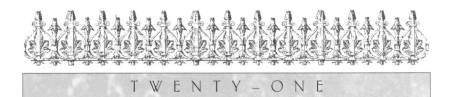

TWENTY-ONE

January returned to New Orleans on the twenty-eighth of February, to find that Emil Barnard—*Doctor* Emil Barnard—had not been idle in his absence. Six other letters had been written to the *Bee*, mentioning that it was the gracious and charitable Delphine Lalaurie whom January had insulted and further stating that he was known to have assisted in the escape of a number of slaves.

"Really, Ben, this is getting intolerable," pronounced his mother, the day of his return. She'd emerged from the back door of the house only minutes after he slipped from the passageway and crossed the yard, too exhausted and depressed to go in and speak to her first. Lying on his bed, he heard the light sharp tap of her shoe-heels on the steps, and closed his eyes in dread. She'd been saving all the newspapers for the preceding nine days and placed them on the end of the bed. "And don't lie on your bed with your shoes on," Livia continued. "I swear, when Bernadette Metoyer came over to tea the day before yesterday I didn't know what to say. Is it true what Agnes Pellicot tells me, that you were carrying on an affair with that Vitrac, that starved poor Marie-Neige nearly to death?"

"Mama," said January, without opening his eyes, "you have only to *look* at Marie-Niege to know that no one starved her nearly to death."

"Ben, that is a most unkind and unfeeling thing to say."

It was the kind of thing she said all the time. "I'm sorry, Mama."

"You're my son." He imagined he could hear the admission stick in her throat. "And you will always have a home with me, even if you can't pay me the rent you owe me right now. I'll give you another few weeks on that. But I will have to ask you to be quiet when you come and go, and not draw attention to this house."

"Ben, you really have to be more careful," cautioned Dominique, a few nights later, when both were invited to Olympe's house for dinner. "Rumors get around so terribly. You can't insult someone like Delphine Lalaurie! Why, she's seen to it that crazy man Montreuil has nearly been run out of business, for spreading those horrid lies about her keeping slaves chained in her attic."

"Those rumors were around before she lived next to Montreuil." Olympe laid down her spoon and regarded her younger sister with boneyard eyes. "I heard things like that when she still lived over near the bank on Rue Royale."

"That's silly," protested Dominique. "Ben's been in the house, haven't you, Ben? Did *you* see any slaves chained up?"

"I doubt she'd give her daughters' piano teacher a tour of the dungeon." January ate a forkful of Olympe's excellent grillades. Dominique hadn't invited him to her house, as was her usual wont, since his return from Grand Isle. *Coincidence?* he wondered. Or an overwhelming dread that news of his unhallowed presence might somehow reach Henri? Or, God forbid, Henri's mother? "The house-maid I saw looked all right."

"So she's not keeping them chained up in an attic, for the Lord's sake!" Dominique gestured impatiently. Small pendant diamonds flashed in her ears. "Monsieur Montreuil's just insane, and an opium-eater too, I've heard. I mean, Madame Lalaurie did manumit old Davince—"

"Who then had to leave the state," pointed out Olympe. "Mighty convenient for her—as it is for everyone who frees a person who's lived in their house and knows their affairs. And she does have her favorites."

"Well, so does everyone. Besides, Henri eats over there all the time, and he's seen her servants. Every white person in town knows that's a lie." Dominique shrugged, and picked at her food, clearly uncomfortable. At the far end of the table the children, from Zizi-Marie to the baby, were following this discussion with interest. "You just hate her because Mamzelle Marie hates her. Blacks are always complaining that their white folks don't feed them. Goodness knows Bella always is, about Mama, and she's certainly not about to die of starvation."

January held his peace. He'd seen his mother count and weigh not only leftover meat so that her cook would be accountable for it, but the burnt stumps of household candles. It was true, he knew, that for every servant who was kept to rice and beans, there was another who made a fair living off selling surplus food and pocketing the profit.

But his mind returned to the shadowed figure in the music-room doorway, to the voice cold as struck gold. *"Begin again. Begin again. Begin again."*

"What do you think of her?" he asked.

"I think," said Paul Corbier, glancing along the table at the four pairs of voracious eyes consuming the conversation as if it were a rare and ravishing dessert, "that little pitchers have big ears."

Olympe's face softened, like a black Benin sculpture melting into a thousand smiling wrinkles. "So they do." But the seeress, the Pythoness, remained in her eyes as they met January's again. "Truth usually lies somewhere in the middle," she said. "But I think Madame Lalaurie's one to stay away from."

Walking back along the Rue Burgundy after depositing Minou at her door—and being asked inside for a placatory cup of coffee—January felt again the stirring of weary anger, the bitter irony that while *his* lies or alleged lies were denounced, *hers* were overlooked, even by his own family. He felt, too, a backtaste of disappointment in his mouth, a grief—when he analyzed it—that stemmed from realizing that the woman who labored so selflessly among the horrors of the fever season was not, in fact, a good person. He had wanted very much to know that there was good in the world.

But what was *good*? Those whose lives she saved or whose ends

she had made more comfortable didn't care whether Madame
Lalaurie kept her slaves chained up or ruled her daughters with an
iron hand. They didn't care that the domineering nature that so
completely discounted danger of the plague would also react with
single-minded venom against what it perceived as betrayal. Betrayal
being, reflected January wryly, anything or anyone that didn't accept
Delphine Lalaurie's arrangements of how the world should be.

It came to him then—and with no great feeling of surprise or
discovery—that it wasn't beyond the bounds of possibility that Cora
had, in fact, not left Madame Lalaurie's house that Friday night. If
that formidable Creole lady had been listening to the conversation in
the courtyard and had heard Cora urge Gervase to run away—if
Gervase had agreed—a quiet word to Bastien would have served to
close the carriage gates. Madame would know that Cora couldn't
protest that she belonged to a third party. And Madame would have
had no difficulty whatsoever in finding a buyer for the girl within
days. If she kept her slaves chained—and January knew of townsfolk
who did—the girl might well have had no opportunity to either effect
an escape or get a message out before the brokers took her away.

The Lalauries were rich, of course, and didn't need the money.
But for a woman who would punish not only her betrayer but all who
had assisted her, money was not the object. Cora had accepted her
help, then tried to take one of her own slaves—her property—from
her. Madame had championed Rose to the bankers, and Rose had
repaid that help by harboring Cora. It would not have taken much for
Madame to learn that from Cora herself.

If that were indeed what had taken place. He shook his head—he
was getting as bad as Monsieur Montreuil. There had to be some way
to find out. . . .

Motion caught his eye. Someone had stepped quickly out of one
of the passways between the cottages and as quickly stepped back. He
thought that whoever it was, had a club.

Déjà vu clutched him for a panic moment: *Roarke.*
No. Brinvilliers.

He canvassed in his mind the other houses on Rue Burgundy,
then walked back two or three cottages and crossed the street, and

knocked on the door of a modest pink dwelling. "It's Ben January," he called to the muffled query from inside.

It was good, he thought, to have neighbors.

"Ben!" Crowdie Passebon was a perfumer, a rotund and jolly man with a carefully tended mustache and black pomaded ringlets that glistened in the dim candlelight within. His wife had been given the cottage years ago, when her white protector had paid her off. January could see her over Crowdie's shoulder, presiding over the table in the rear parlor, playing cards with an assortment of brothers, sisters, and in-laws. Once a woman mended her ways and married respectably, all but the most repressive were willing to forgive.

"Come in, come in! You're out late—nothing amiss with your mother, I hope?"

"Not with my mother, no," said January. "It's just that there's a crowd of toughs lying in wait for me, by her house. I think they're connected with this stupidity Barnard and Louis Brinvilliers have been putting in the papers."

"T'cha!" The perfumer drew him inside. "People don't care what they print, nor what they believe, either. Dirty Americans." He looked around the neat, sparsely furnished front parlor, and picked up a log of firewood as big around as January's biceps. Most of the male relatives at the table were putting on their coats and selecting makeshift armament, too.

"Be careful!" warned Helaine Passebon. "You can be—"

"We can always say we didn't see who they were in the dark, my love, can't we? With those kidnappers operating last summer, surely we can be excused for taking precautions when we go strolling? Let's go."

There was, of course, no one in the passageway when January and an escort of eight or ten Passebons, Lamothes, and Savarys reached his mother's cottage. He thanked them all, and invited them in for coffee: "Now I feel like a fool."

"Better a fool with a whole head than a hero with a broken one," replied Passebon cheerily, and kissed Livia's hand—she had been sewing in her dressing-gown and was not pleased at the sudden intrusion. The following morning January went to the passway by the cottage and found the tracks of seven or eight men in boots, and the marks where they had leaned canes, clubs, and sword-sticks on the ground.

Rose Vitrac returned to New Orleans a few days after Easter.

January had written her whenever he could find a boat bound for the Barataria, sending her books, and news of the town. No real post existed, so he had not heard from her for nearly ten days, when he got a note telling him that she'd procured lodging in a cheap room on Victory Street, near the wharves. Not the best neighborhood in the city, but certainly just down the street from some of them, and at least none of the riverfront gangs was headquartered there. He and Hannibal borrowed a wheelbarrow from Odile Gignac's brother and trundled her books down to her, load after load of them in the hot bright April sun. They bought jambalaya from the woman who sold it off a cart for a picayune a plate and ate it sitting on the steps up to the gallery outside Rose's room, drank lemonade, and devoured Mexican mangoes bought on the wharf, like three children with the juice running down their chins. The local streetwalkers called greetings to Hannibal on their way down to the wharves—he knew them all by name—and January played the guitar, and Hannibal the fiddle, by the light of a couple of tallow candles far into the warm spring darkness.

"Monsieur Lyons, who runs the bookshop on the Rue Esplanade, is paying me two dollars a volume to translate Aeschylus and Euripides," said Rose, leaning back against the gallery post and setting aside her plate. "This place is fifty cents a week; he says there'll be more. And Monsieur Damas on Rue Marigny said he'd pay me a little to help him read the boys' Greek and Latin—he runs the school at the corner of the Avenue of Good Children. And more will come."

Another boarder came up the outside stairs, a young man in clothing stiff with smeared plaster; he smiled at her as he passed and said, "Good evening, Madame Trevigne."

January raised his eyebrows; Rose averted her face a little, said, "Don't say it. I know. I should have more courage but . . . I'm still tender, as if I've had a bruising."

"I wasn't going to say anything," said January. "I just wondered how you came by papers in another name."

"You wound me," Hannibal lowered his violin from his chin and coughed heavily. "You cut me to the quick. I'd have had our Glauk-Opis"—Rose slapped at him, laughing, at being called by the goddess Athene's appellation—"in town sooner if those last few trading-boats to Grande Isle had been quicker—her letter to me asking for papers, and my papers, distinguishable only by their superior spelling from the illiterate scrawls turned out by city authorities for respectable free persons of color, going back the other way."

January laughed, too, and leaned back against the other post, his arm looped over the waist of the old guitar. He wondered how long it would be before he'd have to change his name, wondered whether he would be able to work in New Orleans again. Wondered what else might be in store for him, by way of dirty tricks from Madame Lalaurie and her friends. . . .

A week later he saw her, as he walked down Rue de l'Hôpital toward the market: the black-lacquered carriage drawn up before the great door on Rue Royale, the matched black horses tossing their silkily groomed manes. Bastien was helping her to the banquette, her gown of plum-colored taffeta a somber note against the bright heat of the spring afternoon. Beautiful and flawless, like a queen.

On impulse, January leapt over the gutter and crossed the mud of the street. "Madame . . ."

Bastien, at the top of the steps already, with the door open for her, stopped and opened his mouth to make some haughty dismissal, but Madame Lalaurie's face warmed with a smile. "M'sieu Janvier." She held out her hand, her friendliness as gracious as a bright-lit window seen through rain. "It has been a long time."

"Too long." January bowed, taken aback as the image of her shadow in the corridor, of Mademoiselle Pauline's haunted eyes and the dim shape of men with clubs and swords, melted away, suddenly ridiculous, as fevered as Montreuil's dreams. He found himself saying, "I trust the young ladies are well?" as if Emil Barnard had never written all those letters. As if Cora had never disappeared.

"Quite well, thank you." Behind her, Bastien still stood in the half-open door. Through it January could see a corner of a hall table, cypress wood waxed to a mirror shine, a dark-covered book and a pair of mended gloves. "And all is well with you?"

So caught was he by that generous charm, that January almost said, *Yes, perfectly well, thank you.* . . . In a way, it was as if she would not permit any answer but that. As if no other possible answer existed in the world she created.

Instead he said, his eyes properly cast down, "In fact it isn't, Madame." It cost him an effort to speak the words. "And if you've read the letter columns of the newspapers you would know something of it."

His eyes went to her face as he said it, and saw there the frown of puzzlement, the inquiring look in those dark eyes. . . . "Oh, good Lord, don't tell me Dr. Barnard still carries his grudge!" She leaned forward a little, and touched his wrist lightly with one gloved hand. "I was appalled, just appalled, when someone spoke to me of that letter."

"He wrote eight of them, Madame," said January. "Eight that I know of. Please," he went on, as she opened her mouth to speak again. "If I have offended you in any way, if there is the smallest basis for what he says about offering you insult or betrayal—"

She held up her hand. "No, no, Monsieur. It is *I* who should ask *your* pardon, for not looking into the matter immediately. My husband's partner is a hot-headed man, a man who nurses the most foolish grievances. And if you must know," she added, dropping her voice, a sudden twinkle in her eye, "Barnard's a most abominable little pest. I will speak to him of the matter."

Bastien held the door a little wider, as if to remind Madame of her obligations; January saw that the book on the table was Mercer's *Conversations in Chemistry More Especially for the Female Sex.* Rose had that one, too. It surprised him that Madame Lalaurie would share her interest.

"I am truly sorry to impose, Madame," he said. "But I apologize. . . ."

"No," interrupted Madame firmly. "No, I will hear no apology. It is I who should apologize, for not taking steps to keep that dreadful man in proper bounds. And I will do so, M'sieu, believe me. Yes, Bastien," she added, with her quick, beautiful smile, "I am now done." She caught January's eye, as if to say, *What can one do?* and ascended the steps into the house.

The carved door closed.

Was it that simple? January resumed his way down Rue de l'Hôpital, shaking his head. He had built her into a monster in his mind, he thought, a malevolent ghost of the fever season. And like a ghost, she had melted, when confronted, into something else.

If she was telling the truth, whispered the voice in his mind.

If she had any intention of doing as she said.

Did her desire for perfection run so deep, that she had to be seen as saintly even by her enemies? Or was the wall so high, that divided the gracious queen from . . .

From what?

(From the beginning, please. . . .)

He stopped at the flash of something black-and-red in the corner of his eye and, turning, saw an old pralinniere go past him with a willow tray of her wares on her head and Geneviève's old shoes on her feet.

The shoes that Rose had passed on to Cora.

He felt as if he'd tripped over something in the road; the momentary sensation of not quite knowing how to react. He'd been watching so long for either the shoes or the dress that he doubted for a moment they were the same. But there was no mistaking the scarred leather on the left toe, the fading lampblack dye, the white laces.

"Madame!" He rounded the corner, pushed through the crowd of the Rue du Levee. "Madame!"

She turned, weathered walnut face puckered with annoyance. She was shorter even than Cora, her headscarf frayed and faded but tied into a fantastic arrangement of points that stuck out in all directions under the weight of the tray.

"What?"

"Your shoes. . . ."

To his surprise she whipped the tray from her head, set it down on the nearest cotton bale, and balancing gamely, pulled off each shoe in turn and slapped them into his hands. "You want the shoes, you take them! I'm tired of all this concern over a simple pair of shoes!"

She turned to go.

"Wait! No!" He stood foolishly, with the frivolous shoes like flat little pressed flowers in his hands. "Please. . . ."

" 'Where had you those shoes?' And 'Did the nuns say where they got them?' They're just *shoes*! And a hussy's shoes, by the look of them. I should never have taken them. It'll be summer soon, and what good are shoes in summer?"

"What nuns?" asked January, bewildered.

The pralinniere stared at him as if it should be obvious. "The Ursulines, fool! What other nuns are there?"

She snatched up her basket, turned on her naked pink heel, and was gone, muttering to herself, "What nuns, indeed?"

Still holding the shoes in his hands, very like the idiot the old woman had called him, January started along Rue du Levee at a run.

Rose wasn't in her room on Victory Street. "I think she gone out," called the girl who worked at the grocery, coming into the yard while January stood irresolute in front of the crudely latched shutters of Rose's door. "That lock don't work, you can probably go right on in."

And remind me never to put YOU in charge of my belongings, thought January wryly. But he'd seen the girl—her name was Marie-Philomène—a number of times in the past week, and she knew him to be Rose's friend.

"Did you see her go?"

Marie-Philomène nodded. "She went out to market this morning, then 'bout three, four hours ago she come runnin' back here, and change into her nice dress, the pretty blue one with the white collar." It was the dress Rose had worn to impress her backers at the school—merino wool, a little worn but neat and businesslike. "Gloves and everything. I think she might have been goin' to that school she works at; she had a book with her, anyway."

Like a Dutch still life, January saw in his mind the mended gloves, the *Conversations in Chemistry More Especially for the Female Sex* on the corner of the hall table. . . .

She'd gone to Madame Lalaurie's.

Everything they had spoken of concerning that lady rushed back to him in a scalding flood: her vindictiveness, her connections with slave-dealers, her power. Her ability to seem like the kind of person who could not possibly do ill. He'd been a fool to believe her, to accept her graciousness and charm. . . .

Rose had recognized Geneviève's shoes, and had learned from the pralinniere that they'd come from the charity bin of the Ursuline Order. And the only way they would have gotten there, he now knew, was through Madame Lalaurie.

Rose had gone to Madame Lalaurie's.

And like Cora, she hadn't come back.

Lieutenant Shaw was out. "Captain Tremouille got a bee up his behind again about the blacks sleeping out." Sergeant deMezieres, on duty at the desk, shook his head. "I don't see what business it is of anybody where they sleep, but seems a couple of those Americans whose boys were kidnapped last fall have taken it in their heads to sue the city over it. No, I don't know when he'll be back."

January knew a handful of the Guards from a couple of encounters during the past year, but knew also that none of them would back him if he tried to tell them he thought a colored woman was being held prisoner by one of the town's most prominent society matrons, particularly not in the face of Barnard's newspaper campaign. More than likely Captain Tremouille, who was connected to three-quarters of Creole society himself, would simply ask Madame Lalaurie about it, get a startled and indignant no, and that would be that.

He said, "Thank you, sir," and took his leave.

The sun was sinking over the glittering river, the new moon following it like a lovelorn suitor, pale and thin. The day had been a clear one, spring heat melting already into the promise of summer. Another fever season on its way. Whatever the Lalauries intended to do to keep Rose quiet—and surely she knew too much English, and too much about her own rights, to sell even to the crookedest broker—they'd do so at night.

Hannibal wasn't at his last known lodging, the shed behind Big Annie's house of assignation near the Basin. The cook there directed

January to the establishment of Kentucky Williams, on Perdidio Street. By the time he reached there the river's long curve was a bed of fire, the mucky gulch of Perdidio Street blue with shadow among its weeds and sheds. Few lamps were lit, and drunken, louse-ridden bravos jostled from tavern to tavern; January nearly trod on a flatboatman who came flying out of the Cairo Saloon and plowed into the mud almost under his feet.

In a two-room shed built of old flatboat planks, January found Kentucky Williams, as tall as some men and with arms like a keelboat's tiller, dispensing *something* from a barrel with a tin cup. January mused a little that in her five-word inquiry as to the nature of his business, three of those words were obscenities. She was already dippering up liquor for him, though. A few feet away the woman Railspike was engaged in a screaming quarrel with a prospective customer. *How do these girls ever make any money?*

"He's gone out," said Williams. When January indicated he wasn't interested in drinking she shifted her cigar to the corner of her mouth, took a swig from the tin cup herself, then dumped the rest of its contents back into the barrel. "You a pal of his?"

"I'm Ben January. He might have spoken of me."

She smiled, her pockmarked face transforming, like a good-natured bulldog. "You're Ben? Pleased to meet you." She held out a dripping hand. "There's some fandango tonight, they're payin' him to play at. Don't he play a treat, though? Last night, with that little thing he plays—da-da-deeee-da"—she made a stab at getting the tune known as "The Beggar Boy"—"he made old Railspike cry."

Railspike kicked her suitor—a bearded Irish bargee—bloody-mouthed into the street. She began picking up teeth from the dirt floor and pitching them after him, screaming curses all the while.

"Hannibal's the best fiddler I've ever heard," said January truthfully. "Paris, Italy, anyplace. You happen to know where he might be playing?"

"Some bunch of rich stinkards." She spit into a corner. "Pigs, all of 'em. Sure you don't want a drink? You can have one free, 'cause you're his friend."

"Thank you, m'am," said January, "but I need to find him fast, and I got no head for liquor, not even a tiny bit. Another time."

She winked. "Another time, then."

Blue shadows, and the day's heat dense and stinking around the makeshift buildings. Another corpse—or maybe it was only a drunk—had materialized on the ground outside the Tom and Jerry. January stopped back by the Cabildo, but Shaw was still gone.

Did he *really*, he wondered as he walked up Rue St. Peter, think that Delphine Lalaurie had Rose locked in an attic someplace, waiting for dark to turn her over to the slave brokers? For a moment he felt as he had back in September, when he'd realized he was ready to bolt for the swamp at the shadow of Henri Viellard's groom. Rose on the Lalaurie doorstep saying, *I know you sold Cora Chouteau into slavery.* And then what? "Oh, Bastien, could you please come in here and knock this girl over the head and lock her in the attic?"

Ridiculous. The woman who held the dying against her breast with that look of holy ecstasy in her face? The woman who'd reacted with such embarrassed horror at what Dr. Barnard had written? Who'd held out her hand with a twinkling smile?

And yet, January thought, wasn't that her entire defense? That "a woman like her wouldn't do such a thing"? A woman like her wouldn't force her daughters to go through that scene at the piano, either—and he remembered, again, the look of terror in Pauline's eye.

Why terror?

Jean Montalban came back to his mind, professor of law and pillar of his Paris neighborhood. Hannibal's voice saying, *One's always hearing about domestic tyrants. . . . No one in the family dares speak of it. . . .* And Rose: *I don't want a woman I've looked up to, as I've looked up to her, to be vindictive. But I don't know.*

And he could not help remembering that Delphine Lalaurie's house was closed in, a walled enclave—a fortress, he remembered thinking. No word of anything that happened there would ever get out.

Absurd, he thought. *Absurd.* But it was the memory of Pauline's fear, as well as of the book on the table, that turned his steps back to his mother's house.

Once there, January carried a pottery jar from the kitchen up to his room, and from beneath the mattress took the powder-bottle he'd acquired from the late Mr. Gotch. He emptied its contents in the bottom of the jar, ran a fuse into it, packed the rest tight with hair and feathers from Bella's store of fever smudges, then added as much sawdust as he could gather—Rose had mentioned it made for a more impressive explosion—from the bottom of the kindling bin. With this under his arm, he made his way down Rue St. Peter again, and along the levee to the market.

"You men want to earn half a dollar?"

It was nearly the last of his meager savings. The two carters sitting by their mule conferred, and accepted. January spent another five cents on an empty packing crate labeled TREVELYAN BROTHERS—ST. LOUIS, scooped it full of dockside garbage to give it weight, and pounded shut the nails on it again. "When the man comes to the gate, you keep him talking," instructed January. "Ask for money. Tell him this was ordered for that address, but say you don't know who at that address."

The men exchanged a glance, and one of them bit the fifty-cent piece he'd given them. If they had any concern about the possible legal repercussions of what they were being asked to perform, the silver content of the coin allayed them. "You got yourself a argument, brother," said one. "But if the Guards shows up, we gone."

"Go with my blessings," said January. Two minutes later, walking up Rue de l'Hôpital in the thick hot twilight, he thought, *Idiot. You shouldn't have paid them in advance.*

The tract of land on which the Lalaurie house was built had only been sold off by the Ursuline nuns a few years ago, and though fewer than five streets separated it from the noise and taverns of the levee, it was an area attractive to the wealthy in quest of lots on which to build houses larger than those close to the center of the old town. Several houses were in various stages of construction on the opposite side of the street in the direction of the levee, heaps of bricks and timber lying between the half-erected walls.

The builders' men had gone for the day. January picked his way through the tangle of beams and potholes to the rear wall of the next-door quarters, moved forward until the high wall of the Lalaurie compound was in view, and waited, the pottery jug at his feet.

A little to his surprise, the two carters did exactly as he had asked them. The shorter and darker man pounded on the gate while his gangly, saddle-colored partner held the mule's head. Below the bed of the wagon January could see the bottom of the carriage gate, the gate through which he had been admitted dozens of times last spring and summer, to give lessons to Louise Marie and Pauline. As he sat waiting a thought crossed his mind, detached and abstract: he had never seen pets in the Lalaurie house. None at all.

The moment he saw the gate open, and saw the polished pumps that had to be Bastien's, he scratched a lucifer match on the brick wall beside him, lit the fuse, left the makeshift bomb *(Thank you, Rose— Thank you, Geneviève)* where it lay, and walked quickly up the down-stream side of the street, counting off seconds in his mind.

The carters could have played in Shakespeare at Caldwell's The-atre. Bastien tried to shut the gates; the shorter man held it, arguing volubly. January crossed the street, came down along the wall on the upstream side, inconspicuous in the near-darkness in his rough cloth-ing, seeing now Bastien's sleek black curls, his plump, muscular back in that neat violet livery.

"Now I been told to get the money for this here lime from you, 'cause I paid for it at the dock," the carter was saying, throwing just the slightest hint of inebriated drawl in his voice.

"I'm terribly sorry you were such a fool as to do so ill-judged a thing," retorted Bastien, "but this is not my affair and Madame has placed no such order."

"Oh, Madame tells you all about every order she place, does she?" put in the taller carter sarcastically.

"In fact, Madame does." Bastien drew himself up, stung. "I realize it's inconceivable to someone of your sort that—"

At that point, January's homemade bomb went off. There was a crack like a cannon-shot, and a great gout of stinking smoke and burning sawdust bellied forth from behind the wall. To his credit, Bastien jerked the gate shut behind him before running toward the place, only steps behind the shorter carter and any number of idlers from Gallatin Street and the wharves who came pouring up the street at a run. The taller carter was hanging on to the mule's head for dear life as the animal reared and snorted, and as January slipped through the gate and closed it behind him, the man winked and signed him good luck.

The house was tall. Both the main block and the kitchen wing towered three floors, the galleries impenetrable shadow. Lights on the ground floor of the main house, glowing slits through shutters already bolted; none above. If there was a fandango somewhere tonight it was a good guess Madame and her husband were in attendance. Either that or they were out looking up some of Jean Blanque's old slave-trade contacts to dispose of Rose.

Over the wall he could hear men's voices, rough nasal American. Of course at the slightest promise of trouble every drunk filibuster and out-of-work roustabout on Gallatin Street would materialize in minutes, eager for loot or diversion or whatever the confusion might bring.

Keeping under the shelter of the kitchen gallery, January headed for the stairs.

The kitchen, as usual, was shut and locked, but the dimmest suggestion of redness outlined the louvers; and as he passed its door he felt the glow of the stove's heat within. As warm as the day had been it must have been like an Indian sweat-bath in there. Foolish to keep it closed up, even if no supper were being cooked tonight. The rooms above it would be ovens. . . .

He heard the soft clink of chain on bricks within.

No supper, if they were at this fandango tonight. No one in the kitchen. *Not the attic, the kitchen . . .*

He pushed open the door, and, conscious of Bastien's imminent return, stepped through and closed it swiftly behind him.

"I'm not doin' nothing," whispered a voice, a broken plea out of the darkness. The smell of urine struck him, pungent and vile in the heat, half-buried under the slurry of other kitchen smells. "Not doin' nothing, just getting myself a little water. Please, Mr. Bastien, don't tell her I was bad. Don't tell her. Please."

A woman crouched on the other side of the big pine table, near the shelves and cupboards of the far wall. The open hearth, banked though it was, threw enormous heat but almost no light. Still, January could see that the woman was far smaller than Rose. An emaciated face, cheekbones stabbing through stretched skin, haunted eyes pits of shadow under a white headscarf, and a dark dress hanging baggy over bony limbs.

The dress was sweat soaked, the smell of it stinging, but it was buttoned down to the wrists and up to the woman's collarbone.

There was an iron collar around her neck. She was chained to the stove.

"Don't tell her, Mr. Bastien." Her voice was barely louder than the scrape of a hinge. She pressed her cheek to the wooden doors of the cupboards against which she crouched, trying to hide behind one blistered hand. "Don't let her know I was bad."

January's heart locked in his chest. All he could seem to see was the way the soft brick of the floor was worn in a shallow groove between the stove, the table, the cupboards, and the chamber pot in the corner—the only places where this woman was allowed to walk—and all he could smell was the stink of the dress she didn't dare to unbutton for the sake of coolness, and the piss she wasn't even allowed to pass outside. All he could think was, *She has Rose here somewhere. She has Rose here.*

Then as if a door opened somewhere inside him he saw Montreuil again, and Olympe's bleak eyes. *Those rumors were around before she lived next to Montreuil. Dear God,* he thought. *Dear God.*

He opened the kitchen door a crack. Outside, Bastien shut and double-barred the gates—they would have done for a medieval city—and walked over to the stable, to check the carriage-team. Satisfied—by his step he was satisfied—the coachman crossed back to the main house. January gave him a few moments to get away from the rear windows, then slipped out. Moving with the utmost caution to the outside stairway, he climbed warily, listening it seemed with the whole of his body and trembling with shock.

Lights came up in what had to be the rear parlor downstairs, muzzy patterns of gold on the herringbone bricks. Minutes later one of the second-floor windows bloomed with candle glow. A shadow briefly darkened the slitted louver lines.

Servants wouldn't be active in the main house at this hour. One of the family, then. Did the crippled Louise Marie attend balls? Or was she at home?

Barely breathing, he ascended the second flight. The smell that lingered on the third-floor gallery, even with the doors of the chambers shut and locked, told him he had found the place he sought.

There was a candle in his pocket, and a screwdriver. Though it froze his heart to make a light he did so, shielding it with his body, to examine the lock. It was of a simple latch kind, yielding to the removal of the the metal plate on the doorjamb. He slipped the latch free, eased the door open, then stepped through and shut it. The smell here was a thousand times worse in the thick trapped heat of spring: feces, urine, moldering blood. The strange, slightly metallic smell of maggots. Ants made trails along the walls, up the studs, across the rafters. Flies attacked the light in swarms.

The room was empty, but beyond the shut door at its far side, someone groaned.

I don't want to do this. I don't want to do this. The words gyred stupidly through his mind as he crossed the tiny room, hoping weirdly that the door on the other side would be locked. Hoping like a child in a nightmare that he wouldn't have to see what he knew he was going to see.

At first they didn't look human, or anyway not like living men who had once walked the levee, sang to ladies, maybe eaten mangoes with the juice running down their chins. The way their arms were chained—elbows together above and behind the head, wrists together in a travesty of an upside-down L, ankles locked to the bands around their waists—it took January a few moments to understand that they were men at all, and not misshapen fetishes carved out of knobbed brown-black oak. Unable to move, they knelt in their own waste, on the other side of a table where a whalebone riding whip and a cat-o'-nine-tails lay with items only barely guessed at. Starvation had rendered them almost unrecognizable as men. It was only when the thing hanging on the wall moved and tried to make noise that he realized that it, too, was alive.

It was Cora.

He didn't know why he recognized her. Maybe by her size, rendered still more childlike by advanced emaciation. Her tiny feet, hanging ten or twelve inches above the floor in their heavy leg irons, looked no bigger than a turkey's claws. There was an iron gag in her mouth, the kind he'd seen in old museums labeled a Scold's Bridle, locked behind her head and forcing her mouth open. Flies crawled in and out, over a thin, constant stream of drool.

January's mind stalled, blocked by what he was seeing. He realized he hadn't the faintest idea what he should do. These people obviously couldn't walk, couldn't make it down two flights of stairs. He had heard the phrase, *ran screaming*—he hadn't known what it had meant, he realized. All he wanted to do was flee, shrieking, down Rue de l'Hôpital, blotting this sight from his mind forever. . . .

His hand shaking so badly he could barely manipulate the latches, he unfastened the iron cage around Cora's head, pulled it off as gently as he could. The girl made a horrible noise in her throat, then spat out maggots. "Gervase." She nodded to the room's inner door.

It was locked. January set his candle on the table, looked among the horrors there for a piece of thin wire that he could use to work the pawls—theoretically, at least. He'd never picked a lock in his life, though Hannibal had assured him it wasn't difficult. In the watery uncertainty of the single flame the tools were terrible, each a silent word of pain: levered clamps, intricate mechanisms of screw and strap, something like a half-unfurled speculum mounted on a screw. Ants and roaches crept over the caked blood.

From among them he picked a vicious little hook, turned back to the door. There was a dim scraping behind him, one of the chained men trying to wriggle across the floor. January brought the candle close to the lock, bent to work the hook.

He heard Cora scream and started to straighten up, his head moving straight into the numbing blow from behind. His body hit the wall. He had a brief glimpse of Bastien raising an iron crowbar for another blow, and remembered nothing more.

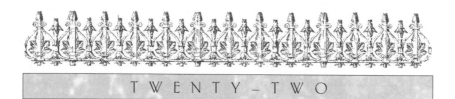

TWENTY-TWO

Pain brought him to, unbelievable pain in his neck, back, shoulders. He thought someone must surely have run iron needles under the scapula, through the cervical joints, into his ribs, everywhere, but in the utter dark, the abyssal stench and heat, he couldn't tell. He couldn't move, was too disoriented to even judge in what position his body was pinned. He threw up, the spasms rending his shoulders like the rack, and the vomit ran warm down his naked chest and belly. Blinding pain drilled through his skull, enough to stop his breath.

He passed out.

He came to from the pain of being moved. Even the light of the branch of candles near the door was pain, gouging through his eyes to his brain. He threw up again, doubled over this time, his wrists manacled behind him, being drawn steadily up. He tried to straighten, tried to move to lessen the agony in his shoulders, but the rope or chain on the manacles kept pulling up toward the ceiling, dragging his arms up behind him. Hannibal had spoken once of his lunatic uncle, fixated on the Spanish Inquisition, and January recognized what this had to be, from old woodcuts: a ceiling pulley, a set of wrist-chains, a rope, and a demon to pull on it until the victim's feet lifted from the floor and his arms were wrenched from their sockets. The light was like an ax in his skull.

"Did you tell anyone?"

That mellow golden contralto: *Begin again.* The rope twisted up a few more inches and he cried out.

Thin and flexible, the whalebone training-whip tore the backs of his naked thighs.

"Did you tell anyone?"

"No."

A cut across his belly. He felt blood.

How he knew what she wanted he didn't know. Maybe because she was white.

"No, m'am."

It was hard to look at her, hard to make his eyes focus. She wore a ball dress of turquoise silk with what they called a Mary Stuart bodice, the candlelight salting her black lace with gold. Queenly, gracious, lovely as she had been that afternoon, apologizing for what Emil Barnard had written. Black-lace mitts on her hands. On the floor beyond her skirts another woman lay with arms and legs folded into an iron contraption that locked between her ankles; January could just see this slave woman's eyes, brown and huge, staring incomprehendingly at him.

Delphine Lalaurie beat him until he fainted again, beat him without a word or a sound and without change of expression on her face. The agony in his shoulders brought him to twice, when he slumped; he wasn't sure when he woke up the third time if it was true consciousness. He only knew that his ankles and wrists were being locked together behind his back, and that her skirts were close enough to his head to smell the patchouli in their folds.

He thought she said—if he wasn't dreaming—"You say Suzette must have seen him come in?"

"She must have, Madame. The kitchen door was open."

"And, of course, she didn't bother to tell you about it."

"No, Madame."

Hallucinatory in the candlelight, he saw Bastien put a shawl around her shoulders. Sweat bathed her face and made black circles in the armpits of her gown, and she'd taken her hair down, as a woman does for her husband. In the leaping shadows the gray did not show; it hung crow black below her hips. The few pins still snagged in it winked like rats' eyes.

She put out her hand, resting it on Bastien's shoulder. No expression changed her face, but she closed her eyes. Straight and cold, for a moment it seemed to January that Delphine Lalaurie was strapped into the self-shouldered bonds of her own perfection, like one of her husband's infernal posture-correction devices. In the silence he heard her draw breath and release it, like a woman convincing herself that she has to be strong. Whatever the cost, she must go on, to some end known only to herself.

"After all I have done for her," she said. "After all I have done."

"Yes, Madame."

"For the girls. For Nicolas." Had she been anyone but Delphine Lalaurie she would have trembled. In her face was the echo of that yearning ecstasy it had worn in the fever wards, as she held a young man dead in her arms. "Not one of them knows how much."

Then she opened her eyes, calm and reasonable and flawless once more. In utter control, obeyed in all things. "I'll have to speak to her."

She picked up the whip from the table and went out.

He was dead.

He was dead and in hell. Though Bastien had taken the candles—as if suspended in space somewhere above the yard January could see the two of them, descending the square-angled spiral of the outside stair—he could see also, clearly, Liam Roarke sitting slumped against the wall near the door, the contents of his opened veins a black slow-spreading ocean around his thighs and his bright blue eyes fixed on January.

"You know you didn't have to tell your smelly friend Shaw, Soublet's name," Roarke said, with an evil smile. "You'd told him it before. He knew."

January couldn't argue with him.

There were other people in the room. Sometimes he could only hear them, twisting and groaning softly in the darkness: could smell the blood and filth, and hear the scrape of metal, and the sobbing of the woman on the floor. Sometimes in spite of the darkness he could see them, by the light of red flame whose heat consumed them all: his father, Rose, Ayasha. Ayasha, lying on the bed, raised her blackening face and shook back the long coil of her hair, and said, "You didn't come. And now you're chasing some other girl. You didn't come because you were lying with Rose." Then she threw up all her intestines, and the child she carried inside her, and died again, her hand reaching for the pitcher of water.

January tried to say, "I'm sorry," but only the serpents of hell crawled from his mouth.

Ants covered him in a gnawing wave, eating his flesh to the bones.

Distantly, Hannibal played the violin, a jig that had been popular in Paris two summers ago, before the cholera came.

If he could only get to his Rosary, thought January, he'd be safe, he'd be all right. The Virgin Mary would get him out of this.

Delphine Lalaurie would be returning. From his vantage point above the courtyard he could see her, gathering up her heavy skirts to climb the stairs. Her husband Nicolas was with her this time, a sheaf of notes tucked under one arm and one of his experimental postural correction devices in his hands.

Virgin Mary, get me out of this.

Heat consumed January, smoke rising through the floor to suffocate his lungs. The building was on fire, plunging down like an avalanche to Hell.

The building was on fire.

He woke and knew it.

There was a little light, coming in through the cracks in the barred shutters that led out onto the gallery, enough to let him know that it was day. Smoke was pouring up through the cracks in the floor.

The woman on the floor, skeletal with prolonged starvation, began to writhe in her shackles, her breath coming in little puffs of pain. One of the men on the beds—there were two beds in the room, he now saw, the manacles dangling from the ceiling pulley between them—stirred and groaned, then lay still again. The man wore an iron collar around his neck, and some kind of iron contraption on one or maybe both of his legs. January's own shoulders were lost in a maze of pain. Agony shot up through his leg muscles, his back, from every welted, bloody inch of his skin.

In the smoke that filtered up through the room the flies were humming wildly around the ceiling, their drone a frantic bass note to Cora's voice—it had to be Cora's—making inarticulate shrill grunts beyond the thin wall. January tried to move and was instantly sorry, his head throbbing, so dizzy he nearly fainted again.

But he had to get out. He had to get out. They'd all burn. . . .

Somewhere he heard shouting, a yammer of voices below. "Sir, I'll thank you to mind your own business," came the yapping tenor of Nicolas Lalaurie's voice, and a deeper voice, harsh but familiar—Judge Canonge's?—replied.

"It's a grave allegation and I think it needs to be looked into."

"Do you call me a liar? I'll have my friends call on you in the morning, sir."

"You have your friends do whatever you want, sir, but I'm going to have a look upstairs."

"This man would say or do anything to discredit me and my wife, sir. For years he's spread rumors. . . ."

"You can't tell me that child didn't fall off the roof, two months after you moved into this place!" That was Montreuil's voice. Behind it there was a clashing, a distant thump of feet. January squirmed, gasping in an ocean of heat. If he cried out—maybe if he cried out they'd hear him. . . .

"Judge!" called someone else. "Here, sir! Here's where it started!"

Inarticulate sounds, a woman's voice; then, louder, "I couldn't bear more, sir. I couldn't bear more. After last night . . ."

"She's been beaten, sir. Severely, it looks like."

"And you're going to punish *me*," demanded Dr. Lalaurie furiously, "because this slut tried to avenge herself after correction—well deserved, I might add—by firing my house?"

"They're in the attic," persisted Montreuil's voice. "They're in the attic, sir, chained up and tortured. Sometimes at night I hear them scream!"

Shut up, thought January dully. *Shut up, you whining little toad! They're never going to believe you!*

"The woman is a fiend incarnate, I tell you! A devil! A female Nero! She . . ."

January recalled the little man's bulging eyes, his rank breath and nervous hands, and his heart sank. A fanatic with a grudge, and a well-known grudge. And, if Dominique's casual remarks were anything to go by, Madame Lalaurie had evidently taken pains to discredit him by gossip as well. Whispers of opium addiction and Montreuil's half-crazy hatred were Madame's best defense: that, and the people who would never admit that their sons and cousins had married into the family of a madwoman. Who did not have the imagination to completely comprehend the word *façade*.

"I think maybe you'd better hand over those keys."

January felt the swaying weight of many men ascending the outside stairs. He gritted his teeth in rage, tried desperately to cry out again—his tongue so swollen with thirst he could barely make a sound—when they went through the long, obligatory delay of searching the second floor: *The attic, you idiots! Didn't you hear Montreuil say "attic"?*

Axes crashed on the outer door. Evidently Dr. Lalaurie hadn't handed over the keys after all. Then the stunned silence, the appalled whispers, as even through the choke of the smoke the stench of the place came to them.

More crashing, purposeful as they cut through the second door. The smoke was already lessening, though the heat remained unbearable. The fire brigade must have come swiftly. Where was Madame Lalaurie this morning?

Then men were in the room, white men and colored, kneeling beside him, unlocking the manacles from his ankles and wrists. Murmuring in shock and horror at what they saw on the beds, on the floor, on the wall, on the table. In the background Montreuil hopped up and down, shrieking, "I told you so! I told you so! I told you so!"

January wanted to slap him.

The courtyard was jammed with people. Black and white and colored, French and American. All fell back, silent with shock, as the first of the men were brought down the stairs, carried by Canonge and Montreuil and a handful of others. January stumbled, not able to walk, supported by a couple of hairy Kaintucks from Gallatin Street and blind in the mid-morning glare. He had a jumbled awareness of the others being brought down behind him, but the wound in his head was making him dizzy and sick, and it wasn't until many days later that he was able to put his recollection of images, voices, events into anything like order. One of the emaciated slaves kept gasping "Food! Food!" and he saw a number of the market-women press forward to give it to them, the bony hands grasping and snatching.

He reeled and staggered, and someone caught him, lifted him up. As he was carried through the gate he saw Nicolas Lalaurie, small and dapper, standing by the second-floor parlor window of the house, looking expressionlessly out. Beside him, for a moment, Madame Lalaurie appeared, clothed as she had been at the Ursulines' during the plague, in a plain but devastatingly fashionable dark dress. Calm as always. Perfect as always, as if none of this had anything to do with her. Then she turned away. He saw her through a window, directing the maids in replacing the furniture that the firemen had overturned.

His mind didn't fully clear until sometime later, when he and the others were sitting or lying in the courtyard of the Cabildo, and people were filing past. Now and then officials would emerge; January guessed from the mutter of their voices that they didn't know exactly where to take the victims or what should be done with them. Market-women, brokers, and dealers from the businesses on Rue Chartres and Canal Street came by, stevedores from the levee, planters, dressmakers, artisans. Their faces formed a blur in January's mind as they stared disbelieving at the mutilated bodies of the men and women on the cots and chairs set in the court, and at the implements that covered the whole of a long table set near the brass fountain in the courtyard's center. How many of them were having second thoughts about the power a master could have over a slave, January wondered. How many were simply taking mental notes of things to be used should they need a little more domestic discipline at some time in the future?

A splotch of black caught his eye. Emily Redfern, leaning on the arm of the Reverend Micajah Dunk, in front of the makeshift cot where Cora Chouteau lay. The bulging blue eyes widened with recognition, and Madame's lace-mitted hand went to her throat, where lay a double-line of moon-gold pearls.

January said to a man near him, "Help me up."

He'd guessed Mamzelle Marie would be in the crowded courtyard somewhere, and so she was. It was easy to find her, once he was standing, by the seven points of her orange-and-red tignon. He made his way unsteadily through the press, and when she saw him coming toward her she stood up—she was washing the wounds of the woman who'd been in the iron spancel—and swiftly closed the distance between them.

"You should sit. I'll get to you."

"I don't need to be got to," said January. But he allowed her to lead him to the stairs that went up to the galleries where the cells were, and by the time they reached them he was out of breath and trembling, his head still pounding from the daylight. "I need to talk to you."

She folded her hands before her and stood looking down at him, bronze face calm.

"I know you gave Madame Redfern the poison she used to murder her husband." He spoke softly. There was so much noise around them that there was little danger of being overheard. "I have what's left of the poison, and the tin. I found them in her room at Spanish Bayou. And you were seen, by her house at Black Oak, where the tin was hidden."

"Only by a slave girl." She didn't seem in the least surprised or discomposed. "Her word is no good in a court of law."

"A slave girl who's just come back from death and Purgatory," he said. "Who's going to be a nine days' wonder with the newspapers. And who's now going to be arrested for a crime you know and I know she didn't commit. She couldn't have, she was gone from Spanish Bayou hours before the poison could have been administered; gone by the same boat that took Reverend Dunk away with the five thousand dollars on him that Madame Redfern wanted to keep, out of all the wreckage of her life."

Mamzelle Marie said nothing, nor did the dark serpent eyes shift.

Somehow, after having seen Madame Lalaurie standing in the

doorway in her turquoise gown, the sight of this tall bronze-hued woman before him—poisoner and witch and worshiper of the Damballah serpent—could no longer frighten him. He'd seen worse.

For the rest of his life, he would always know in his heart that whatever happened, he'd seen worse.

"What I'd like you to do," January said, "if you would, is speak to her. Tell her that unless she writes out a paper of manumission for Cora Chouteau—unless she comes up with some alternate explanation about what happened to that five thousand dollars that disappeared, and it better be a good one—you're going to tell the police what she did. The police and her husband's creditors."

Mamzelle Marie started to speak, then closed her lips again. Her eyes were a world of black salt and graveyard dust.

Then she smiled.

"You know why Emily poisoned that man?"

January nodded.

"Tell me."

"Because he'd bankrupted himself and her. Because he kept her from being what she wanted to be. Because he was carrying on an affair, in her house and under her nose as if she were no more than another wench on the property. Because he told her it would go the worse for her, if she dared get rid of the girl—who never wanted to share his bed in the first place. Cora only fled because she found the poison and feared for her life."

"Ah," said Mamzelle softly. She reached down her long-fingered hand, and touched—very gently—the swollen, hurting mess of his shoulder. "I'll do as you ask, Michie Janvier. Certain things are bought with pain, God's favor among them. But you should know it wasn't me that sold the poison; and it wasn't her that bought it."

"You were there," said January. "Cora saw you."

"I was there," she said. "Otis Redfern brought me up there. He offered me the place at Black Oak, to be mine after his wife was dead. Her father tied the place up in trust. It wouldn't be Redfern's to sell, until her death. He had a key, you know."

"So did she."

"As well for her." She folded her arms. "He didn't know that. He told me he'd taken the only one she had. *He* bought the poison, from a man name Dr. Chickasaw, not a good man, but he have the knowledge; he's out by the end of the Esplanade. It's like her, to have made a copy of that key."

And watching her, as she made her leisurely way through the crowd to Madame Redfern's side, January thought that it was, in fact, very like Emily Redfern to have a spare key. In like circumstances his mother would have had one, too.

"Ben!" It was Rose. She caught his hand, then put her arms carefully around his shoulders—It wasn't fit, he thought dimly, although someone had lent him a pair of rough osnaburg trousers. He pressed his head to her arm, tried to hold her.

She was, he saw, dressed neatly in yellow sprigged with blue, as if for a day's work translating Catullus. His blood and the sweaty filth from the attic floor left great blotches on the crisp cloth.

"I thought you'd gone there," he said. "I saw your book, and your gloves. I thought you saw Cora's shoes."

"I went early in the day, when I knew she was out, to leave a note about Dr. Barnard's letters," Rose said. "It was stupid of me, to leave the book. Later I had an appointment with a Dr. Groeller in Carrollton—he operates a boys' school—and I was nearly late, trying to find you. I left word with Olympe, and with Dominique, and your mother, to tell you that Cora's shoes had turned up at the Ursulines'. Her dress was there, too."

A few feet away one of the men who'd been brought out of the attic was groaning, writhing on his makeshift cot. His belly was hugely swollen, from gorging himself on the market-womens' berries and fritters, the rest of his body a handful of sticks. Dr. Ker knelt beside him, daubing with alcohol at the galls on his wrists and waist, at the jagged wounds left by a spiked collar in his neck. Past them, Hannibal knelt by Cora, talking gently while she clung to the hand of one of the exhausted skeletons—it had to be Gervase—as if she would never release it.

"They didn't know who had brought the shoes in, or how long they'd been there," Rose said. "I thought I should find you, and ask what should be done."

"I was afraid you'd gone to Lalaurie first."

Rose shook her head. "I knew she'd only lie."

His eyes went to the two dark forms, of the Reverend Dunk and Madame Redfern, standing now in a corner of the courtyard talking very quietly, very earnestly, with Mamzelle Marie. Mamzelle Marie shook her head and said something with an air of patient repetition. Dunk retorted, eyes blazing, and Emily Redfern pulled hard on his sleeve and told him to hush. Dunk looked as astonished as if a pet cat had given him an order. But he hushed.

From there January's gaze traveled up to the third-floor gallery of the prison: the womens' cells. Rose had been locked up there, he thought. Locked up with the drunkards, the prostitutes, with madwomen and women like Kentucky Williams. Lying on dirty straw and sick with grief over the death of her girls, over the collapse of everything she had worked for so hard.

He felt strange inside, hollow; empty of everything that had shaped his life for months. But she hadn't moved away from him, or made even the show, as another woman might, of protecting her dress from the muck that covered him. Her hand, resting lightly where his shoulder muscles met his neck, was cool in the spring morning heat.

"What did she say," he asked after a time, "when they brought her in? Madame Delphine?"

Rose's mouth folded tight, and for the first time he saw a flash of anger behind those round spectacle-lenses.

"They haven't brought her in," she said.

Rose would not leave Cora, and told him not to be stupid. Hannibal, who was still with Cora when Rose and January returned to her, told him not to be stupid as well. "I can stand," said January doggedly.

"So does my violin bow, if I prop it up very, very carefully."

In the end Hannibal and Paul Corbier walked with him down Rue Chartres, to the big green house on Rue Royale.

The doors and the carriage gate were shut. Men and women, several hundred strong, were gathered outside in Rue de l'Hôpital and the Rue Royale, muttering among themselves, little gusts of sound, like the wind a coming storm makes in trees. About half seemed to be idlers from the levee, Kaintucks and whores from Gallatin Street, people who ordinarily would have stepped over the body of a dying black in the gutter, or at most paused to check his pockets. But the lure of scandal was strong. Self-righteousness is a heady drug.

Mixed with them were the folk of the market, vendors and farmers and shopkeepers; colored stevedores and Irish workmen and householders, catchoupines and chacalatas, their anger and outrage the summer pulse of bees. Though the fire had been doused, the smell of smoke hung heavy on the air, like the stench of the fever season. The smell of lies and rumors, hearsay and the assurances that everything is fine.

Through the windows January could see into the second-floor parlor, where he had taught piano. Delphine Lalaurie was pointing out to a couple of men—Creoles, friends of hers, January thought, by their dress, people who probably never would believe their lovely friend guilty of anything—where to replace a marble-topped table. She went herself to position a gold-veined vase on its top.

In any crowd January was the tallest person present, with one exception, and that exception he saw at the fringe of the mob, near the carriage gate.

"What are you waiting for?" he asked, when he'd made his way over.

The lanky Kentuckian regarded him with deceptive mildness in his cold gray eyes. "Judgment Day, belike," Shaw said. And then, when January frowned uncomprehendingly, he added, "What she done weren't a crime, Ben."

"What?"

"Well, misdemeanor mistreatment of her slaves, maybe." Shaw spat in the general direction of the gutter. "Last time there was a complaint she just got a fine for it."

"I," said January, his voice icy with rage, "am not her slave."

"Maybe," agreed Shaw placidly. "But she's related to every member of the City Council from Mr. Prieur on down, and to every banker in the city to boot. She holds mortgages on half the property in this city. And those she don't hold mortgages on need her to invite their daughters to the right parties so they can catch husbands."

For some reason January thought of Roarke's attorney Mr. Loudermilk, buying free drinks among the keelboatmen and riverrats of the wharves, trying to organize a jail delivery. Of whatever threat it had been, that had decided the kidnapped Grille brothers and their sister not to testify against Roarke after all.

There was not so very much difference between Rue Royale and Gallatin Street. Only that Roarke's crimes had been, at least, comprehensible.

"So you're telling me the police are going to sit back and do nothing."

"I'm telling you," said Shaw softly, "that in ten years, this won't have happened." His eyes swept back to the tall house, the lace curtains moving in the windows, the walls like a self-enclosing fortress, only slightly streaked with smoke. "Nice lady like that? *They* didn't see nuthin'."

"Well, *I* sure saw somethin', me!" A heavyset countryman pushed close to Shaw. "Me, I been to the Cabildo. What you sayin', she gonna get away with what she done?"

"What you say?" Kentucky Williams jostled up behind the man. "That French cow-whore gonna get *away* with that?"

She had a voice like an iron gong, and the murmur rose around them, angry, disbelieving. Someone got a brick from the building site where January had blown up his bomb, and lobbed it through the window on the ground floor; someone else shrieked, "Monster! Murderess!" in English that grated like a saw.

Fists began to pound on the gate. Around the corner on Rue Royale others hammered at the door. More bricks were hurled at the house; there was a tinkling smash of glass. "Now see what you done started?" murmured Shaw mildly and put a surprisingly gentle hand on January's arm to draw him back.

Hannibal asked, "I take it you're not on duty," and Shaw looked down at the fiddler in a kind of surprise.

"I been told off special by Chief Tremouille not to cross the Lalaurie threshold," he said. "So I guess I won't."

A couple of Gallatin Street toughs and an Ohio boatman got a cypress beam from the construction and began to smash at the gates with it like a ram. The voice of the mob rose to an angry baying, French and English—*"Like the howling of Irish wolves against the moon,"* Hannibal murmured. More bricks were thrown, and a dead rat from the gutter. Men appeared from the levee as if drawn by the noise or by the sudden, whiffed promise of loot.

Shaw checked the pistols at his belt. "I ain't seen the daughters all mornin'. I been watchin'. But I can't stand by if they offer her harm."

"Let them," said January coldly. His brother-in-law had lent him a jacket, too short in the sleeves, sticking to his back from the scabbed welts left by the whip, and had had to put it on him. He still could not move his arms. The mob thrust them back, pushing at the gate, and Shaw snaked his lean body forward, working his way to the front.

He was thus almost knocked to the banquette a moment later when the heavy black gates flew open. Black horses reared and plunged in the archway, eyes rolling in terror; January saw Bastien on the box, wielding a whip in all directions. The mob fell back before the plunging hooves, maybe thinking the coachman was taking his moment to escape. Only when the carriage lunged forward did January see the woman inside, dark-veiled, calm, unbreakably perfect, gazing out over the heads of the rabble. Bastien cracked the whip again and the horses threw themselves forward. Someone shrieked a curse, and the mob surged after the carriage. But the horses were swift. The carriage rocked and swayed as it picked up speed, up Rue de l'Hôpital to the Bayou Road, and out toward the lake.

Some of the mob ran after it, hurling bricks and cursing. The rest turned back, pouring through the open gates, into the wealthy house, and began to loot.

January felt a touch on his side. Looking down he saw that Rose had joined him. There was a crash as someone hurled the gold-veined vase down from the second-floor parlor, men scattering and laughing at the sound of the stone shattering. Someone else yelled in English, "Watch out below!" and the piano was thrust over the edge of the gallery, squashing like a melon as it hit the banquette. Bodies jostled January from all sides, crowding to be in at the carnival of destruction and theft.

January sighed, and with the effort of his lifetime put his arm around Rose's shoulders. She hesitated, then leaned very gently into his side.

"Let's go home."

It's always difficult to write a fictional account of a historical crime, particularly in cases where the writer has to make a judgment about whether any crime was committed or not.

Newspaper accounts of events in New Orleans in the 1830s could be exaggerated, libellous, poisonous, self-serving, or misleading—all uniformly refused to acknowledge epidemics of yellow fever until hundreds died, for instance—but the April 10, 1834, editions of the *Gazette* and (more significant to my mind) both the English and the French editions of the *Bee* contain accounts of the fire at the Lalaurie mansion, the discovery of the seven mutilated slaves in the attic, and the subsequent mobbing and sacking of the house. The *Bee* also contains the deposition of Judge Canonge, one of the most notable local jurists, as to the finding of the slaves. Barely two years after the events, Harriet Martineau, an Englishwoman passing through New Orleans, spoke to numerous eyewitnesses and attests that the debris from the Lalaurie house blocked the street for some time. George Washington Cable and his two assistants, and later Henry Castella-nos—who was born and raised in New Orleans—had ample opportunity to speak to firsthand witnesses as well as to examine documents: neither of them appears to have had any doubts that the events did take place.

In 1934, one hundred years after the event, New Orleans journalist Meigs Frost printed a "vindication" of Marie Delphine de McCarty Blanque Lalaurie, claiming that the story could not be true on the grounds that the Lalaurie house on Rue Royale itself was clearly undamaged. Frost also claimed that the house dated from the late eighteenth century—which was completely untrue—and neglected to mention that the structure was substantially rebuilt by one Pierre Trastour in the late 1830s, so badly damaged had it been. Since Frost's account also contains a quaintly romantic, but provably untrue, legend about Madame Lalaurie as a young woman voyaging to Spain to plead for her first husband's life with the Queen of Spain (Don Ramon de López y Angula was called back to "take his place at court" in full honor, but died in Havana). I found it difficult to place much credence in many of Frost's assertions.

There are a number of possibilities and suppositions involved in the case, but in my judgment—and I thought long and hard about this before undertaking this project—the fact that Monsieur Montreuil next door had been done dirty by a member of Madame Lalaurie's family does not outweigh the fact of Judge Canonge's deposition or the fact that, when she and her husband fled New Orleans in 1834, Madame Lalaurie apparently made no attempt to deny the allegations made against her or to countersue Montreuil, Canonge, or anyone else. Most accounts state that thousands of people filed through the courtyard of the Cabildo that April afternoon in 1834 and saw not only the seven mutilated slaves, but implements of torture (unspecified) that "covered the top of a table." At least one account adds that two of the tortured slaves died from overeating immediately after their long period of starvation; others were so badly injured as to be pensioners of the city for the rest of their lives.

Following her escape from the house on Royal Street, Delphine Lalaurie crossed Lake Pontchartrain to Mandeville. There she stayed for some ten days, evidently hoping that the whole matter would blow over. When it did not, she and her husband signed over power of attorney to the husbands of her two married daughters (she had four in all) and took ship, first, it is said, for New York and then for Paris. There, some stories allege, Delphine Lalaurie lived out her days. One account says she died hunting boar in the Pyrenees.

However, notarial records exist stating that she was back living quietly in New Orleans by the late 1840s; for in 1849 she petitioned to manumit a middle-aged slave named Orestes. Every one of her detractors has made it clear that Delphine Lalaurie did have favorites among her slaves, notably the faithful coachman Bastien; and she is recorded to have manumitted another slave while living at the Royal Street house in 1832. Bastien the coachman was said to have been killed when, after driving Madame and her husband to safety at Lake Pontchartrain, he tried to return to the house and was torn apart by the mob. What Bastien thought of his mistress's activities in the attic, and why he attempted to return to the house can, of course, only be conjectured.

Too many modern cases exist of men who imprisoned one or several youths or girls in their homes or in improvised dugout cellars, over periods of months, as sex slaves or for purposes of torture, before killing them, for me to believe that Madame Lalaurie "couldn't" have done what it is alleged that she did.

Records from the 1840s also indicate that next door to the widow of N. L. Lalaurie in the Faubourg Marigny lived her two unmarried daughters. Most stories add that Madame Lalaurie was buried secretly in St. Louis #1 Cemetery, but no one knows the location of her grave.

Please remember, however, that this is a work of fiction, not a scholarly biography. I used the sources that were available to me and made the best decisions I could from what I read about what the situation and circumstances might have been like, if what the newspapers said was in fact true. If there is further information conclusively vindicating Delphine Lalaurie, I would be delighted to see it. I have tried above all to keep the flavor of place and time and not do violence to my source material.

The house that now stands at 1140 Royal Street in New Orleans has been so extensively rebuilt that very little remains of the original structure. When one of the McCarty plantations was subdivided into house lots, one of the streets was named Delphine Street and remains so to this day.

Barbara Hambly
July 1997